GARDENIAS

GARDENIAS

· · · · · · · · · · · ·

Faith Sullivan

For Kelly,
Thank you for
a great time—

Faith Sullivan

MILKWEED
EDITIONS

© 2005, Text by Faith Sullivan
Milkweed Editions, 1011 Washington Avenue South, Suite 300, Minneapolis, Minnesota 55415.
(800) 520-6455
www.milkweed.org

Published 2005 by Milkweed Editions
Printed in Canada
Cover design by Kevin Putz
Author photo by Kate Sullivan
Back cover photo by Wallace Kirkland, *Life*, February 9, 1942 / Time & Life Pictures / Getty Images
Front flap photo by Harold Carter, *Life*, November 5, 1945
Interior design and illustration by Barbara Jellow
The text of this book is set in Sabon.
05 06 07 08 09   5 4 3 2 1
First Edition

Cover illustration: *Jasminum ram uniflore, pleno, petalis coriaceis*, by Georg Ehret from *Plantae et Palilliones
rariores*. Used by permission of the Arnold Arboretum, Harvard University, Cambridge, Massachusetts, USA.

Special underwriting for this book
was contributed by an anonymous donor.

Milkweed Editions, a nonprofit publisher, gratefully acknowledges support from Emilie and Henry Buchwald;
Bush Foundation; Cargill Value Investment; Timothy and Tara Clark Family Charitable Fund; DeL Corazón
Family Fund; Dougherty Family Foundation; Ecolab Foundation; Joe B. Foster Family Foundation; General Mills
Foundation; Jerome Foundation; Kathleen Jones; Constance B. Kunin; D. K. Light; Chris and Ann
Malecek; McKnight Foundation; a grant from the Minnesota State Arts Board, through an appropriation by
the Minnesota State Legislature, a grant from the National Endowment for the Arts, and private funders; Sheila
C. Morgan; Laura Jane Musser Fund; an award from the National Endowment for the Arts, which believes that
a great nation deserves great art; Navarre Corporation; Kate and Stuart Nielsen; Outagamie Charitable
Foundation; Qwest Foundation; Debbie Reynolds; St. Paul Travelers Foundation; Ellen and Sheldon Sturgis;
Surdna Foundation; Target Foundation; Gertrude Sexton Thompson Charitable Trust (George R. A.
Johnson, Trustee); James R. Thorpe Foundation; Toro Foundation; Weyerhaeuser Family Foundation;
and Xcel Energy Foundation.

Library of Congress Cataloging-in-Publication Data
Sullivan, Faith.
Gardenias / Faith Sullivan.— 1st ed.
p. cm.
ISBN-10: 1-57131-045-2 (acid-free paper)
ISBN-13: 978-1-57131-045-3 (acid-free paper)
1. World War, 1939–1945—California—San Diego—Fiction. 2. Mothers and
daughters—Fiction. 3. Women—California—Fiction. 4. San Diego (Calif.)—Fiction. I. Title.
PS3569.U3469G37 2005
813'.54—dc22
2005008404

This book is printed on acid-free paper.

In memory of my cousin Gil.

And for his sisters and brothers,

Alice, Marlys, Chuck, and Joe.

And for my brother Brian.

And for book groups,

the two I am a member of and the thousands of others

who sustain the continued life of books.

. . . .

We all need the waters of the Mercy River. Though they don't run deep, there's usually enough, just enough, for the extravagance of our lives.

JONIS AGEE, *Sweet Eyes*

. . . .

Acknowledgments

With gratitude to H. Emerson Blake, my editor at Milkweed Editions, for his great skill, patience, and humanity. And to the entire staff of Milkweed. A more supportive and talented crew is nowhere to be found.

Thanks as well to the peerless Douglas Stewart, my agent at Sterling, Lord, Literistic–friend, wit, and hand-holder extraordinary.

Deep appreciation to Women Who Wine, writer friends–Alison, Judy, Julie, Kate, Lorna, Mary, Pat, Ping, and Sandy–who walk the walk, talk the talk, and feed me besides.

And last but never least, thanks to my husband Dan, and to our three children, Maggie, Ben, and Kate, all of them writers of enormous talent and friends of enormous heart.

GARDENIAS

Preview of Coming Attractions

THE *WEBSTER'S COLLEGIATE DICTIONARY* that Miss Borgen and the fourth grade had given me at my farewell party fell open in my lap. Without looking, I placed an index finger on a silky page: *kismet*. A Turkish word meaning fate or destiny.

Once a day—even on the train—I was going to learn a new word, and each word would be a link between me and the fourth grade back in Harvester, Minnesota. Tears began oozing into my eyes and I brushed at them with the back of my hand.

Then the heavy door to the outside thrust open, and along with the roar and clatter of the train, a gust of icy air blew down the short passageway and into the club car of the City of Los Angeles.

The glamorous woman I'd noticed in the Omaha depot glided in, accompanied by an older man in a gray pinstripe suit. Although she no longer wore the slouch hat, she still sported the houndstooth pants and the satiny white shirt with its collar falling gracefully away from her throat. Over her shoulders was flung the fox jacket, as if it were any old thing she'd grabbed in a hurry.

She was short and seemed tall, thin and seemed curved. She flowed between retreating banks of uniforms, and people fell silent or spoke in murmurs, eyeing her glancingly. Two sailors at the last table relinquished their club chairs.

Her hair was jet, glossy and liquid. Cut in a simple Prince Valiant style, it slid forward to shield her from sidelong glances when she dipped her head.

Her skin was the color of unbruised gardenia petals, and her hooded eyes made me think of cooled tar, which when you crack it open is as shiny and polished as a gem inside. She wore no rings or bracelets but carried a little red satin bag that gave the effect of a jewel.

"Who's that?" the young lieutenant sitting beside us asked.

"I don't think I've seen her in the movies," Mama offered, "but she must be an actress or an heiress."

Like sandalwood perfume, calamity hung in the air around the woman. Some scandalous act, perhaps still unconceived, followed her. I loved her. Instantly. Forever. And I wished that I could warn her. But I had barely courage enough to look at her.

January 1942

SINCE THE CITY OF LOS ANGELES wouldn't take us all the way to San Diego—where Mama was dragging me and Aunt Betty—after a night resting up at Mrs. Healy's boarding house in L.A. we climbed on another train for the last leg of the journey.

As the San Diego train pulled out of Los Angeles, Mama was stooped beneath the weight of responsibility. She was not, she would insist, a woman of ruses; she'd been raised to play fair, but our money had dwindled to almost nothing, so now she was prepared to bend a scruple.

Thus it was by trickery that she got us a place in the government housing project in San Diego. She never explained to Aunt Betty, and she wouldn't have told me but I was there when it happened, perched gingerly on my old grip in the aisle beside Mama's seat.

When we boarded the train, it was crammed to overflowing, with soldiers and sailors squatting on their duffle bags in the aisle, so Mama and Aunt Betty split up, each sitting in a different coach. Mama found herself next to a finely dressed although otherwise nondescript gentleman, nearly Grandpa's age, who stowed a handsome leather briefcase in the rack above.

Mama observed later that this was the sort of man who often turned out to be important: not the ones wearing Shriners' rings with big diamonds, but the ones whose wives would have trouble remembering their faces from one day to the next.

When the conductor punched our tickets and moved on, Mama asked the gentleman, "Do you live in San Diego?" She was hoping he had information about jobs.

The man studied her for a moment. "Not any more. I'm back on business. Do you live in San Diego?"

"No. My little girl and my sister and I are going to San Diego to look for work." She smiled wanly, as if barely keeping a rein on her sadness. "We're from Minnesota, both of us widows, and we thought we'd start over out here."

Widows? I sucked in my breath. She'd bareface-lied.

"What kind of work do you do?"

"I ran my own small business in Minnesota—Erhardt Typing Service," Mama told him. "I traveled all over the county, doing office work for businesses too small to hire a girl, or ones that needed an extra hand now and then. I was starting to do well but then my husband was killed and my heart went out of it." She twisted her handkerchief uncharacteristically.

I felt like somebody'd knocked me down. Talk about your movie actresses.

The man reached over and gave Mama's hand an avuncular pat. "You've had a hard time, little girl," he said.

Mama turned her head away as if to spare him tears.

"You won't have any trouble getting work," he went on. "A smart, capable young woman like yourself. Go down to Consolidated Aircraft or any of those defense plants. They'll snap you up."

"I hope you're right."

"Of course I'm right. You know anybody in San Diego?"

"No. We'll try to find a rooming house to start out."

"Places to stay are scarce," he warned. "Lots of servicemen's families and defense workers coming in."

"We don't need anything fancy. A clean bed. Lark can sleep on a rollaway, or even the floor temporarily."

The gentleman stood and reached down his briefcase from the rack above. Across his vest a watch chain stretched, but when he pulled the end of it from the fob pocket only a set of small keys was attached. With one of these, he unlocked the briefcase lying on his lap and withdrew a leather-bound address book, unlocking this with yet another key. From an inside pocket of his jacket he retrieved a fountain pen and a pad of paper, copying a name and address from the leather-bound book and handing it to Mama.

"Don't lose that. You go to that gentleman and tell him that John Holyoke sent you. Tell him you need one of those units that're opening up this next week. They're out there around Pacific Beach."

Returning the pad and pen to his pocket and the address book to the briefcase, he explained, "This is government housing, mostly for defense workers. Nothing fancy, but decent and cheap." He set the briefcase down at his feet. "Ordinarily you'd have to get on a waiting list," he said in a lowered voice. "But I know you'll be discreet."

Mama offered her hand, and Mr. Holyoke shook it.

. . . .

THE DAY WE MOVED from the rooming house was a Sunday as cold and gray as a dull nickel. Carrying our grips, we retrieved our four boxes from the claim window at the San Diego depot and hauled everything on the bus out to the housing project, garnering cutting glances and rude remarks from bus passengers determined to trip over our worldly possessions.

"Trash," an elderly man observed to the bus driver. "Trash blowing in from everywhere." He glanced around to be certain we could hear. The driver was silent. Perhaps he'd recently blown in himself.

"Okies," a woman sitting two seats behind us pronounced. "Everywhere."

Aunt Betty, who was wearing her old Minnesota coat with the collar and cuffs worn shiny, began to weep soundlessly.

As our street drew in sight, Mama pulled the cord and rose to leave, casting a disdainful glance back at the woman whose remarks we had overheard. When we reached the front of the bus, loaded down with our cardboard boxes, Mama shooed me and Aunt Betty ahead of her into the exit well while she turned to the elderly man sitting behind the driver.

"If Pacific Beach, California, was paradise, which it's not, you'd never get beyond the gate, old man."

As we climbed down from the bus, the heavy clouds opened, relieving themselves on us, and by the time we reached the door of 136 Piñon we were soaked. Mama's hand shook till she could barely get the key into the lock.

I glanced back at the winding, rising, blacktopped street, now filling up like a dry creek bed. In half an hour, the water would be up to our calves.

The sidewalks were narrow blacktop strips leading to people's doors. They cut paths through unplanted plots of sand striated with yellow clay, which was bleeding into the street.

The Project was laid out in no particular pattern, streets wandering willy-nilly over foothills, this way and that, like the fine veins on old china. And on each street, row upon row of identical tan clapboard buildings, barefaced and earnest—government issue—paraded away, platoons marching up and down, up and down, always following the blacktop. Each long duplex unit was one-story high, with a low peaked roof, and a square yard of entry stoop at either end.

A far cry from Harvester and the Cape Ann.

. . . .

BACK IN HARVESTER, when we lived in the depot, Mama and I had planned to build a cottage that a brochure from Rayzeen's Lumber Yard called the Cape Ann. The brochure's picture showed it tucked in among graceful old trees, a brick walk winding to the front door.

Well, all that was before Pearl Harbor, before building materials were frozen, and before Mama left Papa. Now here we were, moving into a house that looked as if a strong wind would blow it halfway to Oz.

Setting my boxes down inside the door, I wandered from room to room, flicking on lights, peering out rain-shrouded windows, turning on bathroom faucets, and studying the empty medicine chest.

In the kitchen, I looked into the broom closet, opened the cupboards, inspected the refrigerator, tried all five knobs on the stove, and noted the space for a table and chairs—had we owned any.

I hated it all. I'd come to California under protest, and a broom closet and real bathroom were not going to buy me.

"Which bedroom is mine? Or do I share?"

Mama looked at Aunt Betty. The natural thing would be for Mama and me to share a bedroom and let Aunt Betty have one to herself.

"Why don't you take the bedroom nearest the bath?" Aunt Betty said. "Your mama and I'll take the other one."

When we had unpacked the boxes, which contained blankets, towels, and a few kitchen items such as a tea kettle and a frying pan, the house looked as bare as it had before.

"What're we going to sleep on?" I asked. "And sit on?"

"For the time being, the floor."

"We don't even have pillows," I pointed out.

"We'll fold our coats and use them."

"It's so cold, we'll have to sleep in our coats."

"Well, we've got this nice little gas heater in the living room."

But when we turned the knob, all we heard was the hiss of escaping gas, no "pffffffouffff" of a burner lighting, no ticking of metal as it heated. The pilot had not been lit and we could find no place to light it. The project office was blocks away and we had no phone. In any case, it was Sunday and no one was likely to be in the office.

"Can we go back to the rooming house?"

"We don't have enough money."

"Didn't you get any money from your boss yet?"

"That's got to last the next two weeks."

"What about the money that Aunt Betty got from her boss?"

"That paid the rent here."

"I'm cold."

"What's the matter with me!" Mama said. "We can turn on the oven!"

When I'd warmed myself in front of the oven, I complained that I was hungry. Complaining relieved my misery a little.

"We've got to go to the store, wherever that is," Mama said.

"There was a place two or three miles back down the road," Aunt Betty recalled. "I saw it from the bus."

"Can I come?"

"We don't have a bus pass for you," Mama said. "Every time you ride, it costs money. Please don't cry."

I was sitting on the living room floor, back against the wall, knees drawn up. This was my worst day since Hilly Stillman killed himself.

Half an hour later, I dragged a handkerchief from my beat-up red patent leather purse, wiped my eyes, and blew my nose. Okay. Now, how in hell was I going to get back to Minnesota?

LATE TUESDAY AFTERNOON, when Mama came home from work, I was enlisted to help lug groceries from Jon's Market on the west side of Pacific Beach. Mama hated spending the bus fare for me, but she couldn't carry everything herself.

I wished I had a bus pass like Mama's. These buses made me feel grown up. I didn't know how to drive a car, but I knew how to ride a bus. And I knew how to ride a train. I'd grown up living in a railroad depot back in Minnesota, where my papa was still a depot clerk. I was four years old the first time I rode the train alone to Grandma Browning's.

Across from us on the bus sat a runty, sun-burned fellow holding a big lunch pail on his knees. He wore a Consolidated Aircraft identification badge on his shirt. Next to him, another country-looking fellow, hair water-slicked, white shirt yellowed from lying folded in a box, slouched against the window, looking wistful. They discussed the strangeness of employment practices at the plant.

"It's like the army," the runty fellow said. "The thing you're least suited t' do is the thing they'll give ya t' do. They take them tiny little women and make 'em riveters. I never see it to fail. Them rivetin' guns'll jar your liver loose. Absolutely loose."

Delivering himself of this wisdom, the runty fellow gazed forlornly into the downpour beyond the bus window and began to suck a tooth, as if further truths were lodged among its crannies.

A couple of stops later, the two descended into the leaden twilight, lunch pails over their heads to ward off the rain. They had no jackets, however, and their shirts were soaked before the bus was out of sight.

"Why didn't those men have jackets?"

"Next paycheck," Mama told me.

. . . .

SITTING ON THE LIVING ROOM FLOOR after dinner, I asked Mama, "What's a riveter?"

"Somebody who shoots rivets into airplanes to hold them together. Rivets are kind of like nails only they come out of a thing called a riveting gun. It's loud like a machine gun."

"I'm glad you don't do that," Aunt Betty said.

"Everyone says it was a miracle, my getting a job in the personnel office. I'm glad I wore my decent navy blue skirt and good white tailored-looking blouse. I looked like someone who knew her way around an office." I was disappointed by Mama's job. "You're not going to build airplanes?"

"Well, not with my actual hands, if that's what you mean."

"If I was working there, I'd want to build them with my actual hands. When an airplane bombed a Jap ship, I'd want to know that I'd helped."

"You're getting too caught up in the war," Mama said.

But in San Diego, everybody was caught up in the war. You couldn't help it. You were surrounded by servicemen wherever you turned. I couldn't look at them without thinking, "Maybe that one will die." I saw them, like Hilly, with their brains blown out and I'd get tears in my eyes and turn off my mind.

Another reminder of the war was the pretty little boarded-up bungalows you saw on the bus ride into downtown San Diego, their yards dusty and overgrown. In a city where housing was scarce, they were a curious sight. When I asked Mama why they were empty, she said they belonged to Japanese-Americans sent away to detention camps.

Another sight on the bus ride into town was war ships in the harbor, every kind of gray ghost slipping in and out: battleships and destroyers and aircraft carriers and submarines. I hadn't known anything about ships when I lived in Harvester, but now I was learning to identify them.

Mama was proud that San Diego had such a grand harbor. It reflected credit on her. Standing in the aisle of the bus, hanging on for dear life as we bounced over streets pot-holed and heaved from the rains, she'd say to Aunt Betty, "Look at that battleship, Betty. Isn't that beautiful? Can you believe that somebody made that? Aren't you glad I brought you here? War would be wonderful if no one got killed."

All over the city, posters reminded us to buy war bonds, give to the Red Cross, write to servicemen, and conserve rubber. We were admonished not to reveal war secrets or waste food. In their spare time, good Americans volunteered for air raid duty, rolled bandages, or collected scrap metal. They were alert and kept their eyes on the skies and on their fellow workers, who might be Axis saboteurs, a word I looked up in *Webster's Collegiate Dictionary*.

Mama and Aunt Betty did a lot of those things. On Tuesday evenings, Aunt Betty stayed in town after work and rolled bandages. She had not applied for a job at Consolidated, where Mama worked.

"I can't work in an airplane factory," she'd told Mama.

"Why not?"

"I might do something wrong and someone would die."

"*What?*"

"I might put a bolt in wrong or forget to put it in, and the plane would fall apart. I can't do it."

"If you were on the assembly line, you'd feel like you had a real part in winning the war," Mama pointed out. "You can't imagine how exciting it is, planes lined up in different stages of construction, men and women going from plane to plane doing their particular job. And you might even meet a nice 4-F."

"I'm going to apply for a job in a department store," Aunt Betty said.

"You won't make any money."

"I know something about working in a store. I worked in the Ben Franklin five and dime."

That was true. After Uncle Stanley left for California to look for work in '39, Aunt Betty had moved in with Grandma and Grandpa Browning in Blue Lake and eventually found a job at the Ben Franklin there.

Mama said Aunt Betty wouldn't have gotten into the mess with Mr. Miller, her boss, if Uncle Stanley hadn't strung her along in such a cruel way, promising and promising to send bus money, which never came.

I didn't know what the mess with Mr. Miller was but it had something to do with a one-day trip to Minneapolis in Mama's little coupé, a trip from which Aunt Betty returned white as a sheet, bleeding, and nearly dead.

At any rate, now Aunt Betty went to work selling ladies accessories at Gilpins' Department Store and rolling bandages for the Red Cross on Tuesday evenings. On Thursday evenings she served snacks at the U.S.O.

One thing neither Mama nor Aunt Betty did was air raid duty. Our neighborhood already had a great sufficiency of wardens. Until Aunt Betty and Mama could afford heavy window shades, no fewer than three wardens advised us that light was escaping through the sheets we had hung over the windows, signaling to Japanese planes so they could blast us to bits.

"Give people an armband and a helmet and they think they're J. Edgar Hoover," Mama said.

Because I was too young to be left alone at night and we couldn't afford a babysitter even if we'd known one, Mama spent her evenings on the living room floor making lists: things to buy when we had money; things to do when we had money. After securing a library card, she also read. She had finished *A Farewell to Arms* in a flood of tears. "Different war, but one damned bullet's just like another."

In February, the war came close to us. "Did you hear about the Jap sub?" my teacher, Miss Dubitsky, asked when I walked into the fourth grade room. She was an emotional woman, given to alarms.

"What Jap sub?" I laid my notebook on my desk and hung my sweater over the back of the chair.

"A Jap submarine surfaced off the coast up by Santa Barbara and it was shooting at some oil derricks or something."

"Did anybody get killed?" Dazed, I sat down, quaking inside. Mama had assured me that California wouldn't be attacked. What would they be thinking back in Harvester? Would Papa be out here on the next train to get me?

"I don't know." Miss Dubitsky slipped her lunch pail into the bottom left-hand drawer of her desk. "But if they ever got a submarine into our harbor and lobbed in shells, they could hit us where we sit, we're that close."

When Mama got home, I met her with the story of the Jap sub. At school they had talked endlessly about it. "The last time anybody saw it, it was headed for Los Angeles."

"I heard that navy planes went after it," Mama told me. "In a few days they'll find out it was sunk, mark my words." Rinsing out her thermos, Mama said, "I wonder why they attacked up there? San Diego is much more important." She sounded peeved with the Japanese.

I was sitting on the floor amidst the blankets where we slept, eating peanut butter and soda crackers. "They said people on shore were signaling to the submarine. Were those spies?"

Mama shrugged. "Most likely people imagined that." She slipped out of her shoes. "Finished your homework?"

I was attending the little jerry-built, clapboard elementary school they'd thrown together to accommodate us Okies and Arkies in the housing project. Although I was in the fourth grade, the lessons were ones I'd already had in the third grade back home.

"I don't have any homework. I got it done at school."

Mama looked troubled. "What do you do at school when you've finished?"

"I write."

"Letters?"

"No."

"What?"

"I write about home."

For now, making up stories about home was the only way I could get there. The stories made me forget where I was. When I wrote, everything else—San Diego, the Project—went away.

"Home?"

"Harvester. I make things up. Usually it's summer, and I live in a pretty house, and Hilly helps me plant a garden in the back. I'm about fourteen usually." Instead of nine.

"What else?" she asked, sitting down beside me on the floor.

"Remember how Papa wanted to buy the Linden house?"

"That was just to keep us from leaving." She pressed her lips hard together, remembering.

I said nothing. What was the point if she was going to get angry?

"Remember how we used to pretend that you were Mrs. Brown?"

Mama recalled, changing the subject, "and you had a husband and a little girl named Myrna Loy?"

I couldn't pretend to be Mrs. Brown anymore, not even to please Mama. My little girl, Myrna Loy, was gone and I couldn't get her back. Sometimes I tried, in my room after school, before Mama got home from work. I took out the doll I'd brought from Harvester, a soiled, rubber baby doll. I put on Mama's black high heels and a smear of lipstick and held the baby Myrna Loy in my arms. She was cold and hard and lifeless. In frustration, I bit off two of her fingers one day, then felt foolish and guilty. I tossed Myrna Loy into a corner of the closet, where she disappeared beneath a pile of dirty clothes.

I was too old for Mrs. Brown and Myrna Loy, too old even for the other fourth graders in my strange, one-story wooden school. It wasn't so much that I felt superior to them. I felt old and alien. We were all aliens, including Miss Dubitsky, late of Wauwwatosa, Wisconsin. But the other students soon hung together in little clots of humanity while I floated free, ancient, like someone who has outlived all her friends.

"I'm too old for that," I told Mama.

"It's hard being a child," Mama said. "You have to do what your parents want and live where they want, even if it makes you sad and old."

How ruthlessly reasonable adults were. "Why can't we do what makes me happy?"

"Because I'm selfish. Grown-ups are selfish. They do what they want and the children get dragged along. It's the way things are."

Did the beautiful woman on the City of Los Angeles have children? Did she ever do what *they* wanted?

From the bedroom that would be mine when it had a bed, I fetched the tablet and pencil I'd brought from Harvester. "The beautiful woman climbed up the bus steps. She said to the driver, 'My car has a flat tire and I need to get to the El Cortez Hotel. Do you go there?' Then she looked around and saw a little girl whose front teeth were still too big and who was holding an old red patint lether purse. . . ."

3

AND NOW I WAS LEARNING acrobatic tricks on the monkey bars at school. Girls who were daring and skilled on the monkey bars were respected. I spent hours leaping and swinging and flinging myself into space, a place without handholds, where my stomach felt empty.

Although strong, I was not a natural athlete, nor was I overly courageous. I had to talk myself through every leap and twist, no less so the two-hundredth time than the first. I would always be a foreigner in the land of the monkey bars.

This particular Friday afternoon in March was windy and gray. Grit blew into my eyes and mouth as I hung upside down, so I gathered my lunch pail and library books and headed home.

What a sorry-looking place Piñon Street was, I thought as I climbed the curving blacktop road, dusty with silt, toward number 136. West of the Project lay established neighborhoods with trees and grass where people lived long before the war. And beyond these, several miles distant, was the ocean. But here was spread an endless challenge to the human need to create home and yard out of whatever lay at hand. Few of the renters had yet planted grass on their plots, and not a tree marked the entire street.

In the mailbox beside our door were two letters from Papa, one of them for me; one letter from Grandma Browning addressed to Arlene, Betty, and Lark; and a packet of mail that had first been sent to general delivery, Los Angeles, and was only now reaching us in San Diego. In this batch was an envelope addressed to Aunt Betty in Uncle Stanley's graceful hand. It had traveled to Harvester, then back to Los Angeles, and now here.

Uncle Stanley had left Morgan Lake, Minnesota, during the Depression, and he lived in Los Angeles, painting sets at Paramount Studios. I missed him and was sorry we hadn't looked him up when we went through there; he didn't even know yet that Aunt Betty was in California.

During the bad times, Uncle Stanley had been ashamed to tell anybody that he wasn't making money out on the road selling farm implements, and he and Aunt Betty practically starved. After Aunt Betty was nearly carried off by uremic poisoning and their baby was born dead, Mama had the idea of pooling the family's pennies and sending Uncle Stanley west to look for work. Everyone hoped he might hook on at Paramount, where a distant cousin had found work.

As soon as he had the money, Uncle Stanley had promised to send Aunt Betty enough for a ticket on the Greyhound. But some emergency, some pressing need for his extra funds, always arose, and eventually people began to think of Uncle Stanley as if he were dead, although he did occasionally write to Aunt Betty.

Mama scorned Uncle Stanley and called him a four-flusher. But Aunt Betty was still crazy about him, even though she wouldn't look him up in Los Angeles because, she said, she had her pride. If he wanted her, he had to send the bus fare.

Now here was a letter. What if he wanted to get back together and he had sent Aunt Betty bus fare? And there we'd been, already in Los Angeles, not knowing. I held the letter to the light, but Uncle Stanley had used a privacy envelope with a blue lining.

Laying all the mail except my letter from Papa on the kitchen counter, I sat cross-legged on the living room floor and carefully slit the envelope from Papa with my fingernail. Two sheets of lined paper trembled in my hands as I unfolded them, and a dollar bill fell into my lap.

Dear Lark,

How's my little girl? Are you missing your Pa? You've probably got so many California friends now, you don't have time to worry about Harvester and the pals you had here.

But we're worrying about you. Beverly stopped by the depot office yesterday to inquire about you. She said she hadn't had a letter in some time and she was worried maybe the Japs had bombed San Diego. Ha ha.

I told her she'd have to be my little girl now and go fishing with me when bullhead season opens. She thought that was a swell idea.

I can't believe your Ma ran off and took you with her. I did everything in my power to make her happy.

Maybe she'd come back if you were to tell her how sad you are, being so far away from your Pa.

I've got a cold that settled in my chest and acts like pneumonia. I'm running a pretty good fever but couldn't locate the thermometer, which your Ma no doubt took.

I plan to take a vacation later and come out there. I won't say when. It'll be a surprise. Some day I'll just turn up on your doorstep.

In the meantime, go to Mass every Sunday and say your rosary. Light a candle and ask God to look after your Pa, who loves you.

This letter is for you, not your Ma, so put it where it will be safe.

It was signed "Pa," and there was a P.S. "The dollar is to pay for candles at the next few Masses."

Although I loved and missed Papa, his letter made me feel anxious, as if a big, black bird were hovering above me, waiting to land on my head. Folding the note, I returned it to the envelope, slipping it and the dollar bill beneath my underwear in the tan grip in my closet.

What should I do about the money? When the priest in Harvester refused to bury Hilly Stillman because Hilly had blown his brains out, I quit the Church and didn't intend on going back.

Dinner that night was a strange occasion, all of us affected by our letters. Mama and Aunt Betty, unraveling along their seams, were by turns garrulous, abstracted, and frightened.

"Mama says Donald Hanson enlisted in the Coast Guard," Aunt Betty said, poring over Grandma Browning's letter while she ate hot dogs and macaroni salad standing at the counter. Tucked into the pocket of her long-out-of-date beige chambray dress was Uncle Stanley's well-traveled letter. She was saving it for dessert, however disappointing it might prove.

Mama and I were sitting on the kitchen floor.

"Who's Donald Hanson?" I asked.

"He used to take me to the dances before I met Uncle Stanley," Aunt Betty explained. She stabbed a piece of hot dog but her hand froze and the meat remained on the plate. "I didn't know they were taking men as old as Donald Hanson."

"If they're breathing, they'll take them," Mama told her.

Aunt Betty lifted the fork to her mouth, chewing very slowly.

Mama said, "Stanley's got a good job at the studio. I doubt he'd enlist at his age." She carried her plate to the sink. "It's not as if he had a hero's reputation to live up to."

"That was mean," Aunt Betty cried, throwing down Grandma's letter and running out of the kitchen.

Where was she going to hurl herself, into the empty bedroom? Dignity was difficult in a house without furniture.

. . . .

Later, buried among the covers, lying between Mama and Aunt Betty, I heard them murmuring in the dark.

"What makes me so mean?" Mama wondered aloud. "I'm sorry. What did Stanley have to say in his letter?"

"Nothing new," Aunt Betty told her.

Mama said nothing.

"There was mail for Erhardt Typing Service," Aunt Betty said.

"The last accounts receivable. Fifty-one dollars."

"And Willie?"

Exhaling angrily, Mama pulled the covers tight around her. "He says he's coming to drag me back."

"Can he do that?"

"He's going to get a court order, he says. If I won't go, he'll take Lark. He says he's seen a lawyer."

"Do you think he has?"

"I don't know. Willie's treacherous."

Aunt Betty stretched out a hand across the lump that was me and Mama put her own into it.

The distant boom of coastal anti-aircraft guns shook the house.

Preparing to leave for work the following Saturday morning, Mama drew me into the kitchen while Aunt Betty plucked her eyebrows and put on her face in the bathroom.

"Here's a bus token," Mama told me, pressing it into my hand. "I want you to meet me in the plaza at half past twelve."

On Saturdays Mama worked only half days.

"Why?"

"It's a surprise."

"Who for?"

"All of us."

"How can it be a surprise if you already know? Is Uncle Stanley coming? Are we going to meet him at the depot?"

"This has nothing to do with Uncle Stanley. Just mind me and don't say a word to your aunt. I want her to have a happy surprise." She looked at me closely. "Do you understand?"

I nodded, understanding very little.

At twenty past eleven I climbed onto the bus. I would be downtown at least half an hour before Mama arrived. During that stolen half hour, I circumnavigated the plaza, relishing the drugstores and haberdasheries, straying into side streets to appreciate the pawn shops and the jazzy music from cheap bars.

At twelve-thirty I settled onto a bench close to Mama's bus stop, my ratty-looking red patent leather purse, with its treasure of seven cents, resting on my lap. My brown oxfords—my only pair of shoes—were a disgrace, the toes scuffed to threadbare, and the laces indecorously knotted where they'd broken.

Most of the time, I didn't notice my shabbiness. There were plenty of down-at-the-heels kids in the fourth grade. But when I was thrust among hundreds of spiffy servicemen and their dolled-up girlfriends, I stuck out like a sore thumb.

Next to me sat a Marine, as clean and brand-new looking as a magazine illustration. He smelled of cigarettes and Aqua Velva.

"Waiting for your mother?" he asked, studying me as if I reminded him of someone.

I nodded and tried to hide my shoes under the bench.

"You look like my sister's girl, Marianne. She's about your age. Eight, nine?"

"Nine." I spoke with my lips barely parted. No point in showing him my teeth, which were still way too big for me.

"Well, you're a pretty little girl," he said. Then, spying his Marine friends, he rose to join them.

"Thank you," I called after him. I was saddened by his kindness because I knew that I was anything but pretty. With my thin, mousy hair, which Mama no longer had time to curl, and a Minnesota dress that was too short for a child my age, I looked like a Polish war orphan.

I thought of the beautiful woman on the train in her houndstooth trousers and fox jacket. What caprice of nature or God accounted for such a creature existing in the same universe as Lark Ann Browning Erhardt? But after the death of Aunt Betty's baby and the suicide of Hilly Stillman, I no longer looked to God for plans that made sense. If He had a plan, it was eminently callous.

Still, I didn't resent the Houndstooth Lady's beauty. She was a happy accident, like a shooting star streaking suddenly through my sky. I wished I could wash the dishes at her house.

A busload of Consolidated workers pulled to the curb, and Mama in her navy skirt, white blouse, and "stylish but sensible" Cuban heels, waved to me from the crowded aisle. Soon she appeared on the sidewalk, swinging her navy purse and black lunch pail. Her hair was swept into a pompadour in front while the back fell into a snood like the assembly line girls wore. But for the brown roots pushing up beneath the henna, she looked like a lady on a War Effort poster.

Before we'd left Minnesota, both Mama and Aunt Betty had splurged on a trip to the beauty parlor, from which Mama had emerged the redhead she'd dreamt of being. Aunt Betty was by nature a pinkish blonde and perhaps Mama envied her that. In any case, Grandma Browning had nearly collapsed upon seeing Mama's new hair color. "A Minneapolis streetwalker" was what Mama looked like, Grandma said. With her hair cut short and pulled into a mass of short curls at the back, Mama looked to me like Norma Shearer in *The Women*.

"Can you tell me the secret now?" I asked Mama, falling into step with her as she turned left, legging purposefully away from the plaza.

"We're going to buy some furniture," she said, parting the Saturday afternoon throng with her headlong march. "Melba's uncle owns a furniture store in our price range." Melba was Mama's friend in the personnel office at Consolidated.

"Where did we get the money?"

"I got fifty-one dollars from Erhardt Typing Service."

"Is that enough?" I was running to keep up.

"It's a start. We'll charge the rest."

"Grandma says charge is the road to perdition."

"I don't want to hear what Grandma says. Grandma's not sleeping on the floor."

Our first stop was Victory Furniture, just beyond the central and most congested part of downtown. With a representative display of furniture arranged on the sidewalk, Victory Furniture crouched low, haunch by hindquarter with other cut-rate businesses.

Ignoring two salesmen—one outside, leaning against an indigo sofa and trimming his cuticles, and a second just inside the door, appreciating himself in the mirror of a walnut bureau—we headed for the quarter-acre of desk piled high with a clutter of sales agreements, *Police Gazettes,* and *Wild West Tales.*

Later, when Mama had bought a sofa and chair, two beds, and three bureaus, she cast a doubtful glance at an old Negro man with skin the color of dark honey who sat on a kitchen chair beside his ancient truck at the rear of Victory Furniture. A hand-lettered sign on the truck's cab read, "Hauling—Any Sort."

The old man, who said his name was Lou, assured Mama that he and his truck could haul whatever she'd purchased.

Mama started to walk back into the store.

"Ma'am?"

"Yes?"

Hat in hand, eyes fixed on an invisible point of reference in the middle distance, he hesitated. Then, slapping the felt hat against his leg, he asked, "You want to ride with me in the truck when I deliver your furniture? You could sit on the divan in the back, if you want. And if you got other stops, I could taxi you where you got to go."

Never in her life had Mama been this far in debt, she confided as we watched Lou secure the last bureau. Four hundred dollars. Fourteen dollars a month for the next three years.

Climbing into the truck, Mama said, "Trustworthy Second Hand is the next stop." She gave Lou an address and the directions her friend Melba had provided. "Also, I need a cheap little radio and a deck of cards."

The old man laughed. "Sounds like you been short on entertainment."

We creaked and clattered toward Trustworthy Second Hand, which was considerably south of downtown, and on the way Lou pulled to the curb in front of an electrical repair shop.

"Might be you'll find a cheap little radio here," he said.

We had an entire shelf of unclaimed radios to choose from, but the man behind the counter, who inquired, "That Lou out there?" suggested a Zenith table model with a handsome walnut case as our best bet.

When we stopped next, Lou asked, "You got twenty-five cents, ma'am?" and he climbed down from the truck and disappeared through the side door of Slattery's Pool and Billiards. "These folks get cards cheap from Mexico," he explained minutes later, handing me two sealed decks of playing cards.

The cavernous Trustworthy Second Hand was shadowy, filthy, and sinister. A place from which children might be kidnapped and women sold into white slavery, Mama observed, grasping my hand.

Stepping gingerly, she examined tables and lamps. I tiptoed among a wicked maze of stacked-up odds and ends. Rounding a tower of tables piled every which way, I half swallowed a scream.

On a musty, disintegrating Victorian sofa, a body was laid out in threadbare tweeds, with a tweed cap over its face. Scuffed brown shoes with stained spats covered the feet.

"What's the idea o' startlin' a man out of his slumber?" he muttered crossly from behind the cap.

"I thought you were dead," I whispered. "It's spooky in here."

Sitting up, he rubbed his eyes with his knuckles, like a child. "Spooky? This treasure house of sweet rejectamenta? You're surrounded by beauty out of season. Tragedy by the square yard."

"I'd like to buy some of it." Mama appeared at my elbow. "For the right price," she added.

"Price is a word I resist. I put no price tags on my collection. No more than y'd put a price on an orphan."

Rising to his feet, the little man thrust tweedy-looking hands into his hip pockets and rocked back and forth on the disreputable brown shoes.

"To what sort of treasure did y' wish t' give home?" he asked, digging into his breast pocket for a toothpick.

"I need a kitchen table and chairs," Mama told him. "Also lamps and a bookcase. I have thirty-five dollars to spend."

He ran freckled hands through freckled hair, worrying a freckled scalp as if scruples were tearing at him. "Well, then, y' must look around and select the pieces y' fancy. When y've done, I'll say whether it's a deal."

Mama wandered in one direction, I in another. Propped against a table leg in a particularly stygian corner, I found an oil painting in an ornate and out-of-favor gilt frame. Jumbles of paintings and prints and family photos littered the store, but this one, with its serene familiarity, drew me. A log cabin stood among snow-shawled evergreens. Snow lay deeply drifted in a lane that led to a sturdy door and windows, where an ochre glow cast a welcome across the snow. Against a deep blue night, the lantern moon led the traveler.

I lowered myself onto a horsehair fainting couch, staring my way into the oil painting, past the sturdy door and into the dim, warm room where a fire leapt in the grate. On a table pulled up close was a plate stacked with toast, and beside that a substantial cup with "Rayzeen's Lumberyard, Harvester, Minnesota" printed on the side. Steam rose from the cocoa, where melting marshmallows floated. Shucking my coat, galoshes, and oxfords beside the door, I crossed the room and climbed into the armchair, stretching my stockinged feet toward the fire. I reached for the topmost slice of toast, dunked it into the cocoa, and sucked the chocolate juice. Hilly would feel safe in the remoteness and warmth of this cabin. And he would laugh to find the cocoa waiting. Three and a half months had passed since his death, but it was as painful now as in December.

"Do you favor that?" the freckled man inquired, nodding toward the painting.

"Yes."

"It's on sale for a dollar. Have y' got a dollar?"

"No."

"Pity," he clucked.

"Mama gives me ten cents a week," I told him, "but I've spent it." Papa had sent me a dollar for candles, but I couldn't spend that for a painting. It would be a sin.

"I suppose I could sell it t' y' on credit," he allowed.

"Is that the same as charge?"

"Correct."

"Charge is the road to perdition," I said.

"Whoever told y' that?"

"Grandma Browning."

"Ah, well, maybe I could take an IOU."

"What's that?"

"It's where y' sign a piece of paper that says y' owe me one dollar and that y'll pay it to me by . . ." He calculated. "By June fifteenth of nineteen hundred and forty-two." His gaze considered the painting. "A cunning piece, ain't it? Makes y' feel right at home."

"What does?" Mama materialized from around the side of a china cupboard.

I pointed to the painting. She took it in slowly, then appraised me through narrowed lids, two perpendicular worry lines appearing between her eyes.

"It's on sale today for a dollar," I explained. "I want to sign an IOU."

"It doesn't go with our new sofa and chair."

"It's for *my* room."

"How will you pay for it?" she asked in a pinchy voice, as if the painting were a disloyalty.

"I'll save my allowance. Please, Mama?"

Afraid that she would say no, I rose and walked away.

"Lark," she called in the same pinchy voice.

Clasping my hands over my ears, I hurried on.

"Lark!"

To my right was a dark, towering beadboard cupboard, like one in the cabin. I opened it, stepped in, and pulled the door to. Its dimness smelled of dust and age and grandmothers. I crouched in the corner, pressing my face against the wood.

At length, there were rustlings and murmurings close at hand and the door was opened. "All right," Mama said in a dry, displeased tone, "you've had your way. You can sign an IOU."

From my red patent leather purse I extracted a soft old hanky with yellow chrysanthemums printed on it. Wiping my face and blowing my nose, I climbed out of the cupboard.

Mama had worries and responsibilities; I had longings and memories. She didn't want to think about those because they would lie on her like yet another responsibility. Since coming to California, we knew each other less and less. I felt as if I were waving good-bye to her from the deck of a questionably seaworthy vessel, bound across dangerous waters.

WHEN THE TRUCK WAS LOADED, the second-hand dealer stood at the curb, addressing Mama but surveying the furniture we'd taken possession of.

"I know y'r a woman who'll treat these dears with the respect they deserve," he murmured.

Lou lifted me into the back, where I sat on the new sofa from Victory Furniture, clasping the oil painting.

"They've got character and worth," continued Mr. Trustworthy, his hand on the door of the truck, loath to part. "And history. One day y'll lay a hand on the wood, and y'll hear such a story, comin' to y' through y'r skin. It's happened t' me." He let go of the door then and waved us away.

Although these parting words were spoken to Mama, I appropriated them. It could happen. You'd lay your hand on a piece of furniture and hear stories. Mr. Trustworthy knew what he was talking about.

When we had made one final stop, the old truck rattled past the harbor, airport, and Consolidated, heading north and west to Pacific Beach. With much scraping of unwilling gears, we turned off of Garnet onto Piñon.

"Might as well back the truck right up to the door," Mama told Lou as we approached 136. "There's no grass you can hurt."

We set up the beds first, so that I could make them while Lou and Mama arranged the remaining furniture. When we were nearly finished, Mama sent Lou out to move the truck to the street.

"We don't want Betty to suspect. And bring in that bag on the front seat," she added.

Our last stop had been for rum and half a dozen bottles of Coca-Cola.

"You'll have a drink," Mama told Lou as he plugged in two living room lamps whose tattered silk shades would need replacing when we had the money.

"Maybe half," he said, screwing a light bulb into its socket.

"It's pleasant to sit by lamp light, isn't it? I don't like overhead light. It makes everything look like a depot waiting room." Mama was sitting on the new beige sofa, Lou on a kitchen chair. I stood hugging to myself the safe, smug feeling furnishings can give you, even in a place where you don't want to live.

Mama was flushed and fluttery, gabbing on as if to a girlfriend. "My sister Betty will probably fall over in a dead faint when she sees all this furniture. She's been depressed. She's separated from her husband. But when she sees this, she's going to perk up. Now we have a real home. I think that's important, don't you, to make a place a real home?"

"Yes, ma'am, I do," Lou said.

In Minnesota, Negroes were as scarce as gardenias, so sharing a drink with Lou lent an element of the exotic to Mama's and my life. I kept expecting him to do or say something Negro, something foreign that would be a mystery to me and that I would attribute to our different colors. But everything he said and did made perfect sense and was the sort of thing that Grandpa Browning would say or do. For instance, he held his hat on one knee the way Grandpa did, and said, "You got to be careful who you take into your home, ma'am. Like me, for example, I wouldn't do no harm, but you wouldn't want to invite every fellow who hauls furniture, you understand?"

"I appreciate the advice."

I thought Lou was growing uncomfortable. Maybe his family was waiting his dinner.

"Do you have family, Lou?" Mama asked.

"Yes, ma'am. Boy's getting ready to enlist. Girl works at Gilpins'."

"That's where my sister Betty works. Where does your daughter work? What's her name?"

"Her name is Esther and she works in the ladies' restroom."

"Well, Betty will . . . go in and say hello." Quickly off on another tack, Mama inquired, "Have you always lived in San Diego?"

"No, ma'am. Moved from Virginia to New York long time ago. Nineteen hundred. After my mama passed on. Couldn't see no future in Virginia."

"Nineteen hundred." Mama whistled. "That was a long time ago."

"Yes, ma'am. Moved to California in 1921." He wet his throat with a small swig from the rum and Coca-Cola, then rose, handing me his glass and saying, "I got to go."

Mama got her purse from the bureau in the bedroom. "I want to give you two dollars, Lou."

"You paid me, back at Victory Furniture, ma'am."

"But you ended up carting me around all day. I won't feel right. At least take a dollar."

"I like to leave it just like it is, ma'am."

"Do you have a telephone?"

"No, ma'am. But I'm usually back there behind the furniture store."

We watched him head out into the thickening twilight. The engine of the ancient truck moaned and sputtered but finally caught. Lou turned on the truck's low beams, the upper portion of which had been painted black to comply with wartime regulations, and nudged the old vehicle out into the street as one might encourage a venerable nag with gentle prodding.

Closing the door behind us and throwing her arms up in the air, Mama whooped, "Isn't it beautiful? Isn't our house beautiful?"

She drifted around the living room, repositioning pieces of furniture, then patting them as if they were well-behaved children. "I mean, it still needs plenty of work, rugs, curtains . . . but it's *home* now, Lark!"

Aunt Betty was coming up the stoop, and Mama giggled and squirmed. "We'll holler, 'Surprise!' when she comes in," she whispered, grabbing my hand and dancing up and down.

The door opened.

"Surprise!"

6

If we imagined that Aunt Betty was going to dance the tarantella, we were mistaken. She stood inside the door in her threadbare Minnesota coat, purse clutched to her breast, and looked around, doing calculations. "How much?"

Running a hand nervously along the back of the pale rose chair from Victory Furniture, Mama smiled without purpose, explaining, "The radio and the things from the second hand store I paid for with my Erhardt Typing Service money. The rest is on time payments. In my name. I never mentioned your name. If I die, you won't have to pay a dime."

Aunt Betty had been poor and miserable in Minnesota. Now she was poor and miserable in California. In Minnesota Mama had been the bossy one, the one who had her way, and she still was. This despite Aunt Betty being five years older. When was she ever going to get out from under? All this lay on Aunt Betty's shoulders, hunching them round, like an old woman's.

Slowly my aunt began removing her coat. Folding it over her arm, she fondled its shabbiness and slumped against the door. I could hear our breathing over the whisper of the gas heater.

Fifty-two cents an hour plus commission was what Aunt Betty drew from Gilpins'. But in ladies accessories you could half kill yourself and never reach the minimum sales beyond which commission was paid. So far, Aunt Betty had earned a dollar and three cents above her salary.

"I need a new coat, Arlene. I haven't had a new coat since I was married. When I go to work, I take off my coat before I walk through the revolving door so no one'll see it." Despite the words, Aunt Betty spoke mildly, and her mildness carried away Mama's giggles.

"I've got pieces of cereal box in the bottom of my shoes to cover the holes. So has Lark," my aunt went on with no more emotion than if she were saying her rosary. "I own one brassiere and keep washing it out. If that isn't dry in the morning, I wear it wet." She drifted into the kitchen and out, then into the bedroom she was to share with Mama. We heard her at the closet, hanging up her coat.

Mama moved to the bedroom door. I followed. Aunt Betty was undressing and pulling on her flannel night gown.

"I'll get supper on," Mama told her.

But Aunt Betty turned her back and knelt beside the new bed, arms resting on top of it, hands clasped. Crossing herself, she began to say her silent prayers.

Except for "please pass the syrup," Mama and I spoke hardly a word during supper, sitting at the new second hand table. Aunt Betty did not appear.

"I shouldn't have spent the typing service money at Trustworthy Second Hand," Mama allowed, picking at her pancakes and Spam. "I should have used that money for shoes and coats. Sometimes I don't stop to think."

. . . .

WHEN *YOUR HIT PARADE* WAS OVER, Mama made herself a weak rum and Coca-Cola—the celebratory one she'd intended to share with Aunt Betty—and handed me a half glass of Coca-Cola.

Had Papa listened to *Your Hit Parade?* If I knew the programs Papa was listening to, I could tune them in and we'd be connected by radio.

That was less threatening than his turning up unexpected on our door-step. I curled up on the beige sofa; Mama settled into the rosy chair, patting and caressing the arm.

"I got into a furniture frenzy today," she said, staring into the glow cast beneath the raggedy lampshade. "Something drove me." Her voice hummed with vehemence, but also bewilderment. "Sometimes I need to feel . . . powerful. I need to feel in control. When you spend money, you feel powerful." She looked at me. Did I understand?

Some.

She glanced toward the bedroom, as if explaining to the sleeping Aunt Betty. "I also wanted this place to be cozy and pretty." She laughed a jerky little laugh. "Those are the two things I want, Lark: to be pow-erful and to have things cozy." She started to lift the tumbler of rum and Coca-Cola, then paused, staring at something in her thoughts. Was there something else she wanted?

"Did you want this place to be like the Cape Ann?" I asked, wishing that we could talk about that.

Mama looked piqued. "*This* is our new beginning," she said, flour-ishing her glass to indicate 136 Piñon, *not* the Cape Ann.

When Mama and I had planned to build a house in Harvester, she had picked out a lot, one block east of Saint Boniface Catholic Church. She dreamed up pretty ideas for every room, and I planned a garden where Hilly Stillman and I could plant flowers. The Cape Ann was to be the new beginning for Mama, Papa, and me.

I carried my untouched glass to the kitchen and put it in the refrigera-tor. "I'm going to bed," I told her.

"Don't you want to talk?"

"No, thank you."

Before turning the covers back, I stood my painting on the new bu-reau opposite the new bed. I could see Mama in the living room in the rose chair, staring at the wall over the gas heater and playing with her hair. I'd forgotten to ask her what the black and tan was. Mr. Trustworthy had mentioned troubles with an officer of the black and tan back in '20. It was nothing to do with putting your hand on a piece of furniture and hearing stories, I was sure. Tomorrow I would put my hand on the new end table. And when I saw Mr. Trustworthy again, I'd tell him what I heard.

Reaching for the *Webster's Collegiate Dictionary,* I opened it and poked a finger at a page: *crosier.* A cross-shaped staff carried by a bishop, abbott, or abbess. Well, you couldn't expect to get a useful word every time. Now, *kismet,* that was a useful word.

When I woke Sunday morning, I thought I was at Grandma's house in Blue Lake, because I was lying in a real bed. Finally it came to me. Then I thought, today Aunt Betty's going to Mass.

Up to now, our lives had been so torn up that no one, not even my aunt, expected us to make it to church, which was a long bus ride away. But starting today, Aunt Betty was going, and she wanted me to go along. Well, no.

When Hilly was refused burial in the Catholic cemetery, Father Delias had admonished me to forgive the Church as I would forgive my dearest friend. Mama had warned against cutting off my nose to spite my face, and Aunt Betty had alluded to pride going before a fall. Papa had assured me that if the Japs bombed California, I would go directly to hell since my soul was not in a state of grace.

Sometimes at night I thought of burning in hell, and tears of self-pity wet the pillow. But if I went to church only to save my soul, I would despise myself for turning my back on Hilly. If the Japs came, I'd take my chances.

In the living room, Mama was telling Aunt Betty, "I'm putting change beside your purse. When you come back from church, would you bring a Sunday paper?"

"You're not going?"

"No." Both Mama and Aunt Betty were converts to Catholicism, but Aunt Betty's conversion had "taken" better than Mama's.

"And Lark?" Aunt Betty asked.

"I can't make her go."

"Of course you can. She's only nine years old."

"She'll go when she's ready."

"What about you?"

Mama didn't answer. She blamed the Church for Papa's weakness. She'd once said, "When a man can go out on Friday night, get drunk, lose his paycheck gambling, and then go to confession on Saturday, and by Sunday he's Saint Willie of Harvester, what chance does a wife have? According to the Church, if a car hits Willie between Saturday night and Sunday noon, he'll go to heaven. He'd better make an appointment with death."

While Mama took a bath, I knelt on the sofa, closed my eyes, and laid my hands on the end table. For five minutes I remained kneeling while a story passed into my fingers, not like an electric current, but like a stream of warmth.

In the bedroom, I took up the tablet and pencil and began writing.

Grandma Spencer lived in a cottage at the edge of a little town. She grew beautiful flowers in her yard. Daisies and lilaks and peeonies and clematis and other ones too.

When her grandchildren whose names were Becky and Marie were small they loved to visit and help with the garden. Grandma Spencer let them pick bookays for the dining room table and for the end table in the living room and for their bedroom upstairs.

But the girls were ladies now and they lived far away with their husbands and their houses. And they only came to visit at Christmas.

On summer afternoons when Grandma Spencer was done working in her yard, she made a pot of tea and sat on the sofa, looking out and remembering Becky and Marie digging in the dirt.

Looking at the end table beside the sofa she remembered the water glasses filled with flowers that Becky and Marie had picked.

Then Grandma Spencer put her hand on the table. The children touched this table she thought. Now I touch it and we are close to each other through the wood. And it was true. When she put her hand on the table they were there with her for a little while.

When she died they found her sitting on the sofa with her hand on that table.

I tore the pages out of the tablet and laid them on the bureau. I would send them to Mr. Trustworthy to let him know that he'd been right.

Later, when I had pulled on an old pair of shorts that rode up in the crotch and a blouse with smocking across the shoulders that made me feel like a baby, I poured a bowl of Wheaties, going light on the sugar. Sugar was scarce. Mama's friend Melba said we could get all the sugar we wanted in Mexico, and when we had money she would drive us down to Tijuana.

I sat at the kitchen window, looking out on the bare ground on either side of our stoop. We needed to plant something there. If I had Grandma's Burpee catalog, I could look up flowers that grew in washing-away sand and hard yellow clay.

"Mama, let's talk about flowers."

"Flowers?" Breaking the color capsule with her thumbs, Mama leaned against the kitchen counter, massaging a bag of oleo, working the saffron color through the margarine.

"We need to plant flowers. And grass. This place looks awful."

"We don't have any money."

"Couldn't we just talk about it?" She wasn't in the mood. "Please, Mama?" I wheedled, dragging her out the door. She was still kneading the ole as we stood in bright sunlight and I pointed out, "We could plant flowers there, along the west side of the house, so you wouldn't see the bottom of it."

Constructed atop large concrete blocks, the houses—each of them two back-to-back units—had shadowy, open crawl spaces beneath, where I'd been told by schoolmates that black widow spiders and rattlesnakes lived. With flowers, we could maybe box the spiders and snakes in.

Mama squinted off into the Land of Slim Prospects. "What kind of flowers?"

From around the opposite end of the building lumbered a pair of overweight English bull dogs, merry as fat old men on vacation.

"Cecil, Percy!" a throaty voice called.

In no mood for commands, Cecil and Percy trotted toward me.

A tall woman, about Aunt Betty's age, wearing a garment splashed with pink, red, and blue blossoms, strove to overtake the dogs while keeping her wrapper closed.

"Percy, Cecil, don't frighten the little girl." She turned toward me. "Most people are frightened to death of those faces, but they won't bite."

I bent to pet first one and then the other. The woman adjusted the furled silk scarf that held her shoulder-length graying blonde hair away from her face.

"My name's Fanny Dugan. My husband's name is Jack. Those are our two children, Cecil and Percy." She laughed a rasping laugh. "We're from Chicago."

Pulling a pack of Spuds from her pocket, she lit one, inhaled profoundly, and blew smoke rings into the morning air.

"I work half days at the elementary school. In the office," she told Mama. "Jack works at Consolidated. You too?"

"Yes, Consolidated," Mama said. "I'm Arlene Erhardt. This is my daughter Lark. My sister Betty lives with us. We're from Minnesota."

"I saw you and Lark—isn't that a pretty name?—looking at this . . . desert," Fanny Dugan said, pointing with her cigarette to the side yard we shared. "Jack bought a spade and rake yesterday. We're putting in daisies up along the edge of the house. If you'd like daisies, we could work something out."

"Thank you."

"We're all strangers here. It'll be a damned long war if we're not neighborly." Again she swallowed a deep drag from the cigarette. How did her meager chest hold it all?

"Have you met your other neighbors?" she wondered, releasing smoke from her nose like a benign dragon and pointing again with the cigarette, this time at the door of the next unit, the door facing our own across a shared sidewalk leading to the street. No more than twenty feet separated the two entrances.

"They're a brother and sister, Belle and Beau. Let me think. What was the last name? Ellery? Everett? Eldridge. Yes. Belle and Beau Eldridge from a spot in the road in . . . North Dakota? Or Nebraska?"

As if we'd inquired, she added, "He might be forty or fifty. She could be fifty or sixty."

The two dogs were sniffing around the Eldridges' front steps.

"Cecil! Percy! You do your job there and I'll box your ears!" They turned sad faces toward Mrs. Dugan and, one after the other, lifted a leg against the Eldridge stoop.

"Naughty boys," Fanny drawled. She clapped her hands to summon the animals. "Shall I get the leash? They hate the leash." She swung about as if to return to the house for the leash.

Percy and Cecil stood on their short, crooked legs, cocking their heads at her. "Oh, hell," Fanny sighed, then laughed. "Jack will bring them back. They mind Jack."

Just then, Fanny's husband appeared, heading toward us. He was shorter than his wife by an inch or two, but strong and wiry. The sleeves of his shirt were rolled to the elbows, revealing knots of muscle and lending the impression that he might plunge into vigorous labor at any moment. "Need help, Fan?"

She pointed to the dogs, chasing each other up the row of houses along Piñon. Placing a thumb and little finger between his teeth, Mr. Dugan whistled sharply. The dogs skidded to a halt, turned to inquire, then bounded back.

While Mama and the Dugans were discussing the dogs and the yard and the war, Aunt Betty returned from church, carrying both a newspaper and a many-colored bouquet of giant zinnias.

"Twenty-five cents," she said, holding them up.

"Aren't they riotous?" Fanny exclaimed.

"Like your bathrobe," I observed.

"It's a kimono," Mama said.

Shortly after Mama introduced Aunt Betty to Fanny and Jack, the gathering broke up, the Dugans fetching Cecil and Percy into the house, Aunt Betty, Mama, and I heading in to read the Sunday paper.

Aunt Betty filled an empty mayonnaise jar with water, arranged the zinnias in it, and placed them on the table beside the sofa. Sitting down with a section of the newspaper, she said, "I could hardly wait to get home from church and sit on the sofa and read the paper."

She had forgiven Mama.

I flopped down on the floor to read the funnies. "We need a rug."

Mama tossed the first section of the newspaper aside. "Burma, Java, the Philippines. It's all retreat, retreat, retreat. When do we start advancing?"

My head jerked up. "Are the Japs coming?"

"No."

"Why not?"

"Because it's too far."

"Then how come we keep having air raid drills?"

"Because in wartime you have to be ready for everything, even if it doesn't happen."

"I wish I could be an air raid warden."

"Why, for heaven's sake?"

"So I could wear a helmet and arm band and be important when the Japs come."

Aunt Betty said, "Here's a picture of that woman on the train, the one you were so taken with."

"The one with the fox jacket?" I jumped up to see.

Aunt Betty handed me the rotogravure section of the paper. There she was indeed, coming out of the Coconut Grove night club with the same cigar-smoking old man.

"'European prima ballerina Alicia (Arkovsky) Armand and Hollywood producer Harvey Alch after Coconut Grove fund-raiser for displaced European children,'" I read aloud. "She's a ballet dancer?"

"That's what it says."

"She's got on a crown. Is she a princess?"

"It's a tiara and I doubt it."

"Can I cut this out? I'm going to collect pictures of the famous people I meet."

"You didn't meet her," Mama said.

"If we went up to Los Angeles and visited Uncle Stanley, I might."

"We're not going to visit your uncle," Aunt Betty said.

"What did Stanley say in that letter you got?" Mama wanted to know.

Because Mama usually sent me outside to play when they started talking about Uncle Stanley, I snatched the funny papers from the floor and headed for the bathroom, where I locked the door and began running water in the sink. With the bathroom drinking glass, I pressed my ear to the door as I'd seen someone do in a Thin Man movie.

"Nothing new," Aunt Betty was saying. "He talked about his friends from the studio who've enlisted. He says they're hiring new people. It was all like that, lots of writing without saying anything." She paused. "He sent a twenty-five dollar money order."

"Well, that's news. He never sent money before. Was it for a bus ticket, did he say?"

"No, he didn't. He said he thought I probably had uses I could put it to. It's like alimony."

A long silence followed.

"Don't you think?" my aunt said.

Mama didn't answer at once. Finally she said, "Maybe he's ashamed to ask you to come, since so much time's gone by."

"Do you think that could be it, that he's embarrassed?"

"It's possible."

Aunt Betty blew her nose, and when she spoke she sounded brighter. "I'll put it in the bank in case he asks me to come."

"Buy yourself a new coat," Mama told her.

"No, I'll write and thank him and let him know we're here. Then if he wants me he'll write and tell me to come and I'll have the money."

"Are you sure you still want him?"

"You've always hoped I wouldn't."

"I never said a word against him until the baby. We almost lost you when Baby Marjorie was born."

"Arlene, you tried to talk me out of him long before that, almost from the beginning."

Mama said nothing.

"Do you remember how handsome he was?" Aunt Betty said. "Such pure features. Like a choir boy, you said."

"He had beautiful eyes."

"And soft curly hair. When I cut it, he used to say I left it too long so

I could play with the curls." Aunt Betty had grown peaceful and dreamy amidst her reveries. "He always put me in mind of a baseball player. Such broad shoulders. Remember? A lovely body."

"Yes," Mama said. "An athlete's body, like one of those marble statues. A lovely body." A long, lazy pause. "I remember."

8

BEFORE SCHOOL LET OUT FOR THE SUMMER, I thought I had made a friend. Falling in together on the way home from school, Shirley Olson and I discovered that we both hated California. And, like me, Shirley meant to run away.

Shirley's mama and papa had been housekeeper and hired hand on a cattle ranch in Wyoming, along the Wind River. When she was four years old, Shirley had a pony, and when she was six she was bitten by a rattlesnake and nearly died.

"You ever been to Wyoming?"

"I don't know."

"You'd know if you had. Along the Wind River is God's country."

"How come your folks left?"

"Couldn't make enough money, Pa says." She didn't sound convinced. Now her mama and papa worked at Consolidated, "Rakin' in the moola. I'd rather be piss-poor in Wyoming."

Vehemence, like electricity, zigzagged through Shirley's limbs, compelling her to pitch herself up the sidewalk in a hopping, skipping burst of anger, sun-bleached pigtails bouncing wildly.

Catching up with her, I asked, "Will your mama and papa go back to Wyoming?"

"They *say* they're saving up to buy a ranch after the war," she said, an odd tone of contempt in her voice. "But I'm not waiting." She scooped up stones and hurled them across the street.

"How much money have you saved—for running away?"

Her shoulders lifted.

"And how much would you need?"

"Ten, I figure."

How on earth could a child save ten dollars?

Glancing along the treeless, grassless street toward the barren foothills beyond the Project, Shirley snorted, "Did you ever see anything so ugly?" Her memories of the Wind River were as sharp and insistent as mine of Minnesota.

We had reached 136.

"Would you like to see my oil painting?"

"I don't care."

"Someday I'm going to have a house like the one in the painting," I told her, unlocking the door.

"You got a nice place," she murmured, running her hand along the back of Mama's rose-colored club chair.

We still didn't have curtains at the windows, although Mama had purchased a pale green Axminster rug for three dollars and fifty cents from a family over on Corte Colinas who were moving back to Florida. If it wasn't luxurious, the place at least looked homelike.

I flopped down on my bed. "There's the painting."

Propped up on my bureau, the picture of the log cabin was the last thing I looked at before falling asleep and the first thing I turned to in the morning.

Shirley stood in front of the bureau studying the painting. "Looks like Wyoming."

"It looks like Minnesota."

"Right by the Wind River is what it looks like. Where'd you get it? I want one."

"Trustworthy Second Hand, but they don't have any more. Not like this one." She looked half prepared to make off with mine, so I told her, "They've got a lot of pictures. Some of them have horses and barns. The next time Mama and I go there, you can probably come along. Mr. Trustworthy let me buy this one for ten cents a week. It'll be paid for in two more weeks." Changing the subject, I asked, "Did you have a nice house in Wyoming?"

"It was okay. I had a sheepskin rug by my bed and a swell Indian blanket, but we had to leave them there because they went with the house."

"Whose house was it?"

"It belonged to the Fergusons. They owned the ranch."

"When you go back to Wyoming, where will you stay?"

"I got somebody'll take me," she said, settling herself on the edge of the bed.

"Relation?"

"That's for me to know."

Again she gazed at the painting. "That's Wyoming, all right."

"If you keep saying it's Wyoming, I don't want to play with you."

"You call this playing?" she scoffed. "This isn't playing. This is sitting around doing nothing."

"Go home," I said. "You're making me tired. I'm going to take a nap."

She hopped down from the bed, tossing me a look of great scorn.

"Babies take naps." Without another word, she was gone.

I felt at once sad and relieved. I was impressed by Shirley's pluck but frightened by the way she had appropriated my painting.

I stared hard at the cabin, at the Minnesota snow and moon, reclaiming them. Then, exhausted by the effort and the force of Shirley's personality, I fell asleep.

. . . .

A week after I sent the story to Mr. Trustworthy, I received a note from him scrawled on the back of a blank invoice.

"Dear Lark Ann Browning Erhardt," he wrote. Browning was to have been my only middle name, but the priest who baptized me told Mama that I must also have a saint's name. Mama assured me that the long moniker would stand me in good stead when I was famous.

> In receipt of your story about Grandma Spencer, I am grateful and touched. The tale brought back my own dear mam, rest her soul.
>
> I am pleased to learn that a story came to you through a piece of sweet rejectamenta. Yes, that is gratifying, indeed.
>
> If you find you have time, you might try laying your hand on the bookcase. I'd be much surprised if it didn't yield a story or two.
>
> I will be forever in your debt should your kind heart prompt you to share your next tale with your devoted friend,
>
> Padraic O'Faolin

I taped the note to my bedroom wall, then lay my hands on the bookcase. Mr. Trustworthy was right. I felt a story.

The Ghost Dog

Jim Smith was 8 years old and he wanted a dog for his birthday but Mrs. Smith said they couldn't have one because they lived in an apartment and the owner didn't like dogs. The owner said dogs made too much rackett.

Poor Jim. He cryed himself to sleep because the world was full of dogs but not one of them was his. Sometimes we keep hoping for something even though it's impossible. We just don't know how to stop. That's the way it was with Jim.

His mother was afraid he would make himself sick with disapointment. But what could she do? She thought and thought. It was almost time for Jims birthday.

The night before the birthday she got an idea and the next day she drove downtown.

She invited Jims friend Bob Daly who lived in the house next door to come over for a little birthday party. After they sang Happy Birthday Mr. Smith brought out Jims present which was a bookcase half filled with books about dogs.

Jim liked the bookcase and the books and he knew that his mother and father had tried their best so he put on a good face. But inside he was very disapointed. Inside he was crying. Books were swell but they were not a dog.

The next day Bob Dalys dog Buster got run over. Bob cryed hard and Jim cryed with him. Jim had loved Buster as much as Bob had loved him.

Mrs. Daly said "we will get you another dog, Bob." That cheered Bob up a little but he still cryed because even if you can have another dog, you still love the old one.

The day after Buster got killed Mr. Daly bought a new dog and Bob named him Fritzy. Fritzy was white with black spots.

That night Jim lay in bed sad because he didn't have a dog and Buster was dead and Fritzy was nice but he wasn't the same as Buster. And that was for certain.

It was dark in Jim's room because his mother had turned out the light but when Jim stopped crying he thought he saw something by the foot of the bed. He sat up and rubbed his eyes. He did see something. A dog. And that dog was Buster. He was even the same brown color and had the same white chest and paws.

"Buster" he wispered. Buster came to the head of the bed and licked Jim's hand. His tung wasn't wet and he didn't make any noise but just looked at Jim and cocked his head.

Jim reached out to pet the dog but he couldn't feel anything. Then Buster jumped up on the bed and laid down beside Jim but he didn't even make a dent in the covers.

Buster was a ghost dog. Jim didn't mind because he was just so happy to have a dog. After that Buster showed up every night and slept beside Jim and since he didn't make a single yip the apartment owner never guessed that there was a dog on the premises.

Writing a story for someone who waited to read it made me feel more useful than cleaning house did.

After school the next day, I remained on the playground to practice tricks on the monkey bars. I was becoming adept at hanging by my heels from the third bar up, grasping the lowest bar with my hands, pushing off from the heels, and swinging to earth. It looked impressive, but it was easy. You just had to remember to tuck your legs before landing. If you came down extended, you'd break your ankles or knees.

Hurling through my slim repertoire of flashy-looking tricks, I imagined myself to be Alicia (Arkovsky) Armand, lithe and elegant. I had asked Mama for a Prince Valiant haircut, but she said I had too many cowlicks.

The younger children had left the playground. Only a knot of marble-playing sixth grade boys remained, huddled at the opposite side of the courtyard around which the school was built. Occasionally they glanced up from their game, eyeing me sideways. When I had been practicing for about an hour, one of the boys separated from the others and began to cross the open space. I sat on a top bar watching him approach. I didn't know him. He was tall and loose-jointed. He walked head down, studying the ground ahead of him.

As he drew near, he looked up at me, then over his shoulder at the others who were squatted on their haunches, watching. A strange, lopsided smile twisted the boy's mouth, making him look uneasy and arrogant at the same time. Reaching the monkey bars, he leaned against one of the corner uprights in a pose of masculine nonchalance, like a movie gangster intimidating somebody. But his eyes shifted from me to his friends to the empty classrooms. Instinctively I unhooked my feet, edging backward toward the interior of the monkey bars.

"What's the matter, little girl?" he asked in a whiney voice that mocked me. "You scared?"

I shook my head.

Beyond him I saw two of the other boys rise and start toward us, laughing, teasing each other, saying things I couldn't hear.

"Pull up your skirt," the boy at hand told me. "Show me your underpants."

Clamping my knees together and tucking loose folds of cotton skirt under my thighs, I shook my head again.

"You better do what I say," he warned, "or I'll push you off of there."

Stupefied, all I could do was shake my head. Nothing of this sort had ever happened to me. Harvester boys had teased and said naughty things sometimes, but they never threatened.

I wanted to believe that this was a peculiar kind of joke in which sixth graders engaged and if I knew the proper retort the boy would laugh and go away.

Instead, he climbed onto the lowest rung and stood staring at me over the top one. "Pull up your skirt or I'll pull it up for you."

The two approaching boys drew near. Across the way, the remaining two boys stood. One withdrew, loping off in the direction of the Project, the other headed toward the monkey bars.

I squeezed the bars until my fingers grew numb. My ankles were wrapped tightly around the uprights.

"Pull up your skirt," the first boy repeated with a snicker and yet with more threat. He was emboldened by the presence of the two additional boys, one to my left, one in front of me.

Mesmerized, I could not remove my gaze from the first boy's face. The others I glimpsed only peripherally, including a fourth who drifted in our direction. Maybe he would stop them.

"You want us to pull down your panties for you?" the first boy asked, as if I had agreed that my panties were coming down and it was only a question of who would do it. "You know what we'll do to you when we get your panties down?"

I shook my head. What *would* they do? I heard a "thung" as the fourth boy climbed onto the monkey bars behind me.

The boy to the left had said nothing. Now he swung himself through the outer bars into the next section of the structure. Only one square remained between him and me.

"Skeerd?" he asked, tilting his body toward me. I leaned away, holding on more tightly, my limbs beginning to tremble. He was so close that I saw dark crusts of sleep at the inner corners of his eyes. The top button of his shirt was undone and his bony chest showed in the vee, his skin the color of skim milk.

He thrust out a hand to lay it on my thigh and I yanked away.

"I'll tell," I said, but it came out in a whisper.

"She said she'd tell," the white-shirted boy said, giggling. "Tell" sounded like "tail."

In front of me, a boy with straight, clean black hair, long, curved lashes, and very dark blue eyes, spoke for the first time. Clinically, like a teacher explaining a lesson, he said, "You won't tell. If you tell, I'll cut off one of your fingers with my jackknife."

He looked at me unblinkingly. Now he, like the other boy, swung himself inward, grabbing onto the next row of bars, never taking his cool, untroubled eyes from me. This was a signal for the rest. As one, they moved inward, through the grid, fastening onto me.

I couldn't scream. I didn't even try. If someone came, the boys would say they'd been teasing, and of course they would be believed because teasing was what boys did.

The boys to my left and right each grabbed one of my feet, untangling it from the upright where it had kept me balanced. I teetered helplessly, pushing my attackers away as best I could, snatching at anything to keep from falling. Behind me a boy yanked at my skirt, trying to pull it from beneath me.

"Hang on to her, Burton," yelled the black-haired boy who owned a jackknife and was himself pulling at the front of my skirt, shoving it up my thighs. Burton clamped his arms around my chest from behind, squeezing until my ribs seemed to crack.

"No," I sobbed, "leave me alone!" I kicked, but the black-haired boy was wedged between my knees and my legs struck iron gridwork.

A sudden, deafening reverberation caught us mid-motion. For a second, the boys froze, and then they were fleeing like squirrels as an older boy appeared from nowhere, running around and around the monkey bars, pounding the metal with a baseball bat and howling like an Apache.

Pursuing my enemies across the playground, my rescuer called to me, "Run."

Swinging to the ground, I ran, sobbing, glancing back once or twice to be sure no one saw where I ran or which house was mine.

Inside, I locked the door and dashed from room to room, lowering the shades. Wrenching off my blouse and skirt, I stuffed them under the pile of dirty clothes in my closet.

When I had run the tub full of water as hot as I could stand, I scuffed off my shoes and socks, slipped out of my underpants, and stepped in, scrubbing myself raw. Later, I pulled on a nightie and climbed into bed, shivering and tugging the covers around me.

9

"LARK, THE TABLE ISN'T SET," Mama said, opening the door to my room. "What have you been doing all afternoon?"

"I don't feel good."

She crossed to the bed. "What's the matter?" she asked, laying a hand on my cheek. "Do you hurt anywhere?"

"My head."

She left, returning with aspirin and a glass of water. "Do you feel like supper?"

I shook my head.

"Try to sleep then," she said. "Do you want me to close the door?"

"Yes, please."

Reaching for the door knob, she said, "You'll feel better in the morning."

No, I wouldn't. All summer the boys would be free to roam the Project, hunting for me. I squirmed, recalling their sniggering voices and clumsy, unpitying touch.

And where had God been this afternoon? It was no good saying He sent a rescuer. By that time, too much had happened. And if the boys came to cut off my finger, I could not hope for my rescuer to appear again.

Where had he come from with his baseball bat? His face, turned back toward me as he called "run," had reminded me of Hilly. His eyes were dark, his brow broad and smooth, the curve of his cheek gentle like Hilly's.

Hours later, I woke, chilled, and slid out of bed. My old pink bathrobe hung on the bedpost, and I slipped it on. I was tying the sash when the scene on the playground came rushing back.

I clutched at the bed and waited for substance to seep back into me. Wobbling to the window, I raised the shade and leaned against the sill.

Across the blue-black coastal sky, airplanes pulled lighted targets. The big anti-aircraft guns on the cliffs above the beaches shook the earth. When the shelling stopped, the howl of a coyote up in the foothills floated down the void. This was all unfamiliar, somebody else's childhood, and I hated it.

Before she left for work the next morning, Mama came into my room, reminding me of my Saturday chores. "And don't forget to water the gardenia bush," she said.

Mama was so sappy about gardenias that for Mother's Day Aunt Betty and I had given her a gardenia bush. Jack Dugan next door had dug a hole for it at the corner of the house.

Now, still in my night clothes, I plodded to the kitchen, found the empty lard pail under the sink, and filled it with water. Opening the outside door, I peered around, sprinted out, and dumped the water at the base of the plant.

Back in the house, I slammed the door and stood with my back pressed against it. Across the street, a boy who didn't belong was ambling along, casual as you please, craning his head and looking at all the units.

Mama had raised the shades earlier. Now I lowered them and climbed back into bed.

It was nearly noon when I woke. Unless she stopped somewhere after work, Mama would be home within the hour and hopping mad when she saw my chores not done. Saturdays were given to housecleaning and errands. Errands. I'd forgotten about the errands Mama sent me on, to the post box or the Project office, out on the street in full view.

I had dusted and picked up the bedrooms and the living room when Mama unlocked the door.

"Why're the shades drawn?" she asked, stepping in and setting her purse on top of the bookcase.

"I . . . I was playing air raid," I said as she began raising them.

"You haven't even started the kitchen," she said. "I suppose the bathroom's not done either."

All afternoon, as I cleaned the kitchen and scoured the bathroom, I expected to hear Mama say, "I want you to run to Jon's Market," or "Take this rent check to the office," but she was preoccupied and kept to her room.

When the laundry man delivered our bundle—a knock at the door that stopped my breath—I paid him from Mama's purse and sorted the wash into piles. Carrying Mama's and Aunt Betty's to their room, I noted that Mama was seated on the bed, back against the headboard, scratching on a writing pad.

"Should I put these things away?"

"What?"

"Should I put these things away?"

"Uh . . . no. Put them on the bureau."

"Are you writing to Papa?"

"Hmmmm?"

"Is that a letter to Papa?"

She stared at me. "What? No, it's to . . . a friend."

"Bernice McGivern?" Bernice McGivern was Mama's best friend in Harvester.

"Yes. I haven't written to Bernice in a dog's age."

I closed the bedroom door behind me. Another lie.

Tossing in bed that night, my head ached with worry about the boys. I wished I were at Grandma Browning's. I wished I were lying on the daybed on her screened porch, in the spilled light of the streetlamp, listening to adults around the dining room table.

I recalled how they drank oceans of iced tea and lemonade, and ate salted peanuts and butter mints while they played five hundred. Laughing and cursing and pounding the table, they bid and outbid and overbid in a noisy competition of wits and wills, Grandma and Grandpa and aunts and uncles and cousins, four at the table and as many kibitzing and waiting their turn.

When they had forgotten that I was on the porch, they hashed over family gossip, some freshly shocking, some with its disgrace worn to a romantic patina.

Lying on the daybed on Grandma's sleeping porch, hearing stories and making up new endings for them, that was what I should be doing. That was where I belonged.

I tiptoed to the bedroom door, closed it, and stuffed dirty clothes at the bottom so light couldn't escape. From under the bed, I slid out the writing tablet.

10

THE NEXT MORNING, while Mama filled the tea kettle at the kitchen sink and Aunt Betty pulled on her stockings in the bedroom, I sneaked out to the living room and opened Mama's purse. Easing the envelope out, I read, "Stanley Weller, 1344 Hyacinth, Hollywood, California."

Early the following Wednesday morning, yanking on a pair of corduroy trousers and an old striped polo shirt, I slipped out with the lard pail. As I stepped onto the stoop, I saw that the door across from ours was open. From beyond the screen I heard radio voices.

I'd never laid eyes on the Belle Eldridge whom Fanny Dugan had mentioned, though I saw her brother Beau now and then. I remembered their names because I'd never known anyone named Belle or Beau.

Watching Beau trudging up from the bus stop, returning from work, I'd thought the name was wasted on him. He had a forlorn, beaten-about-the-head-and-shoulders look. And he was going to flesh, as Grandma Browning would say.

When I'd finished watering the gardenia bush, the radio voices in the Eldridge house were silent and in their place I heard the kind of twittering noise people make trying to coax a bird to sing. So the Eldridges had a canary.

I was reaching for the handle of our screen door when Fanny Dugan called, "Lark."

Fanny was returning from a walk with Cecil and Percy, the dogs on leashes. Displeased at being tethered, they crossed wickedly back and forth in front of her, tangling the leads. She looked worn out by their tricks.

Forgetting the boys who were coming to cut off my fingers, I ran to meet Fanny. She handed me the leashes as the two bulldogs jumped up and down and wove themselves around my ankles.

"Can you come over?" Fanny wheezed, not quite shuffling toward the Dugan end of our building but going carefully.

She let us in, telling me, "Make yourself at home," before vanishing into the bedroom, coughing as she went. Aunt Betty said that Fanny had a smoker's hack and ought to quit cigarettes.

I sat down on a comfortable sofa, covered in a green-and-white jungle print of ferns and palm fronds. Aunt Betty had called the upholstery extravagant after she and Mama stopped in to discuss the daisies, but Mama said it was very chic.

Obviously trained not to jump onto the sofa, the dogs scrabbled at my feet, whining. At length they retreated to what must have been their chair, an enormous poufy circle with a curving back, covered in an emerald damask and trimmed along the bottom with a deep satiny fringe. Over it, Fanny had thrown an old piece of green-and-white drapery to protect it from the abuses of two bulldogs. The chair was large enough for both of them.

On a table by the window sat an array of photographs in silver frames. In a group photo taken on a wide lawn sweeping down to a lake shore, Fanny stood at the heart of the gathering—her Chicago family, I guessed. Much younger, she had a strong, brand new look.

When he was planting Mama's gardenia bush, Jack had spoken in a bantering way of his wife as "Mary Frances O'Neal of the Chicago O'Neals," as if her family counted for something. Now here she was, living in the Project.

In the Project, you didn't ask questions, Aunt Betty said. You took people as they were. If they wanted you to know, they would tell you.

I thought Mama was grateful for this indifference to history, since she was a woman who had run away.

Doubtless other runaways lived in the Project, escaping not from husbands but from the Depression. As the man on the bus coming out to Pacific Beach had complained, they'd blown in from everywhere. They hadn't had a pot to pee in before the war, Mama said. Now they had gas stoves and heat, electric iceboxes and electric lights. Some were black sheep who could finally start over. Some were tramps who'd had to ride the rails looking for work until Pearl Harbor came along.

Returned from the bedroom, Fannie had changed into one of her vivid, flower-strewn wraps. Looking peaked, she nevertheless managed a smile.

"Would you like a cup of coffee? What time is it? Nine-thirty? I don't think it's too early for cake."

She drifted toward the kitchen. The dogs and I followed.

"Coffee and cake would be ambrosial," I said.

"Now that's not an everyday word."

"I got it from my *Webster's Collegiate Dictionary.*"

I felt very fine sitting at Fanny's table. The wood shone. Mama said the table was Duncan Phyfe and had cost someone a fortune. Mama knew about furniture. She used to subscribe to *Better Homes and Gardens.*

Fanny served us each a giant slice of yellow cake, blanketed with thick maple frosting and lying on a delicate china plate. She had heated milk in a pan and when it was warm she added it to our two cups of coffee. From one drawer she withdrew silver teaspoons and forks, from another, linen tea napkins.

She didn't ask, "Does your Mama allow you to drink coffee?" She simply served me as if I were old enough to say no.

I waited while she put a tiny piece of cake in each of the dog dishes, folded herself onto a chair, unfurled her napkin, and sliced off a bite of cake. Then I lifted my fork.

"Did you live in a nice house when you were a child?" I asked, wondering at the splendid formality of the linen, china, and silver.

"Yes," Fanny finally answered, "I suppose it was. It was a wonderful, sprawling place on Lake Michigan, with a lot of nooks and crannies to hide in."

"Mama and I were going to build a cottage east of Saint Boniface Catholic Church in Harvester," I told her. "The plan was called 'Number One Hundred and Twenty-seven: The Cape Ann.' It had two bathrooms, one up and one down, and three bedrooms, counting the sewing room."

The focus of our hopes, the Cape Ann had provided Mama and me with endless hours of dreaming. My room was to have a dormer window with a window seat. In the back yard, Hilly and I would grow vegetables and flowers where no one could frighten him.

"If we had built the Cape Ann, I don't think Hilly would have killed himself," I concluded, forgetting that Fanny knew nothing about Hilly. Then, because my eyes were stinging, I changed the subject. "Do your mama and papa still live in that lake house?"

Fanny drank off the remaining coffee in her cup, not hurrying, then blotted her lips on her napkin. Smoothing the linen across her lap, she stroked it absently. Had she heard me? During my brief acquaintance with Fanny, I had not seen her this quiet. Ordinarily, she laughed and chattered in her cigarette baritone, gesturing grandly and inclusively, drawing you into a safe, indulgent place.

Fanny's eyes—large, gray-blue, and hooded—diverted attention from the meatlessness of her cheeks and jaw. Her sculpted temples had a mauve, vulnerable shadow to them, and her lips, when not lipsticked, were pale and thin. However, one rarely saw her without rosy lipstick and a blush of rouge.

I thought Fanny was lovely. Her appearance was undeniably theatrical. Mama said that Fanny was striking rather than pretty. If I were to choose between striking and pretty, I'd take striking every time.

"Who was Hilly?" Fanny asked, returning from her thoughts.

I spent half an hour chronicling Hilly's story. The early parts, I knew only through hearing them retailed by others.

Hilly Stillman had been the first boy in Saint Bridget County to enlist to serve in the Great War. He'd been brave in combat and selfless in the rescue of fallen comrades. In 1918, with his physical wounds mending and with medals in his knapsack from the governments of France and the United States, Hilly had been mustered out with a permanent limp and an addled brain. The doctors explained to Hilly's mother that his mind had retreated to childhood, age five or thereabouts.

These same doctors were optimistic that Hilly would recover. And although he did slowly regain his adult sensibilities, they were fragile. When the Japanese bombed Pearl Harbor, the half-acre of trust he had cultivated was destroyed. On a bitter December night, in his pajamas, he stepped outside onto the landing and, in the aloof darkness, put a gun to his head.

Although I had seen Hilly's coffin lowered into the cold ground in the Harvester Protestant graveyard, for me he was not dead. He was more a part of life than Papa was. Hilly had come with me to California, and Papa had not.

It was nearly eleven when I said good-bye and thanked Fanny for the cake and coffee.

"Next time I'll teach you to play gin rummy," she offered, leaning against the door jamb and shooing Cecil and Percy back into the living room.

Grabbing the lard pail from the top step, where I'd left it, I carried it to the kitchen and opened the cupboard below the sink. Tossing the pail in, under the pipes, I finally noticed that something plunked around in the bottom of it.

Mistrusting the kitchen light, I ran outside, emptying the pail onto the ground beside the stoop. The hair on my arms stood up. Ants scurried back and forth across a hard bit of earth and over a small, gray paw, still sticky with its own blood.

11

I WAS SCREAMING. The boys had broken down my bedroom door.

"What on earth?" Mama's voice was conciliatory. She sat on the bed. "Nightmare?"

I stared at her, absorbed her. No, she was not the boys.

She jogged my arm. "Are you awake?"

It was still daylight, and Mama was home from work.

"Yes." I brushed back my damp hair.

"Well, what's wrong?"

"The lard pail. . . ." The image of the bloody paw lying on the hard earth came back with awful clarity. "A paw. . . ."

"A paw?"

"And blood. In the lard pail."

"Where?"

"Outside, by the steps." My stomach rose up against my breast bone and I lay down again, pulling the sheet over my shoulders.

"I'll see," Mama said, unsure whether I was dreaming.

She returned in a few minutes. "It looks like a kitten's paw," she said. "How did it get into the lard pail?"

"I don't know." I explained that I had watered the gardenia bush, then been invited by Fanny to have cake.

"Boys," Mama said. "There are boys who do mean things, like killing little animals."

Later, Mama brought me supper on a tray, something she had not done since my last bout of tonsillitis a year and a half before: a bowl of

Campbell's tomato soup, a Velveeta-and-sliced-onion sandwich, and a cup of tea.

Aunt Betty was putting in an extra evening at the Red Cross, assembling little packets of amenities—razor blades, soap, and such items—for our boys overseas, so Mama brought her own supper into my bedroom and we ate together.

When she carried away our trays and turned out the light, I flew to the cabin where Hilly ladled cocoa into two generous cups.

"Wouldn't it be nice to have a gray kitten, Hilly?"

. . . .

THE NEXT DAY, which was Thursday, I stayed in bed, rereading *The Message in the Hollow Oak,* a Nancy Drew. How spunky and self-reliant Nancy was. She made it seem natural to be stalwart, even audacious. What was wrong with me?

I lost myself in Nancy's adventure, living the confident, sophisticated life of a girl who drove her own roadster and whose father was a well-known attorney in River Heights.

I had imagined, back in Harvester, that if we built the Cape Ann I would become a confident girl, one not too shy to recite "The Night before Christmas" when we gathered at Grandma Browning's. I had believed then that if we lived in a pretty cottage instead of a converted storage room in a railroad depot, Papa would stop gambling and hitting the bottle, Mama would stop looking for more than she had, and I would stop blushing and hiding. We would all conform to the charm of our surroundings.

On Friday I scrubbed the bathroom and kitchen, ran the dry mop around the house, and dusted the furniture and woodwork. If I kept the house neat and clean, passing my imprisoned days in household good works, not only would I avoid the boys with their knife, but I would also store up righteousness.

On Friday night, when I had bathed and pulled on my nightie, I wandered out to the kitchen, restless with confinement, loath to climb back into the bed where I'd spent much of the week.

In a box on top of the refrigerator were a handful of very hard gingersnaps. Reaching them down, I tried biting into one but they'd dried rock hard.

At the kitchen door, Aunt Betty suggested, "I'll make tea. We can dunk the cookies."

When the tea was steeped, Mama joined us, fresh from her shampoo and bath and carrying a dish of bobby pins and a comb. We gathered around the table to sip weak tea and dunk old gingersnaps while Mama set her hair in pin curls.

"I've got to get to a beauty parlor," she said, as she had said at least once a week for months, "and do something about this hair. It needs a cut and, well, I don't know what else."

"Most of the henna's gone," Aunt Betty assured her. "It doesn't look as bad as you think."

"That's a great relief," Mama laughed, clamping several bobby pins between her teeth to have them handy.

Aunt Betty smiled and shifted on her chair, gathering her robe about her like a bird settling down in its nest. In the past few weeks, she had begun to shed the haggard, whipped look that had haunted her for so long. She'd regained some of the flesh and color she'd lost over the past three years. And although transporting joy would elude her until she was reunited with Uncle Stanley, she had reached a calm place, out of the storm of loss and upheaval. The routine of usefulness—Gilpins', the Red Cross, the U.S.O.—brought her order and satisfying weariness.

Mama, however, had not grown peaceful. For her, there was a crucial difference between peace and victory. And she would not rest until Aunt Betty was victorious.

But what was victory? Aunt Betty falling out of love with Uncle Stanley? Uncle Stanley begging Aunt Betty to take him back? Was that what Mama had written to my uncle about?

12

THE FOLLOWING WEDNESDAY MORNING, moving from window to window, raising the shades, Mama admonished, "Try to keep the place neat."

"I have been," I told her, pouring puffed wheat into a bowl.

"Well, sweep the stoop and sidewalk. And don't forget to water the gardenia," she said as she left for work. Something in her manner suggested a cat on hot bricks.

The postman left a penny postcard for Mama from her friend Bernice McGivern in Harvester, and a letter for me from Papa.

I lay them aside while I washed the morning dishes and cleaned the countertops.

When I set the table, I laid Mama's postcard from Bernice beside her plate. To have her mail laid neatly beside her plate was one of Mama's airs and graces.

Despite flouting society by dyeing her hair and leaving her husband, or perhaps because of it, Mama clung to certain niceties and still reminded me periodically that her great-great-grandmother had been a lady-in-waiting in the English court. The family had lost its fortune and come to America, she said, but we must remember who we were.

When she returned from work, she complained that I hadn't watered the gardenia bush, but she was mollified by the tidy house. "Get out there now, before you're in trouble."

Beau Eldridge, lugging his lunch pail, came lumbering up the sidewalk from the street.

"It's still alive," he observed of the gardenia bush.

I nodded.

"It likes plenty of water," he said in the same expressionless voice, mounting the Eldridge stoop. "I read that in the newspaper."

These were Beau Eldridge's first words to me. Although spoken without élan (page 320 of my *Webster's*), they were uttered in a pleasantly resonant voice. His plodding gait and pudding shape had led me to expect something entirely different.

I stood staring after him.

That evening, Aunt Betty brought out a map of the world, three feet by four, and tacked it to the kitchen wall. She handed me a box of thumbtacks.

"From now on we'll keep better track of the war. At the U.S.O. the boys come and go so fast. And when they go, I don't know *where,*" she said, as if they fell into a foreign void, someplace beyond the horizon.

We sat down at the table. So far, the war had been a drama, stirring and colorful, but impersonal, happening on a distant stage, like the outdoor pageant back in Blue Lake, where Grandma Browning lived.

Aunt Betty's hands were folded, one over the other on the table, and she leaned toward the map, her lips working in concentration. Except for Uncle Stanley, I knew little of my aunt's passions. She was deep, Grandma said. Mama always bridled at the implication that she, by contrast, might be shallow.

I sat motionless, holding the box of thumbtacks, waiting for instructions.

At length Aunt Betty turned to me. "We're going to keep track of the battles, Lark. When the Allies win, we'll put a white tack on the map where it happened. And when the Axis wins, we'll mark that with a black tack. You'll be in charge of tacks."

I was flattered to be enlisted in this way. "I'll read the Sunday paper and listen to the radio."

Mama, who had been wiping out the bottom shelf of the refrigerator, looked sideways at Aunt Betty. "What brought this on?" she asked.

"These boys are people, Arlene. We ought to care what's happening to them."

Mama straightened and turned toward my aunt. "I do care. I just wondered why it was today that you brought home a map."

Aunt Betty ran her hand across the table's oil-cloth, smoothing invisible wrinkles. "There was a Mrs. Jellison in fine china. I didn't know her except to say hello." As if a stitch of pain had caught her, Aunt Betty put a fist to her breast. "Her son was in the navy. He was killed last week. Well, at least that's when the word came."

"I'm sorry," Mama said, tossing the cloth in the sink and joining us at the table.

Aunt Betty traced with a forefinger the yellow checks in the oilcloth. Finally she said, "Mrs. Jellison fell in front of a streetcar this morning."

"Fell?" Mama asked.

"She was Catholic," Aunt Betty said. "I remember she came to work with a smudge on her forehead last Ash Wednesday."

. . . .

LATER, I NOTICED THE UNOPENED LETTER from Papa. I was reluctant to read it. I hadn't written as often as I should; I hadn't been to Mass and I didn't intend going.

I climbed into bed. You couldn't not open a letter from your papa.

I picked at the flap, tore it a little, then screwed up my courage and tore it a little more. It was like working a baby tooth loose. But all at once I snatched out the typed page and down fluttered another dollar bill.

Dear Little Lark,

It has been several weeks since I heard from you. I hope you haven't enlisted in the Marines. Ha ha. Your letters are all that keep me going, so I pray to find one in the mail tomorrow.

I'm sending another dollar so you can light candles and ask God to make us a happy family again.

I went fishing at Sioux Woman Lake after work yesterday. Caught a dozen bullheads. Remember all the times you and I went fishing together? [There'd been three or four.] And the great times we had hunting night crawlers? [Once.] Maybe if you say a lot of prayers and tell your ma how sad you are, we'll have those good times again.

All my love,
Your Pa

I put down the letter and closed my eyes, expecting love and remorse to fill me. Instead, I felt nothing.

I was becoming a cold-hearted little girl.

By Friday, the dot on Aunt Betty's world map called Midway Island was covered by a white thumbtack. Since we'd had few victories in the war so far—the news from North Africa, China, and elsewhere was mostly bleak—I thanked God for this one. And while I was at it, I asked Him to send the families of the four boys back to wherever they'd come from.

God was an enigma. One minute he was silly, unreasonable, and unloving, demanding godliness from creatures He'd purposely created weak (He did nothing without purpose, did He?). The next minute, He was a loving, forgiving, compassionate Jesus. He reminded me a little of Papa.

The admonitions of the nuns notwithstanding, it surprised me that no one ever criticized God. To me, creating people weak only to punish them for it smacked of some sort of cat-and-mouse game. After all, He had created hell before he even made Adam and Eve, so he knew ahead of time that they were going to fall. So free will didn't even come into it. The need to please both God and Jesus gave me a headache and made me crazy.

One half of me wished to be five again, when I had believed everything I was told. The other half, suspecting that that was dangerous, listened for alarming information and stored it away against the day when it would be translated into knowledge.

Mama's secret letter-writing to Uncle Stanley was alarming information.

Putting the top back on the box of tacks, I asked Mama and Aunt Betty, "Have you seen any WAACs yet?"

Women were joining the army. In *Life* magazine they looked noble and at the same time stylish in their olive drab uniforms. Even their dowdy, sensible shoes had an air of purpose and patriotism.

Mama pulled Old Dutch cleanser from the cupboard and began scouring the sink. "If I didn't have you," she told me, "I'd enlist in the WAACs myself."

"I've heard they're a pretty wild bunch," Aunt Betty said.

"That's what they always say when women want to do something interesting," Mama observed.

All that week Mama was twitchy, nervous. Friday she was late getting home from work, arriving half an hour after Aunt Betty. "Are you sure she didn't tell you she'd be late?" Aunt Betty asked twice, each time going out to stand on the stoop and search the street.

The macaroni and cheese grew cold, its many small parts congealing into a single, rubbery thing that could be lifted whole out of the bowl.

When Mama came strolling up from the bus stop, I could see that she'd had something to drink. Her limbs moved indifferently and her eyes glittered.

13

"Saturday we're going down to Trustworthy Second Hand, you and I," Mama said. I was sitting on the toilet, watching her apply make-up. "You can pay for your oil painting and I'll look for a treadle sewing machine." She blotted her lips.

We still had no curtains, but Mama could make some if we owned a machine like the one we'd left in Harvester, the one Papa hadn't sent.

I followed her to the kitchen, where she drank the last of the tea in her cup and slammed a sandwich and thermos into her lunch pail. Glancing around the room, assessing it, she blew me a kiss and left. A minute later she was back. "Forgot my purse." She had ants in her pants.

Sitting beside the window at the kitchen table and pouring milk over puffed wheat, I glanced across at the Eldridges' kitchen window. Our houses were mirror images. I could see a woman moving about. "Billy, Billy, Billy, sweet, sweet Billy," she crooned.

I craned to look at the sky. The hot sun had burned away the sea haze, leaving the sky vast and deep. The boys would be out wandering around.

Pounding at the door. My heart stopped.

I set my spoon down, shoved the bowl aside, and lay my head on the table. I wanted to pray but all that came to my lips was "Bless us, oh Lord, and these, Thy gifts, which we are about to receive from Thy bounty. . . ."

"Lark Erhardt! I know yer in there."

Shirley Olson. The girl who'd started to be my friend.

When I finally opened the door, she was sitting down, waiting.

"Where were you, on the pot? You took long enough."

I didn't answer, but opened the screen door to let her in.

Shirley was wearing an old pair of blue twill trousers with the knees scraped out and a plaid flannel shirt big enough to be her papa's. Her feet were bare and her hair had not been combed.

She followed me into the kitchen and sat down at the table without being asked. If I hadn't been glad to see her, I'd have pointed out her bad manners. She watched me return the milk bottle to the icebox. I should have offered her cereal, but the presumptuous way she'd sat herself down made me feel contrary, so I ate my cereal as if she weren't there. She stared, eyes following the spoon up and down. Now I felt guilty, but also angry that she could waltz in, making me feel mean.

"You want some toast?" I asked. Offering her toast wasn't the same as giving in to her silent demand for cereal.

She jumped to her feet. "Where's the bread?"

I indicated the cupboard. "There's jam and ole in the icebox."

Shirley was soon slapping together jam-slathered bread and filling herself up with sweet sandwiches.

"You want to go out and play?" she asked when she had eaten three sandwiches, licking jam from her dirty fingers.

"I can't."

"Why not?"

"Just can't."

"That's dumb. Come anyway." She rose and, uninvited, fetched a glass from the cupboard and poured herself milk.

I shook my head.

"Your ma say you can't play out?"

I nodded, lying.

"Well, I can't stay then," she said and drank off her milk, preparing to leave.

"You going home?"

She shrugged. "I might go to the beach."

"On the bus?"

She shook her head, wiping her milk mustache on the back of a flannel sleeve. "Hitch a ride."

The words filled me with anxiety. If I were to hitchhike, Mama would spank me till I couldn't sit down. "Alone?"

"Maybe. Maybe with some other kid."

"Does your mama know you hitchhike?" Shirley was only a child! Nine or ten years old.

"She don't care."

Was Shirley lying, trying to impress me? I put my dirty dishes in the sink. "Want to see my oil painting?"

"Sure." She turned and led the way.

We sat on the bed, backs against the headboard and studied the painting. Shirley rattled on about the Wind River and Wyoming, telling me why this painting was undeniably a rendering of that place. When she wound down, I told her about Hilly and the gray kitten and drinking cocoa in front of the fire.

"You're loco," she said.

"What's loco?"

"Crazy."

"I am not."

She cackled.

"Don't you ever imagine things?" I asked.

"I imagine I'm back in Wyoming," she said, adding with another cackle, "I don't imagine an old soldier with his head shot off and a dead cat living with me."

"Mama's taking me to Trustworthy Second Hand Store Saturday.

That's where we bought the picture. It's too bad you think I'm loco or maybe you could come."

"Well you are loco, and what do I care about a secondhand store?" she said, hopping down from the bed.

"Are you leaving?"

At the bedroom door, she turned. "If you give me the painting, I'll stay and I won't call you loco."

I shook my head, dumbstruck that she could ask.

. . . .

FRIDAY MORNING, WHILE I WAS DUSTING the living room bookcase, Shirley showed up again.

"Can you play?" she wanted to know, thrusting past me into the room when I opened the door.

"I have to clean house."

"Don't you ever go outside?" She plopped down on the couch, snatching up a *Life* magazine that Fanny Dugan had passed along.

"Sometimes."

"I never see you."

"I have to help my mama," I told her, dusting the tops of our small assortment of books. "Don't you have to work at home?"

"Lookit this," she said, feigning interest in an article and holding the magazine up for me to see. "Who're those girls?"

"Princess Elizabeth and Princess Margaret Rose."

"Who're they?"

"They're the princesses of England." What did she want? Why was Shirley here, riffling through a magazine in which she had no interest?

She tossed the magazine aside and chewed a hangnail. Spitting a tiny piece of dead skin across the room, she asked, "You still going to the secondhand store tomorrow?"

"Yes."

"Ask your ma if I can come." She rose, hitching up the old blue trousers she'd worn on Tuesday, and headed for the door, bored by dusting and English princesses.

"What do you do when you play outside?" I asked.

She shrugged. "Different stuff. Sometimes I go down to the school and play on the monkey bars, or I play Japs and Americans with some kids over on Camino Padero."

"Do you ever play store or house or school?"

She rolled her eyes and screwed up her face. "I like games where you run around and kill people." She opened the door. "Ask your ma if I can come."

Half an hour after Shirley left, a manila envelope, stiffened with cardboard, arrived in the mail, addressed to Lark Erhardt. The return address was Wheeler, Harvester, Minnesota. Sally Wheeler was one of my two best friends, the other being Beverly Ridza.

The envelope was addressed in Sally's neat, Palmer Method hand. Just out of fourth grade and her handwriting already looked like a school teacher's.

I used to sit and stare at Sally, even when we were in kindergarten. She had black braids as thick as my wrist, shining and perfectly plaited. Her eyelashes matched her hair, black and thick and curled.

Sally was beautiful and quiet and sad, rarely cruel like most little children. Sometimes she withdrew from us, however, and wouldn't play or talk. That was mainly because she was embarrassed by her mama and probably worried too; her mama was a well-known crier, breaking into unexpected tears even in public, surprising everyone, including herself.

Mama had told Bernice McGivern that Stella Wheeler was going through the Change, whatever that was. But it seemed to be taking forever. And who would she be when she'd finished changing? No wonder Sally didn't always feel like playing.

But now Sally had sent me a package. I tore the envelope open and pulled out two shirt cardboards, between which were pressed a note from Sally, a snapshot of her taken in her backyard, and a gray, cardboard picture frame, the folding kind that holds a studio portrait. Setting aside the note and snapshot, I opened the frame.

Hilly. It was the photograph Mrs. Stillman had displayed in her living room, eighteen-year-old Hilly in his army uniform, a blameless amiability to his handsome features and a dreamy, expectant look in his eyes, as if in the distance he saw better times.

He had been forty-one or -two the last time I saw him, thin, haunted, lost-looking, but even then the sweetness of the photograph had clung to him.

Staring into the familiar, open face, I began to bawl—worse than Mrs. Wheeler—shaking and falling on the floor. I cried until my throat ached and my chest hurt.

When the crying stopped and only sighs wrenched up from my insides, I staggered to the bedroom, cradling the photo. Late morning sunlight from the east-facing window warmed the rumpled covers. Sighing and hiccoughing, I curled up, the scene in the oil painting drifting toward me, expanding and engulfing me. Me and Hilly and the gray kitten.

14

AT TEN THE NEXT MORNING, Shirley was back, pounding on the door. She was sporting the plaid shirt and blue trousers again, but this time she wore oxfords from which someone had cut half-moons so her toes hung out over the end.

"What'd your ma say? Can I come?"

I wanted to give her a shove but, imprisoned in the house all summer, I wasn't likely to find another friend. In any case, Mama had said that Shirley could come. "If you have bus fare," I told her. "Both ways."

From the pocket of the shirt she pulled a ragged pink bus pass, the sort grown-ups bought weekly for going to and from work. "My ma's."

On the ride downtown, Shirley grew quiet, and as we jumped down from the bus into the swirl of the Saturday plaza she contracted until she was as stiff as a pencil. I had to pull her through the crowd toward the center of the little park where Mama was meeting us.

We sat down on the dusty grass to wait, Shirley gawking. Finally she asked, "What're all these people doing here?"

"Catching buses, shopping, just walking around. It's always like this, especially on weekends."

She half disbelieved me.

"Is this the first time you've been downtown?" I asked, relishing her abashment. I glanced around as if the milling throng of servicemen and defense workers were a staple of my life. I had been to the plaza three times.

"Sure I been here," she lied, "I just never noticed all the people."

Mama didn't flick an eyelash when I introduced Shirley, but merely said, "We have to get on one of those street cars over there." She pointed to a trolley clack-clacking up the street.

Shirley never turned from the window or released her grip on the seat during the ten-minute ride to Trustworthy Second Hand. She couldn't have been more fascinated or apprehensive if we'd taken her to China.

Stepping down from the streetcar, I related how, on our first visit to his secondhand store, we'd found Mr. Trustworthy sleeping on one of the sofas.

"His name isn't Trustworthy," Mama laughed.

"Then why is it called Trustworthy Second Hand?" I demanded, embarrassed.

"He wants us to trust him."

"I bet his name *is* Trustworthy," I said. "I'm going to ask."

The broad front window was piled with the usual jumble. Displayed prominently amidst the beauty out of season, as Mr. Trustworthy called it, was a ponderous mahogany library table as vast as a bed. Indeed, it was piled with an assortment of faded cushions, and Mr. Trustworthy lay sleeping among them, wearing a childlike smile. On his feet were the same soiled spats, the same cracked and crumbling shoes. Like Aunt Betty's and mine, Mr. Trustworthy's were lined with pieces of cardboard. As before, his freckled hands were arranged piously over a tweedy vest.

We entered without disturbing him and Mama set out at once to find a treadle sewing machine all of whose parts were operational. Shirley and I wandered through the "museum of the misunderstood."

"Whadya suppose that thing's for?" Shirley asked, studying a tall cabinet of tiny drawers.

"It's one of those chests the dentist keeps his stuff in."

Shirley nodded. We drifted in separate directions. I found the towering beadboard cupboard in which I had hidden. Climbing in, I pulled the door to, breathing the same delicious odor of dust and grandmothers.

When I slipped out again, I overheard Mama discussing sewing machines with Mr. Trustworthy. They stood near the front of the store and I was in the antipodes among sideboards, hat racks, folding screens, wounded plaster nymphs, and scarred cupids. The darkness here breathed of old people. I could live quite happily among belongings sloughed off by grandparents on their way to the grave.

Turning from the cupboards, I spied a slack-witted moose head gazing down upon my solitary game of hide and seek. Nearby, a stuffed brown bear, missing one of its glass eyes and two claws, reared up on its hind legs.

Beside the moose head hung a large photo of a woman in a simple, dark dress. She wore a dramatic little cloche with a long feather that swept down along her cheek, emphasizing the delicacy of the bone. Her eyes contained melancholy and tender rue, at once forgiving and mocking. They reminded me of one of the fights between Mama and Papa before we left Harvester. In sadness, Mama had cried out, "You poor thing, you can't hurt me any more!" Strange, how the photo brought that to mind. And wasn't it a strange thing for Mama to say, as if she mourned for the long-ago Papa who had been able to hurt her.

I didn't understand the way men and women loved, which was so different from the way children loved. I had noticed this in the movies as well. Men and women loved each other for peculiar reasons, except William Powell and Myrna Loy, who appeared to love each other for kindness and humor.

Uncle Stanley had been kind and funny, and yet Mama seemed to hate him. Then it dawned on me—just like that, for no good reason—

Uncle Stanley was the one for whom curtains had to be made. Mama had written him and now she was making preparations.

"Lookit this," Shirley said, startling me in my speculations. "Lookit these horses. They're like Mr. Ferguson's." She thrust in front of me a framed print of frightened horses galloping straight at me, as if the devil were whipping them and they didn't see me in their path.

"The Mr. Ferguson who owned the ranch in Wyoming?" I asked, studying the bulging, glazed eyes, the manes tossing like waves in a storm.

She yanked the picture from my grasp and held it to her narrow breast. "He had Arabians like these."

Then Mama called, "Time to go, girls."

"We just got here."

"I have to get home and start sewing," Mama said.

"I wanta buy this," Shirley declared. "How much is it?"

Mr. Trustworthy, laying a finger beside his nose, squinted his eyes and cocked his head, first noting the picture, then studying Shirley.

"And where d' y' come from?"

"Wyoming."

"They've darlin' horses there, I've heard."

Shirley nodded, regarding Mr. Trustworthy closely, trying to take his measure.

"Horses—they've got souls, y' know. When they perish, their souls sprout wings, like Pegasus, and off they fly to heaven. Zeus turned Pegasus away with a gadfly bite, you know, but your own God lets 'em fly in at the gate. When y' die, y'll see the horses y've loved, them you left behind in Wyoming."

Shirley frowned to keep from showing her pleasure.

"You want to buy the picture? Well, I've got t' think what it's worth."

I could hear Shirley suck in her breath.

" . . . Half a dollar," he concluded. "Or I could take an IOU the way I did with this young lady's oil painting."

Finally Mama told Shirley, "I'll pay for it, and you can take it home. But every week, you'll bring me a nickel or dime until you've paid me the fifty cents."

Mama and Shirley were first out the door. I turned back and opened my purse, extracting three sheets of folded tablet paper. Shoving them at Mr. Trustworthy, I explained, "I put my hand on the bookcase, and you were right."

Shirley was so pleased with her picture that she kicked me on purpose as we climbed back onto the streetcar. Strutting up the aisle, she swung into an empty seat as if she'd been riding streetcars all her life. "He'd hadda snootful," she said.

"What?" I sat down beside her while Mama took the seat behind us. "The old geezer at the second hand place had a snootful in him."

I knew what a snootful was. On Papa's side I was descended from men who often as not had a snootful on Saturday night, but Mr. Trustworthy?

I turned back to Mama. "What's the black and tan?"

"The black and tan?"

"Mr. Trustworthy said he'd had some tragic dealings with the black and tan."

"I'm not sure," she said. "Something to do with war in Ireland, that's all I know."

Having seen what war did to Hilly, I wasn't surprised if it caused Mr. Trustworthy to have a snootful before noon. Tonight I'd finish the new story I'd started for him.

. . . .

WHILE WE WERE CLEARING SUPPER DISHES, Lou appeared at the door with Mama's sewing machine. When he'd rolled it into the living room, Mama offered, "A cup of tea?"

"Thank you, no, ma'am. Got to get straight home to dinner." Lou wiped the back of his perspiring neck with a blue bandana. "Special tonight. Woodrow—my son—he's leaving tomorrow for the army."

"He enlisted?" Mama wiped her hands again and again on her apron.

"Signed up to be a foot soldier, like his old man," Lou explained, nodding.

"You were in the army?" Mama asked, her voice rising on a note of incredulity.

"Oh, yes, ma'am. Twenty-five when we sailed to France. A growed man. Three sixty-ninth from Harlem. Saw plenty fighting."

Mama stood leaning against the kitchen door frame, staring at Lou, who hesitated by the front door, folding the bandana and returning it to his hip pocket. Now he tugged an old watch from the twill trousers, opened it discreetly and eyed the time.

Still Mama studied him. At length Aunt Betty appeared in the kitchen doorway, dishtowel in hand. "How much do we owe you?" she asked Lou.

Closing the watch, Lou stuffed it back into the watch pocket. "A dollar?" he asked Mama.

Mama woke from her abstraction. "I'm sorry," she said, and hurried to fetch her purse from the bedroom.

Seeing the drayman out, she called, "Tell Woodrow . . . tell him to be careful." Closing the door, she drifted into the kitchen. "Did you know Negroes fought in the Great War? No one ever told me that."

. . . .

Taking a break from two hours of frenzied curtain sewing, Mama wandered into my room while I prepared for bed. Drooping against the bureau, she massaged one shoulder, then rubbed her eyes with the heels of her hands.

Slapping across the room in her house slippers, she picked up Hilly's picture from the bedside table. Propped against the lamp, next to Hilly, was Sally's snapshot. Now Mama plucked that up and studied it.

"Sally's getting tall. But look at that forlorn backyard. Not a flower or bush or bench." Returning the pictures to the table, Mama shook her head. "And what's to become of Sally?"

If Mama were still in Harvester, she could look out for Sally and Stella Wheeler as she'd tried to look out for Hilly and Mrs. Stillman. Of course, Sally and her mother had Mr. Wheeler but, as Mama often pointed out, he had his hands full with Mrs. Wheeler being so incapacitated by her Change.

"Well," Mama said, straightening, "this isn't getting the curtains done."

"Why do you have to get them done tonight?" I wanted to needle her for lying about the letter she'd written Uncle Stanley.

"To get something up at these windows, why do you think?"

"We got along all this time, we could get along another week or so."

"I want it done and off my mind," she said. "Now, get into bed."

I got into bed and she bent to kiss me, admonishing, "Lights out in five minutes." As the door closed, I pulled Sally's letter from under my pillow.

Dear Lark,

When Mrs. Stillman heard how sad you were in California, she asked me to send you this picture of Hilly. She said she had another one. I am sure you will be glad to get it.

Mrs. Stillman is very good to me. Beverly Ridza and I have cookies and tea at her apartmant.

I gave your address to Mrs. Stillman but the arthritis in her hands is bad, so she told me to send you her love.

Mommy still cries. She misses your mommy and I miss you. Come back when you can or send for me.

Your friend,
Sally Wheeler

15

Once more I slid the tablet from beneath the bed. Mama was too busy sewing curtains to notice that I hadn't turned out the light. Sharpening my pencil with a little ten-cent sharpener from Jon's Market, I began.

The Cabin by the Woods

Three people and a gray cat live in a cabin by the woods in Minnesota. One of them is a girl named Ann Browning. Another is a dead man named Hilly Stillman. The last one is a dead toddler named Marjorie Weller. The cat which is also dead is called Fala.

To some people a dead soldier, a dead toddler and a dead cat living in a cabin would seem unusual. Some people might be afraid to visit. Well in a way that is a good thing because it keeps away people who are just trouble anyway.

Anybody who is dead and shouldn't be is welcome to live with Ann Browning, Hilly Stillman, Marjorie Weller and Fala. If a lot of good dead people come Hilly Stillman says that he will build more rooms.

Ann Brownings grandmother says that ghosts are real. And she says sometimes ghosts are like angels who look out for us. Ann Browning isn't sure about angels because she isn't sure about god but she's sure about ghosts if that's what you want to call Hilly and Marjorie and Fala.

The furniture in this cabin is mostly sweet rejectaminta because that is the kind Ann and Hilly like. It reminds them of their grandmothers. Also when they lay their hands on the furniture it tells them stories so they are never board.

Ann Browning has a good friend who lives in California and his name is Mr. Trustworthy. When the furniture tells Ann stories she writes them down and sends them to him.

Ann says that stories can keep people from being too unhappy. Stories take their minds off their troubles. And sad stories show people that things could be worse.

In the *Webster's Collegiate Dictionary* I tried to check the spelling of words I wasn't sure of but I couldn't find a listing for "rejectamenta" so I had to guess.

I tore off the two sheets of paper, folded them, and began a note to Mr. Trustworthy.

> Dear Mr. Trustworthy
> I have written another story. But the thing is that it isn't very good because nothing happens. But I hope it takes your mind off the troubles with the black and tan. In the mean time I will work on the story and see if I can correct whats wrong.
> Yours truly
> Lark Ann Browning Erhardt

I had meant to begin a letter to Sally but I was getting sleepy, so I flicked off the light and lay in bed thinking of ways to improve the story.

In the living room, Mama was telling Aunt Betty, "There were two or three pianos at the second hand store."

"We can't afford a piano."

"Not right now. But down the line? Wouldn't it be swell to have a piano? There was this black one that reminded me of Mama and Papa's. And guess what it cost. Fifteen dollars! The chair you're sitting in cost that!"

She treadled a moment, then stopped again. "And you can bet they're going to stop making pianos till the war's over—like everything else. All the old ones are going to be snatched up. I was lucky to get this sewing machine."

Grandma and Grandpa Browning's piano was an ancient but tuneful black upright built by the Starr Piano Company of Madison, Wisconsin. Aunt Betty had played it before I was born, and at the holidays after she was married to Uncle Stanley.

As a girl, she had owned all the latest sheet music. The piano bench was stuffed so full that bits and pieces stuck out even when the lid was closed.

Mama hadn't mentioned pianos until she thought I was asleep. She didn't want me begging for one. But it would be swell to have a piano. I couldn't picture boys hurting a girl who had a piano.

"Down the line we'll get one," Mama concluded. A moment later, the treadle was rackety-racking as she returned to the frantic curtain sewing she'd begun after supper.

Waking the next morning, I found simple white curtains hanging at all the windows. Mama must have worked most of the night.

When Aunt Betty arrived home from Mass, carrying the Sunday paper, Mama still hadn't stirred from bed but I was curled up on the sofa writing to Sally. As she laid the paper on a chair and removed her battered navy blue straw hat, Aunt Betty gave me a rueful look.

Mass was a mixed blessing for her. On the one hand, it filled her with a sense of being shepherded by someone more judicious than Mama. On the other, it nagged her to return her two strayed sheep to the fold. She came home with a sad, evangelical glow—sad because her effort was doomed.

"God missed you at Mass," Aunt Betty said. "Today is Father's Day, and the priest said we should pay special honor to our Heavenly Father as well as our earthly one." She picked up the furled newspaper from the chair and sat down. "Did you remember to wish your papa a happy Father's Day?"

"I didn't know." Not quite true. There'd been ads in last Sunday's paper. Shirts for Father's Day. Ties for Father's Day. It hadn't sunk in. I was forgetting that I had a father.

Sitting on the bed, I wrote:

> Dear Papa,
> I am sorry I didn't write to you for Father's Day. Mama and I were so busy. But I should not forget.
> Mama bought an old sewing machine for two dollars and made curtins for every room in our house.
> I have a friend named Shirley. She is from Wioming. She had a pony when she lived there. And she was bitten by a rattle snake.
> That is all the news for now except that I am sorry for forgetting Father's Day.
> Love xxxxxooooo
> Lark

I was in a hurry and didn't look up all the spelling. Wyoming didn't look right to me. When I had addressed an envelope, Aunt Betty gave me a stamp from a little book of them in her purse.

"Did you write to Uncle Stanley?" I asked.

She hesitated. "Nooooo," she said, drawing the word out. "It would hurt him to be reminded of Baby Marjorie."

"I wish you and Uncle Stanley would get back together and have a baby."

"I can't have any more babies."

"Why?"

"Where the babies grow, inside, is messed up."

"But couldn't you adopt a baby?"

"I'm almost too old. They don't let people adopt when they're too old. I'll be thirty-four next Sunday."

And by the time she and Uncle Stanley got together, if they ever did, she'd be older still. No wonder Mama was impatient to get Uncle Stanley down here.

"Babies get left on people's doorsteps sometimes. I've heard of that."

She didn't answer, but went to the kitchen to put on an apron and begin mixing pancake batter.

I followed, warming to my subject. "There's a story in *Happy Stories for Bedtime* about a poor woman who left her baby on an old couple's doorstep. Babies like that are called foundlings. Mama said that's because you open the door and find them." I got out plates and began setting the table. "I'm going to ask God to leave a baby on your doorstep."

"We shouldn't ask God for miracles."

"Why?"

"Because then He has to disappoint us."

"He doesn't *have* to disappoint us. If I was God, I'd do so many miracles they'd stop calling them miracles. They'd just be *life.*"

"Because Adam and Eve ate from the Tree of Knowledge, God can't do that," she reminded me.

"But He's God, so He knew ahead of time that they were going to eat from the Tree of Knowledge. He planned the whole thing!"

Pouring batter into a skillet, Aunt Betty advised, "We should ask God to make us strong and good and content with our lives."

Mama stood in the doorway in an old peach satin nightgown that had once been her best but was now ratty and frayed. She laughed. "Don't you dare get content with your life, Lark. God helps those who help themselves."

Like Adam and Eve?

Later, as I lay on the floor reading the funny papers and letting my mind run to miracles, Mama noted, "There's another feature in the rotogravure about your Alicia Armand." She tossed that portion of the paper to me.

A postage stamp-size photo of Alicia Armand, just her head with her hair skinned severely back from her face, stared at me, eyes dark and smudgy, mouth slightly open as if in appeal.

> Alicia (Arkovsky) Armand, under contract to Twentieth Century Fox, today makes her home in the Hollywood Hills, but only a year ago she was sheltered in a barn in the French countryside waiting to make a dramatic escape from Gestapo-controlled France.
>
> "I cannot detail my escape," she told this reporter. "There are those who might yet suffer for it." She did reveal that it was aboard a Turkish freighter that she was spirited out of Marseilles.
>
> A Jewess, the beautiful Miss Armand was a featured dancer with a number of French ballet companies and dreams of the day the war is over so that she may return to France and the dance stage there. Until then, she will raise money for displaced children by acting in American films and, when possible, dancing with U.S. ballet companies.
>
> Our hats are off to Alicia Armand and to the Free French!

"Can I cut this out?" I asked.

Mama nodded, preoccupied with the war news. "It looks like Tobruk is going to fall," she informed Aunt Betty.

"What's Tobruk?" I asked.

"A place in North Africa. Libya. Looks like Rommel's going to take it."

Rommel, I knew, was a German general. "Should I put a black tack on the map?" I wondered, trailing out to the kitchen to find this latest bad news name on the world map.

"Not yet. The British may hang on."

I did locate Tobruk, however. There it was, on the Mediterranean coast of Africa, opposite Crete and Greece to the north. Off to the west, on the south coast of France, was Marseilles, from which Alicia Armand had escaped. I slid onto a kitchen chair and sat staring at the map. From France to Hollywood was a long way.

I included the actress in my daydreams. In this way, maybe I could rescue her from loneliness. Was that possible? Could you wish a person out of themselves and into your dreams? Maybe if I ran into her on the street in Los Angeles sometime, she would recognize me from my dreams or at least wonder if we hadn't met before.

There was a pounding racket at the door. Hadn't anybody ever taught Shirley how to knock? Invariably she pounded as if announcing a Japanese invasion.

Aunt Betty answered, calling to me uncertainly, "Someone wants to see you, Lark."

"Tell her it's Shirley." Shirley's rough voice sounded mushy, as if she were chewing a caramel and talking at the same time. When I reached the door I saw that the side of her face was swollen and a bruise extended from her jaw to her right eye, the lid of which was puffed and blue. A shallow cut had left a thin red line across her cheekbone.

"What happened to you?" I asked, ushering her into the living room. Mama laid aside the newspaper and was studying our guest. Aunt Betty, who had retreated several steps, stood hovering.

Shirley glanced from one of us to the other, all the while rubbing her grubby palm down the side of her pants leg. "I was playin' tag," she said slowly, "and . . . I ran into the side of the house."

"When?"

She looked at me wildly, as if I were a teacher testing her on material she didn't know.

16

"Where does Shirley live?" Mama asked when my friend had left.

"I don't know."

"You've never been to her house?"

I shook my head. "She never wants to play at her house."

"Do her parents work at Consolidated?"

"I guess. She doesn't talk about them, only that they worked on a ranch in Wyoming."

Somebody might wonder why Mama and Aunt Betty were so concerned about Shirley. But Grandma Browning once complained, "Those two girls will cart home every stray dog that limps across the road." Papa called them do-gooders.

I didn't see Shirley again until Thursday morning. By then, the bruise had turned yellow and green and purple, and it made me half sick to look at it.

When she had eaten enough toast to owe me something, I asked, "Where's your house? On Piñon?"

She shook her head and picked at the small scab on the back of her hand.

"Caliente?"

Negative.

"Camino Padero?"

"None a yer business, Minnesota trash," she snarled, pitching herself out of the kitchen and out of the house.

She came pounding on the door that afternoon while I was in bed writing to Sally Wheeler. I clamped my hands over my ears and hummed until I was sure she'd left.

"Dear Sally," I had written.

> Thank you for your letter. I really needed to hear from you.
> I don't have any friends here except for adults. There is a girl named Shirley who comes around a lot but she is not my friend I can tell you that. She is the meanest girl I ever met.

Now I continued:

> And believe me she is not pretty. Just the opposite. And she is not smart. So nobody at school wants her for a friend. I almost would feel sorry for her if she wasn't so mean. But I don't want to dirty this paper talking about her!
> So I won't.
> Tell Mrs. Stillman thank you for the picture of Hilly. When I saw it I cried for about an hour and it made me hurt inside. But I am so glad to have it. It makes me happy. Do you understand?
> You are the prettiest and nicest girl I know.
>
> Your friend forever even after I am dead,
> Lark Ann Browning Erhardt

. . . .

TWO LETTERS FROM PAPA arrived in Friday's mail, one for Mama and one for me. They'd been sent from the railroad depot on Monday, when Papa knew for sure that I'd forgotten Father's Day.

> Dear Little Lark,
> Father's Day came and went without even a postcard from my little girl to wish her Pa a happy day.
> Some people still think pretty well of me, tho. After Mass

yesterday Magdalen Haggerty and Dora Noonan from the Loon Cafe invited me to have lunch down there, "on them."

There was quite a gang of Knights of Columbus swells who'd stopped after Mass, but Magdalen and Dora treated me like the biggest swell of all.

I think I'll stop by the draft board. If I was in the army or dead, maybe you'd remember me in your prayers. I'm sending two dollars. Light twenty candles and say twenty prayers, and God will forgive you, like I'm trying to.

Love, Pa

I burned with shame. Grasping the dollar bills by the corner as if they were on fire, I carried them to the bedroom closet.

Papa's scolding shamed me, and so did the cold stone I found in my chest where a soft heart should be. What kind of child was I?

I wouldn't tell Mama about Papa's letter. My forgetting Father's Day could become a weapon she could use against him. "Lark has started to see through you, Willie," she might say.

Was I seeing through Papa? It was not the business of children to see through their parents. Children ought to be raised by their grandparents, that was all. Grandparents never worried about being seen through. It didn't cross their minds.

What if I started seeing through Mama? What would I see?

At about half past three in the afternoon I woke, heavy with shapeless anxiety. From the kitchen broom closet, I dragged the housekeeping gear and set to work to purify the house.

"Looks like we're expecting Eleanor Roosevelt," Mama laughed when she saw the clean house. She was always jolly after work on Friday; only Saturday morning remained until her day-and-a-half off. Not that she resented her job. "Everything and everyone passes through personnel, one way or the other," she liked to say. All the plant gossip and politics, all the war talk and labor troubles.

Besides, Mama was learning about offices and how they worked. "When the war's over, I'm going to walk out of there with a business education," she told Aunt Betty.

Now Mama tossed her purse onto the rose chair and carried her lunch pail to the kitchen, humming "Chattanooga Choo-Choo." I trailed her, emptying the lunch pail, rinsing the remaining few drops of coffee from the thermos. The letter from Papa was on the table.

"Damn," she breathed.

"Are we having tomato soup and Velveeta sandwiches?" I asked, hoping to distract her. We often had those on Friday, both for Aunt Betty's Catholic sake as well as for the war effort.

"Oh, for heaven's sake, I suppose," Mama snapped, snatching up the letter and heading to her bedroom.

Since the table was set, I fetched *Heidi* from my room and sat down on the sofa to wait.

. . . .

MAMA'S FACE ACROSS THE SUPPER TABLE was puffy, her eyelids red. She sat stirring her tomato soup long after it was cool. When the dishes were washed, she jerked herself from room to room, distracted and aimless.

At nine, she came into my room and sat on the edge of the bed. Although her voice was subdued, the conversation concerned pleasant things.

"Sunday is Aunt Betty's birthday," she reminded me. "After work tomorrow I'll run downtown and buy presents. I was thinking we might give her a pretty brassiere and panties. She needs them, I know. And maybe a pair of stockings. What do you think?"

Dull as dishwater was what I thought, but I nodded.

I wished I could buy my aunt a bracelet or a book or a bottle of perfume. It did not occur to me to use the money from Papa.

Mama picked at the bedspread. A suggestion of a smile pulled at her lips and her lowered voice grew more conspiratorial. "Wouldn't it be swell if Uncle Stanley showed up for Betty's birthday? He might. He just might." She hugged me in a little spasm of pleasure. I hugged back, dubious.

17

On Saturday morning, I cut appropriate words and pictures from old *Life* magazines, pasting them onto a folded piece of paper with flour-and-water paste, but the birthday card for Aunt Betty dried so knobbly that it resembled a stretch of rough, treeless terrain on a topographical map. I pressed it under three or four books and even ironed it with the electric iron, but in the end it looked ancient and oddly threatening.

"It's the sentiment that counts," Mama said, arriving home at three-thirty and studying the outside of my card, where a pretty face, strongly resembling Aunt Betty's, tilted skyward and admonished, "Remember Pearl Harbor." The message inside, clipped from ads for Ponds cold cream and Sal Hepatica laxative, proclaimed, "She's lovely! Gentle and speedy!" These words of admiration were accompanied by a photograph of an attractive young debutante rolling bandages, just as my aunt did every Thursday evening at the Red Cross. Beneath all this a long line of X's and O's marched across the page along with "Lark Ann Browning Erhardt."

"Shouldn't it say 'Happy Birthday' somewhere?" Mama asked.

When Mama had had a leisurely bath, shampooed her hair, and dabbed cologne behind her ears, she pulled on an old housedress from our Minnesota lives, a red cotton frock sprigged with white daisies. The fabric was faded but the princess lines and short, puffed sleeves showed off her figure and firm, girlish arms. She had pin-curled her hair and tied a scarf around it, and now she looked scrubbed and pert and hopeful.

Papa's letter was filed away in a battered purse on her closet shelf, out of sight and out of mind.

We wrapped the brassiere and panties, the stockings and new garter belt, each in a separate little folder-box provided by Gilpins' department store. "If you put each present in a different box," Mama said, "it seems like more."

Thick, lazy afternoon sun fell across the rug where we knelt tying each small box with pink satin ribbon. This afternoon was like life in Harvester, where time had been endless.

Mama's face was lit by secrets. When the presents for tomorrow's birthday were wrapped and stacked on top of the bookcase, she straightened towels in the bathroom, smoothed the spread on her and Aunt Betty's bed, and finally strayed outside to water the gardenia bush. I sat on the stoop.

Up the walk trudged Beau Eldridge, returning from Saturday afternoon overtime. Coming abreast of Mama, who was fussing with the gardenia bush, removing a couple of dead leaves, he noted, "It's still alive."

Mama nodded.

"I wouldn't have thought it could live in this soil."

"You never know what will live."

"Yes." He shifted his lunch pail, unfastening the two clasps that held it. From the interior he withdrew a small, waxed paper package and held it out to me. "Have some cookies? I'm trying to lose weight," he said. "You'd be doing me a favor. My sister's way too generous when she packs the pail."

I took the wrapped cookies, thanking him.

Closing the pail, he lodged it under his arm and thrust his hands into his trousers pockets, striking an unguarded, sociable attitude.

"You're from North Dakota?" Mama asked.

Hesitating, he jingled change in his pockets and looked toward the street as if something there had caught his eye. "I . . . came from there. But we lived a long while in Nebraska. My sister and I." Before Mama could respond, Beau asked, "You're from Minnesota?"

"Harvester. A little burg of about two thousand people."

Beau nodded, then said, "That's a pretty dress." This was unexpected. Even he seemed surprised.

Mama's eyes widened, but she smiled. "Thanks. It's old as the hills."

From someplace inside their house, Belle Eldridge called, "Beau? It's nearly dinner."

"I'd better mind," he said, moving off and up the steps, closing the screen door behind him.

"A sad old dog," Mama called Beau at dinner, recalling their meeting to Aunt Betty.

"He's not so old," I told her.

"Well, how old do you think he is?" she asked, setting a plate of bread on the table.

I thought for a moment. "About Uncle Stan's age."

After supper Mama pulled the bobby pins from her hair and combed out the curls into a bouncy fluff around her face. She was full of needles that pricked her to restless sweeps of the house.

Aunt Betty, exhausted by a long day at Gilpins', had hung up her dress and drawn on an old robe over her slip. She sat on the sofa, writing a letter to Grandma and Grandpa Browning, thanking them for the two dollars they'd included with their birthday greetings.

She looked up as Mama rose from the club chair and glided past. "Are you all right?"

"What?"

"Are you all right? You're as nervous as a dog with fleas."

"I'm fine. I thought I'd make a pot of tea. Would you like a cup?"

"We just finished supper."

Mama, who had in fact been headed toward the bathroom, altered her course and slipped out to the kitchen, where she sat down at the table, forgetting the tea.

I shadowed her. I'd never seen her this way, drifting and dreaming, trailing sighs and expectations. Uncle Stanley's possible visit had her all twitchety.

"All dressed up and no place to go?" Aunt Betty wondered, having set aside her correspondence and followed us to the kitchen. She lit the stove under the tea kettle.

"I wouldn't call this old thing 'all dressed up.'" With two fingers Mama flicked the hem of the dress scornfully.

Still, when the weak tea was brewed, she carried her cup to the stoop and sat in the chilly late twilight following the westward flight of three B-24s.

The next morning, while Aunt Betty was at Mass, Mama made a birthday cake, chocolate with seven-minute white frosting. "It's a good thing we don't use sugar in our tea," Mama observed. The small cake and its frosting required nearly two cups of the government-rationed sugar.

From her purse on the bureau, Mama withdrew a tiny white paper bag containing five big pink gumdrops and one green. Between sheets of waxed paper sprinkled with powdered sugar, she rolled the green and all but one of the pinks with the rolling pin, flattening them until they were nearly as wide across as your hand. Then, with a paring knife, she cut slits toward the centers of the pink circles and trimmed the outermost corners, making them into petals, rounding them, even as flower petals are rounded. With a few deft twists, she gave each petal a tug and a turn, and when she was finished a big, pink gumdrop lay on the yellow-checked oilcloth, transformed into a wild rose.

Mama sculpted four roses, jammed a little white birthday candle into the center of each, and placed them in a cluster on top of the cake. The green circle she cut into small leaves and stems, which completed the nosegay.

"Why four roses?" I inquired.

"Aunt Betty is thirty-*four*," she explained, setting the cake on top of the refrigerator, wiping off the table, and handing me the sixth gumdrop, pink and intact.

Thirty-four. I couldn't conceive of being thirty-four, especially an unhappy, deserted thirty-four. Yet Grandma Browning had cried out and clutched her breast when Mama had suggested that Aunt Betty get a divorce. Only one woman had ever continued living in Blue Lake after her fall from marriage, and she had money. People respected your money if not your character. Grocerymen and committee women did not turn their backs on your money.

Again Mama had donned the red dress blooming with white daisies. She'd tied a narrow band of white ribbon around her head and smudged a blush of rouge on her lips and cheeks. Her feet were tucked into last summer's open-toed wedgies; her red-painted toenails, squeezed together, peeked out daringly.

Yesterday's air of expectancy still clung to her, but a wrought-up, frantic quality had crept into it. As the day wore on into afternoon, Mama's mood darkened. She claimed that her short temper resulted from reading the Sunday paper—Tobruk and Sevastopol had both fallen to the Axis, and the Japanese were in possession of Attu and Kiska in the Aleutian Islands.

"The Aleutian Islands!" Mama exploded. "Practically our doorstep! Why isn't someone *doing* something?" Aunt Betty and I stared as Mama bolted for the bathroom and slammed the door.

Returning ten minutes later, she explained, "The war's getting on my nerves. I'm sorry."

"It's depressing," Aunt Betty agreed. She showed me where to place the black tacks: one in North Africa, one in the Ukraine on the Black Sea, and one in the North Pacific between Alaska and Japan.

The nimbus of festivity surrounding Aunt Betty's birthday dimmed as vexation at Uncle Stanley drove Mama into a fit of contrariness: Nothing was right. There wasn't enough vanilla flavoring in the cake frosting. The pink of the undergarments we'd given Aunt Betty was too vivid—cheap looking—and the stockings ought to be sand, not taupe, though she'd had hell's own hard time getting even the taupe pair.

Aunt Betty knelt beside Mama's chair. "I love my presents. They're just what I wanted and needed. And how did you ever make seven-minute frosting with that old hand beater?"

"It's all wrong," Mama sobbed. "The war is driving me crazy."

In the next day's mail, shuffled between the monthly statement from Victory Furniture and a vacation postcard from Bernice McGivern postmarked Lake Okoboji, Iowa, lay a letter for Aunt Betty in Uncle Stanley's hand.

It was light and slim, one thin sheet of stationery, probably. Maybe a birthday letter, yet it had a morose look. Not a flourish nor a grace note to it.

Since Aunt Betty never read his letters aloud, I thought of steaming it open. In the end it wasn't so much scruples that stopped me as knowing that I would have to reseal the envelope with flour-and-water paste.

I set the mail on the kitchen table, grabbed the lard pail from under the sink, and peered out to be sure that neither Shirley nor the boys were anywhere in sight. Emerging into the open and perilous world, I closed the screen door silently behind me.

The air smelled exotic—a mix of eucalyptus, sea brine, and from the foothills, sage. I sat down on the top step to soak in the morning warmth. Drawing my legs toward me, I hugged my knees, laying my head on them and closing my eyes.

Behind her kitchen curtains, Belle Eldridge cooed nonsense syllables to the canary: "tweeee tweee tweee" and "looo looo looo." They were lulling sounds and soon my mind floated into the dim foyer of sleep.

"Why, why, why, Billy? Sweet Billy. Cruel Billy. Billy who killed me killed me killed me. Oh, God, Billy."

Now I was fully awake. I knocked over the pail and it clattered to the sidewalk. The Eldridge kitchen window slid silently closed. Uncertain whether I'd been dreaming, I examined the *why, why, why's* and the rest. I must have been dreaming. You wouldn't accuse a canary of killing you. But a patch of clear sky in my brain insisted, *You heard her just fine.*

I carried the lard pail to the spigot and filled it. "Okay, roots, here it comes," I announced, pouring the water into the depression at the base of the gardenia bush.

Yesterday morning, while Mama and I were fussing with Aunt Betty's birthday cake, Jack Dugan had planted daisies along the edge of the crawl space on this western, street-facing side of our shared building. Instead of sowing seeds, he'd put in plants with yellow blooms already bobbing on their little stems. A jaunty band, they paraded from the Dugan's corner, under their windows, then under ours, to within a couple of feet of Mama's gardenia bush.

They were drooping a bit, in need of watering before the sun rose over the house and hit them. Virtuous as a nurse on rounds, I filled the lard pail again and again, soaking the ground around each daisy plant. Maybe Fanny would come out later to water and discover that a secret helper had been here first.

As I mounted the stoop and grasped the handle of the screen door, something drew my eyes to the street. On the opposite side of Piñon, arms looped over each other's shoulders, three boys lounged in a slack posture as if they'd been standing just that way for some minutes, peering at me.

18

RETURNING HOME THAT EVENING, Aunt Betty carried Uncle Stanley's letter to the bathroom while Mama kept supper warm. When she joined us, my aunt looked desiccated, her vital juices extracted.

"A letter from Fortune's Stepchild?" Mama asked. Setting a bowl of fried potatoes on the table, she pressed, "Well? What did he say? Did he wish you a happy birthday? Did he inquire about your health?"

"He didn't mention my birthday," my aunt said without bitterness. "He talked about his work and the war and his car. He's having trouble getting parts and tires for it."

Aunt Betty's plate was still bare. I passed her the potatoes and she stared at them. At length she scooped out a scant tablespoon and set the bowl down. She hadn't noticed the ring bologna or the ketchup, so I slid those toward her. With abstracted daintiness, she ate the fried potatoes, then wiped her mouth with the paper napkin and scraped back her chair.

"He sent another twenty-five dollars," she said, and left the room.

His picture remained on her bedside table—a candid shot of him leaning against the driver's side of the old Model A, a foot resting on the running board. Dressed in his Sunday-best dark pinstripe trousers, matching vest, and white shirt, he clutched a gray fedora in his left hand against his hip and smiled seductively into the camera. The black-and-white picture, taken in Grandma and Grandpa Browning's drive, against a wall of lilacs, captured his easy charm.

. . . .

AFTER AUNT BETTY'S THIRTY-FOURTH BIRTHDAY, the photo and the twenty-five-dollar money orders were our only reminders of Uncle Stanley for a long time, as Aunt Betty did not speak of him.

Mama, on the other hand, was ever more obsessed, more disapproving, more dissatisfied, more vocal. She was working herself into such a fury of disdain and blame that no matter what miraculous turnaround Uncle Stanley might effect, it would never be enough.

About Papa, Mama spoke less and less. She was erasing him from the pages of her life. But Willie Erhardt was not someone you could easily erase. His determination to hang onto Mama was in his letters, and in our letters from Grandma Browning, with whom Papa corresponded erratically but emotionally.

"Willie says he'll kill himself or you or both, if you don't come back," Grandma wrote in one letter to Mama. "For Lark's sake and Willie's, I think you should." Usually Mama burned upsetting letters and I didn't get to read them, but this one she'd stuck between the pages of *Leave Her to Heaven*.

Papa continued to write about coming to California. "If I have to," he'd written me, "I'll drag your Ma back here by her dyed hair." But the trip did not materialize in 1942, and I suspected that the money needed had been lost at poker, a game Papa loved but had no talent for.

Failing a trip to California to drag Mama home or kill her, would Papa talk the draft board into taking him? He desperately needed to cause a stir, to reassert himself in our lives.

Mama said that the army wouldn't have him, that he had a bad leg from a broken bone being improperly set when he was a boy, but I'd heard stories of men wangling their way into the service with all sorts of handicaps. Mama said Papa was more likely to wangle his way out than in.

Papa might not be saving enough money for a trip to California, but he was still sending me dollar bills for votive candles, and I was stuffing them into my galoshes. I didn't count them. I didn't want to think about them.

When school resumed in the fall, I found myself in Miss Carlyle's fifth grade. We had regular scrap drives now, mainly for old rubber and metal, to aid the war effort. I couldn't contribute much because I couldn't go out collecting door to door. Instead I brought things from home: rubber bands, a hot water bottle with a bad leak, a bag of tin cans.

The boys had passed from our elementary school to a junior high school out of the neighborhood. By running home at two forty-five when school was dismissed, I could pretty well avoid them during the week. But they still lived in the Project. Two or three times during the fall, one or another of the fifth grade girls invited me to her house after school, but I said no because I didn't dare be caught out on the streets.

And Shirley Olson wasn't a girlfriend. At recess she never talked about movie stars or songs on the Hit Parade. She talked mostly about the Fergusons and the ranch, or about killing Japs. After a while nobody listened.

Shirley rarely came to my house and she never asked me to hers. At my house, she ate our food without being asked, riffled through magazines without interest, and studied my painting with a wolfish eye. As time passed, she took no more kindly to personal questions than she had before, and she was contemptuous of the pictures of Alicia Armand that I had torn from magazines and newspapers and tacked to my bedroom wall.

More and more, in her publicity, the dancer-actress was called by her real last name, Armand. She had taken the name Arkovsky for her career in ballet, but American movie audiences liked short names on the marquee: Betty Grable, Myrna Loy, Irene Dunne, Alicia Armand.

Her growing fame thrilled me, because I had discovered her. On the City of Los Angeles, when the average movie fan had never heard of her, I had fallen under her spell.

With her first two films, *The Contessa Goes to War* and *West of the Volga,* the French performer had "caught the imagination of the movie-going public," according to *Stars of the Screen.* In her spare moments, she lent her pure, pale presence to war bond rallies in Hollywood, Seattle, Chicago, and Boston, and she worked tirelessly raising money for children displaced by the war.

For my birthday in September, Aunt Betty treated me to *The Contessa Goes to War,* a comedy about a contessa who sabotages the Nazis after they commandeer her castle. Gathered into the plush lap of the Fox Theater, I absorbed the radiance and sadness of Alicia Armand as a Christian receives the Host: gratefully, with some hint of the pain and sacrifice it represents.

In December, Mama took me to *West of the Volga,* a film depicting the German occupation of a small Russian village and the execution by boiling water of a lovely Russian patriot (Alicia Armand, of course) who had lured individual German soldiers to their deaths at the hands of villagers. I covered my eyes when they dumped her into the huge vat.

"That movie," Mama said when we came out, "is far too mature and bloody for a fifth grader." We had nevertheless remained for the entire showing. And anyway, tragedies and atrocities were reported in the newspaper every day. What of the Canadian soldiers slaughtered at Dieppe, a massacre late in August and represented on the kitchen map by a black tack? Although things improved toward the end of the year, 1942 was bleak for the Allies, and not a high-water mark for me.

Turning the corner in September from age nine to ten had brought none of the rewards of double-digit age that I had anticipated. My teeth were still too big. When I smiled, I imagined people saying, "Where are those teeth going with that little girl?" And I was beginning to see through people.

Age ten meant swimming (or drowning) between the two shores of dependency and autonomy. Grown-ups began to shove you away from the near shore, expecting you to maneuver for yourself out there in the deep water of twelve, thirteen, and fourteen, expecting you to solve your own problems, live with your own fears, conquer your own loneliness. Weren't they sorry to be saying good-bye to you?

19

THE SATURDAY BEFORE CHRISTMAS, Mama brought home a four-foot Christmas tree and a stand. "We'll set the tree on one of the living room tables," she said. In Harvester, we'd had a tree that reached nearly to the ceiling. But then we'd owned a car to haul it home.

When Aunt Betty arrived from work, she was lugging a Gilpins' bag containing a string of tree lights, a few glass ornaments, a pack of various-colored sheets of construction paper, and a jar of real paste, like the ones at school, with a little brush applicator in the lid.

She handed me the paper and paste, saying, "We'll need plenty of paper chains."

Sitting on the living room rug, cutting construction paper while Mama and Aunt Betty strung popcorn, I listened to Lionel Barrymore play Scrooge on the radio and summoned my own Christmases past.

Last year, Hilly was buried on the sixteenth of December, when a blanket of snow covered the ground. A bitter wind spit snow in our faces as we stood beside the grave. A few days later, Papa gambled away the money Mama had saved for a down payment on the Cape Ann and Mama said, "That's it."

All day Sunday, I cut out and pasted paper chain, yards of it, too much for the small tree, so Mama hung it over the living room windows and around the doors.

On Monday, I snipped out paper stars, candy canes, and snow men to hang on the tree, later wrapping the two clay dishes I'd made at school for Mama and Aunt Betty. They were meant to be bowl shaped, but the rims had collapsed under their own weight and they looked like strange-colored mashed potatoes with the centers depressed for gravy. Aunt Betty's was a muddy pink and Mama's bluish red. I felt too old to be turning out such failed trifles, but that was age ten for you: too old to be cute, too young to be clever.

On Wednesday night, Aunt Betty brought home a bag of assorted hard candies from Gilpins' and dumped it into a cereal bowl. Striped, curled red-and-green ribbons of sweetness; round, flattened white pieces with tiny pine trees in their centers; red raspberry-shaped candies, hard on the outside, soft and chewy in the center; and pillow-shaped candies of different colors. With sugar she'd saved, Mama made gingerbread men.

Thursday morning, I cleaned house. Straightening my bedroom closet, I tipped the galoshes out, dumping the dollar bills from Papa onto the floor. The rainy season was coming and I would be needing the galoshes. Borrowing an idea from *The Contessa Goes to War,* I tucked my running-away money into an envelope and taped the envelope to the wooden backing on my oil painting.

I didn't own a dress-up dress anymore. I'd outgrown my Minnesota dresses and since I didn't go to church or parties Mama hadn't replaced them. I chose the prettiest of my school dresses, a red-and-blue plaid with white collar and cuffs.

For nearly an hour, I fussed with my hair—I was letting it grow. Then, as the December light began to fail, I set the table, plugged in the Christmas tree lights, and curled up in the rose chair to admire the tree in the candy-colored half light.

Around four-thirty, as high clouds rolled in and damp evening air crept into the streets, I lit the gas heater. Straightening, I heard the groan of an old truck turning up Piñon, lumbering to a halt at the foot of our yard. Pulling the shade aside, I made out Lou's truck in the near dark.

From the passenger seat, Mama jumped down, tossed aside her purse and lunch pail, and began waving her arms, directing the turning and backing of the truck onto the sidewalk and no farther, as both Jack Dugan and Beau Eldridge had planted grass. Another figure, lithe and dark, rose from the truck bed and called instructions to Lou in the cab. I ran outside as the truck ground to a stop and Lou set the brake.

On the back of the truck, strapped in and covered with old blankets, was the elephantine shape of an upright piano. Although it seemed impossible that two men, one of them old, could haul the piano off the truck, up the sidewalk, and into the house, they did, while Mama and I shoved the bookcase out of its customary corner.

When the piano was rolled into the corner, the two men wiped sweat from their necks and brows and laughed as if their hard work were a private joke.

"Now I want you two to sit down," Mama told them. "You're not leaving till you catch your breath. It's almost Christmas Eve. I'm not sending you home without some cheer."

"Be all right if I try the piano to make sure it works?" the younger man called to Mama.

"Heavens, yes," Mama yelled from the kitchen. "Lark, this is Lou's son Woodrow. He's home on leave from the army. Woodrow, that's my daughter Lark. She's home on leave from the fifth grade."

"Pleased to meet you," Woodrow told me, sitting down at the piano. Running scales up and down the keys, his ear cocked, Woodrow judged, "This instrument don't sound too far off the mark."

Mama carried in drinks for Lou and Woodrow, then returned to the kitchen for a plate of Ritz crackers spread with pimiento cheese from a jar.

Woodrow took a cracker and ate it, washing it down with rum and Coca-Cola while Lou looked on, proud and uncomfortable. Mama raised her glass. "Here's to Woodrow. And . . . absent friends."

The men raised their glasses. Setting his drink on the floor, Woodrow began picking out a melody with his right hand, one I knew because Aunt Betty used to have the sheet music. "For All We Know."

Gradually he added a few bass notes, keeping the arrangement as simple as a piece from a child's first piano book. Almost imperceptibly, the left hand grew more complex. Eventually the two hands ended in a kind of philosophical summing up. Woodrow seemed to be laughing at his own seriousness. *All this and a nickel will buy me a cup of coffee.*

As hastily as he had sat down, Woodrow sprang up, reaching for his glass and drinking the remainder of the rum and Coca-Cola.

"You play better than the people on the radio," I told him.

When I looked at Lou, his eyes, fixed on his son, were grave.

Mama hurried for her purse and wrote out a check. Reaching for it, Lou turned quickly away, muttering "Thank you, ma'am" as he descended the two steps to the walk. Woodrow, close behind, called with heavy nonchalance, "Slow down, old man."

Mama stood at the door until she heard the dray turn the corner, heading back into the city. When she swung around, she was catching tears at the corners of her eyes.

"What's wrong?"

"Imagine how Lou must feel. If you were going off to war, I'd never stop crying."

20

I SAT ADMIRING THE TREE and the watery glow the lights cast on the ebony finish of the piano, and the way it lit Aunt Betty's face as she stepped in from the damp night, a Gilpins' bag again grasped in her arms.

Twisting around to shoulder the door closed, she spied the piano in the shadows. Opening her mouth as if to protest, she squealed like a child. "A piano! A piano!" She ran to the kitchen, still carrying the shopping bag. "Arlene, you fool, it's wonderful!"

Mama took the bag. "You like it? You're not mad?"

"There's sheet music in the bench," I told my aunt.

Aunt Betty flung her coat on a chair, and struck up "O Come All Ye Faithful," following it with "God Rest Ye Merry Gentlemen." Tunelessly humming along, Mama sliced tomatoes for salad, opened cans of peas, and breaded the fresh tuna.

We didn't linger over dinner and dishwashing. The piano waited. But hardly had we hung up our towels than someone knocked at the door—Fanny and Jack Dugan, Fanny holding out a three-pound box of assorted chocolates and Jack thrusting a bottle of Wild Turkey whiskey at Mama.

"Come see our piano," I urged Fanny, taking her hand. "Isn't it beautiful? Mama got it at Trustworthy Second Hand." Mama was pressing Jack to sit down and have a drink of the whiskey he'd brought. He was saying he didn't mind if he did.

"Do you play the piano?" I asked Fanny.

She ran the back of her fingers lightly across several keys, not depressing them, only brushing their surface.

"Mind if I take this off?" Jack stood and eased out of the handsome tweed sport coat.

"Let me hang it over this chair," Aunt Betty said.

Jack loosened his tie and settled himself again on the sofa, draping an arm along the back. He studied Fanny, who stood at the piano.

"Fanny, what are you drinking?" Mama asked, handing Jack his whiskey and water.

"Nothing, thanks," she said. "Maybe later." The fingers of her right hand picked out a soundless tune.

"Do you play the piano, Fanny?" I asked again.

She didn't seem to hear the question, but from across the room Jack answered, "She does," his eyes admiring his wife.

Fanny sat down and for a moment merely looked at the keyboard. Then, without ado, she began playing what Papa called long-hair music and what Aunt Betty later explained was a mazurka, following it with a Chopin waltz and a Mozart sonatina, all played with a skill which hushed us.

When at length Fanny's body hunched, spent, over the last clear chords of "Jesu, Joy of Man's Desiring," we burst into applause.

Fanny swung around on the bench, covering a cough with the back of her hand, and called out, "Hooch for the piano player!"

Mama disappeared to fetch the drink.

"Did you ever play professionally?" Aunt Betty asked.

"Almost," Fanny said. She turned to Jack. "Cigarettes?"

Reluctantly, I thought, Jack fished a pack of Spuds and a lighter from his shirt pocket. Aunt Betty, ever sensitive to people's wounds and reticences, didn't pursue Fanny's piano career but asked, "Jack, do you play?"

Jack held the lighter to his wife's cigarette. She inhaled deeply, closing her eyes and slowly expelling the smoke, as if cigarette smoking were a mystical rite.

All the while Jack observed her, a tamped-down anger at the back of his eyes. But he addressed Aunt Betty's question, returning the cigarettes and lighter to his pocket. "Fan says I play the piano athletically. That sums it up."

Fanny wandered out to the kitchen where Mama whacked a refractory ice cube tray against the sink, swearing at it. Mama was in high spirits, though. In fact, her pique was part of her gaiety.

I sat on the straight chair beside the kitchen door, where I could hear everyone. I heard Aunt Betty ask Jack about his family, heard that his parents had both died of diphtheria many years ago in Detroit. Sad, she said, they must have been young. Yes, in their twenties, both. A childless aunt and uncle had taken Jack to live with them. They too were dead.

Aunt Betty, always tender to the hardships of others, grew more sensitive under the influence of alcohol. A melting quality came over her. Her features softened and her eyes grew large and liquid.

"But I've got Fan," Jack reminded my aunt. "An uncommon woman." Lifting his glass, he drank deeply.

Sitting sideways, I ran a hand down the lapel of Jack's sport jacket, which hung over the back of the chair. A muted blue-and-tan tweed, it complemented his coloring, his slicked-back sandy hair and intense blue eyes. Jack put me in mind of Alan Ladd in *This Gun for Hire*—an odd combination of muscular urgency, tension, and geniality.

"How did you and Fanny meet?" my aunt wondered. She sat in the rose chair, still in the navy blue dress with lace-trimmed collar and cuffs that she'd worn to Gilpins'. Her pale red hair, pulled back from her face, fell about her shoulders.

"I was a union organizer when Fanny and I met. One tough son of a bitch." He laughed, then shifted as if something pinched him. "Could I trouble you?" he asked, holding out his glass.

Aunt Betty carried the glass to the kitchen. Jack unbuttoned his cuffs and rolled up his sleeves. Rising, he stood with his back to me, hands shoved into his hip pockets, staring at a window whose shade was drawn. His shoulders worked up and down, relieving tension.

"Jack?" Aunt Betty held out his glass and spoke to his back. "Your drink?"

Although he turned to take the glass, Jack remained at the window, staring at the shade. His back was to my aunt when she sat down again, which struck me as a strange way to carry on a conversation.

"I was working out of Detroit," he said, "commuting back and forth to Chicago every week, trying to organize O'Neal meatpacking. One night I met this good-looking girl in the dining car. What I didn't know was she was Frank O'Neal's daughter. I sure as hell wouldn't have searched out Fanny O'Neal for a sweetheart. A guy could get killed."

"Killed?" Aunt Betty twisted around to look at Jack.

"She had that same whiskey laugh back then." Smiling, he turned around. "When the train got to Chi, I took her to a blind tiger on the South Side for a drink. Damned if the barkeep and all the help didn't know her by name. 'Lady Fan,' they called her. Everybody was crazy about her, telling her the latest jokes and gossip and asking after her family.

"I never tumbled, do you believe it? Never connected her with Frank O'Neal and the meatpacking business. Fan told me she'd spent some time in Europe. I figured her for an art student, y' know. The truth was, she'd spent two years in a TB sanitarium." He rocked on his heels and worked his jaw as if to loosen it, although that seemed unnecessary.

"Kept me in the dark about a lot of things. Wouldn't let me see her home. Always took a cab. I wondered if there wasn't a crazy husband lurking around with a gun in his pocket. Chi was a rough town in those days. Nineteen twenty-seven.

"I started seeing her once or twice a week, regular. She'd meet me. I didn't pry, and it never occurred to me to follow her. Whatever the deal was, it was Fan's deal."

A fire burned in Jack. I thought he'd had a drink or two before leaving home, and the whiskey kept the fire hot. His account of meeting Fanny was told with defiance, as if he was forbidden to speak of this. He glanced repeatedly at the kitchen door, daring Fanny to stop him.

Fanny sat at the kitchen table with Mama, clinging to Mama's words, relieved to listen to someone else's problems.

"A damned Christmas card with the Virgin and Child," Mama huffed. "*Sensitive*. And twenty-five dollars. That was it." She shook her head. "Betty'd be better off if he left her alone. But, no. The Virgin and Child! After her losing her baby."

Jack was standing by the piano now, studying the keyboard. My aunt waited for him to continue. He sank down on the bench, swearing, "I had nothing to do with Pat O'Neal getting killed."

At the kitchen table Mama had concluded the list of grievances against Uncle Stanley.

Fanny studied our war map. "Do you have someone in the war?"

"No one close. You?"

"A nephew, Dennis, in the navy." She looked down at her hands, then clasped them tightly together so the knuckles shone white. "His father died when he was two."

In the living room, Aunt Betty assured Jack, "No one would think you had anything to do with someone getting killed."

He laughed. "Fan's people did."

Why tonight of all nights was Jack telling my aunt this story? Was he drunk?

"Two workers from the O'Neal plant were beaten to death and dumped in the Chicago River the day before Thanksgiving—guys who'd been working with the union. The other workers figured management was warning them. A month later, Pat O'Neal was shot driving home from the plant, Christmas Eve."

Fifteen years ago.

"We'll never know who killed him or if it had anything to do with the union. Could have been a gambling debt or mistaken identity. Fan leveled with me then, told me who she was."

With a ragged, impatient gesture he swept back a shock of hair.

"Pat was Fan's favorite. He was the oldest; she was the baby. He'd always looked after her. He had a wife and a boy, two years old." Jack scrutinized his brown wingtips, the corner of his mouth screwed up. "Fan was beside herself. Frank O'Neal twisted arms up and down city hall to have me arrested. I was investigated from hell to next Thursday, hauled in at all hours. They played rough."

Mama was making popcorn. Back and forth, back and forth across the burner she shoved the big iron skillet. I pulled my chair closer to the piano bench to hear the rest of Jack's story. Aunt Betty, too, inclined her head.

"My alibi was thin. Fan and I had met for a drink at a speakeasy around two that afternoon, but we'd each gone our own way at three. She was heading home for the family Christmas. I was invited to spend the evening with the family of one of the men fished out of the Chicago River, so I went back to my room to get cleaned up.

"I was in the bathtub at four-thirty, when Pat was shot. No witnesses. The union brought their lawyers and investigators in, but it ended in a stalemate. The police couldn't prove I did it and I couldn't prove I didn't. I wasn't arrested, but . . ." He tipped his glass and finished the bourbon. ". . . I was never cleared, either."

Aunt Betty nodded.

"So that was it. Except for her grandmother O'Neal, none of Fan's people spoke to her again. Frank disowned her. But Fan stuck with me.

For that I'd be happy to burn in hell." He spun around and faced the piano.

At this moment Mama plunged into our chastened midst, bearing an enormous blue enamel soup kettle of popcorn; in her wake came Fanny with a stack of unmatched cereal bowls.

"All right, you crepe hangers, let's see some smiles and hear some songs," Mama demanded. "Do I have to turn on the radio when I've got three piano players here?"

At once Jack began pounding out "Jingle Bells." I sat down on the bench beside him and Mama freshened drinks. Jack played recklessly, not always hitting the right keys. We sang in snatches, running to keep up.

"Hark! the Herald Angels Sing" followed "Jingle Bells," and after that a furious "We Three Kings." "Deck the Halls" was so rash, even I stopped singing. The others had already fallen by the way. Drenching streams of perspiration streaked down Jack's cheeks and into his collar.

Suddenly he stopped. Rising and pushing back the bench, he stammered, "I've drunk too much. Sorry." Wrenching open the door, he hurtled out.

Fanny, holding a bowl of popcorn, stood beside the Christmas tree, unsurprised. "Sorry," she murmured, echoing Jack. Absently, she set the bowl on a table. "Jack makes himself sick at the holidays."

Aunt Betty lifted Jack's sport coat from the back of the chair. Draping it across her arm, she ran a hand along the fabric as I had, but with great tenderness.

Moving toward the door, Fanny took the jacket. "Forgive us?" she asked, turning to Mama. Her smile was sardonic. "We didn't want to be alone."

I gathered up Fanny's and Jack's glasses and carried them to the kitchen, drinking what remained, then emptying the untouched popcorn back into the enamel kettle and tidying up the kitchen, all the while listening to Aunt Betty relate Jack's story.

"Well, that explains Fanny's mood," Mama said when Aunt Betty concluded. "I thought maybe it was because of her nephew Dennis being out in the Pacific."

"Son of the brother who was killed, don't you think?"

Mama considered. "Probably. Do you think Jack did it? Killed her brother?"

I nearly dropped the iron skillet I was returning to the oven. That Jack might have lied hadn't crossed my mind.

"I don't think so. . . . I don't know."

I heard my aunt rise from the sofa. Her heels clicked on the floor where the carpet ended and then she was beside me, saying, "Here's my glass. You can throw the rest of it away. I have to leave for Mass."

"Mass?" Mama called from the other room.

"I'm going to midnight Mass," Aunt Betty told her, standing at the kitchen door, leaning against the jamb.

"Why?"

"Because it's Christmas Eve. And I need to think."

"Can't you think here?"

"No. I need to think about Stanley and what to do. It's easier at church."

"What about Stanley?"

"I thought he'd come for Christmas. I never thought he'd come the other times, like on my birthday, and he never said he'd come now. But, still. . . ."

"And why shouldn't you expect him?" Mama asked. She had.

Had she written him again?

"Well, I never did before. I don't like feeling mad, especially at Christmas, so I'm going to Mass."

"Mass would only make *me* madder," Mama told her. "I might hear some priest telling me to stand by that four-flusher." She was thinking, Why should her sister turn to the Church when she had Mama?

Nevertheless, Aunt Betty fetched her things from the bedroom closet, including the same forlorn and shapeless coat she'd worn on the trip west. Something about the sight of my aunt pulling it on uncomplainingly drove Mama to scream at her, "Well, go then, but I hope you don't think that Stanley's spending Christmas Eve in church worrying about *you!*"

Aunt Betty looked at Mama with wonder, picked up her handbag from the piano bench and let herself out.

Bursting into tears, Mama charged to the door, flinging it open. "And after I bought us a piano!"

I escaped to the bedroom. Closing the door, I set Aunt Betty's glass— still in my hand—on the table beside the bed and undressed in the dark.

In her strangely distraught state, Mama flicked on the radio and began singing along with Kay Kyser, who was playing "Deep in the Heart of Texas." The next song was "White Christmas." You could hardly turn the radio on without hearing it. Mama switched the radio off and began sobbing again.

Sliding out of bed and carrying Aunt Betty's bourbon and Coca-Cola, I tiptoed to the window and raised the shade. No stars.

People were complicated, way more complicated than I'd realized when I was little. Each person was like the dentist's cabinet at Mr. Trustworthy's: drawer after drawer of different people.

Listening to the moan of the foghorns, I sipped the syrupy tang of the drink and lay my forehead against the cool window pane, summoning Hilly Stillman and Alicia Armand from the shadows of the Project.

21

AUNT BETTY NEVER SAID whether God had any advice about Uncle Stanley. I guessed that His line was busy, as Grandpa Browning used to remark. But Aunt Betty found solace in the piano.

I too was fooling around with the piano, pounding away at it, hopeful that one day I would produce music. I did a lot of pounding after seeing Alicia Armand's new movie, *Dark Sonata*, about a Norwegian concert pianist who traveled through Nazi Germany entertaining the troops and the High Command while spying for the Allies. The film was thick with Tchaikovsky, Beethoven, and Debussy.

As I had once believed that I would awaken one morning to tap dance like Eleanor Powell, I now presumed, despite that previous disappointment, that I would awaken one morning to play concerti like Jose Iturbi.

Aunt Betty bought *Wee Ones Learn to Play* and the beginner's John Thompson book and began giving me lessons. Beginner lessons were not piano-playing, though; they were exercises in tedium. After a few weeks, I lost interest and went back to pounding, still hopeful.

Returning from church the Sunday after Christmas, Aunt Betty changed into an old housedress and a pair of knitted slippers that Grandma had sent. After pulling on a shabby cardigan and turning up the flame of the heater, she made a pot of tea.

I sat at the piano with *Wee Ones Learn to Play*, giving it another shot. Plink plink plink, right hand. Plink plink plink, left hand. Plink plink plink, down the keys. Plink plink plink, up the keys. Every third note I struck was wrong and I started over each time. I had no *dexterity* (page 277 in *Webster's*).

Shirley Olson's face, peering in a living room window, startled us. Recoiling, Mama frowned, made a shooing motion at Shirley, and told me, "See what she wants. She scared me half to death, spying like that." Had Mama, for a second, imagined Papa's face?

Shirley was on the stoop, picking her nose and wiping it on her dirty shirt. "Don't you have a handkerchief?"

She looked at me without comprehension and walked past into the house.

"Wipe your feet," I told her, pointing to the rug in front of the door. "I can't play. I'm going to read the paper."

"I ain't here to play with you. I heard a piana, and also I got money for your ma," she said, marching across to Mama. "That's it now, ain't it? The pitcher's paid for?" She thrust a ten-cent piece at Mama, final payment for the horse picture from Trustworthy Second Hand.

She turned then to listen as Aunt Betty sat down and began a Chopin nocturne. After long minutes of standing stock still in the middle of the room, Shirley sidled toward the chair by the kitchen door and lowered herself onto it, never taking her eyes from my aunt.

When Aunt Betty finally rose from the piano, I was studying the front pages of the paper, searching for Allied victories or losses that I could record on the map. I was finding no victories, nor any great routs either. In Stalingrad, the Russians were finally fighting back; and at Guadalcanal, the American Marines and army were making small headway. No tacks.

Mama put aside the women's section and began pumping Shirley about her family. "I'd like to meet them sometime," she said chattily. "I've never met a real cowboy."

"Where'd you get the piana?" Shirley wanted to know.

"Trustworthy Second Hand," Mama told her. "Would you like to play it?"

"Don't know how," Shirley said, simultaneously side-slipping her way onto the bench.

"Well, I've got to peel potatoes for dinner, if you ladies will excuse me. Shirley, you're invited to stay for dinner if it's all right with your mother."

Shirley was her new do-gooder project.

"It's all right with her," Shirley mumbled.

"You must go home and tell her," Mama insisted in a kindly voice. "I wouldn't like it if Lark stayed for dinner and didn't tell me."

"I'll tell her," Shirley said, laying a grubby hand on the piano keys and depressing one of the white ones, eliciting a soft treble "plink."

My nose in *Hans Brinker and the Silver Skates,* I paid little attention as she played various notes in a random, one-fingered meandering, eventually picking out a one-fingered "God Bless America." I decided to take a bath and wash my hair.

Out in the living room, Shirley was playing a one-fingered "Home on the Range," and Aunt Betty was encouraging her, telling her that she had a musical ear.

I soaked until I was covered with raisin-skin, then shampooed my hair and reached for the hand mirror on the back of the toilet to see if I looked anything like the pretty young women in *Good Housekeeping* magazine who shampooed with Drene.

Later, dressed in the plaid frock, I brushed my damp hair, trying to turn the ends under in a page boy like Maureen O'Hara's in *To the Shores of Tripoli.* No such luck. I sat down on the living room rug with the scrap book Aunt Betty had given me for Christmas, a bottle of LePage's glue, and the Alicia Armand pictures and articles I'd been collecting.

Across the room, Shirley picked out "In My Adobe Hacienda" while Aunt Betty riffled through sheet music, searching for my abandoned *Wee Ones Learn to Play.* "Here it is," she said.

Within minutes she was pointing out on the keyboard the black notes printed in the early pages of the book. "This is middle C," she said and depressed the proper key, "and here it is in the book. These lines are called a staff, and middle C is a whole step below the bottom line on the staff," and so on as she had done with me.

The difference was that Shirley was nodding and studying first the lines in the book and then the keys, her face concentered, her body curved over the keyboard. When she had groped through several of the one-hand, one-note-at-a-time, truncated melodies in the first pages, she went back to the first with more assurance, then on to the next.

By the time I'd heard these same note combinations four or five times, Shirley was beginning to take liberties with them, holding some notes longer, giving a line a bit of personality.

Aunt Betty intervened, explaining time, note values and other such complexities. Again Shirley's head rose and fell in absorption, dawning comprehension giving her the fidgets to get back to the baby exercises and apply her new knowledge.

She quarter-noted her way through the same old bits of music several times. After half a dozen perfect renderings, she began striking some of the notes sharply, others softly. Her grubby person bent into her efforts and swayed with them, even as Alicia Armand had done in *Dark Sonata.*

Aunt Betty's hand lay lightly on Shirley's shoulder as she encouraged and directed. Now and then she leaned over and placed Shirley's hand, thus, upon the keys. "As if you held a tennis ball loosely in your palm. Keep the wrist up. That's right."

Shirley had no piano at home nor any hope of one, so why try teaching her to play? Something in me was irked by Aunt Betty's attention to Shirley. True, the attention could have been mine if I'd continued my lessons. Still, I hated to see Shirley wedging herself into the middle of my family. But that kind of thing happens if you live with do-gooders.

Around four, Mama advised Shirley, who was glued to the piano, to run home and see if she could eat over. "Why don't you go with her?" Mama suggested, turning to me.

"I can go by myself," Shirley told her.

"I'm sure you can, but Lark needs to get out. She's the color of tapioca pudding."

When we reached the street, however, Shirley swung on me. "You ain't coming with me, tapioca," she said, giving me a shove. "Wait here. If you tell your ma, I'll get you."

So I stood waiting in the dimming light of a late December afternoon, worrying about the boys and chafing my chilled arms while Shirley high-tailed it up Piñon.

Moments later, from around the opposite end of the Eldridge's building, swooping and screeching like a man-eating bird, Shirley descended. Startled, I screamed and collapsed on the grass, holding my arms above my head, while she laughed, throwing her head back, staggering forward and backward.

When she'd exhausted herself laughing, she stood over me, hands on hips, taunting, "Scaredy cat, scaredy cat."

"Why do you come over to play with me, then?"

She snorted, "I don't come to play with you. I come 'cuz your ma and your aunt are nice, and now you got a piana."

"Don't come any more," I pleaded.

"'Don't come any more,'" she mocked, nudging me with her filthy bare foot.

"Why are you so mean?"

"'Why are you so mean?'" she whined.

I struck out blindly at her leg but she dodged.

"You can't even fight!" she laughed, kicking my thigh and turning away to lope up the walk, unconcerned, daring me to attack her, knowing I wouldn't.

Enraged, I dragged myself to my feet and followed.

"Wash your hands and faces," Mama told us.

Shirley emerged from the bathroom with distinct lines of dirt-demarcation at her wrists and around the periphery of her face. The towel she left behind was gray, and the sink looked like a stormy sky. I washed my hands under the bathtub tap, leaving Shirley's mess for Mama or Aunt Betty to discover.

At dinner Mama and my aunt twittered over Shirley's talent. "Anyone would think you'd been taking lessons for months," Mama told her, piling scalloped potatoes with Spam onto Shirley's plate while Aunt Betty dished up a mountain of green beans beside the potatoes.

"You'll be playing by ear in no time," Aunt Betty said. "Still, a musician should know how to read music."

Dinner continued in this vein, Mama and Aunt Betty heaping food and praise on Shirley. For dessert, Mama produced the box of candy from Fanny and Jack and placed it before Shirley, saying, "Take four pieces. Two for now and two for tomorrow."

Shirley studied the top layer of chocolates, picking up a number of pieces and exploring their surfaces for clues to their contents. Then she lifted the cardboard dividing the layers and peeked at the lower selection, a thing Mama forbade me to do. For that matter, Mama never allowed me to pick the pieces up and examine them, either. My hands beneath the table were tied in knots of crossed fingers, a charm against Shirley choosing the caramels.

After hours of poking and inspecting, during which Mama and Aunt Betty stood by smiling and winking across the table at one another,

Shirley chose the four caramels in the box, lifting them out in their little fluted brown paper cups and laying them beside her plate, not even saying, "Thank you."

Mama passed the box to Aunt Betty, who looked for the smooth, rounded tops of chocolate-covered cherries and removed two, passing the box to me. I withdrew the two gold foil-wrapped pieces, even though I knew the foil-wrapped candies were usually a bland vanilla nougat or some other uninteresting flavor. But I also knew that Shirley had been sorely tempted by them because of the pretty wrapping. Mama in her turn chose a peanut cluster and a chocolate-covered toffee wafer.

"Now, then," Mama began, addressing Shirley, "you must feel free to come over and practice the piano during Christmas vacation. When school starts, you can come home with Lark and practice before supper." She paused, continuing in a voice at once serious and gentle, "but you mustn't let the piano interfere with homework."

Homework? Shirley? I didn't know how Shirley'd been passed from fourth grade to fifth. She rarely turned in homework and never volunteered answers in class.

But that was all beside the point. The point was, why did Mama invite Shirley to come over and not ask me first? I was the one who'd have to deal with her. The vanilla nougat I was chewing tasted like paper. I drew my chair back and was about to carry the second candy and the two gold wrappers to my room.

"Can I have one of them gold papers?" Shirley asked.

I turned back, staring in disbelief.

"Can I?"

Mama told me, "You've got two."

"But *she* took all the caramels."

Mama laughed. "But she's *company*."

"Not if she's going to be coming here all the time."

Mama gave me a pointed look. I was in trouble if I didn't give Shirley one of the gold wrappers. Hatred both of Mama and of Shirley knotted my stomach.

"I'll walk you home," Aunt Betty told Shirley, trying to neutralize the charged atmosphere. "It's dark out."

Shirley sprang from her chair, grabbing up the caramels. "Keep your paper then," she hissed, rushing out the door.

"Now look what you've done," Mama said, hurrying to catch Shirley.

Aunt Betty and I began clearing the table. We were washing dishes by the time Mama returned.

"I couldn't find her," she said breathlessly, as if she'd been running. "If anything happens to her, I will hold you responsible, Lark."

"She didn't run away because of me. She ran away because Aunt Betty wanted to walk her home. She doesn't want anybody to know where she lives."

"She ran away because you hurt her feelings."

"That's not so. She wouldn't let . . ."

"That child has nothing in this world but grief, you don't have to be around her ten minutes to know that, and you can't show her the smallest kindness," Mama said.

I spun away, slamming my bedroom door. Setting the oil painting aside, I shoved the bureau in front of the door so Mama couldn't get in. I might have saved myself the effort. She didn't try.

How did Mama know that Shirley had nothing but grief, I wondered, pulling off my dress. And why should that make me like her? Half the time, I had nothing but grief.

From the bedside table, I took one of the gold foil papers and folded it carefully until I had a band the width of a wide wedding ring. I held it around my finger and studied it. In the morning I would cut a red paper jewel for it.

Did Alicia Armand own a gold ring with a red stone? I began day-dreaming the scene on the city bus after her car developed a flat. I was sitting near the back of the bus and she made her way toward me.

"I'll tell you when we reach your stop," I assured her, noting on her right hand a beautiful gold ring with a red stone.

"You are vairy kind," she said. "Wooed you like to hayve lunch wiz me at the El Cortez Hotel? I aim looking for a leetle girl to be een my naixt movie."

22

MAMA AND AUNT BETTY had unleashed a musical monster. Who'd have dreamed that within that grubby, scabbed blot of a girl lay an appetite for piano beyond all reason or understanding? She spent hours at the piano; I spent hours in my room with the door closed, reading and working on the story for Mr. Trustworthy.

After Mama insisted that she or Aunt Betty discuss with Shirley's mama the piano practicing, Shirley did not show up for a week. "Leave me alone or I won't come back," was the message.

Mama enlisted Fanny's help. Fanny, who worked part-time in the school office, dug out Shirley's address from the files, and one Saturday afternoon Mama climbed the winding street.

Had I not fallen asleep on the sofa, listening to *Your Hit Parade* on KNX, I might not have heard Mama in the kitchen tell Aunt Betty, "The door was open and I could hear a radio playing. I knocked and knocked."

The icebox door closed. "You want milk in your tea?" Mama asked, then picked up the story again. "Finally, this woman showed up in a filthy robe, saying she'd just got home from work and what did I want?

"I looked around. There was a stinking old mattress on the floor. No other furniture. The place hadn't been cleaned since they moved in. I can't describe it—empty whiskey and beer bottles, and everywhere cigarette butts ground out on the floor. The place smelled of pee and God knows what else.

"Well, this woman may have come from work, but she reeked of liquor and I don't think she'd had a bath in two weeks. I'd be surprised if she's employed at Consolidated. I'll check."

"What did you tell her about Shirley?"

Now a cupboard door opened and closed. Mama said, "I didn't tell her anything. I kept thinking, I'm going to make things worse for Shirley if I start talking piano lessons and staying for supper and all that. I pretended I was looking for people named Chambers and I got the hell out.

"I stopped at Fanny's to see if there was anything we could do. She said if we try to get the law involved, the Olsons will take off. While they're here, we can at least keep an eye on Shirley."

Another silence, then, "What should I have done?"

"You did what you could."

In any case, the piano practicing continued. On school days I ran home after the last bell and let myself in, relishing the few moments of solitude before Shirley descended. I slapped Velveeta sandwiches together, poured milk into a cup of cold tea, and dashed to the bedroom to do homework and write. On Saturday mornings, I did my chores, working around Shirley.

Had it not been for Sunday servicemen, I might have been plagued by her seven days a week. But one Sunday in April, after a particularly violent Japanese attack on Guadalcanal, Aunt Betty came legging up the walk from Mass in the company of a swaggering sailor.

I sat on the stoop waiting for my aunt, who sometimes brought us a bunch of zinnias or baby roses from the flower stand near the church. The day was misty and the sun not strong enough to burn through. The Project's carefully nursed lawns were a rich, ripened green after the winter rains. A hushed-down quality muffled the foghorns in the bay, and neighbors returning from church moved slowly, silently, as if peopling a dream.

The boy with Aunt Betty was Arnold Nessin, and he cracked his

knuckles and his Black Jack gum as if these were rakish ploys for winning female hearts. He was from Akron, in Ohio, the birthplace of pres-
idents. Only Virginia had produced more, he said.

Mama said that Minnesota, to its credit, had produced none. Arnold
Nessin tilted his head, studied Mama, and dismissed her with a knowing smirk: shrewish, uppity, thought she was clever.

Mama outdid herself preparing dinner so that Arnold would know
what he would be missing when he wasn't invited back. Fried potatoes,
like golden round coins, were piled beside steaming salmon cakes, light
and crisp. Peas and sliced tomatoes lent color to our plates. For dessert,
Mama brought out baked apples, stuffed with raisins, cinnamon, and a
bit of our precious brown sugar.

Under the civilizing influence of Mama's cooking, Arnold Nessin
grew subdued. But Mama did not suffer whippersnappers, and almost
immediately after dinner Arnold was launched out of our safe harbor
into the damp evening.

"What made you drag *him* home?" she asked Aunt Betty when the
sailor strutted, cock-of-the-walk and whistling, down Piñon Street toward the bus stop.

Aunt Betty dried the fried potato bowl and returned it to the cupboard. "He looked so young, so arrogant, I thought he must be very
frightened to look that sure of himself."

Mama said nothing. Emerging from the bathroom later, hair in pin
curls, she tightened her robe, conceding, "I think you're right about that
boy, Betty. I bet he isn't more than sixteen. I'm ashamed of myself."

Writing letters on wispy V-mail paper, Aunt Betty dotted an *i* and
paused. "He *was* smart-alecky."

"But he's a child. And he could be dead next month." Mama crossed
her arms over her breast, hugging herself. "If he's at Mass next week,
bring him home. If he wants to come."

But Arnold Nessin wasn't at Mass the next week. Mama couldn't put him behind us, however, and when we entertained sailors on future Sundays, she inquired of each bluejacket, did he know or had he heard of Arnold Nessin? "He was on a destroyer, didn't he say, Betty? He was from Akron, Ohio."

None of the sailors serving on destroyers had run across him, and none of the Ohioans were familiar with his name.

Sailors came and went, and soldiers and Marines too. Between church and the U.S.O., we never lacked for young men to sit down to Sunday dinner with us: boys who'd not yet found sweethearts, men who were faithful to a wife or sweetheart back home. Grateful and respectful, they drifted in and out of our lives, the young ones boisterous and brash, the older ones sober and stoical and tending to come to us singly while the boys appeared in threes and fours, laughing and cursing.

Not infrequently, Mama and Aunt Betty and I were taken out on Sunday afternoons to the zoo, the Mission Beach amusement park, or the movies, but invariably we ended up back on Piñon Street for Aunt Betty's piano-playing and Mama's cooking.

Those servicemen who had children of their own gazed at me solemnly, their demeanor kind and formal, their occasional gifts educational—books about animals and rocks and native peoples in far-off lands. One time a Marine lieutenant gave me *Roget's Thesaurus*. He had a big crush on Mama.

The younger men almost never brought me gifts. Between visits they forgot that I existed and were generally surprised to see me sitting on the stoop or reading the Sunday funnies on the living room floor. Their interest was entirely in Mama and Aunt Betty, although the two women referred to them as boys and giggled at their green gawkiness. The boys were lonesome for their mothers and sisters, Mama told me, and it was probably true, although their gaze was not always filial.

Sensitive to the ration book and financial limitations on our entertaining, the men brought liquor and Coca-Cola and canned goods and nylons and Lucky Strikes from the PX. The Luckies we exchanged with neighbors for sugar.

Sunday afternoon entertaining was a treat for Mama and Aunt Betty. Without entanglement, the two women brought men into their lives in the name of patriotism. What more could two married but separated women ask? Aunt Betty wouldn't allow Mama to feign widowhood, although she did brook Mama's reference to a husband who was serving "back east."

"You should get one of them service stars for your window," a Marine told Mama. "Like my mom's got."

A silk service star in the window was a serious and prestigious matter, signifying a house under constant threat of loss. If we had such a star, indicating a husband or son in the service, would the seventh grade boys leave me alone? One thing was certain: No boys loitered ominously when soldiers visited us.

If we packed a picnic and took the bus to the beach, two or three sailors swinging along at our sides, I spent the afternoon flying up and down the shore in the delicious certainty that twelve-year-old boys with knives would not set upon me.

One Sunday afternoon in July, Mama, Aunt Betty, and I, with four sailors—Dutch, Bernie, Tim, and Harold—straggled home from Mission Beach, all of us slightly nauseated from hot dogs, cotton candy, and whirling rides.

"How about a game of strip poker?" Dutch sniggered, holding the door for my aunt.

"What kind of talk is that?" she reproved in a firm voice, although she knew he was only kidding.

"What's strip poker?" I asked Mama as she mounted the steps, followed by Bernie, Tim, and Harold.

"It's nothing that decent people know about," she said.

Mama opened the windows and lowered the living room shades partway to keep out the late afternoon sun. The men tossed their sailor caps on top of the piano and sprawled sleepily on the sofa and chairs, their summer whites limp with perspiration and the day's outing.

Aunt Betty offered iced tea. Everyone declined. We were all of us sleepy, and presently Tim and Harold were dozing on the rug, arms and legs arranged haphazardly. Dutch, who was older than the others by two or three years, slipped off his shoes. "Betty, you don't mind if we catch a little shut-eye, do you?"

"Take a nap while Arlene and I start dinner," she told him, and fetched a pillow from the bed.

Bernie in the rose chair had removed his shoes and put his feet on the sofa beside Dutch's. In minutes they were all snoring, except Harold, who slept as silently as an infant, hands folded beneath his cheek, knees drawn up.

Aunt Betty paused for a moment to watch Harold sleep. "He looks six years old," she said, melting into a maternal mood, although she herself had warned Mama that they must guard their emotions. "They're here a few days or weeks and then they're gone—sailing off the edge of the earth."

Mama shoved a couple of chickens into the oven. Aunt Betty turned from the sleeping boys and, slipping her apron from the hook, prepared to peel potatoes. Decent mashed potatoes with decent gravy were a dab of home to most of the boys. "They're sentimental about food," Aunt Betty had observed. Tears had sprung to the eyes of a seventeen-year-old Marine from Utah when he dug into Mama's green-apple pie.

While Aunt Betty attacked the potatoes and Mama chopped cabbage for slaw, I set the table. It accommodated only six, and those six would be squeezed together cheek by jowl. I would eat standing at the counter by the sink. I didn't mind: I was still shy around the servicemen, even the youngest.

We floated contentedly in the pale blue late afternoon. From a row of houses adjacent but built on a higher terrace of the Project came the squeals of small children playing tag. I stood at the east-facing window and looked up the rising embankment to see them tumbling in new grass. The embankment was gentle, and now that it was grassy, children somersaulted down.

Here was I, safe in the house with Mama, Aunt Betty, and four sailors, on a day which would end in a sentimental hour of songs at the piano. As I waded in the warm shallows of these thoughts, a figure loomed at the top of the incline, and although it stood at too great a distance, seemed to peer into my eyes.

Papa.

"Papa." I turned from the window.

"What?" Mama asked.

"Papa! He's up there!"

Tolerant disbelief showed in the slow way she crossed to the window, wiping her hands on a towel. "There's nobody out there," she said, surveying the embankment.

"Up at the top."

But he was gone.

23

Papa did not come that night. After dinner, I went to bed, although the sky was still light, and the four sailors stayed on, singing Stephen Foster and Irving Berlin. In bed, I lay studying the embankment until I could no longer discern it, then pulled the shade and turned on the light to read.

But how could I keep my mind on *Roget's Thesaurus* with Papa out there someplace? Why hadn't he come to the door? And why, when I saw him looking down at the house, hadn't I run out and called to him? Not only had I failed to run out, I had even felt alarm. A squeezing sadness filled my chest. After a year and a half, he was a stranger.

While Aunt Betty rolled her hair at the bathroom mirror, Mama opened my door and gave me a searching look. Did I still think that I'd seen Papa?

"You'd better turn out the light now," she told me, retreating.

The next morning, when Mama had left for work, Aunt Betty sat down at the kitchen table, where I was eating toast and peanut butter. Wearing a crisp, pale green piqué dress with a wide white collar, she was ready to leave for work at Gilpins'.

The store had made many changes in assignments due to men, and some women, leaving for the war. Three times Aunt Betty had been reassigned or promoted. The first time, she was transferred from ladies accessories to better ladies dresses, where she began to accumulate a little commission. Then she was promoted to manager of ladies accessories. Finally, in March she had replaced the manager of better ladies dresses, a Mr. Bettin, who'd been drafted despite having walked around for a week with a peeled onion in his armpit, a trick that was said to produce temporary symptoms of heart disease. For Mr. Bettin, it had produced only a strong odor.

Mama spoke of Aunt Betty's "meteoric rise in the fashion world." Aunt Betty demurred, calling her move up the ladder dumb luck. She accepted each new challenge with a becoming air of surprise, grateful for the salary increase, pleased by what she was learning, and eager to repay the company's faith in her.

"A ninny salesgirl from the Blue Lake five and dime," she called herself. "I hope Gilpins' never takes a closer look." But if you took a closer look, what would you see? Someone as limpid as drinking water. Her sincerity rang clear and true, like a spoon against crystal. This was no less so when she began applying pale apricot color to her cheeks and lips and tweezing the errant hairs from under her brows.

If Mama was the tiniest bit green-eyed that Aunt Betty could have her hair and nails done once a week in Gilpins' Salon and buy pretty clothes at a discount, she kept it to herself. What she couldn't keep to herself was her growing frustration with her own career: a stenographer going nowhere. "I could transfer, but transfer to what? Riveting? Welding? I'm smarter than Mr. Hapgood and Mr. Gross put together, but nobody's going to give me a job like theirs."

"Remember what you said when we came here?" Aunt Betty reminded her. "You'd learn all about offices and after the war start your typing service again, this time bigger and better."

Mama's discontent was dimming her vision of the future, though. And it worried and confused Aunt Betty. "If you buy more war bonds instead of putting everything into this house," she said, "you'll be ready for Erhardt Typing Service when the war's over."

But Mama wanted a carpet in the bedroom. Blue. And some pretty pictures of roses for the walls. For whom? Not for Papa.

Papa.

He was the reason Aunt Betty was sitting opposite me at the table this morning.

"Your mama says you think you saw Willie."

"I did." I wiped my mouth with a paper napkin. "He was up on the slope looking down at the house."

"Why didn't he come to the door?"

"Maybe he was spying on us." The moment I said it, I knew it was true.

"He came two thousand miles to spy on us?" she said.

I nodded.

She studied me, then crossed to the window where I'd stood. "Up there?"

"Yes."

"It must have been someone who looked like him. I've heard of that. There's a funny name for it. I forget the word." She didn't want to believe that Papa would spy on us.

Barely had I washed the tiny stack of breakfast dishes and tidied the living room when Shirley Olson's pounding rattled the door. I would be happy when school reopened in September.

Yanking the door open, I surveyed the vicinity for Papa but saw only Shirley. She'd washed her face, but just the central portion, and combed her mop, but only in front. And she'd scrubbed her hands, but only to the wrists.

I realized that there were no pretty dresses hanging in her closet. I'd never seen her in anything but boys' cast-offs, like these ratty brown trousers with the knees missing and the short-sleeved green shirt with only the top button and a safety pin holding it closed.

Shirley played—scales and exercises and real songs from the John Thompson. I was grudgingly impressed by her doggedness and progress. I was hardly a critic of piano playing, but even I heard improvement and refinement from week to week. From the bedroom, a further element was obvious. Happiness.

What was it in piano playing that created happiness? Was it the sounds themselves or the power? You probably felt powerful playing the piano, *controlling* it, wielding it.

Little teeth gnawed at my heart, and I bled bitterness. Shirley had stolen my family, my house, and my privacy, and for that she was rewarded with happiness. Lifting the oil painting down from the bureau, I lay it face down on the bed and carefully removed the dollar bills from the envelope on the back. Even though I knew how many I had, I counted them again, arranging them in piles of five. Five piles of five and one left over. Twenty-six dollars. Stacking them into a single pile, I held them against my bitter breast. *When?*

Returning the painting and money, I flopped down on the bed with Mama's second-hand copy of *Tobacco Road*, which she'd picked up in a batch of other books. But it reminded me of Shirley, so I tossed it aside and lay gazing out the open window at the slope. Children rolled down and clambered back up, laughing. I did not see Papa.

But I could *feel* him.

Around eleven-thirty, Shirley's music stopped. Shortly after, I heard cupboard doors open and close, then the refrigerator. Shirley preparing lunch. She would make a mess, about which Mama would say nothing.

Mama and Aunt Betty overlooked Shirley's thousands of shortcomings, mainly because she was a waif: wartime flotsam cast upon their shore, a Christian duty. Also, women are suckers for ugly-duckling-into-swan stuff. Plus Aunt Betty's baby had been born dead and maybe she was adopting Shirley to fill the empty space. *And* Shirley never treated

Mama and Aunt Betty the way she did me; only rarely did they see her treat me poorly.

After Shirley resumed practicing, I slipped out to the kitchen and loaded a plate with soda crackers and a cup of cold tea and milk. For half an hour, I stood at the bedroom window watching and eating crackers.

At dinner, Aunt Betty told me, "I remembered that funny word for somebody who looks like somebody else. It's *doppelganger*." She sipped bean soup. "I suppose everybody has a doppelganger somewhere, don't you think, Arlene?"

Mama didn't answer. She passed a plate of toast. "Since Lark ate all the soda crackers, we're having toast," she explained to Aunt Betty. "It's a wonder there was any bread left. She ate most of that, too. I'll have to run to the corner store or there won't be bread for my lunch pail." The "corner store" was two or three miles away, and Mama would have to take the bus.

"Shirley ate the bread."

"You blame everything on Shirley."

"Well, she did eat the bread. I ate the crackers, but she ate the bread." It was a losing situation. To be exonerated for eating the bread was to be found guilty of tattling on Shirley.

Aunt Betty and I washed dishes while Mama went to the store.

"Did Shirley practice?" my aunt inquired, handing me a bowl.

"Hours and hours."

"She works hard."

So did I. On my stories. The difference was, my work was silent, and I didn't share it with Mama and Aunt Betty. I wasn't sure exactly why that was.

Later, I measured bubble bath into the tub and ran water. Reclining beneath the hissing bubbles, I relaxed. The tub was a luxury. We hadn't had a real bathtub when we lived at the depot, only a galvanized steel one that you filled from the kitchen sink.

Padding barefoot into the kitchen, I asked, "Aunt Betty, could you braid . . ."

Mama, purse still dangling from her arm, sat at the table, staring at a sheet of lined paper lying on the oilcloth. Noticing me, she reached for it, but I was too quick.

Pasted to the paper was a frame from a comic book: a bug-eyed woman in a vivid blue dress struggling to loosen the grip of an attacker, who was choking the life out of her. In a box within the frame were the words, "She thought she could escape, but she was wrong."

"Willie," she whispered. "Willie left it."

24

WHEN THE BOYS LEFT a hacked-off kitten's paw in the lard pail, Mama had called it a prank. One part of her knew that the comic book clipping was the same, but another part—the part that was sick with dread and guilt about Papa—took the crude warning to heart.

"It's those boys, trying to scare me," I told her, as bluffly as I could. "I'm not afraid of them. They're just stupid Okies." *Okies* was Mama's catchall phrase for riffraff.

As usual in times of crisis, Aunt Betty ran water into the tea kettle and put it on the stove to boil. A river of tea ran through our kitchen. We each, on occasion, slipped into it and swam for the opposite and higher shore.

"I'll put the groceries away," I told Mama, placing the clipping on the table as if it were a mere curiosity.

. . . .

Before Shirley arrived Tuesday morning, I watered Mama's gardenia bush and Jack's daisies. The daisies had grown into substantial bushes, covered with blooms. At either side of the stoop Mama had managed to keep a few puny hens-and-chicks alive, and I watered those as well. From Miss Eldridge's kitchen, a voice was singing:

> After the ball is over,
> After the break of morn,
> After the dancers' leaving,
> After the stars are gone

On the step I hesitated, straining to hear.

Many a heart is aching,
If you could read them all;
Many the hopes that have vanished . . .

Here Miss Eldridge paused and the last line was spoken with weary bitterness. "After the ball."

I hurried inside, assembling food for the day and carrying it to my bedroom.

Having abandoned the stubborn shabbiness of life in *Tobacco Road,* I began *Tender Is the Night.* These characters did not remind me of Shirley, even the Shirley who now presented herself, tidied up, possibly bathed, with the boundary between pink and gray skin blurred.

Most of the day passed like the previous one, me in the bedroom reading, Shirley either in the living room playing or in the kitchen eating. Around one-thirty, Fanny dropped off the latest copy of *Life* and remained for an hour, coaching Shirley, who opened like a ripening rose.

"Isn't our Shirley wonderful?" Fanny effused. "The touch! The sensibility!"

With the magazine held against my nauseated middle, I slunk off to the bedroom. Behind me, Fanny said, "The little Mozart piece. Try the last few bars again, dear, and this time . . ."

Long after Fanny had departed but before Mama arrived home, when the buttery afternoon had settled into a rancid somnolence, I dozed over *Tender Is the Night,* waking later to find drool on my chin, sweat on my neck and a poisoned feeling in my stomach.

The piano was silent. Voices droned in the kitchen, riven by a sharp blade of familiar male laughter. I leapt up, trembling, and dove beneath the bed, into a stifling, dusty, twilit space. Papa's laughter followed me even beneath the bed. What would he think if he came looking and found me huddled here?

More laughter, more droning. They were in the living room now, and Shirley was playing the piano. "Ragtime Cowboy Joe." Where had she learned that? Was she capable of sitting down and playing *any* tune? Papa was laughing as though this were the funniest, most entertaining ditty he'd ever heard.

The song concluded. Papa thanked Shirley, then said something softly, which I could not make out. The screen door creaked and Papa called, "Come on back tomorrow."

Through the floor beneath me I felt the vibration of the inside door closing. Papa was whistling "Ragtime Cowboy Joe." I scrabbled along the floor to the wall at the head of the bed and pulled myself into a knot. My heart hammered against my breastbone like tiny fists beating to get out.

The whistling was outside my door. I closed my eyes and covered my ears, concentrating on the shower of yellow, white, and red motes floating behind my eyes.

Suddenly a strong hand grasped my ankle. I screamed and kicked wildly.

"What the hell's the matter with you? This the way you welcome your pa?"

"I didn't know it was you," I lied.

"I come two thousand miles and you act like I'm a housebreaker."

"I'm sorry."

"You're so sorry, come out of there. I can see I'm not wanted. I'll leave," he said, adding, "God, what'd I ever do to deserve such an unnatural child?"

"Don't leave," I said, shame driving me out from under the bed. "I'm sorry."

He grabbed me, laughing and hugging me till my ribs hurt. I hugged him back, hoping love would flood in, like water filling a lock in a dam, floating me beyond this place, back to times and feelings past. But my arms felt stiff and my feet couldn't find a natural, comfortable place to stand. Disengaging, I patted his arm as Mama patted me when she wanted to be left alone but didn't want to hurt my feelings.

An unnatural child. I led him back to the living room, asking if he were hungry. He wasn't. He sat down on the sofa. "Who was the kid playing the piano?"

"Shirley Olson. Aunt Betty gives her lessons."

"Sounded pretty good."

"Yes."

"Can you play?"

"No."

"How come is that?"

"I don't have a musical ear." This was an expression I'd heard Mama use.

"What's that mean, 'musical ear'?" he asked derisively. "Anybody can play the piano. Maybe not the long-hair stuff but regular music. You need to *practice,*" he said with meaning.

"I practiced," I told him. Actually I hadn't practiced much, but it bothered me that he made the assumption so readily.

"You don't get anyplace in this world if you're lazy. Play a tune for your pa," he said, laughing, as if the request were a simple, jolly matter, something a loving, natural child wouldn't think twice about. "How about 'Ragtime Cowboy Joe'?"

"I can't."

"Sure you can."

"I don't know how."

"Well, what *do* you know?"

"I don't know how to play the *piano*, Papa. I know how to cook." I was trying to sound reasonable, but I felt events getting away from me. "I could make you a toasted cheese sandwich."

"Anybody can make one of those," he laughed. "When I've come all this way, I want to hear a tune from my girl."

I lifted the lid of the piano bench and riffled through the music until I found the beginner's book. *Wee Ones Learn to Play*. On the cover, in a black-and-ivory silhouette illustration, ringleted tots romped through tall grass, each playing a whistle or drum or tambourine. Carefree, adorable creatures, each of whom could play a tune for their papa.

I opened the book to song number seven, "Up and Down," illustrated with another silhouette, this one of a little boy and his puppy running up a flight of stairs. I chose it because it required both hands, though not simultaneously.

I had not played any of these pieces for a long time, and my fingers stumbled. The first two or three times, I started over. But finally Papa said, "You're right about one thing. You can't play the piano." I put the book away and opened the outside door.

"Maybe there's a breeze," I said, although the curtains at the windows hung lank. "I'd better set the table. Mama'll be home soon." The kitchen and the mention of Mama recalled Sunday afternoon, when I'd stood at the window catching sight of Papa.

Holding a clutch of silverware, I wandered to the living room door. "Why didn't you knock on our door Sunday?" I asked.

"What're you talking about?"

"You were standing at the top of the slope where the little kids roll down. Sunday afternoon. I saw you."

"Well, you saw wrong," he said, reaching for the folded morning paper, to which we now subscribed. Flicking it open, he laughed, "You need glasses."

"Where *were* you Sunday?"

"What the hell is this, the third degree? I was getting on the train in Harvester, if it's any of your business."

My face must have shown my disbelief. "You calling me a liar?"

I turned back to finish setting the table, including a place for Papa. Since Aunt Betty worked at the U.S.O. on Tuesday evenings, there would only be the three of us for supper.

I heard Papa rummaging in the brown satchel sitting beside the front door. Standing by the icebox now, a whiskey bottle in his hand, he asked, "Any ice?"

"In the ice compartment," I told him, folding paper napkins. He set the bottle on the counter, opened the icebox and the ice compartment door. The ice cube trays were frozen to each other and to the metal surface on which they rested. Papa gave them an angry yank, then hit them hard with the heel of his hand. A peanut butter jar flew out, barking his shin.

"Goddamn," he swore, slamming the door so hard that everything inside rattled. "Goddamned inferior piece of shit. Where'd she get *that?*" he asked, rubbing his leg.

"We pay extra on our rent for it," I explained, heating the blade of an old butcher knife over the gas flame and prizing the bottom tray from the ice compartment. The two trays came out together and I ran cold water over them till they separated. Dumping several cubes into a glass, I handed it to Papa.

"She'd of been better off buying a used one."

"But this one works."

"The hell it does." He grabbed the bottle, unscrewed the cap, and poured whiskey. He'd taken a dislike to the icebox.

Sitting down at the table and running his gaze around the room, he seemed to notice his surroundings for the first time. "Jerry-built."

"What?" I searched in the icebox to see what Mama had planned for dinner.

"This chicken coop your ma's brought you to. Cheap, jerry-built stuff," Papa said, tilting his chair back to peer out the window from which the walk and stoop were visible.

"It's got a real bathroom," I pointed out, "and we don't have to carry slop pails."

"How many slop pails did *you* ever carry?" Papa asked.

I couldn't believe my ears. I'd carried slop pails every day from the age of five, when I got big enough.

"Don't you remember? I carried thousands. Except when it was real cold, like twenty below, then Mama carried them."

Papa guffawed as if that were the funniest story he'd heard in years. "Where do you get this malarkey? I never saw you carry a slop pail."

Stunned by Papa's lie, I couldn't remember what I was doing at the icebox. I closed the door and clung to the handle.

"You know what?" Papa chortled, "I think we need to put you into Saint Peter." That was Minnesota's hospital for the insane and retarded. "First you say you saw me on some slope when I was two thousand miles away. Now the slop pails." He slapped the tabletop. "You've been out in the California sun too long."

Papa's words knocked me sideways. The kitchen floor heaved up and rolled away. I clutched the icebox door handle.

"N . . . no," I stammered.

"Yes." He giggled. "I knew your ma shouldn't have brought you here." He rose, came around the table, and started tickling me. "How about a hug, little girl?"

I slipped out of Papa's grasp, unable to bear being tickled by someone who'd just told me I was crazy, even though I did suddenly feel I might be crazy. The kitchen was receding from me, leaving me unsupported, unprotected, and removed from the comfortable reality of checkered oilcloth and iron skillets.

Hands lifted in a gesture of supplication, Papa asked, "What's the matter with you? I tease you a little and you act like I'm poison." Wheeling away, he threw the heels of his hands against the edge of the counter and bowed his head.

Teasing? What did that mean? Had he been teasing when he said that I never carried slop pails or was he teasing when he said that I was crazy?

"I really did carry the slop pails, didn't I?"

"What?" I'd interrupted his unhappiness. "You're still on about slop pails?" he asked as if I were plaguing him.

The radio in Belle Eldridge's kitchen was tuned to the KFI five-fifteen news. (Mama was late.) In Sicily, Allied troops were pushing north. The Russian army was on the offensive in several areas, while in the Pacific, American aircraft had sunk a Japanese destroyer near Bougainville.

Yesterday in Rome, the Pope addressed a fearful crowd following a raid by American airplanes on the San Lorenzo district. "And now, Mothers, a word from the makers of Ovaltine."

25

"GOD, I'M ALL DONE IN," Mama groaned, throwing open the screen door. Tossing her purse on the piano bench, she called to me, "Melba and I had to work overtime. Is supper . . . ?"

In the kitchen doorway, she stopped so suddenly that she lost her balance. "Willie." One hand grabbed for the jamb.

For a moment she teetered between fear and anger, then burst out at Papa, "How dare you come here unannounced and lie in wait?"

"Arlene . . ."

Recalling what I'd told her earlier, she threw her lunch pail on the counter and stood, fists clenched on her hips. "My God, Willie, you've been spying on us. Spying!"

"Spying? What d'ya mean 'spying'?"

"You know damned well what I mean. Lark saw you—out that window, Sunday, so don't try to lie out of it."

Papa returned to the kitchen table and sat down, holding out his empty glass to be filled, smiling at me in a chummy, conspiratorial way. "Lark told me about that," Papa said. "I explained how she was mistaken, how I was getting on a train in Harvester Sunday." He chuckled a little.

"I'll find out," Mama assured him.

I handed Papa a glass with ice and whiskey in it. Mama snatched it back, running water into it and setting it again in front of Papa, daring him to complain. "Don't get drunk before Betty gets home."

"Since when do I take orders from you?"

"Since you're in *my* house."

Papa let this pass. "Make yourself a drink," he said, nodding toward the bottle.

"No, thank you," Mama said, opening the cupboard and withdrawing a couple of cans of tomato soup and a can of Spam, slamming them down on the counter, then crossing to the icebox.

I pulled the key from the bottom of the Spam and began winding the metal seal. While Mama sliced Velveeta for toasted cheese sandwiches, I extracted the Spam, cubing one half of it to fry and add to the soup.

Although I hadn't any appetite and I doubted that Mama had, by going about dinner preparations we might get our bearings. But Papa ached to be the center of a drama. To withhold tears and pleas, to go about our business, was to deny him satisfaction.

Papa had come to California with an unreasonable demand for satisfaction. At best, he would be happily surprised by a wife and child who had fallen on hard times and were ready to come home. At worst, he would be maddened and martyred by the undeniable loss of them.

Papa would allow himself only the two roles: victor or martyr. He did not conceive of himself as one who negotiated, tolerated, or simply withdrew. A dark stream of ancient loss ran through Papa's character, a loss for which he'd spent a lifetime grieving and seeking compensation.

I slid the chair away from the table and took my place. Mama ladled soup into our bowls. On either side of the bowls lay triangles of toasted cheese sandwich.

At the counter, Papa slopped Dutch courage into his glass. "You've turned the kid against me."

"I don't know how you figure that," Mama said, setting the soup pot on the stove and taking her seat.

"How many kids hide under the bed when their pa comes to visit?"

"She was shy. It's been a long time."

"Whose fault is that?" Papa asked.

"It's yours," Mama said. "You could have visited before."

"I begged you not to leave," Papa said.

I remembered that and didn't want to. When he finally saw that Mama was going, Papa had wept and begged, making promises that Mama said he would break: The Linden house was for sale and he would buy it for her. Wouldn't she be grand then, in a house with big, airy rooms, stained glass windows, and a corner lot? The queen of Harvester.

I was certain that a child growing up in the Linden house would have the confidence to sing solos during music class; she would learn baton-twirling and wear white boots with dancing tassels in the Memorial Day parade.

But Mama stood firm against last-minute pleas and promises. She had heard pleas and promises before.

"Come back," Papa said now, and the words were an echo of that morning in the snow when the train had huffed impatiently, waiting for Mama, Aunt Betty, and me to board.

"I see now," he continued, his voice no longer sarcastic, "how much that house—what did you call it?"

"The Cape Ann," I said.

"I see now how much the Cape Ann meant to you, Arlene. We should have built it." His voice held both regret and hope. "There's other houses, though. The Brede house is gonna be sold. Old man Brede's gonna live with his daughter."

Mama stared bleakly at her untouched soup.

"The Brede house—you probably remember—is a block east of the school." Papa hurried on, "Lark could come home for lunch. And you'd be real near Bernice McGivern." To me he pointed out, "Just a block from Sally Wheeler, too."

I was trying to recall the Brede house. "Is it on a corner?"

"That's right."

"And there's a real pretty picket fence?"

"That's the one."

"And a little rose arbor beside the garage." I knew now which house it was.

"By God, you got a memory," Papa said. "The kid's a genius," he laughed, looking at Mama.

A wan smile drifted across Mama's face.

"There's plenty of room for a garden," observed Papa. "I bet your grandpa'd come from New Frankfurt and help lay it out." Grandpa Erhardt was a gardener of repute.

Had Papa really changed? My heart lifted, picturing Papa, as I had once pictured Hilly, digging and planting with me. "Should we make a list, Papa, of what we want to grow?" I started up from the table to fetch a pad and pencil.

"Sit down," Mama told me. "Eat your supper. There's time for lists later."

"You see how excited the kid is, Arlene? She wants to come back to Harvester, don't you?" Papa glanced at me, then back at Mama. "If you care about her, Arlene, you'll come back."

Mama's response was somewhere between a laugh and a groan.

"What's that supposed to mean?" Papa wanted to know.

"Nothing. Nothing." Mama sighed and played with the spoon beside her plate, turning it over and over.

"Well, talk to me then," Papa said, rising to refresh his drink. "What're you thinking?"

"I'm thinking you've turned up on my doorstep out of the blue, with all kinds of assumptions about Lark and me. You expect us to pack our grips and hop on the next train east. Take off your blinders, Willie."

Papa blinked. "If you're going to tell me you don't love me, save your breath. I don't believe it."

"Love doesn't enter into this," Mama told him. "I like being free. Free to make my own money, free to spend it. I'm free to make myself happy, Willie."

"And what about Lark?" Papa asked. "You're draggin' her along behind you like a tin can tied to a Model T."

"All of a sudden, when it suits your purpose, you're worrying about Lark?" Mama shook her head. "I can't make Lark happy if I'm miserable."

"Well, that's just about the damnedest excuse for doing whatever the hell you want that I ever heard." Papa returned to his place at the table, in front of the open window.

I hoped no one was listening. I was embarrassed for Mama and Papa, and angry at the way they could go on at each other for hours, days, years, nothing getting settled. I was even angrier that they thought they knew what I needed. They never listened. Mama once had, but that had stopped a year and a half ago, when what I wanted and what she wanted peeled off in different directions.

Across the way, Miss Eldridge's kitchen window was open. A dim light, probably from a living room lamp, not enough to bring an air raid warden running, gilded the outline of the window.

In our kitchen, we sat in shadows. To light a lamp was to offer hospitality, and Mama would not lest it be interpreted as acquiescence. She moved wraithlike, picking up her plate and bowl. "Eat your supper," she told me.

"I'm not hungry."

I carried my plate and bowl to the counter, then drifted to the east-facing window. Out of the purple darkness at the top of the slope floated the muffled shouts and rat-a-tat-tats of children playing fighter planes and Japs.

At the table, Papa sobbed, "It's been hell. I want you to know it's been hell."

I had never heard a man cry like this. On occasion, Papa had wept, but never in this wild, atavistic way. I was as repelled as if he'd torn off his clothes.

I wanted to run away but I couldn't. I might miss some bit of information that would help to explain our lives. I needed to understand why Papa would chase after torment.

He threw his head down on his arms, keening.

"Papa, don't cry," I heard myself begging.

"A year and a half of hell. I can't go on," he bawled, lifting his head, focusing on the pale cloud by the sink that was Mama's white blouse. "What am I going to do, for Christ's sake?"

"I don't know, Willie," Mama whispered.

"You've got to help me, Arlene. Save me," Papa wept.

I crept past Papa and out of the kitchen. Feeling my way to the table beside the sofa, I flicked on a lamp, then lowered the window shades and closed the outside door. A heavy calm of hopelessness lay over the house.

"You're tired, Willie. I'll make up the sofa bed. We're all tired."

When the bed was ready, Papa capitulated, exhausted by whiskey and despair, and allowed himself to be led, quietly weeping, to the living room. Pulling off his shoes, he lay down fully clothed on the open sofa.

"Turn on the piano light," Mama told me, switching off the table lamp, which shone in Papa's face.

Wordlessly and in near darkness, we cleared Papa's place at the kitchen table and set the room in order. Mama poured us each a glass of iced tea and we sat by the north window, through which few breezes found their way. It wasn't late, but only seemed so.

Mama leaned on her forearms and was quiet. I thought perhaps she'd fallen asleep sitting up, but at length she reached for my empty glass and said, "Say your prayers." Not since we'd lived in Minnesota had she said that.

26

IN THE BATHROOM, Papa whistled "Ragtime Cowboy Joe." Sliding out of bed, I dressed and padded out to the kitchen. It was only eight, but the day was already warm.

I carried a bowl of puffed wheat to the stoop and sat down. The plants needed watering again. Mama's gardenia bush especially, with its several blooms and buds. It had hung on. Any plant could flourish in good soil, Jack said, but for a gardenia to survive in poor soil was a miracle.

Mama and I were both silly over the gardenia's perfume. Sometimes Mama cut a blossom and put it in a glass of water on the kitchen table. The two of us could sit for half an hour taking turns holding the glass and drinking in the fragrance. "Don't touch the petals," Mama always warned. "They'll turn brown. They're very sensitive. We have to respect that."

While I was watering the gardenia, Miss Eldridge stepped out onto her stoop. "My, it's hot."

"Yes, ma'am." These were the first words Miss Eldridge and I had exchanged.

She fanned herself with a circle of cardboard cut from the back of a shredded wheat box. "The day reminds me of the Midwest. The prairie."

"Yes, ma'am."

"Was it prairie where you lived, in Minnesota?"

I considered. "I think it was, ma'am. There were lots of farms."

She nodded. Despite her old-fashioned dress, which was too long, and her narrow lace-up shoes with chunky two-inch heels, Belle El-dridge owned a delicate, besieged comeliness.

"You have someone visiting?" she asked. Her fan paused against her cheek.

"My papa, ma'am."

Staring off toward the bay, she asked, "Are you available to work?"

"Available to work, ma'am?"

"Yes. I have work I need done. I would pay you a little. I can't afford much."

"I could work. Yes, ma'am. That'd be fine." Even working for a lady who accused her canary of killing her was preferable to hanging around the house, watching Papa suffer. And wouldn't Papa be impressed with my get-up-and-go.

Grasping the handle of her screen door, Miss Eldridge looked at me as if nailing a message to my brain. "Come over when it's *convenient,*" she said.

I carried my cereal bowl to the sink.

"Who's she?" Papa asked. He was sitting at the kitchen table reading the San Diego *Union.*

"Miss Eldridge. She lives next door."

"I could see that."

"She's a neighbor, that's all I know."

"Hmmmmph." He turned the page. "Damned Yankees are going to take the pennant." The Cubs were Papa's favorite team, and the Yankees his bane. When the Yankees took the pennant, Papa started right away putting money on the National League team. If the Yankees won the series, he lost his shirt.

I heard Shirley mount the steps and hurried to open the screen before she started her pounding.

Stepping inside, she asked, "Your pa still here?"

I nodded. "What'd you do to your hair?" Her head was shorn like a thatched hut.

"Jealous?"

I was, a little. Except for a tail here and there that she'd missed, Shirley hadn't done such a bad job. She looked kind of like Jackie Cooper in *The Champ*, which I'd seen at the penny movies long ago, in Harvester.

Shirley had also cut off the cinched-up, ratty trousers so they looked almost like shorts. Tucked into them was a white shirt, sleeves rolled up.

Sailing past me, Shirley took possession of the piano and began a tempest of scales and exercises. Her back was straight, as Fanny had instructed, and her head was held aloft, high above her shoulders. Her wrists, too, were up where they ought to be, not draped down over the edge of the keyboard as mine had been, like something hanging on for dear life.

The sofa bed was still flung open, sheets and pillows in a stirred-up heap. I straightened the sheets, stuffed the pillows into a cubby hole beneath the mattress, and restored the sofa to its normal position.

Papa joined Shirley at the piano. Shirley said something about "that skunk Hitler," which set Papa to giggling. Then Shirley launched into "Right in Der Fuehrer's Face," singing raucously. Papa joined in, lending grandiose fart sounds where called for, and roaring with laughter.

Shirley charmed Papa with her talent and audacity. I queased with envy. What if I were to join in singing "Praise the Lord and Pass the Ammunition," which Shirley had taken up? What if I clapped in time to the music, tapped my foot, smiled and sang with them?

Like reciting "The Night Before Christmas" in front of the relatives, it was possible only in dreams.

In the midst of my stifling self-pity, I recalled Miss Eldridge. "I told Miss Eldridge I'd help her," I shouted over the pounding chords of "Over hill, over dale."

The deep gold matelasse bedspread-drapes in Miss Eldridge's living room were closed, but in the corner beside the old burgundy mohair sofa a table lamp shed honey-colored light through its parchment shade. On the floor between the sofa and a matching armchair sat two open cardboard boxes. Clipped velour cloths whose dark red-and-green designs were faded to pastel protected the tops of two lamp tables, one at either end of the sofa. Though dim, the room was not oppressive, merely withdrawn.

The living room would have been airless, but the kitchen windows were open for Billy's sake, and Miss Eldridge had set an enormous oscillating fan on a little mahogany table beside the kitchen door, training it on the corner of the room where we were doubtless to work. The ponderous to and fro of the fan, punctuated by a barely audible click of the oscillating mechanism at each end of its lazy swing, was lulling and familiar.

I was transported to Grandma Browning's dining room, where the whirr and click of a great, pale green fan was part of summer's vernacular, like watermelon and iced tea. It gave me an eerie but pleasant start, then, to hear Miss Eldridge say, "Sit there and I'll bring us a glass of iced tea."

Edging past the cardboard boxes, I sat in the burgundy chair, its pile worn bare along the arms. I had an overwhelming need to be at home in this room, to lay my head on the bosom of its familiarity. I ran my fingers over a spot on the chair arm where wheat-colored threads of warp and woof shown through.

"Down at the heels, isn't it?" Miss Eldridge said, entering with a glass of tea in one hand, an empty plate in the other. She set the plate on the lamp table beside me, then placed the glass on top of it. "Tea stains are forever," she explained.

I rose. "May I help you, ma'am?" I was startled to hear the civility in my voice.

"You may carry the plate of cookies," she suggested, and I followed her to the kitchen while she fetched her own tea.

"My Grandma Browning made antimacassars for her living room suite," I told Miss Eldridge, setting the vanilla wafers on the table beside our glasses. "She crocheted them."

"I used to crochet when I was a girl," she said when we were settled, she on the sofa, I on the chair. "I remember making lace trim for a shirtwaist." She wiped her glass with a napkin and laid its cool dampness against her cheek. "Mama said it was a fool thing to do. My lace wasn't at all suitable, she said."

Miss Eldridge pronounced *Mama* in an odd way, emphasizing the second syllable. She had closed her eyes. Now she opened them and fixed me ferociously, inclining her body toward me. "A parent can be the worst thing that happens to you," she hissed.

I was shaken. And disappointed. I had hoped she would be like Grandma Browning and her living room would be a sanctuary where stories were related, like those around Grandma's dining room table, of fires and drownings, parties and picnics, babies born with fur on their chests, and old women who could levitate their beds while lying on them; stories, in short, to carry Miss Eldridge and me away from the Project and the boys, away from the war and our own dreary baggage.

Had she perhaps heard Papa's carrying-on last night? Was that why she'd said parents could be the worst thing that happened to you?

Miss Eldridge settled against the sofa, the tea glass trembling in her hand, and cast me an uneasy glance. "Forgive me."

Then, setting the tea aside, and with a heaving of her breast, she explained, "These two boxes must be sorted through." She bent to lift the flaps of one, revealing its contents. "I'm much older than Beau, and I'll be dead long before he is. This must all be set in order for him."

What we had to set in order was a mass of photographs and documents: baptismal and marriage certificates, transfers of property and such—a history of Belle and Beau's family.

"Most of this came to me when Mama passed away last year," Miss Eldridge said, her voice breathy.

"Your mama and papa lived in North Dakota."

She nodded. "Papa owned half the county. Our farm began at the edge of Elgin and stretched west for miles. Papa built Mama a grand big house five miles out because Mama disdained small-town society. Hoi polloi, she called it. She had her piano and her library, and she oversaw the one-room township school that Papa built. She chose the teacher. And the teacher lived at our house like a paid companion for Mama.

"The first teacher, Miss Swenson, remained for eight years. Then she married an old bachelor farmer and went to live on a rundown spread south of ours. She seemed happy there.

"After Miss Swenson, Mama hired William Bates, who had a four-year degree from the University of Pennsylvania and had come west to write a novel about homesteading. By this time I was going to high school in town, so Mr. Bates was never my teacher, though he did help me with English composition and Latin."

I would never have guessed that Miss Eldridge had such a trunkload of words pressing to burst out.

With a spastic toss of her head, she said, "Mama was very pleased with Mr. Bates. He was cultured." Her voice had grown thin and high. "He was beautiful. . . . The dearest man." Then, with finality, as if Mr. Bates had succumbed in their parlor, "He left us at the end of his third year."

"He died?"

She seemed to consider this. "He may have."

Her eyes widened to dispel gathering tears. In a swift, silent up-springing, she flew from the room, closing the bathroom door behind her.

We hadn't begun our work and it wasn't work I could begin with-out her. Eventually I carried the tea glasses and the cookie plate to the kitchen, where Billy hopped about in his cage, rearranging himself on the swing and eyeing me mutely.

Beyond the kitchen sink, in the bathroom, water was running. Miss Eldridge was, I was sure, crying and running water to cover the sound.

Older people weren't supposed to cry, except under the most extreme circumstances. They were supposed to be strong for the sake of the rest of us.

Slipping out of Miss Eldridge's house, I crossed to my own, where no piano music greeted me, nor did any human face. Where were Papa and Shirley?

27

WE WERE ALREADY EATING DINNER when Papa and Shirley returned, Papa exclaiming, "That's a big zoo," and motioning Shirley toward the table.

Mama, who was seated nearest the cupboards, rose to fetch another plate and flatware, laying them in front of Shirley, along with a paper napkin. She also increased the stack of bread and set the peanut butter jar beside it.

"I'll take you all out for a big feed while I'm here," Papa said, eyeing our table.

"How long were you planning to stay?" Mama inquired, making an effort not to sound anxious.

As though the question had gotten by him, Papa enthused, "That zoo is big enough to get lost in, Betty. Been up there?"

"A couple of times."

"How long did we spend," he asked Shirley, "four hours?"

She nodded, her mouth full of fried potatoes.

"We hardly scratched the surface. 'Course we did spend some time stuffing our faces." He laughed and nudged Shirley.

Shirley cast a sideways glance across the table to be certain none of this escaped me.

"Too bad you couldn't come, Lark." Papa's words were fringed with sympathy. "How much money did you make?"

"Miss Eldridge is going to pay me when the job's done."

"That old bat?" Shirley disdained, reaching for a slice of bread. "She's crazy as a bedbug."

"She is not!"

"You ever hear her talkin' to that bird?"

"Lots of people talk to their birds."

Our kitchen window was open.

"Not like her. 'Darling, darling Billy,'" Shirley mimicked.

"Shut up, Shirley!"

"You shut up, young lady," Papa told me. "You don't talk to a guest that way."

"Then make her stop talking like that about Miss Eldridge."

Aunt Betty asked, "What're you doing for Miss Eldridge?"

"We're sorting old pictures and stuff." We hadn't of course. "It's very interesting. Miss Eldridge's papa was rich."

"That why she's living *here?*" Papa asked.

Why was she living here?

"Did she say he was rich?" Mama asked.

"She said he owned half the county. And he built her mama a big house. And they had a library in their *house.*"

"He may have lost everything in the bad years," Aunt Betty said.

After the dishes were washed, Papa, who'd been listening to *Merry Melodies* on KFSD, suggested, "You and I'll walk Shirley home." But Shirley slipped away while Papa was in the bathroom.

Aunt Betty and I took care of our map: The Americans and English had taken the southeastern third of Sicily, a three-cornered island off the toe of Italy, and the Russians were now punishing the Germans on the eastern front.

But despite the victories, or maybe because of them, the list of local servicemen killed or wounded continued without diminution in the San Diego *Union.*

The evening crept across long stretches of uneasy silence, punctuated by infrequent bursts of conversation that sounded counterfeit. Papa chain-smoked Wings and riffled restlessly through *Life* magazine. "So, Betty, what d'ya do at the store?" he asked, his voice in the quiet as startling as a gunshot.

Setting aside the tacks, Aunt Betty explained that as manager of better ladies dresses she had half a dozen women working under her supervision. Along with the buyer, she determined what would appear on the racks.

Papa let out a low whistle. "Half a dozen women. How come you don't get a job like that, Arlene?"

Mama bristled. "I'm fine where I'm at."

Finding it difficult not to pace, Mama finally carried a bundle of underwear to the bathroom and spent half an hour laundering panties and bras before hanging them to dry on a folding wooden rack that she set up by the kitchen window. Wiping her hands on a tea towel, she paused in the doorway.

"I saw a slipper chair at Trustworthy Second Hand a while back," she told Aunt Betty. "For the bedroom. He only wants four dollars. I could make a pretty slipcover."

"What's a slipper chair?" I asked.

"It's a little upholstered chair for ladies' boudoirs."

"Why's it called a slipper chair?"

She shrugged. "Maybe it's where you sit to put on your slippers," she said to me, then to Aunt Betty, "a blue flowered chintz would be nice, don't you think?"

Papa's tolerance for this kind of talk was minimal. "For God's sake," he huffed, tossing a magazine aside, "is that all you think about?"

"I'm trying to make a nice home for us," Mama said, continuing to wipe her hands.

"If it's a nice home you want, come back to Harvester."

Ignoring this, Mama hung up the towel, then returned to inquire, "What about a game of three-hand bridge?"

"Three-hand bridge?" Papa echoed with a note of disparagement. He considered bridge effete, like golf or tennis. If Aunt Betty hadn't been there, he would have pursued Mama's return to Harvester. But he wouldn't fight no-holds-barred in front of my aunt. She still respected him and he considered her an ally.

For an hour and a half, they played. The conversation continued fitfully, but the game itself relieved tension: Each player could pretend that his silence, or hers, was absorption, and the various hands provoked comment. "Eight diamonds in the dummy! I never saw that before," or "I knew you'd finesse my king of spades, but what could I do?"

I lay on the sofa. If I closed my eyes, I could imagine I was lying on the daybed on Grandma Browning's front porch, listening to the voices of grown-ups playing cards in the dining room. Phrases like *grand slam* and *three no-trump* and *unprotected king* filled me with a sense of well-being.

When the game broke up around eleven, Mama nudged my arm. "Time to hit the hay."

"You can use the bathroom first," Aunt Betty told Mama. Sitting down at the piano, she played softly, "I'll Be Seeing You," and "When the Moon Comes over the Mountain," which she knew to be a favorite of Papa's.

Papa sat on the sofa waiting his turn in the bathroom. I stood in the living room doorway, listening to the music, waiting for Mama to finish her *ablutions* (page 3 of *Webster's*) and scold me to bed.

Playing songs so familiar that she didn't have to glance at the keyboard, Aunt Betty made conversation with Papa.

"Is Father Delias still at Saint Boniface?"

"Yeah, but he's getting dotty. Too liberal."

"What did you like best at the zoo?"

Papa thought for a moment. "The bears."

"Really?"

"They were sad," he said. "You could see that. They looked home-sick. When the keeper threw them fish, everybody laughed and clapped, and the bears clapped too, but their hearts weren't in it. Their hearts were someplace else. Back in the woods."

Serious conversation, anything bordering on the philosophical, tended to embarrass Papa, but he had more he wished to say about the bears.

"There's a proper place for a bear to be. You take him away from that, haul him off to a zoo or circus, he'll go crazy, lose his . . . balance. People the same."

Mama came out of the bathroom. "Get to bed now," she told me. "I'll see you in the morning, Willie."

Later, dressed in pajamas, a concession to travel, Papa opened my door and poked his head in to find me reading *The Secret Garden,* a fifth-grade graduation gift from Aunt Betty.

"What's that about?" he asked, advancing into the room.

"A girl named Mary, whose mama and papa die of cholera in India and she has to go to England to live with an uncle."

Papa sat down on the edge of the bed, nodding politely but looking as if I were speaking Armenian. "I don't want you thinking of me like I was dead," he said. "I'm your pa, and I'm going to be for a long time."

I almost expected him to add, "So you might as well get used to it." I was put off, though I could see that he was trying to be fatherly, maybe even reassuring.

"Do you understand?"

"Yes."

"I'm not sure you do," he said gruffly. "Your ma can go to hell and back, but she's still my wife. And you're still my kid." He was weeping again.

I reached out a hand to touch his shoulder and he grabbed me the way drowning people do, desperately, crushing me till I whimpered.

"Don't cry, kid. Your ma and I are getting back together."

28

AGAIN ON THURSDAY MORNING, Papa remained at the table after breakfast, reading the *Union* sports section and smoking a Wings while I made up the sofa bed. When Shirley arrived to begin practicing, I retreated to the stoop. Would Miss Eldridge appear, inviting me back?

Around ten-thirty, I heard her in the kitchen, murmuring to Billy and rinsing dishes in the sink. Moments later she appeared at the screen door. "Good morning," she said in a tired voice. "Your visitor still with you?"

"Yes, ma'am."

She nodded and raised a hand to shield her eyes from the July glare. On the southwestern horizon, B-24 Liberators were lifting into the sky, like the silver souls of heroes rising to heaven. "Will you help me again?"

"Yes, ma'am."

Once more she nodded, not taking her eyes from the planes. Over the ocean, they wheeled in a great, embracing arc and lazily headed east.

Miss Eldridge dipped her head in the direction of her living room and retreated into its darkness. I followed.

"Beau and I are the last of our family," she said once we were seated by the boxes. "The end of the line."

"Maybe you'll get married and have a baby," I offered, "or Beau will." Something about a family dying out upset me.

"I think," she began, ignoring my words and turning to the cartons, "that the easiest way to do this is to divide everything into three piles: before 1850, 1850 to 1900, and 1900 to 1943."

1850 seemed like the dawn of history. That Miss Eldridge had documents from before that amazed me, and caused me to think of her as fairly ancient herself. Indeed, we uncovered an August 1889 clipping from the Elgin, North Dakota, *Argus* announcing the birth of Belle St. Honore Eldridge to Mr. Charles Eldridge and Mrs. Eldridge (nee Celeste St. Honore), making it clear that Miss Eldridge would be fifty-four in August.

For several hours, I poked through the boxes of pictures, clippings, and documents, arranging them in the three groupings. The smaller of the two cartons was filled almost exclusively with pictures, report cards, and other memorabilia of Beau Eldridge's life. Solemn and cherubic as a toddler, he'd grown sad and careful-looking as an older boy. His report cards were rife with A's and Excellents, his only shortcoming being a reluctance to contribute to discussion.

When we'd worked for a couple of hours, Miss Eldridge made chicken salad sandwiches. "Wash your hands in the kitchen sink," she said. "God only knows what smirch you've got on you," she added, as if more than mere dust might rub off on me from the rummaging and sorting.

"Beau graduated from Burning Field, Nebraska?" I asked, recalling the "Payne Photographic Studio, Burning Field, Nebraska" on a folding cardboard frame.

Miss Eldridge, who was fussing with a pitcher of iced tea looked up. "Burning Field? Yes. We lived in Burning Field."

I changed the subject lest she whip off to the bathroom again. "Did you ever gather pussy willows when you were little?" I recalled with nostalgia my own treks out from Harvester along the railroad tracks to gather the long boughs with soft, mouse-colored nubs clinging to them, so furry to the cheek that they seemed more fauna than flora.

"Oh, yes," she said, placing a glass of tea beside my plate and motioning me to sit. "A creek ran through our pastureland. Clumps of pussy willows grew along the banks. Papa would hitch a travois behind my pony and we'd lead him out to the creek to load up."

"You had a pony?"

"A little gray fellow named Galahad." Her hand played idly with the small brooch of opals, seed pearls and sapphires, which she wore at her throat.

Innocent and pleasant though these remarks seemed, they caused Miss Eldridge consternation. The pulse at her temple throbbed visibly. I asked no more questions but finished my sandwich, carrying the dishes to the sink.

Later, sifting through the numerous cross-references of family life, I emptied out a manila envelope from the smaller carton. A couple of dozen glossy snapshots of Beau slid out in a heap, most of them taken in front of a small, white clapboard house with a peaky roof and balustered porch.

In the earliest photo, he sat in a pram, a bonnet tied under his chin; later, when he was maybe three, he held an old-fashioned watering can and bent to water his bare feet. In only one photo was he not alone: Beau, at possibly seven, wearing short pants, stood stolid beside Belle, who was young in figure but old and serious in the eyes.

"Is this in Burning Field?" I asked, holding up the picture of the two of them.

"Yes, yes," she sibilated, a storm of ghosts blowing through her. She wiped her brow and the back of her neck with a handkerchief. Rising from the sofa, she said, "The heat's affecting me. I need . . . a cold cloth." Bumping into a table and nearly knocking over a lamp, she made her way out of the room, like someone wading in waist-deep water.

I got up and pulled aside the drapery. *These windows ought to be open.* But the full blaze of the afternoon sun would beat in if the drapes were flung back. Miss Eldridge needed shades here.

Letting the drape fall back, I returned to the carton of Burning Field memorabilia, lifting out a taupe velveteen-covered folding diploma issued to Beau Eldridge from Burning Field High School in June of 1923. Tucked inside was his birth certificate, dated December 3, 1906, from the city of Minneapolis, Minnesota. Parents, Celeste St. Honore Eldridge and Charles Byron Eldridge. With my index finger, I traced numbers on the carpet. Beau was thirty-six.

I added both documents to the 1900 to 1943 collection. Tipping the remaining items from the smaller box, I flipped through them. Several commencement programs surfaced. On the cover of each, "Cotton-wood Township School" was printed, and the year of the graduation ceremony. Miss Eldridge was duly noted as the teacher.

Although she had taught in a one-room country school, Miss El-dridge had resided in town and driven, presumably by horse and buggy, to her work in the country. Miss Eldridge had been eighteen when she began teaching in Cottonwood Township, and Beau had been a baby.

Very little remained to be sorted from this carton: Beau's college di-ploma, issued from the University of Nebraska in 1927 and granting him a bachelor of arts degree, and a clipping from the Burning Field *Telegram* announcing that "Beau Eldridge of this city has accepted a position teaching English and elocution in the high school of Salt Lick, Nebraska."

Several documents pertained to a property at 308 Meadow Street, in Burning Field. The white clapboard house. It had been purchased in December of 1906, around the time of Beau's birth, and sold in Novem-ber of 1941.

When I'd stacked these items on the pile, only a yellowed envelope lay on the carpet. I lifted the flap and dumped out yet another photo, this one of a young man who, except for the eyes, which were rounder, and the build, which was lighter, might have been the Beau of the high school graduation picture. Turning the photo over, I read a pale, penciled scrawl. "I am not the man you cared about. Forget. Forget. Forget."

29

SLIPPING THE PHOTO BACK into the envelope, I shuffled it in among others. I didn't want Miss Eldridge to know that I'd seen it and read the words "Forget. Forget. Forget." Forget what? And why, apart from Beau's birth certificate, was there no evidence of his and Belle's parents?

I considered the possibility that Mrs. Eldridge had died in childbirth and Belle had raised her brother. But no, Miss Eldridge had spoken of her mother's death as recent. I sat on the worn red chair, tapping my fingers soundlessly on the arms and trying to make sense of Belle Eldridge's life.

She had been in the bathroom ten minutes now. Once or twice, I heard water running as she bathed her face with a cool cloth.

"That's better," she said, appearing in the doorway, smoothing her dress and the back of her head where the hair was lifted up off her neck and fastened with combs. "But I think we need a glass of tea, don't you?"

Nibbling vanilla wafers and sipping tea, Miss Eldridge asked, "What kind of work does your father do?"

"He's a clerk for the railroad, ma'am. He sells tickets and sends telegrams and delivers freight and keeps track of the box cars and things like that."

She nodded. "And he's only visiting here?"

"Yes, ma'am. He's going back to Harvester."

"When?"

"I'm not sure, ma'am. Pretty soon."

"Are he and your mother divorced?"

"No, ma'am. Not yet. Mama's planning on it."

"Divorce isn't the worst thing that can happen," said Miss Eldridge. "Some husbands and wives should never have married."

This turn of the conversation unsettled me. "If you had window shades," I began, abruptly changing the subject, "you could get a breeze through here."

"Shades?" She eyed the heavy drapes that veiled her from the world. "One of these days," she said without conviction.

Mama was home from work when Papa and Shirley rolled in from a day's outing at Mission Beach. Shirley carried a red-and-white pinwheel, a green felt pennant emblazoned with "Belmont Amusement Park, Mission Beach, California," and a sailor doll wearing a navy blue middy, bell bottom trousers, and a white sailor cap.

"Look what your pa won for me," she whooped, tossing the pinwheel and pennant on the piano bench and thrusting the sailor doll in my face.

"You're missing all the fun, going off to work every day," Papa told me. "We rode the Ferris wheel and the tilt-a-whirl, and the merry-go-round . . ."

"And the roller coaster!" Shirley cried. "You can see Pearl Harbor from the top."

"You rode the *roller coaster?*" You couldn't have dragged me on that roller coaster for love or money.

"Hell, yes," Papa laughed. "She rode it three times." He headed for the kitchen, pulling a fresh bottle of whiskey from a brown paper bag. "What's for supper?" he asked Mama.

"Baked beans, hot dogs, and salad," she told him, opening and closing the icebox. "Lark, the table's not set."

"I was working for Miss Eldridge," I explained, reaching plates and glasses from the cupboard.

"You want a drink?" Papa asked Mama, fixing himself one.

"No, thank you. Maybe later, when Betty gets home." She stirred the beans in a pot on the back of the stove.

For a moment we might have been in Harvester, with Papa coming in from the depot office. I finished setting the table, a dreamy hope blowing on the back of my neck.

"Where's Betty?" Papa asked.

"Working at the U.S.O."

"What'd you think of that Plunge?" Papa asked Shirley during supper. "Pretty fancy, huh?"

"You went *swimming?*" The Plunge was a beautiful indoor pool beside the beach.

"Sure," Papa said. "We rented suits. How long did they say that pool was," he asked, turning to Shirley, "a hundred and seventy-five feet? Anyway, Shirley and I had a race, one end to the other. She damned near beat me, too." Papa speared another hotdog, slathering it with mustard and ketchup.

"Shirley dove off the high board," Papa went on. "You couldn't get me up on that thing, but up climbs our Shirley like she was just gonna jump off the front porch."

Our Shirley?

"I said to Shirley," Papa gabbed, enjoying the whiskey shine he was starting to feel and settling into man-of-the-house palaver, "maybe she could come visit us in Minnesota. She says she's a fisherman and I said we've got the fish—walleyes, northerns, bass, sunfish. All y've got to do is bait your hook and drop it in Sioux Woman Lake, right, Lark?"

"I only ever caught one little bullhead, Papa."

"What! I remember one time you had half a dozen on your string! More than one time. What're you talking, 'one little bullhead'?"

"The other ones you and Mama caught on my line and pretended I caught. That doesn't count." I was dampening the spirit of the moment, so I added, "But there's plenty of fish, all right. What I like, though, is catching nightcrawlers for bait. Remember, Papa, when we hunted nightcrawlers at Mr. Navarin's?"

But Papa was on another track. We were like two trains traveling side by side for a minute, me heading north and him south.

"I could send Shirley a ticket," Papa went on, gesturing with his knife and fork. He turned to Shirley. "You ever slept on a train?"

Shirley shook her head so hard you could hear her brains rattle.

Papa laughed. "Well, you'd sleep on the train before you got to Harvester! And eat, too. In the dining car."

Nodding and swallowing Papa's gab, Shirley reached for another slice of bread.

At moments like this, I loved the smell of whiskey because it surrounded an open-hearted expansiveness. If only Papa could maintain this pitch of joy and hope. He chattered along easily, like a train on a long level stretch. This was the side of him that his chums saw. No wonder he was popular with them.

Evening fell suddenly, as it does by the ocean. Mama began gathering the dishes from the table. "Give me a hand, Lark."

Papa remained at his place, telling Shirley that tomorrow he was taking us out to supper, including her, "so wear your best bib and tucker."

Before Papa could again suggest that we walk Shirley home, she stashed gingersnaps in her pocket and stole out of the kitchen and out the front door, clutching the sailor doll, pennant, and pinwheel.

Papa careered along on the whiskey track, a little out of control now but trusting that the same whiskey magic that had carried him clickety-clack across the sunlit plains of dinner would transport him safely through the dark and ragged terrain of Arlene's decampment.

Freshening his drink and sitting down again, now in front of the north window, which faced Miss Eldridge's kitchen, he stared off toward the western sky. The anti-aircraft emplacements were beginning their nightly practice. Distance softened the boom, boom, booms till they sounded like a muted bass drum far down the street.

Looking across the room at Mama, Papa told her, "I want you to come back."

Wiping off the counter beside the sink, Mama spoke over her shoulder, "Let's not argue tonight, Willie. We had a nice supper. Let's be friendly." She folded the dish cloth and hung it over the neck of the spigot. "How about a game of honeymoon bridge?"

As though he hadn't heard her, Papa said, "I want you to come back. I've been more than patient. I've given you time to get this outta your system."

"I'm not coming back. I told you that all along. You don't listen." She spoke not fretfully but with weary resolve. Removing her apron and draping it over the back of a chair, she sat down opposite Papa.

"I was just a kid when I married you, Willie. You were the first fellow to ask me. Maybe I worried that you'd be the last." Mama dropped her eyes. "I don't think I loved you, even then."

Papa's breath wheezed as if she'd punched him. He gulped whisky and water, hoping maybe to appear cool and contemptuous, but his hand shook and he erupted in a coughing fit.

Even before he'd stopped coughing, he'd jammed his body up against the table's edge, thrusting his face toward Mama. "You don't think you loved me?" A drop of whiskey slipped down his chin. "You damned well said you did!"

"I thought I loved you. I was only a kid, Willie. What I loved, I think, was getting married." She glanced across at Papa, anxious that he should see clearly for the first time the beginning and how it had been false, not through his fault but her own. "I thought I'd never get tired of keeping house and cooking and making things pretty."

She smiled ruefully. "I didn't realize that you marry *somebody*. I wasn't prepared for that. In a way, I suppose I thought I could be happy married to almost anyone because the main thing was keeping house and having babies."

"And I'm supposed to suffer because you didn't realize you married *somebody*? And Lark too, she's supposed to suffer? No, by God," he shouted.

Pushing violently away from the table, he carried his glass with him to the counter and the bottle.

"You don't know the first thing about being a woman," Papa cried, gesturing at Mama with his replenished drink. "You never did. You wanted to be a . . . a businessman, a hotshot. Being a wife wasn't good enough."

Mama said nothing.

"I know about your men."

"My men?"

"You think because you're out here in California I don't know what's going on. Lemme tell you—everything you do gets back to me."

"My men?" Mama laughed, a serif of hysteria edging the sound. "Willie, are you nuts? What men?"

"The men you entertain, right here, with the kid in the house. I hear about it. You've dragged our little family into the gutter, Arlene, but I'm taking the kid. And there's not a judge in the country'll stop me when he hears about you."

Mama's loathing poured out like thick, black crude. "You lying son-ofabitch. You'll take her over my dead body."

Half holding my breath I backed out of the kitchen and sat on the piano bench rocking back and forth.

Mama went on. "You're a weak, vicious liar, who tells himself the lies so often he believes them. I despise you because you could have been something better. You're pitiful, Willie, the poorest excuse of a man I ever saw. I'd see you dead before I went back or let you take Lark. I . . ." Mama's voice broke off in a squawk.

Feet scuffled and something fell from the counter or table. A rhythmic, muted banging, like someone hitting the wall with a bag of potatoes, sent me flying to the kitchen.

Flicking the light switch, I saw Papa, his hands around Mama's throat, slamming her head against the wall. His breath was ragged, and his grunts were in time with the banging.

Snatching the clean frying pan from the stove, I swung at Papa's head, striking him a glancing blow. His head twisted to one side as if he were inquiring who had hit him, and he slumped to the floor, carrying Mama beneath him.

My mind went blank. Then the pan slipped from my hand, clattering to the floor and rousing me. Mama was gasping and moaning. I grabbed Papa's arm and tried to pull him away.

"I killed him, I killed him."

On my knees, tugging and pushing, with Mama's help I finally heaved Papa onto his back. Mama pulled herself out, disentangling her legs and propping herself against the wall. Her shoes were missing and the sleeve of her blouse was torn from its seam. Her throat was reddish purple and a cut on her brow at the hairline was bleeding down the side of her face onto her blouse. She cradled her right wrist, which was bleeding as well. Just above the wrist, an oval, wine-colored wound oozed blood from two or three punctures. Had he *bitten* her?

I ran to the bathroom for Mercurochrome and a washcloth. Returning, I wiped Mama's arm and swabbed it with disinfectant. The gash on her head was still bleeding, so I rummaged in the linen closet for gauze and tape.

As long as I ministered to Mama, I didn't think about Papa. But when I'd finished bandaging and disinfecting, I asked, "Should I call the cops from Fanny's house?"

Mama opened her eyes and stared at me. "The cops?" she rasped.

"I'll have to go to jail," I explained.

"Why?"

"I killed him."

The corner of her mouth lifted in caustic mirth. "No such luck."

30

I SQUEEZED A PILLOW under Papa's head and he soon came around. The frying pan had left him with a ringing headache and a knob on the back of his skull, but he was in one piece.

Leaning heavily on a kitchen chair, he pulled himself up, easing onto the seat and exploring the wound beneath his hair. Then he eyed me.

"What did I ever do to you, kid?"

Heading once more for the bathroom medicine chest, I returned with the aspirin bottle and ran a glass of water. I uncapped the bottle and handed it to Papa, who shook three tablets into his palm.

"You tried to kill me," he said.

"You were killing Mama."

"Oh, for Christ's sake, I wasn't killing your ma, but if I was, don't I have a right?"

Refilling the glass, I handed it to Mama, along with three aspirin.

"Arlene?" Aunt Betty called from the front door, alarmed that our shades weren't drawn.

When she saw Mama on the floor, blood staining the front of her white blouse, she ran to her. "What's happened?"

"Willie and I had a little disagreement."

Papa said, "We always have fights, Betty. You know that." He had decided to treat it lightly. Wasn't this, ha ha, the way things had always been between him and Mama?

Setting her purse aside and kneeling by Mama, Aunt Betty said, "Pack your bag, Willie."

"The kid nearly killed me, Betty."

Aunt Betty stood and helped Mama to her feet. With an arm around Mama's waist, she turned to Papa. "Pack your bag."

I sat on the sofa, watching Papa gather his belongings into the grip. Sober now, he wept, and I wept with him.

Kneeling beside the bag and fastening its buckle closures, he looked up at me. I wished for Shirley's ability to talk to him. All I could do was sit smoothing my skirt.

When the grip was secure, Papa got up, glancing toward Mama and Aunt Betty's closed bedroom door. He started to say something, then reached for his bag.

Taking his free hand, I walked with him to the door and out, down to the blacktop street, down the street to the bus stop at the corner. Setting the grip on the ground, Papa pulled his wallet from a back pocket and hastily extracted a bill from it, stuffing it into the pocket of my blouse. The war-dimmed headlights of a bus bore down, shedding weak, dirty light and reducing our good-bye to a brief, silent hug.

The double doors closed peremptorily as Papa mounted the steps, fishing change from his pocket. I waved, but the bus drew away and I was waving at pale, retreating taillights.

. . . .

RELIVING THE SCENE in the kitchen was making me crazy. I lay in bed staring at the oil painting but seeing again and again Papa choking Mama, and then the lights of the bus disappearing down Garnet Street.

After about an hour, the painting worked its way through the taillights of the bus and I was seeing the warm light spilling from the windows of the cabin. Oozing my way past the gilded frame and through the heavy door, I reached for the writing tablet.

The Cabin in the Woods Continued

One day Ann Browning put on warm clothes and boots and took her ice skates from the wooden box beside the front door.

"I fed the chickens and left corn on the ground for the crows who live in the woods" she told Hilly Stillman. "Baby Marjorie is asleep so I think I'll go skating."

"While you're gone I'll chop wood for the kitchen stove and the fire place" Hilly said.

So off Ann Browning went down the little road that ran past the cabin. Not far from the cabin the road turned and wound around the woods so that when you got to the pond you couldn't see the cabin and nobody in the cabin could see you. It was quite a ways. Maybe a mile.

Ann loved to skate and she skated a long time doing all sorts of fansy tricks. She didn't notise that it was growing dark until it was really dark. Oh dear she thought. Hilly will be worried.

Back at the cabin Hilly paced up and down. "What do you think could have happened to Ann"? he asked Baby Marjorie who was only two years old. "I am very worried. Maybe she fell in a hole in the ice. Or maybe a wolf attact her." He decided to bundle Baby Marjorie in warm clothes and put her on the little sled he had made for her last winter.

Off they went down the road looking for Ann Browning. It had started to snow and the snow was coming down in bucketts.

Meanwhile Ann had taken off her skates and put on her boots. The fastest way home was not by the road that wound around but through the woods. So she started through the woods which were darker than the inside of a crow. She kept losing her way. There was a moon but it didn't give much light through the trees. If she had gone home by the road the moon would have shown her the way. Oh dear she thought. I am lost.

Meanwhile Hilly Stillman and Baby Marjorie made their way to the pond. And what did they find? No Ann! "Baby Marjorie, how could we have missed her on the road? You don't think that she has gone through the woods"!

In the woods Ann grew very tired and cold and finally she could not go any further so she laid down in the deep snow and fell asleep.

Hilly tramped and tramped pulling the sled behind him and calling Anns name. Up and down the woods he went. "If I don't find her soon she will freeze to death" he said. Then he heard one of those crows that Ann always fed. It was at the top of a tree and it seemed to be cawing at him. "What is it"? Hilly called to the crow.

The crow cawed again and flew to the next tree. Hilly followed it from tree to tree until finally the crow flew down and lit on a hump in the snow. Hilly shined his flash light on the hump. "Could it be"? he asked and ran to brush snow aside and there was Ann asleep.

"Ann, Ann" he shouted. "Wake up. It's Hilly come to save you."

And she woke up and she hadn't quite frozen so Hilly led her home pulling Baby Marjorie behind them. Ann was very happy to see the smoke coming out of the chimney and the light coming out of the windows.

And when Hilly had made a big pot of coco they all sat in front of the fire and drank a toast to the crow.

31

"Where's your pa?" Shirley demanded when I opened the door next morning.

"He and Mama had a fight. He's gone back to Minnesota."

"We ain't goin' out to supper?"

"No."

Shirley glanced about for evidence that I was lying.

"Yer a fuckin' sissy shit," she said, then wheeled and slammed out the door.

. . . .

Despite Aunt Betty's protests, Mama had gone to work. Lying in bed, I'd listened to them argue. "Your face is bruised. There's no way you're going to cover up that cut on the side of your head, and your neck is a mess."

"I'll wear plenty of pancake and a scarf around my neck."

Mama was adamant, packing her lunch pail, enlisting Aunt Betty's help in finding her employee identification badge (on the floor under the kitchen table) and marching off at six-fifteen.

I lay on the sofa, dozing and taking stock, too humiliated to present myself to Miss Eldridge after last night's brawl.

But around eleven, someone knocked at the door, a knock less furious than Shirley's. Miss Eldridge. Never before to my knowledge had she ventured beyond her own doorstep.

"You're coming to work? I do need you."

"I didn't eat my breakfast yet or wash my face. I'll come after that."

She nodded, hesitating, then gave that spastic, Bette Davis toss of her head and declared, "Noon, shall we say?"

Pulling on yesterday's white blouse, I heard a papery sound and dug into the pocket, withdrawing the wadded money Papa had stuffed there. A five-dollar bill.

And he hadn't even told me to buy candles.

At noon, Miss Eldridge ushered me into her living room, saying, "Beau bought us expanding files for our work."

Stacked on the floor beside the sofa were several mottled sienna-colored expanding paper files. Beau had also bought a number of thick photo albums and gummed photo corners.

Again the drapes were closed and today the front door as well. Because the day was hot and the roof uninsulated, the house was sweltering, even with the big fan blowing. Between Miss Eldridge and me, we must have drunk a gallon of iced tea.

In mid-afternoon, Miss Eldridge served us glorified rice. Despite the heat, her mood was light. We were sorting pictures and documents from well before her birth, and that may have accounted for her ease.

By four-thirty, we were droopy, however, and she suggested a recess until Monday, since the next day was Saturday and Mama would doubtless have chores for me. We had accomplished a good deal, filing away everything up to 1880. Miss Eldridge actually sent me away with a smile and two oatmeal cookies in my pocket

As I left the Eldridges', squinting in the sunlight, I wondered where Papa was now. Probably in Nevada or Arizona.

Because my eyes were adjusting to the dimness of the living room, I noticed nothing amiss. Then I tripped over Mama's copy of *A Farewell to Arms*. Pictures were ripped from the walls and lay shattered on the floor. Innards of the sofa and rose chair spilled through gaping wounds; splintered glass from the door of the bookcase was scattered across the floor and books were flung everywhere, many with their covers torn from them, pages shredded. Yanked from the rods, the curtains lay in tangled ribbons. Ketchup bloodied the rug and furniture, its spicy smell filling the hot, airless room with a nauseating reek.

In the kitchen, shards of dishes and glasses crunched beneath my shoes. The icebox stood open, its contents dripping from kitchen walls. An alarm rang in my head and I sprinted to the bedroom.

The oil painting was untouched.

In the tiny hall connecting bedrooms and bath, I stood, exhausted by the scene, then sank to the floor. Maybe the person who'd done this would return and kill me. It didn't matter. I couldn't move. Knees drawn up, I fell asleep.

"Oh, my God! Oh, my God!" Mama shrieked, stumbling from room to room, then dashing to her bedroom. She righted the photo of Uncle Stanley, then turned and saw the closet. Staggering out of the bedroom, she clutched shreds of scarlet fabric, the first store-bought dress she'd owned in years.

"Willie," she howled, standing in the middle of the living room.

Papa? I hurried into Mama's room. On her side of the closet, dresses, skirts, and blouses were torn to rags. Aunt Betty's things were untouched. Mama's bureau drawers lay heaped, with underwear, scarves, and other items slashed and strewn about the room. Perfume bottles, hand mirror, fingernail polish, lamp, everything on her bureau had been swept to the floor and trampled. The wooden floor was white where perfume and polish remover had spilled.

I raised the shades and opened the windows. Stepping over the bureau drawers again, I shambled back to the living room.

"Lark?"

"Miss Eldridge." She stood outside the screen door.

"I heard your mother scream."

I opened the door and led her in. Mama had collapsed sobbing onto the sofa, her face buried in her hands.

"Oh, dear," Miss Eldridge breathed, glancing about at the havoc. She searched my eyes.

"Papa," I explained.

She reconnoitered. Returning, she unbuttoned her cuffs and rolled up the sleeves of her dark muslin dress. "An apron?"

From the broom closet, I withdrew an apron and cleaning supplies. Pulling the apron over her head and tying it, Miss Eldridge said, "We'll do your mother's room first. Then she can lie down."

I grabbed the garbage pail from under the sink and followed. While she sorted through the clothing, rescuing anything salvageable, I swept the floor.

"Now, wipe the floor with a damp cloth," she advised, "to get the fine pieces of glass. And make your mother a pot of tea when you're done." Folding the mendable clothes into a pile, she said, "I need a bag for the rags."

Ten minutes later, she said, "Bring me a basin." She headed for the bathroom and ran the cold water tap. Grabbing a fresh washcloth from the rack above the tub, she carried the basin to the living room and began bathing Mama's red, swollen face and her wrists. "Is the tea ready?"

I fetched a cup. Miss Eldridge had unknotted the scarf from Mama's neck. "Oh," she murmured, seeing the welts.

After Mama drank the tea, we got her into bed. "Bring the radio in here," Miss Eldridge said, "so she can listen to something besides her own thoughts."

I plugged the radio in and tuned it to *Waltz Time* on KFI. How on earth had the radio survived unharmed?

The bathroom, too. Papa could have destroyed everything in the medicine chest, but he hadn't. Maybe he wasn't sure what belonged to whom. In the kitchen he hadn't scrupled. Everything made of glass or crockery was shattered. Only the teapot and the two cups left in the sink from the morning had escaped.

The iron skillet lay on the table. The glasses and dishes that hadn't broken readily had been smashed with that.

While Miss Eldridge swept the kitchen, I wiped up the hallway outside the bedrooms as well as the part of my room where I'd tracked ketchup and glass. When Aunt Betty arrived, the living room alone was unredeemed.

I was on my hands and knees in the hall and didn't hear the screen door. I did hear my aunt's quiet, "Willie."

Tossing the scrub cloth in the pail, I rose. "Mama's in bed."

"Is it all like this?"

"Not my room or the bathroom. Or your clothes."

She ran her hands over the piano keys, relieved to find no damage.

Miss Eldridge appeared at the kitchen door. With a glance at the carpet, she said, "I have an Electrolux in the broom closet." I ran across to fetch it while Aunt Betty changed out of her good clothes.

When the litter had been cleared from the living room, the vacuum run, the ketchup scrubbed up, and blankets thrown over the sofa and rose chair, Miss Eldridge sat down with the torn books to see what could be saved. Aunt Betty made deviled ham sandwiches and opened cans of corn, but there were no plates or saucers so I returned to Miss Eldridge's for dishes.

Mama had fallen asleep and we didn't disturb her. Aunt Betty, Miss Eldridge, and I gathered around the table at eight o'clock, exhausted, but satisfied that we had done what we could.

A war had been waged. We hadn't won, but we'd survived. A lunatic pleasure in our own hard work overtook us and while we drank tea and ate soda crackers, we giggled senselessly.

"The vandalism was the work of Nazi saboteurs," pronounced Aunt Betty, laughing and spewing cracker crumbs across the table.

"Bound to be on the ten o'clock news," Miss Eldridge hooted.

32

THE HOUSE, HOWEVER JERRY-BUILT, had been many things to Mama: independence, sanctuary, self-portrait.

"House-proud," Grandma Browning called Mama, but I understood. The house meant to Mama what the cabin meant to me: refuge. Now Mama's refuge had been violated.

Weeks passed while Aunt Betty waited for Mama to begin repairing and redecorating, but she didn't. She went to work and came home. She cooked dinner and listened to the radio. When Aunt Betty reminded her about the slipper chair at Trustworthy Second Hand, Mama didn't hear.

Her torpor frightened me at first. But when August passed and it was Aunt Betty who saw to my new school clothes, I lost patience.

Mama forgot my birthday in September and went out to dinner with her friend Melba. Aunt Betty arrived home with a birthday cake just big enough for three people, a cake as lovely as a piece of jewelry, with a lark nestled among its frosting gardenias, a ribbon fluttering from his beak, bearing a trill of musical notes and the word *Lark*. An old pastry chef at the El Cortez Hotel had made it. Aunt Betty knew him from Red Cross.

After dinner, my aunt and I ate the entire cake. Then, while I cleared away dishes, she fetched my presents, gift-wrapped by Gilpins' and frou-frou'd with streamers and silk flowers.

I opened Aunt Betty's first, a glamorous manicure kit in a black cellu-loid box lined with pink satin. Nestled in the pleated satin, each in its own tiny niche, were a chamois buffer, a manicure scissors, a file with an ivory celluloid handle, and a cuticle pusher with the same.

A second package from my aunt contained a small, pink leatherette case that opened to reveal four bottles: one clear nail polish and one pale pink, one polish remover, and one cuticle remover. A cardboard tube held cotton.

"I bet these are like Alicia Armand's."

Mama—though I suspected it was really Aunt Betty—gave me a pair of black patent low-heeled slip-ons with black grosgrain bows, a pair of chrome-yellow rain boots, and a matching slicker with a hood.

"Get your bath now," Aunt Betty told me, "and then I'll give you a manicure."

When I slid onto the kitchen chair, I smelled of apple blossom bath salts and held out my right hand. "Your mama's going to be sorry when she remembers it was your birthday," my aunt said.

Would it even register? She'd become a ghost in our midst.

"Willie keeps writing, telling her he's going to have the law drag you back there." Aunt Betty was swabbing cuticle remover on each of my fingers. "Your Uncle Stanley has his faults, but he's a gentle man."

"Will you ever get back together?"

"I don't know," she said. "I used to think that if we didn't I'd get sick and die of it."

"Did you want to die?"

"Oh, yes," she said matter-of-factly.

"Did you think about killing yourself?"

"You mean like Hilly? No. I left it in God's hands."

"And now?"

Aunt Betty lifted the cuticle pusher from my manicure set. "If you don't kill yourself right away when something terrible happens—like Baby Marjorie being dead and Stanley leaving—if you go on living, you become a different person. You're always becoming a different person."

Well, Mama certainly had.

She went on. "The Betty Weller who lived in a little house in Morgan Lake is like a friend I used to know. I'm the Betty Weller who came to the city and found a job and worked her way up. And this Betty Weller doesn't want to die. Does it hurt when I pushed the cuticle back?"

"Not much. Keep going."

"I respect that old Betty," she said, "but I'm not obliged to *be* her."

· · · · · · · · · ·

I SPENT MORE AND MORE TIME with Miss Eldridge, filing documents and arranging photographs. I hoped to solve the mystery of the young man, but the "Forget. Forget. Forget." photo had disappeared and I found no more clues.

The project grew as Miss Eldridge decided to add biographical and historical notes to the pictures and documents. That was fine by me. Eventually, I wondered if Miss Eldridge had first hired me to get me out of Papa's way. No matter. I liked being with her.

But as the work neared completion, I made a mistake. I pried.

We had arranged the glossy photographs from Burning Field in proper order, Miss Eldridge had written dates and biographical notes, and I was licking the backs of the last photo corners.

"How come you don't have any pictures of your mama and papa?" I asked. Somehow I knew that this was forbidden territory, but I asked anyway. I was that perverse.

Miss Eldridge froze and the rubber cement dabber in her hand paused in its course, a tendril of goo threading off with a life of its own. "My purse is on the cupboard in the kitchen. Inside, there's fifteen dollars in a silk bag. Take it. We're done here."

33

Aunt Betty's duties at Gilpins' kept growing: searching out new sources of merchandise as old sources converted to the war effort, mediating staff disputes, spotting trends in women's fashions, and recently, traveling with buyers to acquire an over-all grasp of women's wear. All this she related over dinner, as if it were an enthralling game she was being paid to play.

Unearthing new sources owned by women—that she particularly enjoyed. "I talked with a woman today who started with a single sewing machine in her guest bedroom. It put me in mind of you," she told Mama, "when you taught yourself touch-typing on that second-hand typewriter."

Soon after my birthday, Aunt Betty left with several buyers on a ten-day junket. Rather than neglect Shirley's piano lessons, she asked me to inquire if Fanny could sit in for a couple of sessions. I stopped after school on a Monday and knocked on Fanny's door.

We had seen little of her the past two months. Around the time of Papa's visit, she had been laid up with what she laughingly called ague and la grippe. After Labor Day, she failed to return to the school office.

I was shocked when she opened the door. Above the neckline of the cyclamen-and-purple shift, the bones of her breast stood out as if some delicate structure, a birdcage perhaps, were encased by the skin.

"Lark," she said, "come in." She took my hand. Hers was cold and dry and frangible.

Cecil and Percy jumped to the floor in one of the bedrooms and a moment later waggled toward me with snorts and yips of welcome, their loose, brindle skin jiggling with pleasure.

Fanny clapped her hands and pointed to their poufy green chair. Reluctantly, they heaved themselves onto it, looking from Fanny to me and back.

"They have so little company," Fanny explained, "they forget their manners. Have a seat."

Why *not* visit? I no longer hurried to Miss Eldridge's after school. In fact, I hadn't seen her since she'd told me to take my earnings. Having caused her pain, I didn't feel right about accepting money, so I hadn't taken it, but an envelope containing fifteen dollars appeared in our mailbox the following day. I considered dropping the envelope into her mailbox, but that might compound the injury. In the end I'd stuffed the fifteen dollars into the cache behind my painting. Forty-six dollars.

"Cup of coffee?" Fanny asked, her breath insufficient.

"No, thank you." She ought to sit and rest.

"Your father was here?" She sat on a straight chair. "Jack said he thought your father had visited."

"Yes." I told her everything but hurried on to explain about Aunt Betty's trip. Before I'd concluded, Fanny said, "Shirley's lessons. I'd love to."

The prospect vivified her and she rose, insisting, "Jack brought chocolate cookies home."

While we sat at the kitchen table, Fanny pulled a deck of cards from a drawer to teach me gin rummy. After half an hour, her hands shook and beads of perspiration lay along her upper lip. I excused myself, promising to return another afternoon.

"Yes," she laughed, following me to the door, "my English friends are willing companions but dreadful conversationalists."

Waiting in the mailbox when I arrived home were letters from Papa, one for me and one for Mama. This was my third letter since his visit, and nearly identical to the others.

"I will treasure our time together," he wrote, "even though it makes it harder to come home without you."

No mention of the rampage. I felt definitely crazy reading Papa's letters.

34

"DON'T WORRY, LITTLE GIRL, your ma is coming back here, one way or another, I promise you. The Brede house is still for sale and you'll be living there before you know it."

I supposed that Papa was saying similar things to Mama.

Returning from her trip, Aunt Betty tried again to interest Mama in repairing the damage to the house. My aunt had replaced the dishes, glasses, and other items that could be purchased at Gilpins', but sewing slipcovers for the sofa and chair, painting the kitchen walls, and refinishing the bedroom floor where perfume and polish remover had spilled—Aunt Betty could not undertake all of these.

But no one could waken Mama. Her routine wore a dull path through our lives. Home from work, she washed her lunch pail, changed into a nightgown and robe, and read the mail, all in silence.

When the supper dishes had been put away, she bathed and went to bed, sometimes to read a book. As autumn slipped away, recalling the old Mama was difficult.

Aunt Betty took up some of the household slack, randomly checking my homework, maintaining our war map, and on the Saturday afternoon after Thanksgiving taking me on an expedition to Trustworthy Second Hand.

"Christmas is coming and the house looks like a POW camp," she said over her shoulder, boarding a trolley from the plaza.

The day was mild and brilliant. Even the gray ships at the navy piers looked cheerful, afloat on a glittery harbor. The camouflage canopy covering the highway outside Consolidated was like something from a war movie and put me in mind of the new Alicia Armand movie, *Children of Hell,* which Aunt Betty and I were planning to see during Christmas vacation.

The trolley trip to Trustworthy Second Hand brought back the excursion that Mama, Shirley, and I had taken more than a year ago.

"When will Mama be better?" I asked my aunt when we had found an empty space to stand.

"Maybe Christmas will pull her out of it," Aunt Betty said. "I'm going to invite some servicemen."

A Spanish-speaking man and woman stood up, preparing to alight at the next stop. Another man, this one wearing an aircraft worker's coveralls and identification badge, held the empty seat for Aunt Betty and me.

My aunt stood out in the trolley crowd, commanding the sort of glances men cast over a spiffy automobile. "Wonder who drives that beauty?" "Sure as hell wish I could afford one."

For a moment, I saw my aunt through a stranger's eyes. She wore a kelly green coat-dress, and the green set fire to her strawberry blonde hair. The pale apricot rouge and the deeper coral on her lips were soft and natural, innocent and luscious, like perfectly ripened fruit. Aunt Betty at thirty-five was no longer in the flush of youth but life was carrying her on a long, slowly rising tide toward wholeness.

Parked at the curb outside Trustworthy Second Hand was an old, green pickup truck, much battered, with bald tires and a perilous list. On the doors, "Trustworthy Second Hand—Padraic O'Faolin, Prop." was elegantly lettered.

"You have a truck," I said. "You didn't have that before."

"It's pretty often laid up with problems under the bonnet."

Problems under the bonnet.

To my aunt he lilted, "You've settled on the chest, then, have you?" I was amazed that Mr. Trustworthy knew her. To me, he said, "And your mother's sewin' machine is sewin' a fine seam?"

Although Mama had not used the machine for months, I nodded, not wishing to add to the atoms of disappointment floating in the air above the little man's head.

"And the one who was daft about horses?"

"Shirley plays the piano," my aunt told him. "The piano you sold my sister last Christmas, you remember? She's very talented." Aunt Betty headed down a side aisle.

Touched by this news of a Trustworthy orphan succeeding out in the world, Mr. Trustworthy hooked his thumbs into his vest pockets and said to me, "That last yarn of yours—about being lost in the woods— that was a corker. Will there be more?"

I nodded, blushing, and went poking among the chairs and sofas, filling my lungs with emanation of horse hair and sour kapok. Spotting a Morris chair whose arms extended into carved lion heads that were worn to a simian flatness of feature, I plopped down in it.

Closing my eyes, I explored the lion's features with my fingertips and eavesdropped on Aunt Betty and Mr. Trustworthy in the next aisle. Aunt Betty's voice was low and urgent, as if she were in a confessional. " . . . clothes in shreds . . . smashed the glass from the bookcase . . ."

The phrases were interspersed with Mr. Trustworthy's "mmhhmm" and "tsk." They talked like old friends. When had my aunt visited Mr. Trustworthy? I did recall her bringing home a bag of used piano books and, another time, a tarnished silver soup ladle.

"A Mexican divorce isn't worth the paper it's written on. I've talked to a lawyer."

Footsteps came near. "The child's dozed off," Mr. Trustworthy whispered. "Sit over here." They moved further on.

The clasp on my aunt's handbag clicked and seconds later she was blowing her nose.

"I'm afraid," she said.

Mr. Trustworthy understood the meaning of this, for he protested. "No, no. Y'r sister's a strong woman. I recall the first time she marched in here, pickin' and choosin.' I said to myself, 'There's a strong woman.'" His chuckle sounded forced.

A minute or so of silence passed before Aunt Betty cleared her throat, saying, "Well, I'd better get a move on."

"You want the bombe chest," Mr. Trustworthy said, "and did y' fancy the little slipper chair as well?"

As Aunt Betty and I were leaving, we found her purchases by the door, awaiting Lou's arrival: a graceful little chest with inlay on the drawer fronts—one of the dearest companions of Mr. Trustworthy's solitude, he said. Piled on the bombe chest were a sterling silver candy dish and a tower of dusty, leather-bound volumes, *Masters of the English Language.* Flanking it was a faded slipper chair.

At the last moment, I asked Mr. Trustworthy, "How did you get your store?"

"In a card game."

"You *won* it?"

"From a divil who called himself a *junk* dealer."

I grasped Mr. Trustworthy in a quick, clumsy embrace, inhaling Vick's, rye, and regret. "I'll be waitin' for the next installment," he called after me.

Gilpins' department store operated a restaurant, the Chateau Room, where all the waitresses were middle-aged, rosy-cheeked, and overweight in the style of Mother Goose, their elbows dimpled and their bosoms monolithic.

As they walked, their dark green uniforms whispered and their rubber soled shoes squeaked, lending the impression of a small weather system blowing through. I was impressed by the lace-trimmed white hankies waving from their breast pockets like exotic flowers, and the lace-trimmed aprons, along with lace-trimmed bits of cap secured to hair nets with bobby pins.

The lighting was discreet and the tables linen-covered. The Chateau was definitely uptown, I thought—the sort of place frequented by Nancy Drew and her father.

Bigwig store executives stopped at our table, told me they were happy to meet me, and briefly discussed business matters with Aunt Betty, whose calm manner inspired their confidence.

Aunt Betty ordered only toast and a pot of tea for her mid-afternoon lunch, and she paid little attention to these. I chose beef stroganoff, but when it came I had no appetite. Aunt Betty's conversation with Mr. Trustworthy had put me off my feed.

"I eavesdropped on you and Mr. Trustworthy," I said.

Aunt Betty poured milk into her now-cold tea. Stirring it, she said, "Your mama thinks she'll never have control of her life again. That she'd be better off dead." Stirring and stirring, she added, "That's how Stanley felt before he came to California."

I nodded, flattered and burdened by my aunt's taking me into her confidence. She was saying, *You're eleven now. It's time for you to assume the responsibility of this knowledge.*

"If Stanley had stayed in Morgan Lake," my aunt continued, "he'd have killed himself with drink. If he'd found the money."

And he'd have found the money next door at the German woman's, where he'd gone the night Baby Marjorie was born dead.

But that was a long time ago.

What Aunt Betty was saying now was, *We have to treat your mother with care. She's got problems under the bonnet.*

35

MAMA SPENT SUNDAY MORNING with the newspaper, at one point noting in a pale, boneless voice, "Tarawa. How do you pronounce that? It doesn't matter, I suppose, except that so many boys have died there."

And later, "Bougainville. Wouldn't you think that was a town in France instead of a God-forsaken island in the Pacific?" To be absorbed in battles was to construct a rickety wall between herself and Papa's presence.

When Lou had delivered the bombe chest the previous afternoon, Mama took no notice of the purchases but wanted only to hear about Woodrow in Italy.

"Do you hear often?"

"Often as he can write. He was at Salerno."

Now Aunt Betty said, "I wish you'd look at those fabrics and see what you think." Aunt Betty and I had carted home fabrics from Gilpins', one for curtains, another for the slipper chair.

Mama glanced at them. "They're nice," she said and turned back to the battles in the newspaper.

. . . .

A KIND OF RELIGIOUS FERVOR surrounded Aunt Betty's devotion to Shirley's Sunday lessons. "Nothing about Shirley explains her feeling for music," my aunt said with wonder. "It's a gift from God, a vocation." Aunt Betty attended early Mass so that she could get the hand laundry, ironing, shoe polishing, and other chores out of the way by two o'clock.

Now two o'clock came but Shirley did not. Waiting, Aunt Betty sat at the piano and played from a book of Bach inventions.

I slacked about the house, falling into a Sunday torpor, finally picking up a book from the Trustworthy Second Hand pile. Sprawling on the sofa, I tasted of the Romantic poets, their words singing and flying around my head like swooping birds.

Around two-thirty, Aunt Betty stopped playing and glanced at her watch. Shirley was half an hour late. Usually she appeared early, pounding to be let in.

Rising from the piano, my aunt stepped out the door and wandered down the walk. From the living room window I watched her head up the hill, casting her eye between the houses, combing the monotony for the contrary detail: Shirley.

Ten minutes later she returned. "I finally knocked at the house number you gave me," she told Mama. "I knocked and knocked. No one answered. They were in there. I heard a woman's voice." She turned to me. "Are you sure she didn't say anything about missing her lesson?"

I shook my head.

Still later, she asked, with what seemed like suspicion, "You don't know anything about this?"

"No," I snapped.

But gradually I too wondered: Where was Shirley—she who snatched any opportunity to elbow her way into our house? Another hour passed. Aunt Betty said, "I didn't mean to sound accusing."

"It's all right."

"I don't know why I'm so worried about Shirley, but I have a peculiar feeling."

"I do too."

"Tomorrow at school, find out what happened."

But Shirley wasn't at school on Monday. A prickly feeling crept over me when I saw her empty desk.

At recess, I pulled a cloudy red marble from my pocket and joined three girls playing a marbles game.

"Shirley's absent today," I observed.

No one said anything.

"Whaddya think's wrong with her?"

Bent over the game, they murmured, "Who cares?"

36

W HEN S HIRLEY FINALLY SHOWED UP at school, she looked like pictures I'd seen of Billy Conn after thirteen rounds with Joe Louis. Although she wore a long-sleeved shirt buttoned up to the neck, her face was bruised and scabbed, her eyes swollen nearly shut. Her legs below her cut-off trousers were scratched and on the left shin was a knot the size of a pullet egg.

A whispered conference with the teacher, who held Shirley by the arm and looked her up and down, led to Shirley's being sent to the office in the company of a second child to present her excuse slip to the attendance clerk.

Although Shirley was not popular, she was surrounded at recess. Even the boys crowded in, asking what had happened.

"None of yer business."

"Come onnn, Shirley."

"Fell down a cliff at the beach."

"Really?" A respectful hush ensued.

"A guy who sorta looked like a Jap pushed me," she elaborated, "but I didn't get a good look at him."

A subtle jittering stirred the little flock. Girls hiked up their anklets and scratched sand-flea bites. Boys scuffed their oxfords in the dust and one or two sniggered.

"I hit a bunch of rocks."

A third grader standing at the edge of the group covered her mouth and turned away as if she had this very minute witnessed the terrible event.

"Couldn't even get outta bed yesterday," Shirley boasted, smiling. She was missing a front tooth.

I too turned away. If I'd been hurt like that, Mama would have kept me home for a week.

. . . .

BECAUSE OF RED CROSS, I didn't see Aunt Betty until the next morning, when she stood at the kitchen counter alternately blowing on her fingernails and her tea.

Pouring milk into a bowl of Kix, I relayed the news of Shirley's accident, concluding, "I don't believe her."

"Why is that?" Aunt Betty handed me a spoon.

"I don't know."

"Was it the part about someone who looked Japanese?"

"Partly."

"She probably threw that in for drama," my aunt said.

"Even so, I don't believe her. What can we do?"

"If she swears it was an accident, I don't see what we can do, except be extra good to her."

Swell.

That night at dinner, Mama told Aunt Betty, "Willie's been to see Reggie Albers."

"Who's that?"

"A lawyer in Harvester. Willie says I'll be hearing from him."

"You mean he might give you a divorce?"

"No. He wants Lark."

"He's said that before."

"This time he sent along a cancelled check made out to Albers. When Willie spends money on a lawyer, he's serious."

Trudging up Piñon from school the next afternoon, I spotted Cecil and Percy, running loose and dragging their leashes. Grabbing up the leads, I went looking for Fanny.

Since that day on the monkey bars, I hadn't ventured up along this end of the street, but today I was accompanied by two ferocious-looking English bulldogs.

Three blocks up, someone was sprawled on the grass next to the sidewalk, a splash of brilliant pink against the green.

"So you found the little men," Fanny rasped.

"Did you fall?" I asked, thinking she had twisted an ankle.

She laughed briefly and began to cough, shaking her head to let me know that she was all right. Finally she said, "I just gave out like a leaky barrage balloon."

"Can you walk?"

She nodded and began pushing herself up. "I'm better now. The little men wore me out."

I let go of the leashes and got behind Fanny. Despite her assurances, she was wobbly. Then she leaned on my shoulder and waited for the earth to steady itself. Her bony hand gave me a squeeze and we began our descent, her ferocious little men meek and anxious.

37

Leading Cecil and Percy out for a Saturday morning walk, Jack caught sight of me bent over Mama's gardenia bush.

"Lark," he called, "got a minute?"

I emptied the remaining water from the lard pail.

"I'd like to hire you, if I can, to take Cecil and Percy for a trot after school. Just week days. On the weekend, I can take them." He pulled at the dogs, who were digging in the daisies. "Would a dollar and a quarter a week seem fair?"

I pumped his hand.

Tugging the leashes and leading the dogs down to the street, he called back, "Starting Monday."

Sprinting into the house, I flicked on the radio and danced a jig. For a year and a half I'd been a prisoner. No more. Five days a week, I would walk two murderous-looking dogs.

A dollar and a quarter a week. With this and my allowance, I could buy *two* twenty-five cent defense stamps every week. And put a dollar into my running-away cache.

While I jubilated, Shirley arrived for Saturday practice.

"Shirley, guess what! I've got a job!"

She let the door slam behind her.

"Isn't that great? A dollar and a quarter a week, do you believe it?"

She turned off the radio, sat down at the piano, and began shuffling through the music books. This was her first session since the accident.

"Just for walking Fanny and Jack's dogs. I'll be almost rich by next summer."

Ignoring me, she launched a difficult run of scales. Although note-perfect, the playing was violent.

Swishing the cloth across the top of the piano and running the mop around the bare floor, I went about my business. The mailman came and went, leaving me a letter from my friend Sally in Harvester. I carried it to the kitchen, made a sandwich, and sat down to read.

> Dear Lark,
>
> Mommy is still in St. Peter (the mental hospital) but we hope she'll be home by next summer.
>
> Daddy still teaches history and coaches baseball. He helps with other sports, but baseball is his big responsibility.
>
> Beverly and I both miss you. And Mrs. Stillman always talks about you and wonders how you are. She would love to get a letter from you if you have the time.
>
> We had our school pictures taken. Mine is hideous but I'm sending you one anyway. You can throw darts at it if you want. Have you got a picture you could send me?
>
> Your friend forever even after death,
> Sally Wheeler

I stared at Sally's picture. She was prettier than ever. Grown-up look-ing, despite her lovely black plaits. When she cut those off, I wished that she would send me one.

The piano fell silent and Shirley stood by the table. She looked like a character from a horror movie, yellow and purple patches smeared over her freckles. Was she waiting for me to ask if she wanted something to eat? Why couldn't I be Christian?

Instead of inviting her to eat, I said, "I got a letter from my friend

Sally in Minnesota. She sent me her picture." I slid it across the oilcloth. "Doesn't she look like Hedy Lamarr?"

Darting like a hummingbird, she lunged for the picture and letter, tearing them into pieces.

38

"I GOT A LETTER from Stanley today," my aunt began.

Mama lowered herself onto a chair. "And?" She crossed her arms, grasping her shoulders, one with each hand, as if protecting herself.

"He enlisted in the army," Aunt Betty said, measuring the words out. "He's finishing boot camp and we'll see him for a few days at Christmas." After four years.

My impulse was to jump up and down.

"Why?" Mama whispered.

"He wants to see me . . . us."

"No. Why did he enlist? He didn't have to. He's not a kid." Mama sounded angry with Uncle Stanley for doing something she had sworn he was too cowardly to do.

"He's got to prove something."

"To who?"

"To everyone, I guess. He's never really known how to make up for the baby and for leaving."

"So he's going to make up for leaving by leaving again?" Mama spat the words out.

Aunt Betty answered, "He says that joining up is like a penance for running away, and when he's paid his penance he'll be free to come back, to . . . to ask me to marry him again." She lifted a hand and let it drop.

"You're *already* married!"

"It's a manner of speaking, Arlene."

"And you're going to let him do this? Go off and get killed for a damned Catholic guilt that's like something out of a nineteenth-century novel?"

"He's already done it."

Like a splash of cold water in her face, the news of Uncle Stanley's enlistment woke Mama abruptly from her long sleep. But I wasn't sure which was more alarming, Mama asleep or Mama awake. Now, after a day at the plant, she rushed home to work late into the night, repairing and painting over the damage Papa had caused; scrubbing the living room rug till the last traces of ketchup were gone; sewing slipcovers for the wounded sofa, the rose chair, and the new second-hand slipper chair; running up new curtains.

A set of pale green guest towels appeared on the towel bar behind the bathtub, and above the sofa Mama hung a gilt-framed mirror from Trustworthy Second Hand, lending the illusion of a larger room, as promised by *Good Housekeeping*.

Fetching the dogs one afternoon, I mentioned to Fanny our whirlwind of decorating and repairing. That evening she appeared at the door, bearing a pair of tall silver candlesticks tied with red bows.

"If you insist on dressing this place up," she said.

"We couldn't," Mama demurred.

"Don't be absurd. I have another pair." She thrust them into Mama's hands.

"Come in," Mama said. "It's cold out."

"Only a minute." Shoulders rising, rising, rising as she sucked in air, Fanny lowered herself to the piano bench. "My God," she breathed, casting an eye around, "Who's coming, the Duke of Windsor?"

"The place was a mess after Willie left, and Christmas is coming," Mama explained.

"I thought I heard something about Uncle Stanley," Fanny said, glancing from Mama to Aunt Betty.

I ran to fetch Aunt Betty's old photograph of Uncle Stanley standing by the Model A, smiling his seductive 1937 smile. She gave it a long, speculative look.

"A fine-looking man. Looks a little like Ray Milland."

"I used to think he looked like Leslie Howard," Aunt Betty offered.

"Or maybe Gary Cooper," Mama said, taking the photo from Fanny and studying it.

"A fine-looking man," Fanny repeated.

Still holding the picture, Mama returned to the sofa. Glancing around the transformed room, she said, "None of this is for Stanley." But of course it was.

Then she seemed to lose her place. Seconds passed. "I . . . I'm sorry he's enlisted," she said. "He's too old to be marching around with boys. And too young to die."

39

I HOPED WE'D PUT SHIRLEY on the back burner while we prepared for Uncle Stanley's visit, but Aunt Betty wouldn't hear of it. In fact, she was scouting around for a teacher with impressive credentials to hear Shirley play and offer advice.

As for myself, I had paper chains to cut and paste, popcorn to string, and Christmas cards to design. At school, we were making pincushions and 1944 calendars, so I had a gift for Mama and one for Aunt Betty but nothing for Uncle Stanley and Papa. I liked Aunt Betty's idea: men's combs in fancy, hand-sewn felt sheaths.

On a card for Mr. Trustworthy, I drew a map of Ireland copied from a book an air force captain gave me when he came to Easter dinner. I was no better at drawing than at playing the piano and I didn't really know what Ireland had to do with Christmas, but Mr. Trustworthy would appreciate the thought. Inside I wrote, "I wish this card was Grandma Brownings sugar cookies and divinity. All I've got to send you is x's and o's, so here's a hundred. P.S. I'll send you a story for New Years."

Listening to *Terry and the Pirates* on the radio while I worked was impossible, because the air was filled with an explosion of scales and exercises, increasingly sophisticated inventions, ballades, waltzes, and so on. And it did no good to complain. Aunt Betty was convinced that Shirley was a prodigy. On the Wednesday before Christmas vacation, I took Cecil and Percy out for the usual half-hour walk. Instead of scampering up Piñon, the dogs and I climbed the grassy slope lying to the east of my house, the same slope where Papa had stood staring down last summer.

A far wider and more absorbing landscape was visible from here than from our house below. In the harbor to the south, tiny warships rode like toys in a bathtub. Buses came and went along Garnet. But I turned north, leading the dogs to the northernmost rim of this level, where it fell away into an arroyo.

The dogs whined and strained, lunging toward the arroyo. Finally, they turned to bark at me reprovingly. Rabbits played among the rocks and scrub oaks down below, yet here we stood.

I had to drag Cecil and Percy, mewling like babies, back to where we descended the slope to our building. When I had returned them to Fanny, a Chopin etude greeted me at our stoop. Ripply-rapply, the notes tumbled along like water down a hillside, somersaulting over me, past me, into the thirsty air. Between the mailbox and the siding, a heavy gray postcard had been shoved. I pulled it out.

On one side was a photo of a plump woman, naked except for her high-buttoned shoes. Spread-eagled on a bed, she was mounted by a naked man. Observing were two old-timish men with dark mustaches and a second woman, also naked.

Printed on the lined paper was "Lark Airheart," with an arrow pointing to the woman on the bed.

I had to sit down. What did it *mean?* Why were the people naked and what was the man doing on top of the woman? Why was she tied to the bed and *why* was she smiling?

Then I thought, *The boys know my name.*

I hurried into the house, blindly fetching the box of Christmas projects. One by one I lifted out the jar of paste, the scissors, the ruler, the pencil. Slipping down onto a chair, I began marking off lines on a sheet of green construction paper.

Inside my sweater, the photograph pressed against my ribs, squeezing the little-girlness out of me. Naked people in a dim room. It was about something terrible. But what?

I was unaware of the piano music or its absence until Shirley said, "I got the curse."

"What?"

"I said, 'I got the curse,'" she shouted at me, reaching for the jar of strawberry jelly in the icebox.

"What's that mean, you got the curse? What curse?" Had she too received a photograph of naked people?

Sitting down at the table to enjoy her jelly sandwich, she said, "The curse is when you start bleeding."

My God. "Bleeding?" Was it a stigmata? "Where are you bleeding?"

"From my ass, where d'ya think?"

I didn't want to hear any more. But knowing this, she was determined to tell me everything. "You'll bleed pretty soon."

"No!" I covered my ears.

"When you're twelve or so, you get a pain in your belly and then the blood starts. And then you can have babies," she shouted, pulling my hands away from my ears, her hands very strong. "And you have to wear Kotex!"

Behind Shirley's thunder was a sense of betrayal, in this case betrayal by her own body. Like me, Shirley had assumed that her body was a faithful servant in whom trust was placed without a thought. Now her body had become an *other*, terrifying her with blood, not from an explainable wound but from an interior mystery. The only good thing about it was the opportunity to shock me.

"Your ma bleeds," she said, "and so does your aunt."

"They do not."

"All girls bleed."

Why hadn't I been told? It was true that brown paper-wrapped boxes of Kotex occupied a corner of the linen closet. But so incurious had I been about their use that only vague, unpursued notions having to do with perspiration or sore feet attached to them.

Why hadn't Mama shared the secret? Was it so terrible that it had to be suppressed until it overtook you?

"Are you always going to bleed now?" I needed to know this. If I was going to bleed my whole life, well, I didn't see how I could go on.

"Once a month."

"Just one day?" I could probably endure that.

"Hell, no," Shirley said, picking up the partially eaten sandwich. "You got the thing for about a week."

The fortitude required to be a woman was, I feared, beyond me. But now I needed to know something else. "What did you mean, 'And then you can have babies'?"

Shirley finished the sandwich and rose to fetch a glass of milk. She would play me like a hooked sunfish, taking her time with the milk, drinking it all down.

"You know what fucking is?"

"It's a swear word."

"It's when a guy puts his thing in you," she said.

"His thing?"

"His weenie, you jerk."

"He puts it in *where?*"

"Down below, where your hole is, where you pee."

"No. That's not possible," I whispered.

Someplace close by, Shirley was jawing on, "He puts his thing in you and you maybe get knocked up—get a baby. For Chrissake, you are the dumbest door knob I ever knew. . . ."

I didn't hear most of the rest. Suddenly my whole head was stuffed with cotton. A person can only listen to so much. But I did hear her say ". . . hurts like hell . . ."

40

AT SCHOOL THE NEXT DAY, I groped through the hours, seeing pictures I didn't want to see: a naked woman on a bed, a man on top of her. Was she going to get a baby? What if she didn't want a baby?

At this very minute, two rows away, Shirley was bleeding. Did Miss Braun know that? Did those who bled sense each another's condition? When I began bleeding, I'd stay home.

If it were very painful, you'd want to be at home anyway. Why wasn't Shirley at home? She didn't look to be in great pain. But with Shirley you couldn't tell. After falling down the cliff, she had come to school.

"Hurts like hell," she'd said. But no, that had been something else—a man putting his thing in a woman. Was this the only way you could get a baby? If so, then Papa and Mama. . . . I lay my head on my arms.

Miss Braun was standing over me, asking, "Don't you feel well?"

I shook my head.

"Would you like to go to the office and lie down till lunch?"

She wrote me a pass and I marched off, down the wooden portico to the office. The sun shone on the dusty quad and the little breezes teased the flag hanging in the middle of the courtyard, flinging its grommeted edge against the iron pole with a dull, metallic lament.

. . . .

WHEN I STOPPED AT FANNY'S after school to fetch the dogs, she said, "Jack picked up this applesauce cake yesterday. The frosting's an inch thick. If you don't help me, I'll end up having to throw it away." I didn't feel like eating, but she had asked out of loneliness.

She shuffled away. I followed with Cecil and Percy prancing around my feet, reminding me that I was there to walk them.

"What day is your uncle coming?" She cut a huge hunk of cake and set it before me.

"Next Wednesday, I think."

"What do you think will happen?" she wondered, handing me a cup of tea and milk.

I was flattered that she would ask me that sort of gossipy question, as if I were a girlfriend.

"Uncle Stanley is handsome and a good dancer," I said by way of reply, although it wasn't really an answer.

I hadn't seen my uncle since Baby Marjorie's funeral, when he had picked me up and given me a hug. The kind of hug in which the hugger forgets that he's hugging you and you wonder if he'll ever put you down but you don't say anything because he's sad and wondering how he'll make it through the week. You are a pillow. You cannot do anything real to help but you can let him lay his head on you. If Uncle Stanley had hugged me all afternoon, I wouldn't have said a thing. And that was how people felt about him.

"Except Mama," I told Fanny, concluding my recitation.

Fanny refilled our teacups and tucked a strand of hair into the scarf wrapped around her head. Beneath the scarf, she was now completely gray.

Her hands, grasping the teacup with their long, thin fingers, looked like the delicate tracery of winter-bare vines.

Out of the blue, Fanny said, "The day before he died, my brother Pat and I had a terrible fight. About Jack. Pat warned me against Jack. We had a screaming go-round in my parents' dining room. I slapped his face and called him a selfish, capitalist sonofabitch. The next day he was killed. I never had a chance to tell him that I loved him even if he was a capitalist sonofabitch."

"Don't you think your brother knew?"

"I feel like I pulled the trigger."

"But you're a good person, Fanny."

"Don't comfort me."

"Why?" I asked, confused.

"When you've done a terrible thing, you don't want comfort. What you want is punishment and, someday, absolution."

Absolution. I knew that word from catechism, but it was no good reminding her that she hadn't done anything terrible and that she had been punished enough.

"Christ," she drawled, "it's five o'clock. I've kept you sitting here listening to this drivel, you poor baby." She reached for the dog leashes lying on the counter.

Hesitating, leather leads twisted in her hands, Fanny closed her eyes. "The point I intended to make was, it's an awful business, sending someone away without forgiveness."

I led Cecil and Percy up the slope and along the verge again, the same route we'd taken yesterday. The day was thinning down toward evening and growing raw. I buttoned my corduroy jacket and ran with the dogs to keep warm. The salty ocean breeze carried the citrus-y tang of eucalyptus trees blocks away.

Because of the chill knifing through my jacket, we didn't tarry but made our way, full tilt, wind at our backs, to the rim of the arroyo, where the dogs did their duty. Then, turning about, we headed back, all of us breathing hard, our breath visible on the moist, cold air.

Enough pale light lingered so that I could see people up and down the length of Piñon, returning from the day shift. I spotted Shirley, hastening home from piano practice, hands thrust deep into the pockets of a man's rusty-looking suit jacket. She was approaching the first rising curve in Piñon, arms held tight against her body to keep out the cold.

I pulled the dogs up and stood watching. When she had rounded the curve, she broke into a sprint. I moved north again to keep her in sight.

Veering left, she peered behind her before leaping up the steps of one of the houses, disappearing so quickly, it was like a conjuring trick.

Now, I thought, *I know where Shirley lives.*

Shirley who is bleeding.

41

As usual, Shirley ruined Saturday morning. No *Let's Pretend* or *Grand Central Station* on the radio, not with her piano pandemonium.

Fortunately, Mama returned from work at one and asked Shirley kindly to cease and desist. She, Mama, had to think. Handing me her purse to set on the bureau, she directed me to bring her a pencil and paper.

Shirley did a slow sweep into the kitchen, like a peacock, altogether certain of her worth and privileges. Helping herself to half a dozen gingersnaps, she poured a glass of milk in which to dunk them.

"Your aunt's getting me a real piano teacher," she informed me, sucking milk from a cookie that was in danger of transmogrifying (page 1061 of *Webster's*) into a handful of dog poop. "She's taking me to La Jolla tonight on the bus to play for some old lady who used to give concerts *all over the world.*"

"That's nothing," I said. "She's taking me to the movies tomorrow. We're going to see Alicia Armand."

Shirley laughed so hard, she dribbled cookie mush out the corners of her mouth. "You think *that's* important? Listen to this. Your aunt says someday I'll be playing concerts in places like England and . . . Chicago. People will pay money to hear me."

As I started to leave, she called over her shoulder, "Bet if I ask her, your aunt'll take me to the movie, too."

"Lark," Mama waylaid me. "Here's a list of chores you're to do before Wednesday."

"Can't Shirley do something? She eats us out of house and home and never even says please or thank-you."

"You let *me* worry about that, young lady," Mama snapped.

"It's not fair. If I did the things she does, you'd be mad at me all the time! But she does them when you can't see."

"When I do see, I'll get after her, don't worry. In the meantime, try not to be jealous."

"Of *her?* She's mean, ugly, and stupid."

Mama gripped my arm so tightly I would have a bruise. "Don't let me hear you talk that way again, do you understand?"

"No, I don't understand." My face was hot and I was trembling.

"She doesn't have the privileges you have."

"Privileges? I already did my Saturday chores while she was pounding the piano. What are *these?*" I held up the list. "You don't even like Uncle Stanley. What the hell is this all about?"

The hard slap across my face startled Mama as much as it did me, but she did not apologize. Rather, the slap forced her more deeply into the quarrel. "How dare *you* accuse Shirley of being mean? I don't know you when you're like this."

Tossing the list of chores on the floor, I shrieked, "You don't know me, period!"

. . . .

ALTHOUGH AUNT BETTY seemed perfectly calm and self-governing the next day when we took the bus into town, I felt certain that, inside, her vitals were stretched tight as violin strings and that thoughts of Uncle Stanley played upon them.

But instead of talking about my uncle, she spoke about the previous night's trip to La Jolla with Shirley. "Madame Buchova's the kind of person who says, 'If you practiced day and night for the next twenty years, you *might* make a so-so pianist.' And that's praise," Aunt Betty added.

"Is that what she told Shirley?"

"More or less."

"What did Shirley wear?" I could imagine her in her too-big man's shirt and out-at-the-knees trousers, swaggering into Madame Buchova's house.

"I bought her an outfit," Aunt Betty confessed. "She was so nervous about the audition, I didn't think she should worry about her clothes too."

Shirley nervous? That would be the day.

"I told her the outfit was a Christmas present," Aunt Betty said, "and since she had it, why didn't she wear it to Madame Buchova's? Shirley's very proud and thin-skinned. So you have to be careful not to insult her, not to make her feel . . . like a beggar."

Yah, sure.

"I'm sorry you didn't feel like supper last night," Aunt Betty went on. "You'd have seen Shirley in her dress. I hope you won't mention that I told you this. Well, of course you won't. You're too kind and grown-up."

"How did Shirley do?" I asked, hoping with half my heart that she'd failed miserably and with the other half that she'd excelled. She was a brat, but she was Aunt Betty's brat.

"Well, at first she was stiff—she sounded like a player piano. But she sat so tall and proud, I wanted to cry. And the worse she played, the taller she sat.

"Madame Buchova leaned over and whispered to me, 'Is she going to levitate?' and I burst out laughing. It was nerves, but I couldn't help myself. I wanted to slit my own throat.

"Of course, Shirley thought we were laughing at her. She thought she'd failed. Suddenly she relaxed. What did she have to lose? The rest of the pieces went beautifully, and Madame Buchova is taking her as a pupil." Aunt Betty put a hand to her mouth in a gesture of awe. "Isn't it wonderful?"

. . . .

IN *THE CHILDREN FROM HELL,* which Aunt Betty and I saw that afternoon, Alicia Armand played a French doctor, Monique Savonne, who spirits Jewish children out of Europe. In the end, she is herself captured and tortured by the Gestapo. A young German officer who falls in love with her passes her a capsule of poison and she dies in his arms. In the stirring final scene, the camera finds the young officer smoking a last cigarette before facing a firing squad.

Afterward, to prevent people on the bus from seeing my puffy eyes, I gawked out the window, my lips forming Alicia Armand's lines, "Zah cheeldrain! We muzt save zah cheeldrain!"

42

BECAUSE OF CHRISTMAS VACATION, I collected the dogs at noon on Wednesday and we ran along the incline before flying home to greet Uncle Stanley, who was expected sometime before supper.

The house had never looked so grand, everything polished and festive, paper chains hanging around the doors and windows. We would buy a tree on Friday, Christmas Eve day.

Of course Shirley had been hanging around the house all week, preparing for her first lesson with Madame Buchova, which was two weeks from Saturday. Out of morbid curiosity, I had asked Aunt Betty how much Madame Buchova charged. "Well . . . we haven't worked it out yet." It must be plenty.

After returning Cecil and Percy to Fanny, I lazed in a bubble bath, then washed and braided my hair, dabbed Mama's Tabu behind my ears, and painted my nails with pink polish.

Pleading a headache at work, Mama arrived home an hour early. "Well, I remembered that we were out of potatoes, and Betty wanted baked potatoes with the meatloaf," she said, hurrying to the kitchen with her lunch pail and purchases, which included not only potatoes but also four stemmed glasses and two bottles of Cresta Blanca wine.

We flung a sheet over the table for a cloth and I laid the plates and flatware while Mama washed and polished the wine glasses. "Don't they sparkle?" she said, holding them to the light like someone in an ad for Rinso.

She began scrubbing potatoes and directing me, "Fetch Fanny's candlesticks from the bookcase and set them on the table. And be sure to fold the paper napkins catty-corner. Wiping her hands on a tea towel, she moaned, "Paper's so low class." Then, "You didn't set a place for Shirley?"

"Do I have to?"

"Yes."

"Why?"

"For your aunt's sake. She's going to be all nerves. Think how long it's been."

"What's Shirley got to do with it?"

"The more people are around, the easier it'll be. For everyone."

"I'm sick of sharing my family with Shirley. She's got a family of her own."

"Has she?" Mama said.

Later, I lounged against the sill of the living room window, watching an early sunset exploding like an incendiary bomb.

Behind me, Shirley played a melody of unearthly beauty. The room was full of it the way a pool is full of water. Clinging to a scrap of sill, drifting on Shirley's music, I swung slowly about to look at her and saw someone I didn't know, a girl who contained magic.

Turning back to the window, I glimpsed a pale gray car with a Christmas tree riding in the rumble seat. The car pulled up close to the grass. "Mama, it's Uncle Stanley!"

I had worried that I might feel shy when I saw my uncle. Instead, I sprinted to the street and threw my arms around him even as he climbed from the car. "I'm so glad you're here!"

He hugged me hard, then lifted me, setting me on the fender. "You're grown up," he said, a note of sadness in his voice. "And a looker!"

His words heated my cheeks and warmed my heart, although I knew they were malarkey. Mama always said that Uncle Stanley sliced the baloney pretty thick.

I studied this new Uncle Stanley. The army-clipped curls were graying but still embraced his head like a tight cap. The high, curved brow was maybe a bit higher, but it bespoke the same unpinched nature. The long nose was finely chiseled and the mouth sensuous. From the corners of his eyes, fine lines radiated, but the clear blue had a new steadiness.

He set me down on the street, casting an eye around the Project. "Looks like you women did all right for yourselves."

I grabbed my uncle's hand. "Wait'll you see inside."

"If you carry my bag, I'll get the tree," he said, opening the passenger door and hauling out a duffle bag. "When did you start wearing braids?"

Leave it to Uncle Stanley to notice!

"A few months ago."

"They suit you." He winked and tossed me the duffle bag.

"Betty said you didn't have a tree yet," Uncle Stanley told Mama when we reached the door. It was the right thing to say, sidestepping the usual greetings, which would have to include how long it had been since we'd seen each other.

Mama had changed into a pair of tan twill slacks and a short-sleeved red sweater, and she held the door, saying, "What a beautiful tree, Stanley. Come in. It looks freshly cut. And doesn't it smell wonderful? Here, let's put it, well, let's see, where? Lark, get the tree stand and we'll put it in front of the window."

Although she hadn't had a drink, a nimbus of excitement surrounded Mama and her cheeks were lit with more than rouge. Her fervor helped us negotiate the awkwardness of the first moments.

Shirley was introduced to Uncle Stanley. "Our piano prodigy," Mama said. "Betty's been giving her lessons, but Shirley's starting with a new teacher after the first of the year. A concert pianist, if you please," Mama noted.

Uncle Stanley took Shirley's hand. "My own musical talent you could stick in your ear and never notice a loss of hearing," he told her, "but Betty says you'll be playing Carnegie Hall."

"Would you like a drink or tea or anything?" Mama asked.

"What I'd really like, Arlene, is to get into civvies. We have to wear the uniform in public, but I've got comfortable gear in my bag."

Mama showed Uncle Stanley to her room, turned on the light, and closed the door. "If you want to wash your face or anything," she called through the door, "the bathroom's just around the corner. The green towels over the tub are yours."

I was proud of Mama for the way she was treating Uncle Stanley, for her softness because he was going to war.

"Isn't this a beautiful tree?" she said again, rubbing needles between her fingers and sniffing the scent on her hand. In the kitchen, she lit the oven, shoved the potatoes in, and slipped the pan of meatloaf in beside them.

Dinner was as gay and as civilized as a Greer Garson movie. Even Shirley was courteous and a bit cowed, aware for once of the meaning of please and thank-you. Mama had been right about asking Shirley. With five at the table, there weren't any embarrassing silences during which the grown-ups could recall grievances. Shirley kept Uncle Stanley occupied for long periods, asking about the army and what he did in it.

Basic training behind him, Uncle Stanley was heading east to train as a medical corpsman, he said.

Why that, Shirley asked. After all, shooting Japs and Krauts seemed to her the highest of callings.

Maybe it was because he was an old man, Uncle Stanley said. Maybe you reached an age where killing somebody seemed like a punk idea.

Shirley sniggered at the notion that Uncle Stanley was old. He wasn't as old as her pa, and she guessed her pa would love to shoot somebody.

Aunt Betty spoke least, although she studied Uncle Stanley with a tender pride.

After the butter brickle ice cream and Rice Krispie bars, Mama said, "Lark, you and Shirley will do the dishes."

As I washed and Shirley wiped, we didn't say much. My relatives were the only thing about me that interested her.

In the living room, Mama was asking Uncle Stanley about his parents back in Minnesota. He was stopping to see them on his way east, he said. His father had fallen on an icy doorstep and thrown his back out, but his mother was working at the Northern States Power Company, helping out during the war.

"Ma was provoked when she heard I'd enlisted," he said.

"You're an only child," Mama pointed out. "And beyond the age where you'd likely be drafted."

Silence. Then, "Not being able to make a living is about the worst thing that can happen to a person."

Where was he going with this? Mama must have tried to say something because Uncle Stanley said, "Let me finish, Arlene."

I handed Shirley a wet plate.

"When a man is asked to believe in something, like capitalism, and the system turns its back on him, he feels like a dupe. That's how I felt, how I still feel. I feel guilty for what I put Betty through, but I feel God-damned mad for what the system put me through."

Capitalism? What was that? Uncle Stanley never talked this way back in Morgan Lake.

"I've met some pretty savvy guys in L.A., a lot smarter than me—writers and college professors, people who've been around. They feel like I do."

"If you're that bitter," Mama said, "and I'm not saying you don't have a right, then why enlist?"

"If I'm a decent corpsman, well, there ought to be some self-respect in that. Anyway, I sure as hell wouldn't want to substitute fascism for capitalism, don't get me wrong."

"What would you want?" Mama asked.

"Some sort of socialism," he answered without hesitation. "Some system where the big companies are partly owned by the workers instead of the moneybags who don't know the first damned thing about them except how to squeeze the last nickel out of them and the last drop of blood out of the sucker who's doing the dirty work."

Shirley dried the final pot. I wrung out the dish cloth and wiped off the stove top. In the living room, a silence—not so much uneasy as puzzled—followed Uncle Stanley's speech.

"But Stanley," Aunt Betty said, "people are making good money now, more than they've ever made."

"And how long do you figure that'll last? Till the war's over, maybe a decade or so after, till the S.O.B.s find a way to put the screws on."

Mama voted Democrat, I knew, but I hadn't a notion about Aunt Betty's politics. Uncle Stanley's radical talk took their breath away.

"Hollywood's changed you," Mama observed with a note of admiration.

Later, she made up the sofa bed while Uncle Stanley brushed his teeth in the bathroom. "You're sleeping on the sofa bed?" I asked Mama. "I thought Uncle Stanley would sleep there. Papa did."

"That was different. I . . . don't feel like your papa's wife anymore, so I don't sleep with him."

In bed, I opened a Nancy Drew. You never heard Carson Drew say that his country had turned its back on him, or that he was Goddamned mad at what capitalism had done to him. But of course, the Drews were well-heeled.

I had read a couple of chapters when Mama knocked and opened the door. "Turn out the light."

"It's only ten o'clock. And it's Christmas vacation."

"Turn out the light and go to sleep."

"Why?"

"People need privacy."

"What do you mean?"

"Couldn't you do what you're told, just once, without a song and dance?" She was vexed but trying to keep her voice down.

I sat staring after her. People need privacy? I wasn't bothering anyone.

Oh, God. I lay Nancy Drew aside, snapped off the light, and thrust my head under the pillow, trying not to think of Uncle Stanley on top of Aunt Betty, putting his thing in her.

43

WHEN SHIRLEY SHOWED UP around ten the next morning, Uncle Stanley was still sleeping. I was at the kitchen table with the morning paper spread out in front of me.

Peeling herself an orange, Shirley asked, "Your uncle still sleeping?"

"Yes."

"How long's he staying?"

"Till Monday, I think."

"That all?"

I nodded, turning a page. American bombers on Attu had attacked military targets in the Kuril Islands. That was good. But the Japanese had bombed Kunming in Yunnan, preparing for an offensive against India. That was not good.

"He has to visit his parents in Minnesota on his way back east."

"You think he'll be going to the zoo or Belmont?"

"I don't know."

"I bet he and your aunt did it last night."

"No, they didn't."

"How would *you* know?"

"I stayed up all night reading Nancy Drew."

She cackled derisively at my lie. "I bet your aunt could hardly walk this morning."

"How do *you* know about the pain?"

"If you were any dumber, they'd have to get you a dog license," she said, tossing orange peels in the sink.

Hearing Uncle Stanley running water in the tub, I folded the newspaper and set a place for him at the table. Mama had instructed me to make him four fried eggs, three slices of toast, jam, tomato juice, tea, and anything else he wanted.

Twenty minutes later, dressed in civilian clothes and looking rested, Uncle Stanley sat down to breakfast and spread a paper napkin across his lap. "I'd forgotten what a real bed feels like."

I kept my eyes on the plate I was setting before him and hoped he had nothing more to say about beds.

After pouring him a cup of tea, I sat down. "Uncle Stanley, did you ever meet Alicia Armand? The movie actress?"

"Can't say I ever did. She's at Twentieth Century Fox. Unless they'd loaned her out to Paramount, she wouldn't have been around where I worked. Why do you ask?"

"We saw her on the train when we were coming to California. It was kismet. She is so beautiful, you can't believe it. I've seen all her movies. I truly love her. But I worry about her."

"Why is that?"

"She just looks like someone who needs you to worry about her."

He did not seem to find this strange.

Swooshing the dish cloth round and round in the skillet, I turned my thoughts to Christmas preparations.

Reading my mind, Uncle Stanley said, "I'll string the lights on the tree after breakfast so it's ready to decorate."

Later, I found the tree lights in the linen closet and handed them down. Together we tested the bulbs, adding to each a silver reflector shaped like a flower whose petals glowed dreamily when the bulb was lit.

After we finished stringing the lights, Uncle Stanley stood back exclaiming, "We're pretty damned good at this. We oughta hire out. What d'ya say?" He shook my hand, and I was especially pleased since Shirley was there, plunking away, seeing and hearing it all.

Now he turned to Shirley as she concluded a Haydn piece and asked, "Do you know 'Up on the Housetop'?" It was a song we'd sung at school, and Shirley began to pick it out, tentatively at first, then adding chords with the confidence of one whose mind simply works that way.

Uncle Stanley sang lustily, pulling me to the piano to join him. At certain irresistible moments in the song, my uncle did a little musical comedy dance step and doffed an imaginary hat to me. I felt like Judy Garland.

He was more relaxed and self-assured than I ever remembered. Charm he had always possessed, but back in Morgan Lake in 1939, humbled by adversity, his charm was a guttering flame about to die in the next gust of misfortune.

When Aunt Betty arrived home shortly after noon, she found the three of us singing to Shirley's accompaniment. Uncle Stanley told my aunt, "I suppose when I get home from the war, I'll be paying good money to hear Shirley play."

Didn't that make Shirley simper.

While Uncle Stanley and Aunt Betty spent the afternoon in town together, Shirley hung around the house. When I was out with the dogs, I'm fairly sure she took a bath and washed her thatched-hut hair with our shampoo. When I got back, she smelled suspicious.

When I told Mama that Aunt Betty and Uncle Stanley wouldn't be home until seven, she said, "Well, then, we'll have a late supper, like in the movies." Her voice had that sing-y, bubbling sound a person's voice gets when they're happy. And sometimes they don't even know why.

I kept waiting for Mama's resentment toward my uncle to surface, the gibes and scoffing, but her goodwill continued, like sunny weather in the face of predicted storms.

Dinner again was resplendent, with candlelight and wine. Uncle Stanley stood and raised his glass, looking at each of us, including Shirley. "To the ladies. Wonder women."

"Thank you, sir," Mama said, flirtatiously.

After supper, Shirley and I whipped through the dishes while Mama stood on a chair, digging around at the back of the linen closet for last year's tree ornaments.

Aunt Betty unpacked one of the Gilpins' bags she and Uncle Stanley had toted home: glass ornaments in a rainbow of colors, and tinsel that wasn't real tinsel but strands of something like cellophane. Real tinsel had gone to war.

Uncle Stanley slipped the glass spire onto the top of the tree and hung the ornaments on the highest branches while the rest of us fussed over the lower ones.

Seldom in childhood do you stop dead and exclaim, "What a rare moment!" How could you *know* it was rare? But that hour around the tree—with a glow of colored bulbs lighting our faces—was rare, and I knew it.

Mama made popcorn and served drinks—whiskey for the grownups, Coca-Cola for me and Shirley—while Aunt Betty played some of my uncle's favorite tunes on the piano. Taking my hand and leading me to the kitchen, where he shoved the table and chairs against the wall, Uncle Stanley taught me to fox trot on the smooth linoleum while Aunt Betty played "A Nightingale Sang in Berkeley Square."

The next dance was Shirley's, and Aunt Betty played "You Keep Coming Back like a Song." Shirley followed Uncle Stanley's steps better than I did, and she demanded another dance—a perfect example of the squeaky wheel. Uncle Stanley swept her around the floor to Aunt Betty's "I'll Be Seeing You," at one point twirling Shirley off her feet as if she were Ginger Rogers.

On Shirley's behalf, I must say that after her second dance she took over at the piano, allowing Aunt Betty to dance. Rising from the bench, my aunt riffled through the stack of music, selecting "The Nearness of You" and "White Christmas."

Uncle Stanley flicked the kitchen switch so that they danced in spilled light from the living room. I stood in the doorway, watching as they danced together for the first time in over four years. He held her close and drew their clasped hands to his chest. For long moments, they simply stood in one spot, swaying to the music, eyes closed. At the end of "White Christmas," they kissed, and I turned away.

Then Uncle Stanley called to Mama, who was sitting on the sofa staring at the Christmas tree, her drink forgotten in her hand. "Arlene, come out here and give me a dance." Again, Aunt Betty sorted through the sheet music as Mama slowly roused herself and wandered to the kitchen like a sleepwalker, still holding the drink, which Uncle Stanley set aside.

My uncle did not hold Mama as near as he had Aunt Betty; nonetheless they were close enough that Mama's chin almost rested on his shoulder as they danced to "You'll Never Know."

Uncle Stanley executed some slow but intricate maneuvers, which moved Mama first away from him and then back in a graceful glide. I watched their feet, trying to discern the pattern.

Mama moved as if dancing in her sleep. During the second number, "Goodnight, Sweetheart," she clung to my uncle, and over his shoulder her eyes were starlit with tears.

In my room, horrified, I fell across the bed.

All the years of hate had come to this: Mama was in love with Uncle Stanley.

ONCE, ON KNX, I HAD HEARD a song called "How Long Has This Been Going On?" and on Christmas morning that's what I woke up asking. I dug back in memory. But the things Mama had said about Uncle Stanley over the past couple of years when he hadn't sent for Aunt Betty rang sincere. Could you love someone and not know it? And what the hell did I care? I was fed up.

"The Dugans have arrived! Commence the heathen feasting!" cried Fanny as Jack held the door.

But Fanny's step was doddering as her husband shepherded her into the house. Aunt Betty made her comfortable while Jack mixed drinks.

Within minutes of meeting, Uncle Stanley and Jack were huddled together in the kitchen talking politics and unions, their sleeves rolled up to their elbows, like an ad for the CIO.

In the living room, Aunt Betty asked about Fanny's nephew Dennis.

"Still on a destroyer, and still in the Coral Sea. I think." Her fingers twined and untwined as she caught her breath. "He always seems to be in the thick of things. I wish he were on something bigger than a destroyer. They look so fragile."

Glancing about, her gaze sought Shirley, who was wolfing the petit fours the Dugans had brought and hovering near the piano, hoping to be called upon.

"Shirley, will you play us something?"

Shirley slid onto the piano bench and fell to work on a little Brahms piece.

In the kitchen my uncle straddled a chair turned backwards, his arms resting across the back, while Jack leaned against the wall, rubbing the smooth, tanned back of his neck as he inquired whether Uncle Stanley had joined the Party in L.A.

I tried to be everywhere. While Fanny, Aunt Betty and Mama were draped over the living room furniture listening to Shirley, I loitered in the kitchen, filching olives and eavesdropping.

"I went to some meetings, but I never got around to joining," Uncle Stanley was telling Jack. "Liked the people, though. Worked on a couple of committees."

Jack nodded.

In the living room, the insistent hope of "Jesu, Joy of Man's Desiring," drifted from the piano, one of the pieces Fanny had performed in our living room a year ago. Fanny listened, nodding. As the last notes died away, she summoned Shirley to her, patting Shirley's head and calling her "sweet patootie."

Now Mama and Aunt Betty lifted the roaster from the oven and huddled over the turkey, pushing at the legs and muttering assurances that the bird was done. Mama made gravy while Aunt Betty mashed the potatoes. When the salad was tossed, the peas buttered, and the Pyrex casserole of candied yams removed from the oven, Aunt Betty sent Jack home for kitchen chairs.

Shirley and I had laid the tables: grown-ups at the kitchen table, children at a card table close by. Real cloth covered both, even if the cloth on the card table was just a dishtowel. A jar of giant zinnias from Gilpins' flower stall sat in the center of each table, and behind each plate was a name card, made by me, with hand-drawn and colored holly berries, the berries looking like drops of blood.

With reverence, I lifted a forkful of potato from the gravy-filled reservoir I'd constructed. The snowy vegetable possessed a mystical quality, like Communion Host, only tastier. Manna. Maybe God had sent mashed potatoes to the Israelites in the desert.

At the grown-ups' table, Mama was passing turkey and accepting compliments, all with an abstracted solemnity. I couldn't stand to look at her.

On the sale rack at Gilpins', she'd found a chaste-looking, red, two-piece gabardine dress with black velveteen collar and cuffs. Carefully made up and wearing simulated pearl earrings, she looked shy and innocent.

But when I caught her darting a glance at Uncle Stanley, I felt a wave of physical revulsion. And, as if a telegraph wire stretched between us, Mama sent me a worried look. I stared at my mashed potatoes, then raked my fork through them, spilling gravy over everything.

. . . .

AFTER DINNER, Uncle Stanley and Jack sat on the stoop in the cold darkness, smoking cigarettes and discussing the Eastern Front and the siege of Leningrad. Fanny rested at the kitchen table with a cup of tea while the rest of us cleared away.

Although we kept up a fervid gab about rationing, we were play-acting for the sake of the holiday. Beneath the surface, each of us was churning. Even Shirley was not quite herself. Sitting beside Fanny at the table, she gazed about in a prehensile way, grabbing hold of the scene, owning it.

She had gotten herself up in the outfit Aunt Betty had bought for her audition. From God knew where, she'd pinched a length of wide red ribbon, tied it in a bow, and fastened it to the top of her head like a flapping bird, which now drooped as if shot.

Fanny removed the ribbon and smoothed it on the table, wrapping it around Shirley's noggin and fashioning a smaller bow above Shirley's left ear.

"Very attractive," Fanny said. "You look like a flapper."

"Whatza flapper?" Shirley asked.

"*I* was once," Fanny told her. "A young thing who dressed in short skirts and wore her hair bobbed and had a lot of pizzazz." When she said "pizzazz," Fanny's eyes lit up and she gave Shirley a droll, private smile. "The cat's pajamas."

Soon after this, Fanny and Jack left, Fanny saying she was a little tired. At the door she removed from her purse two small boxes, handing one to Shirley and telling her, "For my musician," the other to me, saying, "For my storyteller. Merry Christmas."

Shirley and I stood open mouthed. Then—incredibly—Shirley snatched up Fanny's hand and kissed it.

"Lark," Mama prompted, "what do you say?"

"Thank you, Fanny," I blurted as Jack guided her out into the night. "Thank you, thank you," I called after them.

Storyteller? What did that mean? Surely not the things I'd told Fanny about Harvester and Hilly and Sally and Beverly. That wasn't storytelling, was it?

Shirley perched on the piano bench and tore open her box. Inside the first was a second, smaller box, this one covered in deep blue velvet. Lifting the lid revealed a white satin lining with a gold ring nestled into its folds. She plucked it out and, shoving the empty boxes into the pocket of her dress, ran a fingertip over a little emerald with opals on either side.

"Lookit inside," she said, shoving the ring in my face. "My name's in there, see? It says, 'Shirley.'"

Grabbing the ring back, she kissed it with a loud smack.

"Lark, aren't you going to open yours?" Mama asked.

I was half sick to see my gift, but when Mama asked, perversity seized me. "I'm going to wait till we open presents tomorrow."

When Aunt Betty and Uncle Stanley left for midnight Mass, Mama made up her bed again on the pull-out sofa. In my nightgown, I padded around the kitchen, finding myself a snack of pumpkin pie and whipped cream.

Since discovering that Mama was in love with Uncle Stanley, I couldn't bear being near her. When she set a tea cup on the table and pulled out a chair, I moved to the far end. But there was something I needed to know.

"Is Fanny going to get well?"

"No."

How dare she sit stirring tea in that stupid way?

"Fanny has a heart condition," she went on. "And she'll die of it. Maybe tomorrow, maybe in six months."

"Who told you?"

"Jack told your aunt. Please don't tell Shirley."

I rose, shoving aside the pie. "Why did you tell *me*?"

"Because you asked."

As I rushed from the table, she put out a hand to catch me.

"Don't touch me! Don't ever touch me."

45

As I crossed to the window and raised the shade, I wondered if this would be Fanny's last morning. How could she stand to leave morning behind?

She hadn't died yet, but knowing that she would, and soon, I felt as if she had already, a little. I didn't want to feel that way. Fanny was part of my family now. Jack too. When you lived in a place like the Project, leaving most of your real family behind someplace, you adopted people. Fanny and Jack were my new aunt and uncle. I began to weep.

Uncle Stanley tapped on the door. "Your ma says get your face washed. Breakfast's almost ready."

Shirley showed up in time to eat. If we'd eaten at five a.m., she'd have been on the stoop at four fifty-five.

After breakfast, Shirley dashed for the living room, throwing herself down at the base of the tree and pleading, "Can I please pass the presents out?"

Days before, I'd told her how I looked forward to passing out presents; how it made me feel like a mailman delivering good news.

"No!" I said. "*I* pass out the presents in my house. You can pass them out in your house. It's not fair for you to come here and take my job."

"Girls, girls," Aunt Betty said, "take turns. First Shirley, then Lark."

With a face as mild as the Virgin, Shirley lifted a package wrapped in red tissue paper and frowned over the tag. "For Stanley with love from Betty," she stammered after several false starts, which the adults found only slightly less charming than the twittering of baby birds.

Then it was my turn, and I grabbed the box containing Fanny's present. I didn't want Shirley's hands on it. "You can pass out the rest of the presents," I said. That would take the wind out of her sails.

But even *I* knew that passing out presents wasn't a life-or-death matter. If Shirley had asked whether I minded if she helped, it would have been different.

I unwrapped the small box, preserving the gilt paper. A ring like Shirley's lay inside, only it had my name engraved in the band. But whereas Shirley's stones were an emerald and opals, mine were a sapphire and pearls—a superior combination.

When the wrappings were gathered from the floor and stuffed into the trash, I retired to the bedroom with my gifts. I wanted to be alone with *Jo's Boys, Arabian Nights,* and *Mythology* by Edith Hamilton, all from Aunt Betty and Uncle Stanley. Also, I didn't want to watch Mama trying not to look at Uncle Stanley.

I put away the clothes from Mama and dabbed my neck with Evening in Paris. The money from two sets of grandparents and Papa, fifteen dollars in all, I added to the running-away fund. If I squirreled my earnings from walking Cecil and Percy, by April I'd have almost seventy-five dollars. I was getting there.

Around one o'clock Mama called, "Come play Monopoly with us." Play Monopoly with Mama?

"I'm going to deliver Miss Eldridge's Christmas card," I called back.

"Well, let's fix the poor soul a plate of treats," Aunt Betty said as I emerged, card in hand.

I was soon on my way, carrying a plate heaped with cookies and seafoam divinity from Grandma Browning, petit fours from Fanny and Jack, chocolates and hard candy from Gilpins'.

Seeing Miss Eldridge's fine-boned face and probing eyes, I realized how much I had missed her.

"Lark Erhardt," she said, holding the door. "What's this?" She took the card and read aloud.

Merry Christmas, Miss Eldridge and Beau.
You're folks whom I'm happy to know.
And I'm truly sincere
With my 'Happy New Year'!

"'Whom'?" she said. "Excellent."

"It's the objective case," I pointed out.

"I'm impressed." She took the plate. "Come in. Beau's lying down. He worked overtime every day this week."

Something good-smelling was in the oven, and the living room was neat and dusted.

"Take a seat," Miss Eldridge said, and I went directly to my usual chair, noting with disappointment that the draperies were still closed.

"I've got a goose in the oven," she said.

On the lamp table were stacked *The Complete Jane Austen,* Hardy's *Tess of the D'urbervilles,* and Cather's *O Pioneers!* a book mark in each. Many other titles lined the shelves of a tall bookcase, along with the thick albums of cataloged pictures and family history. "Are you reading three books at once?" I asked.

"Oh, yes," she said. "Sometimes I have half a dozen going. Something for every mood."

"Is the bookcase new?"

"A Christmas present from Beau. Isn't it lovely? Cherry wood." Casting an eye over the stack of books on the table, she said, "I read my favorites again and again, do you?"

I nodded. *"The Secret Garden* and *Heidi* especially. When I was little, I never got tired of *Happy Stories for Bedtime.* Sometimes if I'm low I still read it. I used to read the stories to Hilly."

"Hilly?"

So now I told Hilly's story to Miss Eldridge. She nodded often. "They're martyrs, the gentle ones," she said.

But I was worried about making her sad. When I'd finished explaining how the Church refused to bury Hilly, I changed the subject, drawing a breath and dithering, "I got *Tales from the Arabian Nights* for Christmas. Have you read it?"

She seemed not to hear me, but then she squared her shoulders and reached for the plate of treats, holding it out.

"Thank you," I said, taking a Christmas tree-shaped sugar cookie decorated with green sugar sprinkles. "My Grandma Browning made these, ma'am."

"They're delicious. She must make them with real butter."

"Yes. She buys cream from her friends in the country and makes butter. The cream's so thick, your spoon'll stand up in it. You don't need ration stamps to do that."

"The country," Miss Eldridge said. "There isn't a morning that I don't wake up remembering meadowlarks and mourning doves and the smell of alfalfa."

"I'm going to live in the country some day."

"Are you?"

"In a cabin at the edge of the woods. I'll have a big garden, two or three cows. A horse and some chickens."

"Have you ever lived in the country?"

"No, but . . ." How could I explain about Hilly and Baby Marjorie? It sounded crazy.

"If I had the money, I'd buy a little farm, myself," Miss Eldridge said.

"You can live on mine. You'd be a big help."

She laughed, throwing her head back and clasping her hands at her bosom like a child. The girl in Miss Eldridge lay close to the surface. "I accept." Then, laying a hand on O *Pioneers!*, she said, "You must take this with you. It's about a young farmer woman."

"But you're reading it."

"For the eighth time. I want you to have it."

In Beau's room a radio crackled, and a sonorous voice spoke of our boys at the front on this Christmas day, far from home.

Before I left, Beau appeared, pleased, I thought, that his sister was entertaining.

"Merry Christmas, little Lark," he said.

"Merry Christmas, Beau."

"Was Santa good to you?"

"I don't believe anymore. But Aunt Betty and Mama take up the slack."

"And you have company?"

"My Uncle Stanley's visiting. He's a soldier now and has to leave in a couple of days, but this is the first time I've seen him since I was little."

He came awake. "Where's he stationed?"

"He's being transferred back east somewhere, I forget the name, to be a medical corpsman."

"A corpsman. Good for him."

In the shadow of the doorway, Beau's eyes were hungry. He wanted to be a soldier. Wherever that war broadcast came from, that's where he wanted to be.

But he had a sister to look after, one who was fragile.

46

AUNT BETTY AND UNCLE STANLEY were out when I returned from the Eldridges'.

"They went for a spin," Mama said. "Stanley wanted to show your aunt the car. He's leaving it here when he goes east."

"We're going to have a *car?*"

"Don't get excited. With gas rationing, we won't get far."

"Where's Shirley?" I asked. Riding around like a queen in the rumble seat?

"Taking a nap on your bed."

Whirling, I headed for my room. If I knew Shirley, she'd spent the afternoon pawing through my belongings.

I threw open the door, but she was curled up on the bed asleep, a blanket over her. She'd removed her shoes, the black patent audition ones, and lined them up neatly beside the bed.

Her presents were stacked in an orderly pile beside her, as if someone might make off with them if they were out of her sight. Even in sleep, her hands were balled into fists.

I backed out, closing the door. Scrunching up on the sofa with *O Pioneers!*, I thought almost kindly about Shirley. Seeing her asleep with her presents and her beloved Mary Janes, it was hard to hate her.

A minute later she appeared in the living room doorway. "Where'd you get that book?" she asked, as if I'd stolen it.

"Miss Eldridge loaned it to me. It's about a woman farmer."

"Whatdya wanna read that for?"

"I'm going to have a farm some day."

"You don't know beans about farms."

Just because she'd lived on a ranch, Shirley thought she knew everything about country life. "That's why I'm reading," I said.

"You ever milked a cow or rode a horse? You'd be too scared to even get near one." She threw herself into the arm chair and studied the Christmas tree.

Shirley knew how to take the shine off things.

. . . .

I LAY ON MY BED WONDERING how Mr. Trustworthy had spent Christmas. In the living room, Uncle Stanley and Aunt Betty sat on the sofa discussing matters that couples in wartime must hash out: car registration and dependency checks and life insurance. As for the support money that would be sent to her, Aunt Betty really didn't need it and didn't feel right accepting it. Uncle Stanley argued that if it made her feel better, she could give it to charity.

In the end, they decided to put it into a bank account and use part of it for Shirley's lessons and her other necessities, including bridgework where her front tooth had been knocked out.

Again their conversation turned to politics, which had a powerful grip on Uncle Stanley. He told Aunt Betty about a Communist friend in L.A., a man by the name of Sidney Dangerson, who was the most intelligent human being he had ever met. "The man has read *everything*," my uncle declared. "Proust and Balzac and Dostoyevsky and Dickens and Chaucer and Kant and Aristotle and Virginia Woolf and every major historian since people began writing it down." Uncle Stanley ran out of breath.

"And he wasn't being kind in order to convert me. What he converted me to was *thinking*," my uncle went on. "He's like an Old Testament prophet, full of righteous wrath, but also generosity and humor."

Aunt Betty listened, although she was not caught up by her husband's zeal.

"I want to go college when I get back, honey. What would you say to that? Could you put up with it?"

"Well, of course," Aunt Betty assured him.

"You're a wonderful girl."

"Hardly a girl."

"You'll always be the pretty young girl I married."

"I don't want to be the young girl you married. You're not the young boy I married. You're better. And I'm better. Back in Minnesota, when I was coming apart, I was lucky to have a sister holding me together, dragging me off to California. Thanks to Arlene, I'm finding out who I am. Now, well. . . . You don't really know me."

She had one more point to make. "Not everybody's as lucky as I was. Not everybody has an Arlene. Maybe I can be somebody else's Arlene."

Aunt Betty was not normally given to this sort of talk. What would Uncle Stanley make of it, hearing her speak with such independence?

"We'll make a helluva team," he said. "I wish Sidney could meet you."

Neither of them said anything for a few minutes, and I supposed that they were kissing. Then Uncle Stanley spoke, so softly I strained to hear.

"I'll give you Sid's address. If anything happens to me, I want you to let him know."

"Nothing's going to happen."

"But just in case."

. . . .

MY UNCLE LEFT ON A BLEAK, shivery morning. Both Mama and Aunt Betty went to work late so that they could drive him to Union Station. Insisting that Uncle Stanley sit in the front seat with Aunt Betty, who drove, Mama huddled in the rumble seat in her heavy coat, tears streaming down her face.

I stood at the street to see them off, Shirley beside me, elbowing in. Uncle Stanley kissed her hand and called her "Shirley A. Marvel, the beautiful prodigy of Piñon Street." I thought she'd wet her pants.

When he hugged me, he whispered, "I love you, little comrade. Write to me. Keep me in the picture."

Blubbering as bad as Mama, I promised, "I'll be a socialist, too, Uncle Stanley. We'll be socialists together."

47

"WHAT DO YOU *MEAN?*" The pitch of Mama's voice reached into the bedroom, yanking me out of bed and into the hall.

She stood by the Christmas tree, staring at Aunt Betty; Aunt Betty, on the sofa, stared down at her clasped hands.

"What do you *mean* you're not in love with him!"

My aunt lifted her face, perplexed. "I don't understand, Arlene. You wanted me to divorce Stanley."

"Oh, Jesus," Mama wailed.

"What's happened?" I asked, creeping into the room.

"Arlene, what's wrong?" Aunt Betty asked. "Why are you taking this so hard? I didn't tell Stanley. I won't tell him till the war's over."

"Why *didn't* you tell him?"

"Are you crazy? Send him off thinking I didn't care so he'd jump in front of the first bullet? You can't hate him that much."

"*Hate* him?"

The clock on the bookcase seemed to stop ticking. Finally, Aunt Betty said, "How long?"

"I don't know," Mama groaned.

After several minutes, Aunt Betty said, "So, it could go back before Baby Marjorie's birth." Her voice was too calm. My aunt was wondering if Mama had schemed to keep her and uncle apart, engineering his move to California.

"No!" Mama wept. "No, no, no. You can't think that. Oh, God," she cried, "I never knew I loved him. Not till now."

She ran from the room, pushing me aside.

Aunt Betty spoke to the air. "I told him I was lucky to have you, Arlene."

Again and again Mama swore that she hadn't known she loved Uncle Stanley, certainly not when she raised the money for him to leave Minnesota. But Aunt Betty would never be sure. Finally Mama stopped talking about it. From then on, they lived silently, side by side.

By March, Uncle Stanley was "someplace in Italy." Mama and Aunt Betty were separately fearful, Mama because she loved him, Aunt Betty because she didn't. The death of her love lay heavy on my aunt's conscience.

Aunt Betty threw herself into work. Mama threw herself into servicemen. With a wrought, frantic air, she flew out of the house several nights a week, lavishing on sailors and Marines the affection she couldn't lavish on Uncle Stanley.

Aunt Betty did not concern herself with this. If Mama chose to go to hell in a hand basket, let her. Nor did my aunt worry unduly about me. I was in the sixth grade and old enough to be left alone at night, the Eldridges and Dugans being close at hand.

One Saturday afternoon, Mama dragged her friend Melba home from work and they tried different hairdos on each other. While Melba stood brushing Mama's hair into an up-do, Mama said, "I'm so much older than you, Melba. Am I up to this high life?"

"You've got the energy of an eighteen-year-old, Arlene."

When I asked Melba later what *high life* was, she laughed. "Oh, you know, going to dances and parties, staying out late." One time after that I got up at two a.m. to go to the bathroom and saw that Mama wasn't home. No question the high life meant staying out late.

But I thought there was more to it. Drinking whiskey was part of the high life. If Mama had been out late, the next morning a stale whiskey smell lingered in the living room, where she now bunked.

When work took Aunt Betty out of town, Mama and Melba invited their dates to dinner at our house. On these occasions, the two women were like little girls playing house, conferring over recipes, fussing over the table, and giggling until I was nauseated.

Although I liked Melba well enough, I didn't think she was a good influence on Mama, keeping her out night after night until all hours. Melba was young and single; Mama was not so young and not so single.

By mid-May, the two of them were dating a couple of sailors on a pretty regular basis. Melba's sailor was Buddy Karl from Worcester, Massachusetts, whose family owned clothing stores. Mama's was Buddy's best pal, Ronnie Baker, who had taught English literature at a small college in Missouri before enlisting.

One Sunday, Mama opened the door to Ronnie, who was towing what he called a little brother. Grabbing the younger sailor by the sleeve of his white middy, Ronnie thrust him forward. "Duane Graphensteen, Iowa rustic. Arlene Erhardt, California sophisticate."

Since Aunt Betty was out of town, we all piled into Uncle Stanley's car that afternoon, Mama behind the wheel, Ronnie beside her, Melba in the rumble seat on Buddy Karl's lap, me on Duane's. Off we roared to the Mission Beach amusement park.

Sitting in a tilt-a-whirl seat, waiting for the machinery to crank up, I asked the very young, very blond Duane Graphensteen about farm life and about his family. He told me he had a sister Margaret, my age, who wanted to be a missionary when she grew up. I had once been attracted to the missionary life but, regrettably, it required that a person be religious.

Later in the afternoon, we waited in line for the Ferris wheel. I was frightened but tried to appear no more cowardly than the average eleven-year-old girl. Duane did not, thank God, rock the seat back and forth. He did point out his ship, which lay in the harbor being repaired.

Alighting from the Ferris wheel, we all drifted to the hot dog stand, smearing mustard and relish on foot-longs. While Duane explained how his mother made her own relish, I glanced up to see three of the boys from the monkey bars standing not more than twenty feet away. The black-haired boy who owned a knife was firing a rifle at mechanical ducks. Next to him, another boy punched a third boy on the arm.

Plang. The black-haired boy hit one of the ducks and it disappeared. He continued shooting until the gun was empty. The concessionaire pointed to the bottom shelf, one of several where prizes were lined up. The boy chose a small plaster-of-paris skull for holding pencils.

"Lark!" Mama cried. "Look what you've done. You've ruined your blouse."

Sure enough, I'd hugged the hot dog to me, spilling mustard and relish down my front. Duane grabbed a couple of paper napkins from the counter, brushing off the worst of the pickle relish. I followed up with more napkins, absently rubbing at the stains as I stared at the black-haired boy.

"Something wrong?" Duane asked.

In front of the shooting gallery, two of the boys were making a fuss over the plaster-of-paris skull. Suddenly the boy with the black hair hurled the prize through the air.

My God, I thought, what if it hits someone?

It struck a utility pole, shattering and falling harmlessly to earth. The other boys looked stunned. They would have liked to own that skull. But, recalling themselves, they broke into slavish guffaws, slapping their indifferent young god on the back.

48

As 1944 DRAGGED ON, Miss Eldridge and I grew closer. One day, out of the blue, she suggested that I write a paragraph about nature. "Just a little exercise," she said.

"*Anything* in nature?"

"Anything that interests you."

I spent a week writing and rewriting my paragraph before presenting it to her.

The Gardenia Bush

On Mother's Day in 1942 Aunt Betty and I gave Mama a gardenia bush. Jack Dugan helped us plant it at the corner of our house. Gardenias are supposed to grow in rich, moist soil. The soil at the corner of our house is not rich or moist. We have done our best. I water the bush every other day when we don't have rain which is most of the year. Mama bought fertilizer for it. The bush isn't very big and it doesn't grow as many flowers as gardenia bushes which have better soil but it grows some. They are redolent (page 833 *Webster's*). Jack Dugan says it's a miracle that the bush has lived. Mama says that love alone has saved it but I think the bush has a mind of its own and tries very hard to stay alive and make flowers.

Miss Eldridge read it through twice. Coming to the end the second time, she lay it in her lap, folding her small, deft hands over it.

"I was entertained and informed by this paragraph," she told me. "It contains fact and conjecture. The conjecture invites the reader to stop and ponder, along with the author, what has kept the bush alive. You have anthropomorphized the gardenia bush, an effective technique here."

She wrote something on a piece of paper and handed it to me: anthropomorphize. "Look it up in your *Webster's*."

I appreciated that Miss Eldridge was discussing the paragraph in objective terms. I could learn a lot from her.

"You have committed one or two errors in punctuation," she went on, holding the paragraph in her left hand.

Before we parted on that April afternoon, she suggested that I write another piece. "This one about a family member."

Maybe the Friday afternoons were only a way for Miss Eldridge to entertain. No matter. Her critiques taught me lessons I could apply to my other writing, the pieces I sent off to entertain Mr. Trustworthy. Like Shirley, I was becoming a person who did something. She played the piano. I wrote.

Duane Graphensteen was another bright spot during those days. While he was in the picture, I received no ominous messages from the boys, nor any photographs of naked people.

If I saw Ronnie Baker swinging up the walk without Duane, my heart sank. Duane and I often went for walks and talked to people in the neighborhood. I began to feel like a normal girl.

Duane was easy with people, finding something to talk about with everyone. Girls were taken by his sapphire eyes and smooth, golden skin, their mothers by his boyish deference.

Beau was impressed by Duane's marine knowledge. The whereabouts of the Sea of Okhotsk and Baffin Bay and the Timor Sea were all known to him. Duane could tell you the differences between a blue and a gray whale, a gray nurse and a hammerhead shark, a dolphin and a porpoise.

Mama took to Duane, to his good manners and patience. He'd sit quietly, listening and nodding, whenever she started in about her troubles with Papa, which she did at the drop of a hat. It embarrassed me. For no good reason she'd start rattling off a litany of worries that Papa caused her. I think Duane felt sorry for her.

But Ronnie Baker, after hearing Mama's complaints several times, told her, "Your husband's beginning to bore me." Mama cooled toward Ronnie after that but managed to run around just the same, with Melba and without her.

A couple of times when Duane got an unexpected shore leave and rode the bus to see us, Mama was out on the town. Both times, he stayed anyway, which made me feel that he came to see me as much as Mama. We listened to *The Great Gildersleeve* and Ken Murray on the radio, and made popcorn and played Monopoly and Parcheesi, the Royal Game of India.

Duane told me about someone named Nathaniel Bowditch who was born around the time of the Revolutionary War and wrote the *American Practical Navigator,* which sailors had been using ever since to help them chart their course. Duane was a great admirer of Nathaniel Bowditch.

If it weren't for the fact that he wanted to live on the ocean and I wanted to live in a cabin at the edge of the woods, I might have fallen in love with Duane Graphensteen.

49

SHIRLEY THE DEMON PIANO PLAYER was out of my hair for a while. Madame Buchova had suggested that Shirley would profit from a month in the mountains at a camp for young musicians. Madame taught there during the month of June, so if Shirley attended, her regular lessons need not be interrupted.

Aunt Betty sent the prepared application form to the Olsons for their signature, along with a letter explaining that Shirley's fees would be paid from the Stanley Weller Scholarship Fund, a fudge in the event that the Olsons were touchy about Aunt Betty paying Shirley's way. She needn't have worried about that.

When Shirley returned the signed forms—and to me the signature looked suspiciously like Shirley's—Aunt Betty put together a music camp wardrobe based on Madame's suggestions: shorts and trousers, polo shirts, a couple of sweaters, and a swim suit. These were packed into a jaunty little brown-striped beige grip, along with new socks and underpants. Shirley swanked around like Mrs. Astor's horse.

The upshot of music camp was that I enjoyed an entire month of quiet. After my chores, I read Miss Eldridge's books and wrote letters to my friends in Harvester.

Dear Sally,

My Uncle Stanley is in Italy, I think. You never really know. He is so interesting. Did I tell you he's a Socialist? I think maybe that's what I'll be. It makes a lot of sense the way he describes it.

I have been doing a ton of writing lately. I write essays for Miss Eldridge so I can learn about punctuation and grammar, and stories for Mr. Trustworthy to entertain him.

Maybe you should write stories. They kind of buck you up when you're in the dumps. And I know that you're in the dumps sometimes, with your mother still in St. Peter.

I am completely disgusted with my mother, but I don't want to go into the details. I'll just say that you wouldn't know her, and I wish I didn't. I spend a lot more time with Miss Eldridge.

Anyway, I am saving bushels of money these days, so it won't be long now!

Your friend even after I'm dead,

Lark Ann Browning Erhardt.

P.S. I got the curse. Ugh. How about you?

On the sixth of June, the Allies invaded Normandy—D-Day it was called—and the papers were full of it. Duane was tickled about the invasion, although he himself would probably be returning to the Pacific.

The following Saturday morning, he turned up breathless at our door. "The ship's ready! We're sailing sometime next week." He was restless and pacing. "Let's go for a walk."

When I had washed my face and dabbed Evening in Paris behind my ears, I found Duane sitting on the stoop, talking with Miss Eldridge. They were discussing crops.

"Duane says you're going for a walk." She rose and brushed the back of her skirt. "I made peanut butter cookies yesterday and I'll be brewing tea around three if you want to stop."

"Miss Eldridge took to you," I told Duane as we started up the incline, the route I usually took with Cecil and Percy.

"Why do you say that?"

"She almost never comes out of her house."

Strolling along the verge, we reached the far end of the hill where the dogs and I usually turned back. For a moment we stood looking into the dimness of the arroyo.

"What's down there?" Duane asked. Before I could answer, he started down, loose stones and dust scattering beneath his shoes, rolling away among the scrub oaks.

"Rattlesnakes," I called.

He glanced back, waving me to follow. "I won't let them get you," he said.

I trailed along, slipping and slewing, not really wanting to explore down there but not wanting to stay behind, either.

At the bottom, we halted. The gulch was filled mostly with loose rocks, washed down from the foothills, and dusty little trees that clung to thin soil.

Picking our way along, we discovered an intimate little world, one that gave me the heebie-jeebies, where the trees were all knotty and twisty. But with Duane leading the way, I wasn't afraid.

Suddenly he stopped. "What's this?" he said, bending low and disappearing.

I ran to see.

To the right, concealed by scrub and dead branches that were arranged across the opening, was a little sanctum about five feet high, five or six feet wide, and maybe four feet deep. Scooped out of the hill by some force of nature, it was being used by humans.

"How'd you notice this place?" I asked.

He held out a circlet of filthy hair ribbon, the ends tied together in a small bow. "It was over there, caught in those weeds," he said. The flapper ribbon Shirley had worn last Christmas.

While Duane poked through a heap of comic books, I knelt, my back to him, and eased the lid from an old tea tin. Inside were half a dozen postcards: the same dim room, the same men and women, but doing different things.

Behind me Duane was asking, "Anything interesting?"

Fumbling, I slipped the lid back on the tin. "No. . . . Just junk." I backed out of the tiny cave on my hands and knees. "Let's get out of here."

We arranged the branches again and continued on our way, me stumbling along, dazed. At the end of the arroyo we climbed out and found ourselves near Shirley's house. The path Duane chose took us past her door.

From inside came the sounds of cowboy music playing on a radio. Despite this, the place seemed old and deserted, like a Dust Bowl shack in *Life* magazine.

We'd almost passed when a face appeared at a window. Thin, pasty, its eyes followed us. Where had I seen that face? One of the boys on the monkey bars.

"You're quiet," Miss Eldridge noted when we got back. I was remembering the boy who'd saved me that day on the monkey bars. I often thought of him, wishing I could thank him. He must be in high school now, a junior or senior.

Turning her attention to Duane, she said, "The war won't last much longer now that the boys have landed in France."

Someone was knocking at the door and Miss Eldridge excused herself to answer. Seconds later, Mama swept in. She'd been home from her Saturday half day for an hour and wondered where I'd got to. Yes, she'd love a cup of tea.

Miss Eldridge put the kettle on while Mama brought Duane up to date on Papa. She'd had another letter.

"I finally figured it out," she explained, raising her voice so Miss Eldridge in the kitchen could hear, "Willie thinks I'll stay married in order to keep him from taking Lark. That's what the letters from the lawyer are about."

She picked up a cookie from the plate. "As long as he stays in Minnesota, that's fine by me." Her brow puckered. "Unless of course I wanted to marry again. That'd be another story."

Was she actually dreaming about marrying Uncle Stanley?

That evening, Aunt Betty was late for dinner. "I stopped at Fanny and Jack's," she told me. "She's in bed all the time now." Because of Cecil and Percy, I'd known this.

"I'm going back after supper," my aunt told me. She rarely spoke directly to Mama. "I told Jack to go to a movie."

"Can Duane and I come with you?"

"I don't think so. You know how Fanny is, thinks she has to entertain."

"What time will you be home?"

"Probably not before midnight. Jack's going to the second show."

So Duane and I played Monopoly at the kitchen table and listened to *Your Hit Parade*. Mama, who had a free Saturday night, made rum and Cokes for herself and Duane. I'd never seen him take a drink, not even when the other fellows did. But I guessed that he drank on this occasion to keep Mama company and to avoid making a big deal of his innocence.

Mama nattered on about her bosses. "They think Melba and I should be grateful to be secretaries. Mr. Hapgood says if there wasn't a war on, we wouldn't have jobs at all. 'Wait till the boys come home and you'll be back to ironing shirts.' We'll see about that." She rose, carrying her glass and Duane's to refill. I wished she'd go to bed.

"Duane," she said, "I've talked your left ear off. You are so nice to listen to all this." She set his fresh drink in front of him, looked at her watch, and told me, "Half an hour. Then whoever's ahead wins."

"But . . ."

"No arguments. It's twenty to ten already."

By the time I said good night at a quarter past ten, Mama was giggly and lax-jointed, and she'd found dance music on the radio. "Duane, I'm going to teach you to foxtrot."

I lay in bed thinking about the walk Duane and I had taken, about the secret hideout we'd found, and the tin of pictures.

I dreamt I was in the arroyo alone at night, tangled in the scrub and unable to run.

I woke from the dream, tangled in the sheets and trembling. The clock said twenty past eleven. Extricating myself, I scrambled from bed, whimpering.

As I opened the door, an answering whimper came from the sofa. I padded into the hall. The living room was shadowy, lit only by a distant light in the kitchen. I edged toward the living room doorway.

An expanse of skin moved rhythmically up and down, accompanied by hard, grunting breaths. I looked away as fast as I could, but not fast enough.

50

THAT NIGHT WAS THE LAST TIME I saw Duane. He wrote twice, but I didn't answer.

I did write another essay for Miss Eldridge who asked me this time to describe a place. I wrote:

The Hay Mow in Grandma Browning's Barn

There is a little barn behind my Grandma Browning's house in Blue Lake. Many years ago two horses, a cow and some chickens lived in the barn. Now there is only a Nash.

You can climb the stairs, which don't have a railing, up to the hay mow. It is dusty and smells funny, not bad but like old things. Grandma puts old furniture up there. Things like bird cages and plant stands and broken chairs.

When I visit Grandma and Grandpa I go up to the hay mow every day, especially if I am sad or angry. It's like being a long way away, even though it's only out by the alley. I open the loft door and look out at the alley. I am quite high up. Light comes in and you can see the dust in the hay mow air.

Sometimes I think the tiny dust specks are old thoughts still floating around. When you run the dust mop around the house and shake it out your door you are cleaning out old thoughts. A lot of old thoughts are in Grandma's barn and sometimes I can hear them. Once I heard one say, "I feel like jumping out the loft door," and I wondered who had thought that.

Miss Eldridge gave me a long look when she read about the hay mow, but all she said was, "Your imagination is fine. There are one or two punctuation errors."

When she had pointed these out, she asked, "What does your mother think of your writing? Is she pleased?"

"I don't show her my writing."

She didn't question this and I was grateful.

One day during the last week of June, she asked, "What's happened to Duane?"

I was out with Cecil and Percy, and Miss Eldridge was on her stoop, pounding a bed pillow to freshen it.

"He's gone."

"To sea?" She held the pillow against her breast.

"Yes."

"You must miss him," she said.

I gave a sharp tug to the dogs' leads and hurried away.

. . . .

SHIRLEY RETURNED AT THE END of the month, so full of herself I thought she'd explode. "Fanny wants you to come over and tell her about camp," I said. If anyone but Fanny had asked, I would have forgotten to pass the message along.

Jack had given me a key, so I let us in and led Shirley to Fanny's bedroom. Now that she was very ill, she slept in the little room next to the bath.

"Lark! Shirley!" Fanny greeted us with the measured enthusiasm of one who must conserve her resources.

I crossed to the bed to plump her pillows as I'd seen Jack do. Perspiration surfaced immediately along her hairline and upper lip. I passed her a big handkerchief from the pile of fresh ones by her bedside.

Cecil and Percy stood in the bedroom doorway, cocking their heads, lifting and setting down their front paws, now and then puling softly but never venturing beyond the doorway unless summoned. When they were alone with Fanny, they lay in the doorway and kept guard. I would find them there when I came to fetch them.

"Well, now. How was camp?" Fanny asked.

I sat on a straight chair in the corner while Shirley pulled another up close to the bed. Fanny reached for Shirley's hand.

"It was wonderful," Shirley sighed. "We had classes in the morning. I learned about Bach and Mozart and Beethoven and Rachmaninoff. He died last year, right here in California," she exclaimed, as if California, having hosted Sergei Rachmaninoff, had gained some validation. And I suppose it had.

"I learned about writing music," she went on. "Everybody had to write a piece for their instrument. Only a little piece. But the teacher said mine was . . . promising." She tried to sound off-hand.

"In the afternoon, we practiced, and after that we got to go swimming or hiking or play ping-pong or a lot of other games. A kid named Reginald—isn't that a dumb name?—taught me how to play ping-pong. He called it *table tennis*. Even though he had a funny name, he wasn't too dumb. Not like the freaks around here."

She hurried on. "You shoulda seen the food. You'da died, there was so much, and they gave you dessert at noon and at supper. Pie or cake or bread pudding or ice cream."

Fanny smiled. "You've put on weight, and you look good."

Ignoring the compliment, Shirley said, "We had a recital the last night. I played the Chopin 'Raindrop Prelude.' Madame said it was . . ." She paused, recalling the words, "'quite satisfactory.'"

Shirley lifted her chin sideways, daring me not to appreciate the praise.

Fanny squeezed Shirley's hand. "You have a great gift. And a great soul. I see it back there hiding behind your eyes."

"What's that mean, 'a great soul'?"

Fanny considered for a moment. "Our soul is the possibility we have for greatness. We may be famous. We may be rich. But that's not the same."

Shirley looked unsure.

"Your soul is a burning white light inside here"—she put a finger to Shirley's brow—"that helps you see your way. If you practice kindness every day, the way you practice the piano, it burns brighter and brighter."

Shirley scratched her cheek and stirred restlessly.

Fanny told us about Myra Hess, who was a famous pianist. She had organized concerts in London in the bomb shelter of the National Gallery, whatever that was, so that people would have music even during the blitz. Myra Hess played at these concerts and at hundreds of others in the bombed English cities. And she was still doing it.

"She's married her soul to her talent," Fanny pointed out.

I thought of Alicia Armand raising money for children displaced by the war.

Fanny's voice had ebbed to a whisper. Shirley rose, looking panicked as she saw how weak Fanny was.

"We gotta go now," she said.

Fanny nodded, closing her eyes.

"We'll come back soon," I told her. "Would you like a glass of water or anything before we go?"

She shook her head slightly. I started to leave, stepping over the dogs, who did not budge but lay gazing balefully at Fanny. At the bedroom door I turned.

Opening her eyes, Fanny fixed her sight on Shirley and lay a finger on her own brow.

51

ONE HOT AFTERNOON in early September, shortly after we started back to school, I was paring potatoes at the kitchen sink. The windows and front door were open so that Miss Eldridge, sitting on her stoop fanning herself, could listen to Shirley practice.

I nicked the first joint of my left thumb with the potato peeler and was running water over my hand when Shirley came into the kitchen to get a glass of water.

"Cut my thumb with the peeler," I said.

"You'll live," she said, pushing my hand aside with her water glass.

I wrapped the dish cloth around the thumb. "Yes," I said, "I only wish Fanny would."

Shirley set the glass aside. "Whaddya mean?"

"I wish Fanny wasn't dying."

Suddenly I was on the floor screaming as Shirley beat me wherever she could find an unprotected spot.

Then Miss Eldridge was in the kitchen, wrenching Shirley off and ordering her to get up and stop that this minute. Furious, I cried, "She's going to die, Shirley. You don't get to have everything your way!"

Slamming the bathroom door, I burst into tears.

. . . .

AFTER THE LAST BELL, Shirley and I always hurried away from school, denying ourselves the pleasures of school activities or chatter about nail polish and page-boys. Although we didn't talk, we stood close together on the bus. I was afraid of the boys; I didn't know what Shirley's excuse was.

The key to Fanny's house was on a chain around my neck, along with the key to my own house. Shirley had a key to our house too, which Aunt Betty had long ago provided her. I always left my books and lunch pail on our kitchen table before going along to the Dugans'. Shirley always set to practicing immediately.

On Wednesday, September 27, I let myself into the Dugans' house and went in search of Cecil and Percy, who were lying beside Fanny's bed. Fanny's lunch tray, brought in by a neighbor, lay untouched on the bedside table.

"Fanny?"

She was sleeping, her breath rattling. I had to drag the dogs to the front door and out. Once outside, they trotted along in a businesslike fashion, far more sedate than when we first met. They were preoccupied with Fanny's dying.

We climbed the slope and I led them up and down until they finally relieved themselves. Then we sat down in a spot not far from our house, and I petted them and teased them a little, though they did not have much heart for it.

Gazing down on Piñon Street, I noted a boy on a bicycle delivering the afternoon paper; a vegetable truck turning into the street, bell clanging; and several women stepping out of their houses to meet beside the vendor's wagon as it pulled to the curb near Uncle Stanley's Ford.

At the mouth of the street, three of the monkey-bar boys lollopped along together, one tossing a ball into the air, then swooping forward to catch it.

I did not run or try to hide but sat observing them until they disappeared out of view. Then I rose, slapping my thigh. Cecil and Percy lumbered to their feet.

282 / *Faith Sullivan*

Returning the dogs, I met Mrs. Grey, Fanny's door-opposite neighbor, coming away with the lunch tray. "Didn't touch it," she observed anxiously. "She won't let me feed her," she explained, as if I might think her neglectful. Mrs. Grey was young and expecting a baby in two or three months.

I emptied Cecil and Percy's water dishes, filling them with fresh water. Jack fed them when he got home, but I usually gave them each a biscuit from a box in the cupboard. Today they stared at the treat I offered, turning away and marching to their post by Fanny's bed. I followed.

As I drew near, I heard Fanny speak. Her voice was childlike, weak but urgent.

I hurried to the bed. "What is it, Fanny?"

Eyes closed, chest heaving, she whispered, "Pat . . ."

Her brother.

Tears slipped from beneath her lids. "I never. . . . You know." Her hands investigated the surface of the bedclothes, searching for something.

"Fanny." I grasped her hand, trying to wake her. Lowering myself to the chair beside the bed, I released the hand, which was desperate to search. I got it into my head that she was searching for forgiveness.

Sometimes people needed to be forgiven for sins they hadn't committed. Often people asked forgiveness for what were really God's negligences. And other times they asked forgiveness for sins so tiny they were of no consequence.

Referring to sin, Sister Mary Clare at Saint Boniface once said, "Even a grain of pepper shows up on a white cloth." Well, people can make themselves sick to death worrying about grains of pepper.

"Fanny," I said close to her ear, clasping her restless hand once more. "Fanny, I forgive you."

52

EARLY THE NEXT MORNING, Jack knocked at our door. "Fan's gone," he told Aunt Betty.

Aunt Betty put her arms around him. "I'm sorry." Leading him to the kitchen, she drew out a chair and placed a cup of tea in front of him.

Mama had left for work and I was preparing to leave for school, but I hung unnoticed at the kitchen door.

"She was so young," Jack kept saying. "Thirty-nine." Despite Fanny's long illness, her death was a surprise to him. "Thirty-nine," he repeated, looking at my aunt and shaking his head. Then he said, "She died peacefully." He seemed to find comfort in this.

Aunt Betty inquired, "Did you call her family?"

"I sent a telegram. I couldn't stand to hear what they'd say, do you understand?"

My aunt sat down and put her hand on one of Jack's.

He explained, "What if they said, 'Why are you calling us'? The only ones who cared were her gran, and she's dead, and young Dennis, who's God-knows-where in the Pacific."

"What can I do?" Aunt Betty asked.

He looked at her, trying to think.

"Tell the neighbors? The Eldridges, Mrs. Grey? Who else?"

"There's no one."

"There's Shirley," I said.

. . . .

Considering the small number of mourners, it seemed strange to hold a wake, but Jack said "It's the least I can do," and on Friday night we all gathered in the Dugans' living room to view Fanny in her casket—even Miss Eldridge and Beau.

Fanny was wearing a bright red, silk organza dress, a little shocking and doubtless her own choice. Guilt and defiance. No wonder she'd understood Shirley and me.

Shirley, with a great deal of cerise lipstick slathered on her mouth, sat next to the casket on a straight-back chair. Later, in the bathroom, she reapplied the lipstick with a lavish hand and let me puff a cigarette she'd filched from Jack's pack of Wings.

Her eyes were swollen and I thought she'd been crying.

Mrs. Grey, Miss Eldridge, Mama, and Aunt Betty had all brought food, three times what was needed, everything spread out on the kitchen table.

Jack had set up a bar beside the kitchen sink and people helped themselves. I poured myself a glass of Coca-Cola, as did Shirley, but Shirley added gin to hers when she thought no one was looking. She carried it to her post beside the casket.

I sat with Cecil and Percy on the floor near the kitchen door and listened to the grown-ups. At first their talk was of Fanny. Where would she be buried? In her beloved Chicago, near Lake Michigan.

Mr. and Mrs. Grey left early, Mrs. Grey's ankles being very swollen. Once they had departed, the talk wandered into paths unforeseen, death and alcohol unlatching the gates. A host of dead came to claim the newly dead, Baby Marjorie among them.

"Marjorie's casket was so small," Aunt Betty recalled, using her fork to push bits of marshmallow culled from the Jello salad this way and that.

"Yes," Mama concurred, "hardly bigger than a laundry basket."

"She was a beautiful baby. Perfect little fingers and toes. Her ears and eyelids looked like white marble," Aunt Betty told Miss Eldridge.

Beautiful? Baby Marjorie? She'd looked like an under-done baby bird, scrawny and beaky.

At the kitchen table, Beau spoke to Jack about the war, remarking on the capture of Brest, which he said was "the beginning of the end" for Hitler. Then he added, "Maybe I'll get into it yet." Was that the bourbon talking?

I was surprised to see Miss Eldridge accept a glass of wine early in the evening, and another later. Her conversation was freer than usual, and she spoke knowledgably on a number of topics, embalming among them.

"The Egyptians were embalming people thousands of years B.C.," she informed me. "Sometimes, when archeologists dig up mummies, they find the bottoms of the feet are still soft—after thousands of years!"

I would have liked to hear more of this, but Aunt Betty grabbed the wheel of the conversation, steering it onto Shirley and her piano career.

"On the fifteenth of December, three of Madame Buchova's pupils will play a benefit program in La Jolla to raise money for European orphans. Shirley is the youngest on the program," my aunt said. "Wouldn't Fanny be proud?"

Shirley seemed not to hear this. She sat her vigil, now and then refreshing her glass of Coca-Cola and gin.

"Fanny would be proud," Mama agreed. What a muddler she'd become, unable to bear losing her sister's love yet wanting Aunt Betty's husband!

"It's odd, isn't it, that Mrs. Dugan didn't have a piano here," Miss Eldridge noted.

"But she'd been frail for several years," Aunt Betty said.

"Yes, of course," said Mama, subscribing to Aunt Betty's theory, waiting for another so that she could concur with it too.

"My mother had a grand piano," Miss Eldridge said.

We waited for her to enlarge upon this.

"She was a cultured woman," she went on. Her eyes glittered, her cheeks were flushed, and her soft brown hair had escaped from the bun at the back of her head.

"Cultured and lonely. Yet she wouldn't mix with town folk." Miss Eldridge brushed away a wisp of hair. "She had a library, more extensive and sophisticated than the town library, and she had the grand piano, shipped out from Minneapolis." Miss Eldridge sipped her wine.

"What made her marry a farmer in the first place?" Aunt Betty asked.

Miss Eldridge held out her empty glass and I took it, unsure whether she wanted it refilled but filling it nevertheless from the bottle in the kitchen, where Beau was relating stories of pheasant hunting in Nebraska. Jack smoked and nodded, grateful for Beau's talk of twelve- and sixteen-gauge shotguns, of corn fields and hunting dogs and brilliant autumn days.

Miss Eldridge took the wine. "My mother had been spoiled by indulgent parents and four brothers. The only time she didn't have her way was in marriage. That was arranged. I was told by an aunt that she came to the marriage disdainful."

Miss Eldridge held her glass to the light. "In the end, she pretty much destroyed us all." Although there was nothing funny in what she'd said, she laughed.

Uneasy, Aunt Betty glanced around at Shirley and me. Before my aunt could send us home, we headed for the bathroom, lingering out of sight to listen.

Miss Eldridge told Mama and Aunt Betty about the country school teachers who had lived in the Eldridge house. "Plenty of country schools needed teachers, but few could offer room and board in a house with a grand piano and a library. For William Bates, the library was a strong inducement. He was writing a novel." Her voice faltered.

I sat down on the hall floor and leaned against the door of Fanny's linen closet.

"I'm rambling," Miss Eldridge said. "I don't ordinarily take spirits. Tomorrow I'll be so ashamed, I won't be able to face you."

As I drifted through the living room and into the kitchen, I found that the men had moved on from pheasants to the long hours they were putting in at the plant, sometimes sixty a week.

Beau rose from the table. "Matter of fact, I've got a long day tomorrow, and a half day on Sunday." He shook Jack's hand. "When you're back from Chicago, I'll come by. Take care. Don't get up."

But Jack did rise and follow.

At the door, Beau called to his sister, "I'll leave the door unlocked." In the dim light of the living room, Miss Eldridge's face was indistinct. He hurried down the steps, unaware of her desolation.

Aunt Betty crossed to Jack. "Wouldn't you like to call it a day?" she asked. "We'll clean up the kitchen."

"If you ladies don't mind, I'll take the dogs out."

Aunt Betty and Mama quickly saw to the leftovers, washed the dishes, and tidied up, but it was difficult withdrawing from Fanny. Mama poured herself a shot of whiskey. More surprisingly, so did Aunt Betty. Miss Eldridge, who sat clutching and releasing a wadded linen handkerchief, held out her other hand with the wine glass empty. I refilled it.

The five of us—Mama, Aunt Betty, Miss Eldridge, Shirley, and I—found ourselves sitting like priestesses in a semicircle around Fanny's casket.

"Do they leave tomorrow?" Mama asked.

Aunt Betty nodded.

"When will he be back?"

"The end of next week."

"I can't believe Fanny's people won't be heartbroken," Mama said.

"For them, she died years ago," Aunt Betty said.

"But don't you think people regret those things after a while?" Was she thinking of herself and Aunt Betty?

Again Miss Eldridge laughed.

Aunt Betty took the wine glass that swayed in Miss Eldridge's hand, threatening to slop its contents.

Miss Eldridge's hand flew to find the little brooch of opals, seed pearls, and sapphires. She tossed her head to one side, then dropped her chin. "He gave me this little brooch as a pledge. My God, what she did to him."

Aunt Betty turned to me, threw an arm across my shoulders, and began shepherding me to the door. "Shirley, come along."

Shirley did not want to move, but Aunt Betty was determined.

Miss Eldridge cried, "He was so innocent. . . . He had no experience. . . ." Her lips trembled like a child's.

My aunt opened the door. "You have a key?"

I put my hand to my chest and Aunt Betty shoved Shirley and me out the door.

Behind us, Miss Eldridge said, "She got pregnant. . . ."

Around the corner of the house, I stopped beneath the Dugans' open living room windows. From the other side, we heard, "They came from Canada. My mother's brothers. They beat him so . . . he was nearly dead." Silence, then, "I wanted to care for him, but his family came and carried him back to Pennsylvania.

"Papa wouldn't raise William's baby, so I took him."

53

ALTHOUGH SHIRLEY STILL got on the bus with me after school, she didn't get off at our stop. For all I knew, she rode the bus all night. She did not show up at our house to practice.

Aunt Betty was worried. The week following Fanny's wake, Shirley missed her lesson with Madame.

"What's happening?" Aunt Betty asked one evening as I was feeding Cecil and Percy, who stayed with us while Jack was away. "What's the matter with Shirley?"

"It's on account of Fanny."

"How is that?"

How to explain? "Fanny called her 'sweet patootie' and 'the cat's pajamas' and told her she had a great soul. Nobody ever talked to Shirley like that before, not even you. Fanny was like, I don't know, like an angel to Shirley." And like an aunt to me.

. . . .

JACK CAME TO DINNER the Monday after he returned from Chicago.

"Tell us about the trip," Aunt Betty said.

"Well, I'd been in touch with a school chum of Fan's," he told her as he settled on the sofa. "She handled things at that end, arranged a Mass and a Palmer House gathering afterward."

"Her family?" Mama asked.

"One brother came, but only to report back to the rest of them."

After Jack left with Cecil and Percy, Aunt Betty sat down at the piano and picked out notes among the treble keys while she stared at the bare music board in front of her.

"Please play," I said. I missed Shirley's practicing.

I did not miss Shirley's temper, but when she failed to show up for her lesson a second time I began to worry, while in the smallness of my heart thinking how the mighty had fallen.

Meanwhile Miss Eldridge had gone into an embarrassed seclusion. The problem with being too much of a lady is that you are too easily embarrassed. I knocked on her door. She didn't answer. I wrote her a note. She didn't respond. The curtains were drawn everywhere except beside Billy's cage.

Days and weeks passed. When we had a short letter from Uncle Stanley informing us in his peculiar code that he was with a group that had crossed the Moselle River, I wanted to run across and tell Miss Eldridge. Last time we'd heard, he was in Italy. His outfit had been pulled out and redeployed.

> I'm alive, running my rear end off, and seeing the world.
>
> I hope this finds you well. Do you get out to the movies and to a dance once in a while? I'm sure you're all working too hard. What are Spencer Tracy and Katharine Hepburn up to?
>
> We've been moved around a lot but now seem to be involved in a slower (censored) action, and losses are (censored). I'm grateful to be in the medics. I feel a usefulness and wholeness I never felt before.
>
> How will this all mesh after the war, to make a life? It's exciting to think about, and I can't wait to see.
>
> My love to you, Darling Betty, a hug for Arlene and Shirley, and a kiss from my heart for my little comrade.
>
> Stanley

Later, as she bent over the ironing board, pressing a blouse, Aunt Betty said, "Stanley sees a lot of himself in you."

I was thrilled. "Really? Like how?"

"You're both dreamers. You like to talk about ideas."

"Don't you?"

"I'm always a little embarrassed to hear people jawing about ideas, and all the while they haven't really done anything."

"A lot of times I don't know what I think until I say it. Maybe Uncle Stanley's like that. Maybe that's why he thinks we're alike."

"It wouldn't surprise me," she said dryly, setting the iron down and turning the blouse. She gave the placket a final press and held it up for scrutiny. Slipping the blouse onto a hanger, she cast me a smile. The Madonna of Ladies Ready to Wear.

This same sort of tenderness made Aunt Betty worry about Jack and Shirley. She invited them each to dinner at least once a week. Jack accepted. Shirley didn't.

Jack was gratified to be fostered and indulged. He always showed up with some small offering: a bottle of Roma wine, sheet music for "I'll Walk Alone," a book of card tricks for me or a Ngaio Marsh mystery for Mama.

Usually he brought along his tool box to cut a board for our linen closet or to rewire one of our Trustworthy lamps. Jack could do anything. But his comings and goings had a frenetic quality.

"I worry about Jack," Aunt Betty said.

I looked up from *Tales from the Arabian Nights*. "You are the world's champion worrier."

"He's too . . . busy," she said.

It was Saturday night. Mama and Melba were dancing at the Shalimar Ballroom. I set my book aside.

"Well, he's a man of action," I said. I'd come across that expression in *Life* magazine. "And he's sad. And when he's sad, he has to act, he has to be useful. It makes him feel better."

Aunt Betty rested her chin on her palm. "Yes," she said finally. "Yes, you're right. And I like that about him."

54

I RAN BERSERK from room to room, crawling under beds, ransacking closets. The oil painting was gone.

I'd been the last to leave the house in the morning, and it had been there then. I always gave it a final glance before leaving.

My mind raced off in every direction, over the Project, over the city, as if a thief from the other side of town might have crept in while I was at school.

On the bus, coming home from school, I'd stood beside Shirley. I'd exited at Piñon, and she hadn't. Heading straight for the Dugans', I'd taken Percy and Cecil for a run up on the slope. Minutes ago, I'd returned.

Burying my fists between my thighs, I rocked back and forth. Who'd burgle a house and only take a second-hand painting?

Shirley. Shirley who'd wanted it from the beginning. Shirley who had a key to our house. Shirley. Always Shirley.

Now I was outside, tearing across lawns, up Piñon.

I banged on the door. "Open up, you damned thief! Give me my painting!"

Although it was growing dark, no light shown from inside. But she was there. "Don't ever come to our house again!"

Trudging down the hill, I ached with loss.

When Mama arrived home from work, I was a mess, face red and swollen, head throbbing. She was exhausted and in no mood. "Now, settle down," she kept saying, "And stop the melodrama."

Melodrama? "Go to hell," I screamed. "All you care about is Uncle Stanley and . . . fucking sailors!"

I flew to the bedroom. Flicking on the lamp, I pulled a drawer from my bureau and tipped it over. Thank God I'd removed my money from behind the painting. Otherwise Shirley would have had that too.

I didn't leave my room that night, and Mama didn't try to come in. Nor in the ensuing days did we talk about the things I'd screamed. I expected her to call me on the carpet, but she didn't.

My eyes were still red and swollen the next day. The history teacher asked if everything was all right. Riding home on the bus, I hissed in Shirley's ear, "I know you took the painting."

She said nothing.

I moved to a seat by the rear door.

Shirley did not try to follow.

As for Aunt Betty, she was more concerned about Shirley than about the painting. "Can we sit down and discuss Shirley?" she asked, pulling out a kitchen chair. "She hasn't practiced since Fanny died. Madame had to drop her from the fund-raiser because she's missed her lessons."

"It's not my fault," I told her.

"Of course it's not. But I'm not sure you understand the seriousness of what's happening."

Out of respect for Aunt Betty, I listened.

"Shirley's talent is all she has in the world."

"She's got my painting."

Aunt Betty sighed. "I'm sorry about the painting. If she took it, it was wrong. I'll buy you another oil painting. We'll go down to Trustworthy Second Hand Saturday."

Angry, I walked away.

A week after my conversation with Aunt Betty, as suddenly as Shirley had left, she returned. I was coming down the slope with the dogs and, passing our door on my way to the Dugans', I heard a Brahms piece Shirley had been working on weeks before.

She didn't lift her head when I came in, but played on, *furioso, furioso, furioso.*

55

SHIRLEY WAS DETERMINED to practice her way back into the December twentieth fund-raiser. Maybe she'd thought about Fanny and what Fanny would want. But an angry Madame Buchova refused to say until the first lesson in December whether Shirley would play.

Mama and Aunt Betty agreed that Shirley could practice half an hour in the morning, before we caught the bus, and again for two hours after school. On Saturdays and Sundays, she was allowed unlimited practice during the day. For Shirley's sake, we would accommodate this schedule for a month, Aunt Betty said. For Shirley's sake. For Shirley's sake.

The afternoon of December 20, a bright, cool day, Mama and Aunt Betty fluttered and buzzed around Shirley. Did the black velvet cummerbund lie properly? Was the slip too long? Aunt Betty smoothed a bit of color on Shirley's lips and cheeks so that she would not look washed out under the stage lights. To all their ministrations, Shirley gave way, silently.

A week before, Jack had come to Aunt Betty wanting to know what Shirley would wear. It ought to be special. My aunt agreed. She planned to buy Shirley a new outfit.

"Could I buy her, maybe, a coat, a gift from Fan?"

Now, as she helped Shirley into the new coat, Mama was saying, "Don't be nervous. We'll be there, and we love you."

"It's all right to be nervous," Aunt Betty said. "Nerves will give you that little . . . extra . . . that lifts you up."

Shirley seemed not to hear any of this.

Because the musicians were required to be at the auditorium an hour in advance, Shirley left early, called for by the parent of a fellow performer. Our prodigy, looking smart in lilac taffeta and a camel-colored coat, hurried silently away.

Jack, Aunt Betty, Mama, and I climbed into Uncle Stanley's car for the drive to La Jolla, Jack in a dark gray suit, looking like somebody's big boss.

I wore a new red velveteen skirt, a white sweater, and new black patent dress shoes. The shoes were the only reason I was attending the program. I had refused until Mama said that I would have no new pumps unless I did.

At the concert, Shirley indeed seemed to have been lifted up, playing with more feeling and nuance than ever. After the first tensely correct chords, she drifted away—Shirley, the piano, and the bench on which she sat—to an island where she was unreachable.

Everyone said what a pity it was that Fanny didn't live to hear the performance, but I wondered if Fanny wasn't hanging around the piano, wearing her red organza dress and calling Shirley a sweet patootie.

It was past five by the time Shirley could tear herself away from an admiring throng to join Aunt Betty and Jack in the front seat of the car. Whisking us off to an expensive La Jolla restaurant near the ocean, Jack treated everyone to dinner. Shirley had never been within a mile of anything like it. Neither had I.

The grown-ups fussed over Shirley's triumph till I nearly lost my appetite. I expected Shirley to crow or simper, but she was quiet, only now and then swimming to the surface to answer a question.

Watching her as she toyed with the deep-fried shrimp on her plate, I surmised that she felt safe when she was on the island, much as I felt safe in the cabin. The thought of the cabin and the stolen painting brought tears to my eyes and I excused myself, hoping Shirley choked on her shrimp.

The lounge of the ladies room was deeply carpeted. Along one wall stretched an impressive length of vanity, the mirror behind it rising to the ceiling. On the vanity's highly polished black surface, mirrored boxes of tissues sat waiting, and in front of the vanity plush little stools sprouted like a row of mauve mushrooms.

Sinking down on one of the poufs, I snatched a tissue from a box and dabbed the corners of my eyes. I was not going to humiliate myself by having red eyes. Everyone would think it was a fit of jealousy.

In the adjoining room where sinks and stalls were lined up, I could hear the attendant refilling the roller-towel dispenser. Suddenly, behind me, the outer door flew open and a flash of lilac taffeta whispered through the lounge and into the next room, emitting a soft mewling as it went. I sat staring in the mirror. Was Shirley crying, moaning? I dashed into the other room to find her bent over a sink, vomiting.

"What's wrong? Should I get Aunt Betty?" I looked to the attendant who was wetting a cloth and holding it against Shirley's forehead as the retching continued. The attendant answered my glance with a slight shake of her head.

Finally, Shirley rinsed her face with cold water and straightened.

"Did you eat something bad?" I asked.

"Get out of here!" she screamed. The sound in the ceramic-tiled room was so brilliant that it hurt my eyeballs.

The attendant nodded and I hurried back to the table, trying to appear nonchalant.

"Where's Shirley?" Mama asked.

"Talking to the attendant," I said, slipping into my seat.

"We're ordering dessert," Aunt Betty said.

"Shirley doesn't want any," I told her.

"How do you know?"

"She told me she was stuffed."

"I don't know how she could be," Mama said. "She hardly touched her food."

"She's still nervous from the concert. We should just pretend we don't notice."

"Lark's right," Aunt Betty said. "This was a very big event for Shirley."

When Shirley returned, she wasn't all blotchy or ashen. The attendant had probably fixed her up, powdered her nose and combed her hair. But she was—what? Frightened. Strange, since the concert was safely behind her.

Later, as I was putting my red velveteen skirt away in the closet, I heard Mama say to Aunt Betty, "Isn't it sad the way she has to leave her good clothes here? What would happen to them, do you think, if she wore them home?"

56

By Tuesday, the whole school knew about the concert. One teacher had actually attended, and the others had read a small review in the *Union,* which made special note of Shirley. Someone tacked the review on the bulletin board outside the principal's office. But instead of basking in the admiration of former detractors, Shirley was panicked.

After the final bell, she dashed from school so fast she caught the bus ahead of mine. When I reached Piñon, I didn't see her. But as I headed past our stoop, Cecil and Percy trotting along beside me, I heard her pounding out chord exercises as if she were beating the piano into submission.

Cecil and Percy had grown old since Fanny's death. They still chased cats, but mostly they strolled along, perfect gentlemen. Returning from our walk at a quarter to six, I found Shirley still at the piano. After supper, when it was time for her to leave, she delayed until Mama finally said, "Lark, it's time for bed." And to Shirley, who was seated at the kitchen table poring over a history text with unwonted interest, "You, too, Shirley. Time to head home."

Shirley closed the book and sat staring.

"Is something wrong?" Mama asked.

Scooping up her things, Shirley was gone.

The next morning, I glimpsed her in the hall between classes, two of the boys following her, the handsome, dark-haired one jabbing at her with the pointed end of a protractor, the other laughing.

After school, Shirley fell in with me in the hall, an unheard-of thing, and we waited for the bus together. At the Dugans' walk, we parted, Shirley going on to my house. But a few minutes later, when I passed the door, no music poured out.

The dogs and I marched up and down, Cecil and Percy searching out their accustomed spots to lift a leg. Then we rested together, me talking to them about Fanny and how she looked down from heaven and saw what good dogs they were, Cecil and Percy lying, heads on their paws, enormous liquid eyes fixed on me, following every word.

Without warning, the dogs sprang to their feet and high-tailed it eastward, after a cat. I got to my feet, ready to pursue.

Off to the north, from the direction of the gulch, came a cry, more like a scream. The back of my neck tingled.

I burst across the ragged green and, reaching the lip of the ravine, plunged down, snatching up a twisted tree limb at the bottom and darting along the rocky bed, among the scrub oaks and undergrowth.

And there they were, off to the right, in front of the hideout: Shirley struggling, her skirt shoved up to her waist, a rag stuffed in her mouth, her brother and another boy holding down her legs while the handsome, dark-haired boy, knife in his right hand so that he had to use his forearm for leverage, held Shirley's wrists to the ground. A fourth boy stood unbuttoning his trousers.

As I leapt across the last stretch of rocky ground, the boys looked up with blank faces. Swinging the twisted limb in every direction, I fell on them, landing blows, wheeling around and around. I heard the grunting sound of purpose in my throat, the satisfying *whump* as the branch hit home, the gratifying howl from the victim.

I wanted to kill them, but they wouldn't stand still. They were wheeling, losing their balance, scrabbling, scruffing away, fleeing. And then they were gone.

Chest heaving, I stood, trying not to tremble. Pulling the rag from her mouth, Shirley got to her knees. "My hand," she wept. She lifted her right hand. Blood poured from it.

"Can you . . . hold it real tight?" I asked, not sure what to do. Tossing aside my weapon, I helped her up, and we stumbled up the rugged side of the arroyo.

At the rim, Cecil and Percy came running, whining when they saw that Shirley was hurt. Dashing ahead and barking, they led the way. When we gained the grassy descent to Piñon, I started yelling, "Somebody help! Somebody help!"

I ran to Miss Eldridge's door, wailing and pounding on it. Shirley dropped down on the steps and laid her head on the stoop.

Miss Eldridge yanked the door open. "Oh, my God," she murmured and ran for a bath towel. Returning, she laid it under Shirley's hand and sent me for a clean dish towel and a wooden spoon. Grabbing the towel from me and tearing it into a couple of strips, she wrapped one around Shirley's arm, tying it tightly. Slipping the spoon handle between the cloth and the arm, she twisted, creating a tourniquet.

"Get the keys to your uncle's car," she told me. "Hurry."

As we supported Shirley down the walk to the car, Miss Eldridge demanded, "Where's a doctor?"

I tried to think. In nearly four years, I hadn't been to a doctor. But I recalled a shingle in front of a house on Garnet Street and instructed Miss Eldridge as she helped Shirley and me into the front seat, then climbed in behind the wheel. As we drove down Piñon, turning onto Garnet, she explained how I should twist the spoon and cloth, hold it briefly, release it, wait, twist it again, and so on. I did this, not convinced that it was helping. The bath towel was soaked, as well as a second towel I'd grabbed from our bathroom.

Although it was less than two miles to the place where I'd seen a doctor's shingle, the trip seemed endless. Shirley's head lay against the seat, eyes closed, skin pale and blue.

I whispered, "Does it hurt a lot?"

She moved her head slowly from side to side.

Half a dozen patients waited in the outer room of the doctor's office, but when the nurse saw the blood-soaked towel she hurried Shirley away, telling Miss Eldridge and me that we'd have to be seated. Miss Eldridge said that she would not be seated. "I'm not leaving this child," she said in her schoolteacher voice.

The nurse looked vexed but she gave way, and Miss Eldridge, nodding to me with a satisfied little curl of her lip, hastened down a hallway behind Shirley and the nurse.

People were looking sideways at me, guessing that I was responsible for Shirley's injury. Finding no empty chair, I picked up an old *Collier's* magazine from a table and stood with my back against a doorjamb, pretending to read.

As the minutes dragged by, I grew apprehensive. If the cut were minor, Shirley would have been bandaged and out already.

The others waiting were beginning to look at their watches. Beyond the windows, night had crept on. The nurse came out and lowered the venetian blinds. A woman grabbed at the nurse's arm, asking, "How long?" and the nurse said, "A few minutes." She returned to wherever they had Shirley and people scowled at me. A woman paced up and down, trying to comfort a crying baby, and a toddler threw magazines on the floor. Another woman lit cigarette after cigarette and tapped her fingernails against her handbag. Across the room, an old man coughed and spit into a handkerchief.

Just when it seemed that the room would boil over with aggravation, the nurse emerged, advising Miss Eldridge over her shoulder, "Doctor will want to see her the day after tomorrow. Two in the afternoon. But if she starts to run a fever or you see any sign of infection, get her in here right away." She turned and handed Miss Eldridge two little bottles of pills, then moved out into the waiting room, revealing a dazed and pallid Shirley, Miss Eldridge beside her, an arm around her.

Miss Eldridge led Shirley to the door. I ran ahead to open it, asking, "Is she all right? What'd he do? What'd he say?" I opened the car door on the passenger side and Miss Eldridge, ignoring my questions, helped Shirley negotiate a one-handed entry. The ring finger and little finger of Shirley's right hand were each heavily bandaged, and the gauze wound up and around the palm to fasten at the wrist.

Miss Eldridge shook her head and put the key into the ignition.

57

Mama was waiting on the stoop, Cecil and Percy beside her.

"What *happened?*" she cried, jumping to her feet and holding the door.

"Give us a minute," Miss Eldridge said, leading Shirley through the door and to the sofa.

"Shirley got hurt," I explained. "She cut her hand."

"How?"

I looked at Shirley.

"I was playing with my brother's jack knife," she said, her voice thin as skim milk.

Mama didn't press her.

"Miss Eldridge drove Shirley to the doctor," I said.

"And what about *you?*" Mama went on. "You look like you were dragged through a knot hole backwards."

"The dogs got away from me and I had to chase them into the gulch."

She gave me a skeptical look and fetched a blanket from the linen closet. Arranging it over Shirley, she sat down beside her, brushing the hair back from Shirley's face.

"Will you tell Shirley's parents or should I?" Miss Eldridge asked. "Where does she live?"

"Stay away from them," Shirley whimpered.

Mama looked at Shirley, then at Miss Eldridge.

Miss Eldridge declined to stay for supper. At the door, she cast her eye toward the sofa and told me, "She should stay home from school tomorrow."

Mama said, "She can stay here. The piano's . . ." She broke off in mid-sentence. "The piano." She looked at Miss Eldridge.

"The ring finger on her right hand was nearly severed," Miss Eldridge said under her breath. "And the little finger was badly cut." From one pocket of her cardigan, she extracted a hanky and dabbed at her cheeks; from the other she pulled the two bottles the nurse had given her. "One's to keep down infection. The other's for pain. If she runs a fever, we're to call the doctor." She handed Mama the bottles. "I told them I was her grandmother."

Mama nodded.

Miss Eldridge decided that Shirley ought to stay out of school both Thursday and Friday, so for the next couple of days Shirley shuttled back and forth between the Eldridges' house and ours. On Friday, Miss Eldridge drove her to the doctor's to have the dressing changed.

Shirley's final appointment was scheduled for the following Tuesday, early in the afternoon since school was out for Christmas vacation. Miss Eldridge again chauffeured.

Late that afternoon, when I returned from walking Cecil and Percy, Shirley came over from the Eldridge's, plunked down on the sofa, and began twisting a strand of hair with the fingers of her left hand. All at once, tears streamed down her face.

"Shirley?"

She held up her now unbandaged hand, healing but still looking terrible. "Look!" she bawled. "Look at it!"

"What?"

"That's all I can move it!"

I went closer. "Will it get better?"

"The doctor said maybe. But he just said that to make me feel better." Cradling her arm, she closed her eyes, sobbing, mourning.

I got a wash cloth, wet it with cool water, and wrung it out. "Here," I said, "put this on your forehead and lie down. Would you like an aspirin?"

She shook her head, laying the cloth on her brow, and kicking off her shoes. I sat nearby in the arm chair and tried to read an O. Henry short story in my English book.

What could I say to her? Not a damned thing. Children had the right to be inconsolable. She lay with her hands on her breast, the broken right hand pillowed by the left. I didn't think she was asleep, only removed to a forlorn place where she contemplated life without piano-playing.

Outside, the light began to fail. Shirley and I were stranded together. We were all we had. For half an hour I sat in the thick shadows with her, the only illumination a thin light from the bathroom, the only sounds the ticking of the clock and Shirley's shallow breathing.

On the sofa, Shirley sucked in her breath and exhaled in a tiny sigh.

"I'm going to make tea," I told her. "I'll bring you a cup."

While the tea kettle heated, I made toast. Mama was Christmas shopping in town and Aunt Betty was at the Red Cross.

Squinting and rubbing her eyes, Shirley wandered out and sat at the kitchen table, staring at the map on the wall. Her sweater was buttoned wrong, bunched up here and hanging open there.

"You having supper at Miss Eldridge's?"

"She's fixing pot roast," Shirley said.

I slapped ole on the toast slices and sprinkled them with cinnamon sugar.

"Thank you," Shirley mumbled. "For coming down there."

"When I heard you scream, I knew it was those *Goddamn* boys." I set a bottle of milk and a cup of tea in front of her and the plate of toast between us. I pulled out a chair. "A long time ago they cornered me on the monkey bars at the old school." Talking about it was hard. "They . . . tried to . . ."

"Take down your pants?"

"Yes," I whispered. "One boy said he'd cut off my finger if I didn't let them. He had a knife."

"David."

Such a wholesome name for an evil boy. The shame I'd felt for nearly three years filled me again. "I was lucky an older boy came along and saved me."

"And you got notes from them," Shirley was saying.

"How did you know?"

"It was me that left them. If I did things for them, they'd leave me alone. That's what they said." She sipped the tea.

"They wanted to *get* you," she went on. "Whenever they saw you, you were with a grown-up or you had the dogs. You weren't scared enough. That's what they want, for kids to be scared. Girls, especially." A pause. "And I took your painting."

Somehow I wasn't angry. "Where is it?"

"In their hideout."

"What they tried to do . . . that day . . . was it the first time?"

"No." Hands folded in her lap now, she sat, unnaturally calm, numbed.

"But you could get a baby." The enormity of it shook me. We were only twelve years old.

"Remember when I said a Jap pushed me down a cliff? I fought real hard, and that time I got away." She stared at the map behind me.

How many times had she not gotten away?

"D'ya feel like you're gonna remember and remember and remember? What they did?" she asked.

I nodded.

"It's not like a rattlesnake bite, where you get well and forget."

"Why didn't you tell your mother?"

"Did *you*? Anyway, she don't care. And my brother would just lie about it."

"You were so scared Sunday at the restaurant."

"The boys don't like it if you get . . . above them."

Shirley bit off the corner of a piece of toast.

I rested my elbows on the table, cupping my head in my hands. I didn't really want to talk about these things. But I would if Shirley needed to.

It wasn't merely that I'd shared a space with Shirley, however grudgingly, for two and a half years; and it wasn't pity for what she'd endured and what she'd lost. Those figured in, but mainly we were a club of two members, tainted by the boys.

"You've got to do something," I said.

"I gotta leave." For a moment, her eyes darted, like marbles in a pinball machine. "I gotta get back to Wyoming."

"But your folks are here."

She shook her head. "They're terrible drinkers, worse than no folks at all. They got run off the ranch."

"But . . . how would you get back to Wyoming? Where would you stay?"

"Maybe I could ride the rails," she said. "One time you said something about catching a freight back to Minnesota. If I could get to Lander or Riverton. . . . Hell, if I could even get to Rock Springs I could hitchhike."

I did not like the sound of this. "If we told Miss Eldridge or Jack, I bet they'd help you."

"What would I say? 'My folks drink too much and they don't want me'? Nobody helps you get to Wyoming for a reason like that."

"If you got there, where you used to live, wouldn't they send you back here?" I asked.

"Maybe not. In Wyoming, they know my folks."

My head ached with Shirley's dilemma.

"Where's the depot?" she wanted to know.

"In town. By the harbor."

"I'm going there tomorrow and see if I can figure out how to do this."

"I don't think you should. It's dangerous. My papa used to talk about California railroad bulls. They were like cops to keep people from riding in box cars. Papa said the ones in California were the worst. They'd as soon kill you as look at you. What if they still have them?"

"I could hitchhike."

"It's winter. You'd freeze to death before you got there. Do you have any money?"

"Maybe I could steal some."

"Wait a minute."

Returning from my room, I emptied the manila envelope onto the table and began pulling one- and five-dollar bills from it.

Shirley stared. "Where'd you get that?"

"I've been saving it. Birthdays and Christmases and allowance and walking the dogs." I counted out two hundred and thirty-seven dollars, my hands shaking. I shoved it across the table.

"I can't take that," Shirley said.

"Why not?"

"It's yours."

"You were going to steal from someone," I said.

"Not from you." She pushed the heap away.

"Well, then borrow it," I said and again shoved it at her. "You can pay me back later, when you get a job. Send me a dollar a week or

310 / *Faith Sullivan*

something. If you borrow the money, I won't worry about you so much. You'll be doing me a favor. I'd be grateful if you took it."

Shirley stared out the window.

"When will you leave?" I asked.

"Tomorrow."

Tomorrow.

We bent our heads over the table and began to plan.

58

Dear Sir,

Please sell my eleven year old daughter, Katherine Albers, a one-way ticket to Riverton, Wyoming where she will be met by her grand-parents. I am sorry I can't see her off, but I am laid up with a broken back.

Thank you.

Mrs. Reggie Albers

Before Mama limped home from Christmas shopping, I wrote the note for Shirley to hand the person selling tickets. My handwriting looked grown-up; Shirley's didn't.

I had decided to make Shirley eleven instead of twelve because I knew the fare changed at twelve. This would leave her more of the two hundred dollars to start her new life. She'd refused to accept more than two hundred of the two hundred and thirty-seven dollars, so she'd be poor enough as it was.

Calling her Katherine Albers was to kiss her with luck. Katherine Albers of Harvester, Minnesota, had white leather figure skates, a play house, and perfect little teeth. Surely the name carried some magic. Also, if the FBI started looking for Shirley, no memory of her name would exist at the train station.

I slipped the note into my purse, along with a second envelope bulging with two hundred dollars.

Pulling from the closet the grip Aunt Betty had given Shirley for camp, I packed Shirley's good clothes, keeping back a red plaid two-piece dress with a peplum and lace at the collar. It spoke of innocence and vulner-ability. Her black patent shoes, white lisle anklets, and camel-colored coat would complete the ensemble, as they said in *Photoplay*. Shirley had to look like someone who would never run away from home, some-one who was sent to her grandmother's when her mother was laid up.

Shirley showed up a few minutes after seven-thirty the next morning, when Mama and Aunt Betty had left for work. As soon as she'd eaten, she bathed, washed her hair, and donned the clothes I'd chosen. Then we dabbed her with a little of my Evening in Paris.

Leaving the house, we tiptoed past Miss Eldridge's window. "I wish I could of said good-bye," Shirley said while we waited for the bus. "I wrote some notes to people and put 'em in your top bureau drawer. You can give 'em out at Christmas. I'll be wherever I'm going by then."

I reached for a hanky in my coat pocket.

"Jesus, don't cry," Shirley muttered.

I tried to think of something happy.

"When you're living in Wyoming, will you wear a cowboy hat?"

"Yeah, probably."

On the bus, I told Shirley how to act when she bought her ticket: helpless and sad. And then I told her everything I thought she should know about trains. The main thing all along the line was to be helpless and sad. And not cuss.

It took forever to get Shirley's ticket. When we finally got to the front of the line, the man doing the ticketing had to look up the routing and check everything three times. Before he let Shirley go, he said, "I'm sorry about your mother, Katherine. You're a brave little girl." Nodding at me, he asked her, "Your friend seeing you off?"

"Yes, sir," Shirley replied in a respectful and sad manner. She was getting the hang of it.

Since we had an hour before Shirley's train left, we bought coffee and doughnuts and a box lunch for her. She could still eat in the dining car, but this would tide her over between meals. We took the food and the grip outside to watch trains come and go so Shirley could get a feel for them.

As the moment to say good-bye approached, we fell silent. In the planning, the trip had sounded easy, even fun, but the enormity of it was starting to sink in.

"If nobody gives you a place to stay," I told her, "you've got enough money to come back. You'll come back, won't you, if you don't find a place?"

Gazing intently down the tracks as her train pulled up, Shirley nodded. Her face, long closed tight with anger, had opened a little. I could see the way she was meant to look: delicate bones, long, expressive hazel eyes, and a thin but gracefully bowed mouth.

We found her car and I saw her onto it and to a seat, noting the cast of characters in her vicinity—the grandmotherly woman sitting beside her, the lovey-dovey soldier and his bride opposite, the bride wearing a gardenia corsage. Of course, this threesome wouldn't necessarily be with Shirley all the way to Wyoming, but it was an auspicious beginning.

The grandmotherly woman indicated that Shirley could have the window seat. Suddenly my arms were around Shirley and I was kissing her cheek. "Be sure to put paper on the toilet seat before you sit down," I whispered from my vast store of railway knowledge. And then I was picking my way down the crowded aisle to the exit.

The conductor was crying, "Booooard!" and the engine, way down the track, was emitting those serious steam exhortations that signal leave-taking. I wound my way in and out of the crowd on the platform until I reached Shirley's window, which she had somehow opened.

"Write to me!" I yelled.

"I'm not very good at writing," she yelled back.

"Write me a song then!"

This seemed to tickle her. "Damn right!" she laughed, then glanced at the grandmother. "Sorry, ma'am."

And Shirley was gone.

59

FOR SEVERAL MINUTES, I was unable to leave the station. At length I turned, following my feet. Anyplace but home. When I looked up, I'd wandered into the plaza.

A streetcar stood waiting while passengers embarked. I had money in my purse and a floating, disconnected feeling in my limbs.

At the curb in front of Trustworthy Second Hand, the old green pickup truck was missing. In the grimy front window of the store, a hand-lettered sign said, "I am away." Away? In a bar up the street? On the other side of the world?

I turned, feeling even more disconnected.

Later, I pushed my way through the revolving door of a downtown dime store, wondering where Shirley was by now.

The big-dime-store smell engulfed me: lunch counter fried food, stale popcorn, and cheap scent. Shrugging, I started my Christmas shopping: for Mama, a Whitman's sampler and a package of snoods; for Aunt Betty, a bottle of ink and a big box of airmail stationery. For myself, I bought construction paper and paste.

Standing at the stationery counter, paying for my purchases, I glanced across to the opposite side, where a sailor waited to pay for a fancy boxed fountain pen. He stood in profile to me, leaning an elbow on the counter. As the saleswoman counted change into my hand, he turned.

It was him: the boy with the baseball bat, the one who had saved me from the boys on the monkey bars. He couldn't have been more than sixteen or seventeen. Oh, God. I had never thought of him going off to war. He was so lovely, I could only imagine him living a charmed life, like Laurie in *Little Women*. He didn't recognize me, of course. I wanted to say something—thank him, tell him to be careful—but knew I would cry. I headed for the revolving door, feeling as though I'd lost something but not knowing what.

Outside, I pressed my way along the busy street to Gilpins' and rode the elevator to the third floor. The clock on the wall opposite the elevator said two-thirty. Shirley had been traveling for four and a half hours.

"Lark," my aunt said, surprised, "what are *you* doing here?"

"I want to buy a present for Miss Eldridge—window shades—and I need help."

I was late fetching Cecil and Percy and pitchy dark had come on. The dogs were wild when they saw me. Cooped up all day after Jack gave them their morning walk, they craved a sympathetic voice as well as a chance to relieve their bladders. We tramped along the top of the slope.

Overhead, waves of clouds rolled in from the ocean, covering moon and stars. The wind was middling strong, and I buttoned the last button of my jacket as Cecil and Percy sped along, nosing the weeds and peeing again and again. From the harbor, the wind bore the sad but familiar sounds of foghorns and bells.

How far was Shirley going? A thousand miles? By now, she was rolling along through those mountains and valleys that in the dark looked like the graveyard of the Titans.

As I neared the rim of the arroyo, I shuddered. At my ankles the dogs sniffed and mewled, not fond of idling on a chilly night. Suddenly and without thought, I switched on the flashlight I had brought and plunged down into the sage and tumbleweed, slipping on loose rock and reaching out to catch myself. The dogs too slipped and scuttered, raising dust and snorting.

We scraped along, reaching the bottom and diving into the heart of the black vee that extended north and west. Leaping bushes and dodging scrubby trees, we galloped like the maddened horses in Shirley's picture.

The flashlight cast a stingy illumination and twice I fell, the second time catching a toe on a half-embedded rock and pitching forward with such force that a swooning pain shot through my limbs and torso right up into my brain. The dogs whined and licked my face and nuzzled me till I lurched to my feet and hobbled on.

About seventy feet from the hideout, I saw a pinpoint of light flickering in the shallow cave. The dogs drew close. I bent to pat their backs and felt their hackles raised.

We crept along, my pulse hammering in my neck, my knees throbbing. I kept the dogs on a short lead as we stepped into the small, semicircular clearing in front of the hideout.

On one side of the shallow cave, a candle was stuck into the neck of an empty whiskey bottle, and its light, although dim, revealed my painting propped against the rear wall.

Only one of the boys was there, and when he turned I saw that it was the handsome one with the dark hair. David.

I could not prize my lips apart. My jaws were locked. At my calves the dogs thrummed with menace, a deep, ominous droning rising from their chests.

The boy turned his head abruptly and I guessed that he'd heard me and thought I was one of his gang. The only illumination was immediately round the candle and off to my right, where the pale beam of the flashlight, forgotten in my hand, lit a clump of thistles.

"It's you," the boy said.

I let the leads out a foot or so, and Cecil and Percy strained at them, throats rumbling.

"What d'ya want?" the boy asked, his bravado gone woozy.

Still I could not speak, and I prayed that the darkness concealed my trembling. I let the leads slip out a bit further, so that the dogs were only a few feet from the crouching boy.

"Get them away from me," he demanded, trying to regain his former fierceness. He rose and the dogs lunged, struggling against the restraints, their frightful lower jaws jutting.

"You let those fucking dogs bite me, you'll be sorry."

I took a step forward and the dogs advanced ahead of me. The boy backed, hunched against the far wall of the hideout, looking around for protection. His glance lit on the oil painting.

"You want this?" he asked, holding it up.

Thinking that the boy was threatening me, the dogs thrust their heavy bodies forward, dragging me a step before I could rein them.

"You can have it," the boy cried. "We never wanted it. I don't know why that bitch Shirley took it."

My scalp burned with anger. I took a step. The dogs were at the entrance to the cave.

"All right. All right," he screamed. "We told her to take it. But we weren't gonna keep it."

I could barely understand him over the barking.

"She's a friend of yours. Right? We won't touch her. Get the Goddamn dogs away, and we'll never touch her again!"

Hatred choked me. The dogs inched forward, emitting dangerous, gargling sounds.

The boy quaked, his trousers' legs fluttered. He grabbed Shirley's picture, holding both pictures out to me. "Take them!" he begged. Frantic, he glanced around. The tea tin lay in the corner. Setting the pictures aside, he fell upon the box, emptying the contents on the ground and ripping the cards to pieces. "See?" he implored, as if I'd asked him to do this.

Another tiny step forward. Hate urged me to let go of the leads. Sensing this, the boy fell to his knees, almost within reach of the dogs.

"Please," he entreated, clasping his hands. "I'm really sorry. Christ, don't let go of the dogs." He began to cry.

I watched calmly. He owed those tears to Shirley, and I would describe them to her in detail. When I'd had enough, I dragged the dogs back an inch and waited.

Still on his knees, the boy reached around for the pictures. "I'll carry 'em for you. I'll take 'em up to your house."

Again I dragged Cecil and Percy back, making room for the boy to go ahead of us.

When we reached the house, Jack was sitting on the stoop, waiting. "Are you all right?" he asked, seeing the dried blood on my legs.

The boy laid the pictures and the flashlight beside Jack and moved away quickly, swinging around to make certain I didn't release the dogs. Taking several backward steps, he turned and sprinted up Piñon.

Grinning, I held out the leashes to Jack. Then my legs went watery and I collapsed onto the stoop.

60

NEXT MORNING, I GRABBED THE PAD from the bedside table and wrote to Shirley, care of general delivery, Riverton, Wyoming:

He was down on his knees begging and crying real tears. I wish I had caught them in a Mason jar to send you.

A note from Mama lay on the kitchen table. "When you're done cleaning house, please wrap the presents for Shirley. They're in a bag in my closet behind the shoe boxes."

I slouched at the kitchen table, worrying about Shirley. She didn't have clothes warm enough for Wyoming. It would be snowing there and, according to her, "colder'n hell."

I washed the few dishes and began housecleaning. Shirley did have money, and I supposed that Riverton had stores. But if she spent money for warm clothes, how would she get back to California if no one took her in?

Putting away the dust mop, I watered the gardenia bush, then fetched the presents Mama and Aunt Betty were giving Shirley: a blue cardigan, a blue-and-green plaid skirt, Yardley's English lavender cologne, and a beginner's brassiere. I wrapped them and arranged them under the tree, feeling false and sad.

Again and again, I stopped to relish the painting, restored to its proper place above my bureau. The gilt frame was nicked in several places, and a small scratch sullied the pristine snow in the foreground. No matter.

I'd propped Shirley's horse picture against the wall on my bedside table. When we had a permanent address for her, I'd pack it up and mail it.

Three Christmas cards arrived from Papa. The picture on the front of mine showed a jolly family—mother, father, and little girl—opening the door to carolers. Papa had written on the snowy part, "This is us, next year."

Inside, he wrote:

> I received your hand-made card this week. Drawing isn't your strong suit (haha) but I was tickled to get the card. I think, despite everything, you have a good heart.
>
> I've enclosed a five and a ten. Buy yourself a Christmas treat with the ten and use the five for candles at Mass.
>
> 1945 will be the year you and your ma come back.
>
> Your loving Pa

Stuffing Papa's fifteen dollars and the fifteen remaining from my previous cache into an envelope, I taped it on the bottom of the bureau drawer again.

Mama came in with her arms full of last-minute groceries and carried them to the kitchen. "How come there're only six plates on the table?"

"Shirley can't come."

"*What?* Why not?"

"She just can't."

"You got into a fight with her."

"No, I didn't. Anyway, that never stopped her."

She started shucking off her coat. "Put these groceries away while I get cleaned up."

Of course everyone asked, as we sat down at the table, "Where's Shirley?" to which Mama replied with an edge of sarcasm, "We don't seem to know."

"Miracles do occur. Maybe her family decided to claim her for a change," said Miss Eldridge, to whom I was grateful the entire evening.

Like Jack, Beau appeared at the door wearing a suit and vest. He'd lost weight and was handsome in dark brown. Unusually animated, he tended bar, talked Consolidated news, and offered to carve the roast.

Miss Eldridge wore a smart new dress, shorter than her usual. The russet color set off her brown eyes, and the lines showed off her trim figure. Pinned to the lapel was her signature brooch of opals, seed pearls, and sapphires.

"Your dress is pretty," I told her.

"Thank you. A Christmas gift from Beau."

Miss Eldridge was different, more confident somehow. Whisking Shirley to the doctor and then looking after her had changed her, I thought, made her feel . . . competent and useful.

Dinner talk turned to the grim fighting in the Ardennes. The men spoke of Monschau and Echternach and Bastogne, the women of the hardships of winter fighting.

Mama said little. Uncle Stanley was in that neck of the woods and we'd received no Christmas letters from him, but that didn't mean he'd come to grief. Weeks went by when we didn't hear, then a whole batch of letters would arrive.

The men had retired to the living room for a cigarette and the women were cleaning up in the kitchen. Miss Eldridge screwed the lid onto a fruit jar of leftover gravy. "Beau is enlisting next week," she said casually.

Aunt Betty put down the bowl she was scrubbing and wiped her hands on her apron. She and Mama put their arms around Miss Eldridge.

Aunt Betty asked, "When did he decide?"

"He's wanted to enlist, well, I don't know, maybe since Pearl Harbor. He only stayed to look after me."

"And now?"

"I can manage." She studied the jar of gravy, turning it in her hands. "It was difficult for me, leaving Nebraska. I'd been there so long, I felt . . . almost safe."

"But . . . ," Aunt Betty began.

"You've lived in a small town," Miss Eldridge said. "You know about gossip and disgrace. Beau wouldn't have received a teaching contract if they'd discovered that he was . . . out of wedlock. And they'd have found an excuse not to renew mine."

Mama nodded.

"At any rate," Miss Eldridge continued, "none of that seems to matter here." She opened the icebox and set the gravy on a shelf. "The Project's full of people running away."

"You won't leave us when Beau enlists, will you?" Aunt Betty asked.

"After the first of the year, I'm applying for substitute teaching," she said, "here in Pacific Beach."

. . . .

JUST BEFORE THE CHRISTMAS EVE gathering dispersed, we distributed small gifts to our friends, and Miss Eldridge stared with wonder at the improbably long, skinny package I handed her.

61

I DIDN'T KNOW WHAT TO DO about Shirley's notes. I hadn't wanted to give them out on Christmas Eve and cast a shadow over the holiday. I stuffed them into my purse on Christmas Day, when we left for Jack's, but throughout the afternoon I hesitated, waiting for Shirley to telephone from the Fergusons' ranch—Jack had a phone, so she could call us there. Even when Aunt Betty said, "It's hard to believe she'd miss both Christmas Eve and Christmas Day," I said nothing.

The hours slipped away not unpleasantly. This was the first time we'd gathered in the Dugan house since Fanny's wake, and we felt her presence. But as the light at the window waned and Shirley did not call, Fanny's presence began accusing me. Something terrible had happened to Shirley, and it was my fault.

The grown-ups were draining a last cup of coffee before heading home when I snapped open my purse and withdrew the notes, each in a sealed envelope with a name printed on the front.

"Shirley asked me to give these to you," I said, moving from person to person.

Each turned a wondering face to me. *What was this?*

Mama looked provoked. What mischief involving Shirley had I got up to now? Aunt Betty looked troubled. Why had I withheld information about Shirley when she asked?

I could hardly bear to open my note. Would Shirley remind me how I'd begrudged her every little kindness?

Unfolding the sheet of lined paper, I read:

Dear Lark,

I am not a good speller, but hear goes. I am going to miss you.
You were my only girl friend in California. I was a pain in the ass
so no wonder if you got mad.

I didn't tell the grown-ups in there notes that I'm running away
to Wyoming. I told them I am visiting cousins in Texis for a while
and they shoudn't worry. I'll tell them the truth when I am settled.
Grown-ups do not want to hear the truth from children unless it's
good news.

I left a note at my howse that says I had a ride to Texis with a
family that was going to Dalas, and I was going to visit cousens
which we do have tho we don't keep in tuch.

As soon as I have work I will start to send you money.

Your friend Shirley

"Why didn't she tell us she was leaving?" Miss Eldridge wondered.

Mama was teary. "Why didn't *you* tell us, Lark?"

Aunt Betty was quiet, reading her note several times. "I wonder," she
said, her brow knitting, "is this because of her hand?"

"I hope she hasn't gone off half-cocked," Mama said. "What do we
know about these cousins in Texas?"

"What do we know about Shirley?" Jack asked. "After work tomorrow I'll head up to the Olsons' and get some answers."

As we left, carrying our platters and bowls, Miss Eldridge invited
me to stop at her house. I was afraid she might press me about Shirley,
but she switched on a table lamp and turned to the living room windows, where the old matelasse bedspread was drawn aside. The window shades I'd given her were mounted, and she drew them down now
against the December night.

62

At seven the next evening, Jack stopped by.

"Well, that was an exercise in futility," he said, following Aunt Betty into the kitchen and pulling out a chair. "I pounded on the damned door up at the Olsons' till I finally raised the old man—at least he said he was Shirley's dad—a shifty, snarling little pissant. Said Shirley was none of our lookout. She was in Texas with cousins, and he hoped she'd stay there; she was a snot-nosed trouble-maker.

"He said they'd seen her off with friends of theirs who were heading back to Dallas.

"I asked could we have her address, we wanted to send her Christmas presents along to her.

"'Go to hell,' he said and slammed the door."

"I'm sorry." Aunt Betty sat down opposite. "Police?"

"Not a helluva lot we can do, they say. She had the parents' permission to leave."

. . . .

On Saturday, December 30th, I dolled up. Borrowing Aunt Betty's tweezers, I plucked my brows—God, that was no fun—and helped myself to Mama's Tabu, then screwed on the genuine pearl earrings Jack had given me.

Decked out in a silky white blouse and my red velveteen skirt, I pulled on Mama's best navy blue cardigan. Too damned bad if she didn't approve.

Off I toddled on my one-and-a-half inch heels to meet Aunt Betty at Gilpins' for lunch and then see the new Alicia Armand movie, *Love Affair in London*. Seated in Gilpins' Chateau Room, I ordered lobster thermidor, probably a favorite of Alicia Armand's, washed down with buckets of champagne.

I craved three things before settling down on my farm: champagne in a real champagne glass, a taxi ride, and a telegram delivered by a Western Union delivery boy.

Lunch with my aunt was a series of long silences punctuated by abrupt, trifling chatter: "Oh, yes, the *Hit Parade* is much better with Frank Sinatra," for instance. The rift between Mama and Aunt Betty was creating constraint between my aunt and me. I longed to talk about Uncle Stanley, who was emerging from his former self, new and surprising, like a butterfly from a cocoon. "Betty, darling," he had written, "more and more I think of enrolling in pre-med after the war. Helluva long haul, I know . . ."

Uncle Stanley, the socialist doctor.

. . . .

Josette Delon (Alicia Armand), a young Parisian woman displaced by the war and living in London, was, like my uncle, a person of noble surprises. Early in the film, in a bomb shelter, she met the American pilot Jim Blake (Richard Drew), from Topeka, Kansas. Within minutes, they were in love.

Although Jim protested, "If you loved me, you wouldn't do this," Josette volunteered to parachute into Nazi-occupied France, carrying to the underground plans for the destruction of a strategic armament dump. Jim and Josette parted in anger.

On a blustery English night, Josette boarded the plane that would drop her in enemy territory ("We daren't delay for better weather").

Jim raced across the tarmac and, over the roar of engines and propellers, shouted his love to Josette, who stood in the open door of the aircraft.

Fate is cruel and fond of bizarre coincidences. On his next flight over France, Jim's plane was shot down, although he parachuted to safety, landing near the very armament dump that had been destroyed by Josette and the underground. Making his way to a nearby farm house, Jim discovered Josette, mortally wounded.

To subdued strains of "The Marseillaise," Josette died in Jim's arms. The final fadeout presented Josette's lovely face, large against the billowing clouds of heaven, the tricolor fluttering bravely behind her.

As the audience emptied into the lobby, I excused myself, finding my way to the restroom, where I splashed my face with cold water and thanked God I hadn't borrowed Aunt Betty's mascara.

On the bus ride home, I was in the grip of Alicia Armand, her mix of beauty and tragedy. Even in her comedic roles, melancholy lay just behind her good humor, lending it another dimension.

Had the movie reminded Aunt Betty of Uncle Stanley, who was on the front lines? She was quiet, the onus of not loving him so much greater than the weight of loving him had been.

. . . .

BEAU ENLISTED IN THE ARMY after the first of the year, and we threw a going-away dinner at our house. I had never seen him happier. War seemed to be a place where men went to balance their personal ledgers, and for Beau it was proof of something I didn't understand, something to do with standing alongside other men.

At dinner, glancing at his half-sister, he told us, "When the war's over, I'm going to find my dad if he's alive."

These days, Miss Eldridge sometimes came walking with me when I took Cecil and Percy out. She was substitute teaching, and the walk helped her unwind, she said.

She was a finely tuned instrument. For two or three days at a time, she would say little. She worried about Beau and, I thought, about his father, William Bates as well. His beating haunted her. Did she still love him—he'd given her the little brooch as a pledge—or was it the injustice that she couldn't put aside?

One afternoon, up on the verge, a cool breeze from the west was hauling in high clouds. Miss Eldridge drew her sweater tight and stood looking off toward the bay.

"I wonder if his mind is whole now." Chafing her hands, she added, "So much is owed him. My mother robbed him of his career, his baby, maybe his wits. It overwhelms me."

At times, her resolve failed. One day, seeing me returning with the dogs, she called me to stop in. Settled on the shabby red armchair in her living room, I waited.

"I thought I'd start making enquiries."

I nodded, trying to look encouraging.

"I sat down with pen and paper last night," she explained, picking at the arm of the sofa, "and I didn't know what to say. I mean, what right do I have . . . ?"

"Maybe his mind is whole and maybe it's not," I said. "But maybe his family are all dead and he's lonely. Think how happy he might be to find Beau. He can always say no."

"I hadn't thought of it that way."

As I left, I noted that the photo of William Bates was framed and sitting on the bookcase.

Neither Mama nor Aunt Betty would be home for supper. Melba had talked Mama into seeing *Love Affair in London,* and Aunt Betty was at the U.S.O. On an impulse, I removed money from my cache, slipped into a warm jacket, and raced down to the bus stop.

Alighting from the bus, I hurried toward the gas pumps and blazing windows of the crowded corner store. Requesting change for my dollar bills from the man at the cash register, I turned toward the phone booth, pulled the folding door to, and sat down on the wooden seat. I had never placed a long-distance call. My only knowledge came from movies.

Reading the instructions, I managed to dial an operator and told her I wished to call the Ferguson residence, a ranch outside Riverton, Wyoming. After a minute spent finding the routing, the operator rang through to a local operator in Riverton and explained. The Riverton operator, who sounded as though she were speaking from the South Pole, said that the Ferguson number was 45-ring-3 and proceeded to put the call through. I heard two or three clicks as people on the party line picked up their phones.

At last, a man answered and, with the line open in all the households belonging to the 45 number, he shouted, "How do!" in an uncertain voice.

My operator told me to deposit fifty-five cents, which I did, and then she said kindly, "Go ahead."

"How do!" the voice at the other end repeated.

"Hello, is this Mr. Ferguson?"

"No, this is Buck."

"Is Mr. or Mrs. Ferguson there?"

"No, ma'am. Mr. and Mrs. Ferguson are in Arizona."

"Arizona?"

"Mr. Ferguson's brother Ernest was took bad a couple months back. They went down there to look after him. Me 'n Eddie 'n Barney are runnin' things here. I just come up from the bunk house to get some grub.

Woman comes over from the next place to fix our evening meal while Missus is gone to Arizona. If y'd of called earlier or later, y'd of missed me but as it is I was here."

"Is there someone there named Shirley?"

"No, ma'am, no one by that name. Woman from the next place is Verna. Verna Higgins."

"When will the Fergusons be back?"

"Don't know. Depends. Call back next month, I'd say."

"All right. Thank you. I'll call next month."

I rang off, scooped up the unused change, and left. Shirley had been gone for a month. *Where was she?*

63

AROUND THE FIRST OF MARCH, a lean and tanned Beau came home for a few days' leave. Basic training had been tough, he said, but he'd survived and he was part of a group in a way that he'd never in his life been.

I was pleased to see him but my mind was filled with Shirley. If I'd had the money, I'd have bought a ticket to Riverton and gone looking for her. All I could do was keep calling long-distance to hear that the Fergusons were still in Arizona but would be back around the first of April for certain.

One Sunday evening Aunt Betty said to me, "Are you feeling all right? You've lost weight."

We were in the kitchen, she reading the paper, I at the table staring out the window. I couldn't bring myself to open the paper these days for fear of learning about a twelve-year-old girl found frozen to death in Wyoming.

"Is something bothering you?" Aunt Betty asked. "Do you want to talk about it?"

Of course I wanted to talk about it, but everyone would be out of their minds if I told them I'd put Shirley on a train to Wyoming and that I didn't know if she'd arrived. As it was, they worried about not hearing from her. Talking to Shirley's parents was pointless. If we hadn't heard, they certainly hadn't.

"When she's settled in school, she'll let us know how happy she is," Miss Eldridge said.

But I could hear Mama saying, "You never liked that child, and now look what you've done."

The following Saturday, I did a little housework and read from *Happy Stories for Bedtime*. That's how crazy upset I was about Shirley. *Happy Stories for Bedtime* was like sucking your thumb.

Eventually I filled the lard pail with water and went outside to water the gardenia bush. Jack had recently fertilized it, and it was budding out. *You hang on, gardenia bush.*

When Mama arrived home from her Saturday half day, she slipped out of her shoes, leaving them beside the door, then crossed to the sofa and collapsed, hunched over. Night life was wearing her out.

Someone knocked at the front door and I waited for her to answer. She made no move, so I went.

A boy wearing a Western Union uniform removed his cap and asked if Mrs. Stanley Weller lived here. His bicycle leaned against the stoop. Had Shirley wired Aunt Betty?

"Yes."

"Telegram. Sign here, please?"

"My aunt's name?"

"You can sign yours."

I did and took the pale yellow envelope from him. Hadn't I been thinking just recently that I wanted someday to receive a telegram? This was addressed to Aunt Betty but it had come to our door.

"Who was it?" Mama asked.

"It's a telegram for Aunt Betty. Do you think we should open it? Maybe it's Uncle Stanley saying he's back from France."

"Aunt Betty should open it." Mama laid the telegram on the coffee table. "Your uncle is dead. And if I hadn't loved him he'd be alive."

A remarkable thing happened then. Mama and I each fell asleep, she on the sofa with her head thrown back, I in the chair, my legs drawn up.

Later the front door opened and Aunt Betty stepped in. She flicked on the lamp and peered at Mama and me. "What's happened?" she asked, taking us in.

I rose and gave her the yellow envelope. Without removing her coat, she opened it, read it, and stared at Mama.

"So," she said.

64

AUNT BETTY EMERGED from the bedroom dry eyed but speaking in the half-voice people use at viewings, as though Uncle Stanley's corpse lay in our living room. She asked for the key to the Dugans' house and went to make phone calls.

Mama continued to sit on the sofa, waiting to be dealt with. Except for using the toilet and, later, drinking half a cup of tea, she sat much the same until bedtime.

She did not get dressed the next day, but stayed in bed until Aunt Betty came home from Mass and insisted that she get up. She sat on the sofa as she had the previous day.

Jack appeared at the door in the afternoon and, being almost family, was invited in despite Mama's deshabille. Aunt Betty asked me to turn on the radio. A symphony was playing on KNX. Under cover of the music, Jack and my aunt conferred in the kitchen.

Mama did not go to the plant on Monday, nor on any day thereafter. Aunt Betty urged her to get dressed, to wash her face, to brush her teeth, even to get out of bed. She tried talking to Mama about Uncle Stanley, but Mama shook her head.

"It's all my fault," she said.

Catholicism had taken a stronger hold of her than she'd realized. On her soul, she carried the unexpiated sin of coveting her sister's husband, and for this she was being punished; we were all being punished.

I was going to school each day and coming home to find Mama sit-

336 / Faith Sullivan

ting as I had left her. Miss Eldridge, when she wasn't substitute teaching, stopped in to coax Mama to eat.

A week passed. Mama now floated around the house, from window to window, as if expecting another messenger who might contravene the first. She ate only after being cajoled, and then no more than a bite.

"I've lost my taste," she said with wonder, as if she did not associate this with Uncle Stanley's death.

Why was *she* allowed to collapse? Nobody else was. I had to worry every minute about Shirley while trying to grasp Uncle Stanley's death. And like as not, Mama *had* caused it. The cosmos was a vengeful place. But more than that, I was repelled by Mama's languor.

At the end of the second week, Aunt Betty said to her, "Do you want to go back to work at the plant, Arlene?"

Silence followed, broken only by my fractious breathing. Of course, she'd have to go back.

But, in fact, she didn't. The following week, Aunt Betty handed in Mama's resignation and made hasty plans to transport Mama and me back to Minnesota, to Grandpa and Grandma Browning's in Blue Lake.

"Temporarily, Arlene," Aunt Betty told her. "Just until you're back on your feet. Then you can come back and we'll find you a good job. You were dying on the vine at that place."

Under other circumstances, the return to Minnesota would have been the answer to my three years of prayer, but what joy could I find in this retreat? And how would Shirley find me?

Aunt Betty had vacation time coming, and she arranged to take it now. From Blue Lake, she would proceed on to New York on business.

The day before we left, Lou came to pick up our boxes and carry them to the freight office at the depot. Mama was napping.

Aunt Betty had explained something about our leaving, because Lou looked grave.

"I am truly sorry about your mama," he told me. "She is a good woman. Most kind. Maybe she'll be back again."

As he returned from the truck for the final box, I asked, "How's Woodrow?"

"He's been made a sergeant. We are proud."

"Tell him congratulations from Lark." I handed Lou the money Aunt Betty had left.

Slipping it into his shirt pocket, he said, "And he has got him a row of medals."

I walked out to the street with Lou "The truck's still running," I said.

He gave it a pat. "It hangs on." Opening the door and climbing in, he told me, "Try not to worry about your mama. She'll hang on." He put the truck in neutral and turned the key in the ignition.

That evening we were invited to Miss Eldridge's. Earlier in the day, when I had packed the oil painting and Shirley's horse picture, I stopped by to see whether I could help. She told me to have a seat at the kitchen table while she frosted a spice cake.

"Miss Eldridge, I want to tell you how much I like you. I don't know what I'd have done without you." I was learning that you said these things while you had a chance.

For a minute, she was overcome and simply stood holding the spatula and looking at me. Then she opened her arms and we hugged.

"Child, dear child," she said. "What time is your train?"

"Eight-thirty in the morning."

"Do you want to go?"

"Not like this."

She nodded, making swirls with the icing spatula. "If you had one wish, what would it be?"

"Besides the farm, I'd wish Mama had never loved Uncle Stanley."

"Maybe she couldn't help herself." She handed me the spatula to lick.

"She had *me*. Why did she need him?"

"It's different. You're old enough to understand that," she said.

"Yes, but sometimes you have to *choose*, between hurting other people and hurting yourself. She should have hurt herself."

"Well, maybe she was weak," Miss Eldridge said, pulling out a chair and sitting. "But she didn't mean to hurt you. Someday you'll have to leave her, and that will hurt *her*, but you'll go anyway."

"That's different. That's the way things are supposed to be. Loving your sister's husband isn't the way things are supposed to be."

"Oh, my dear," she said, in a voice she'd never used with me before. "They seldom are."

65

THE NEXT MORNING, Miss Eldridge was on her stoop at seven-fifteen when the taxi turned up Piñon. She hugged me, saying, "Write to me."

"I promise. If you find Mr. Bates, let me know."

She nodded and backed away. "I'll water the gardenia bush," she told us. She stood waving till we were out of sight. And I, in the back seat of the taxi, waved back until we turned the corner at the bottom of the hill.

The morning was mild and foggy. Bells and foghorns sounded warnings in the harbor and chimerical floating castles with smoke stacks revealed themselves and then disappeared, gray slipping into gray.

We had only one suitcase each, mine a new little grip like Shirley's, a gift from Aunt Betty. It should have set me to spinning glamorous daydreams but even the taxi ride, my first, didn't stir me. My first telegram, my first taxi ride. I dreaded to imagine the circumstances of my first glass of champagne.

Getting Mama onto the train was easy enough; getting her to mind her purse and grip was another matter. When we had finally settled into a crowded coach, I bought a morning paper from a boy making his way through the car selling them.

Shoving the furled paper between my seat and the window wall, I helped Aunt Betty stow Mama's things on the rack above, then studied the throng on the platform. How quiet Blue Lake would be. No defense workers and servicemen swarming through the streets; no war planes droning overhead; no anti-aircraft guns shaking the earth; no camouflage netting draping buildings.

I was not displeased. Since Uncle Stanley's death, the war had lost its luster.

As the train pulled away from the station, heading north, I watched the dusty little towns and the orange groves slide past. Pleasant, but not mine.

Was everyone possessed by a place, as I was by Minnesota? And was it always the place where they were born and grew up or were we arbitrarily assigned a spot of earth? To my mind, each person had a compass inside pointing toward the magnetic home.

We had barely rolled into Del Mar before Mama fell asleep. Aunt Betty sorted through papers and letters that she carried in her enormous tan handbag. I noted the telegram among them.

We were staying overnight in Los Angeles because my aunt was meeting with Uncle Stanley's friend Sidney Dangerson. Aunt Betty had called him when the telegram arrived, and again when she realized that she would be in L.A.

While Aunt Betty sorted, read, and made jottings, I extracted my newspaper. On the lower right-hand side of the front page, a headline caught my eye. "Hollywood Figure an Imposter?"

> Clever sleuthing by New York journalist Everett Patten has uncovered alleged evidence that Alicia Armand, thought to be Alicia Arkovsky of the European ballet world, is actually Alice Ayles of Queens, New York, daughter of Herman Ayles, a baker's assistant, and his wife Clarice.

More about the humble Ayles and their humble house in Queens, then "Cont. on page three." On page three was a photo of Mrs. Ayles holding up a school portrait of Alice in the eleventh grade. Clarice Ayles looked thin, angry, and triumphant, although perhaps the grainy wire-service photo did her an injustice.

. . . studio representative stated only that no studio complicity was involved in the alleged imposture. "The studio is as much a victim as the public."

The following paragraph revealed, "Armand/Ayles has disappeared from her home in the Hollywood Hills. Housekeeper Esther Braden told reporters, 'I don't know where Miss Armand is. I haven't seen her since the day before yesterday, when she left for the studio. She went in to look at the final day's rushes of *East of the Yukon*. She's a good girl.' Braden added, 'Look at the money she's raised for children in Europe. And have you seen her films? Another Garbo. What difference where she was born?'"

. . . .

IN DIGGING UP HER BACKGROUND, the reporter had tracked down one of Alice's high school teachers, who observed, "She was a bright girl and talented in many ways, but so shy and quiet, it was painful, really painful. I can't believe she's this Alicia Armand. Yes, I saw one or two of her movies, but I wouldn't have guessed. Alice was a silent little mouse."

But a studio attorney, Arthur Trent, vowed, "We'll call in the F.B.I. We'll hire private investigators. Don't you worry, we'll see that she's put away."

Asked by a reporter whether Ayles had bilked the studio out of money, Trent responded, "Worse. She's bilked us out of our good name. She's broken the public trust."

One mistake and Alicia Armand was ruined. Stunned, I let the paper slip from my hands.

When the train pulled into Union Station, I was still staring. Aunt Betty had to ask me twice to pick up the newspaper from the floor and reach down Mama's coat from the rack.

My aunt had been in touch with Mrs. Healy, and we were staying at her rooming house as we had on the trip out. It pleased Aunt Betty to confirm Mrs. Healy's belief that one could succeed in California. Mrs. Healy greeted us with genuine recollection, observing sotto voce to Aunt Betty, "Your sister looks like you did in 'forty-two."

Showing us to a different room than the one we'd stayed in before, she said, "Mr. Healy bought this bedroom suite at auction from the estate of Melton Fairweather, the distinguished character actor. He played butlers and valets, you know. Died of a broken heart when his son was killed in the Philippines."

The bedroom we'd occupied on the trip out had been furnished with a suite purchased at auction from Bob Halloran, who acted in westerns at Republic. He'd given up the films and moved back to New Jersey.

Later, when Aunt Betty left to meet Sidney for lunch at the Biltmore Hotel, Mrs. Healy returned bearing extra towels. She stacked them on the bureau, smoothing the topmost one and hesitating, as if loath to leave Mama and me.

"Will you be going out for lunch?" she asked.

Mama sat, unhearing, in the great overstuffed chair by the window, her purse in her lap, as though she were waiting for a bus.

"We bought sandwiches and fruit at Union Station," I said, pointing to the white box on the bedside table.

"Well, at least let me bring up a pot of tea."

At the word tea, Mama nodded and shifted her weight.

About to leave, Mrs. Healy asked, "Have you seen the paper?"

I knew what she meant.

"Isn't it awful?" Mrs. Healy said. "But I know one thing: We're not getting the whole story. That attorney for the studio is a slyboots. I wouldn't be surprised if the studio was behind it from the beginning."

"What do you mean?"

"Beautiful young women who escape from the Nazis are the kind of thing publicity departments dream about. They probably created her and now that she's exposed they're getting rid of her. Let's hope she's just run off."

66

MRS. HEALY DROVE US to Union Station the next morning. As I prepared to climb the steps into the coach behind Mama, Mrs. Healy urged, "When your mama's well, you two come back. The future's here." Then, laying a hand on my arm, she advised, "Don't worry about Alicia Armand, dear. She escaped the Nazis; she'll be all right."

The *Los Angeles Times* I purchased at the station had nothing new to report: more interviews with friends and associates extolling Miss Armand's work habits, her love of children, her compliance with studio demands.

"An angel to work with, no tantrums, no ego," one of her leading men reflected. "That kid was no phony," declared comedic actress Sarah Bell, who had played in Armand films and toured the country with her, selling war bonds. "I don't know who Alice Ayles is or where she is, but Alicia Armand was not from Queens."

Who was Alicia Armand?

Human mutability was frightening. Just when you thought you knew someone, they became someone else. "People don't change," I'd heard someone say. But people did change. I regarded Mama, sitting opposite me. And Miss Eldridge. And Uncle Stanley.

In the midst of these musings, I heard Aunt Betty say to Mama, "You would have liked Sidney Dangerson. He's an ardent little man, very kind, very committed to communism. He thought the world of Stanley."

My aunt had taken to carrying on these one-sided conversations with

Mama, as if she would throw a rope of words around Mama and pull her back to life.

"He said Stanley was drawn to communism by his compassion and his desire to help people. He said Stanley was always loaning people money and visiting people in the hospital and doing kindnesses.

"He broke down and wept when he read the letter from Stanley's commanding officer saying that Stanley never took much note of the war itself, only of the people who needed his help."

Later, Aunt Betty insisted that Mama come to the club car. When we were seated in deep-green club chairs and my aunt had ordered drinks, she ruminated, "Stanley was always a sweet man. I wonder when it was he became a good man."

Because of the crush of passengers, we shared a table with a middle-aged couple returning to Michigan from San Francisco, where they had seen their son sail off to war. Two other sons were already serving in the Pacific. The couple seemed dazed but not quite bowed by this third goodbye.

The husband was an executive at Ford and she was active in the League of Women Voters. They were well dressed, well educated and well off, but not the sort of people who pulled strings to keep their sons out of the service.

Aunt Betty chatted with them and encouraged Mama. Mama smiled and once said "thank you," but she could not marshal her thoughts enough to participate.

Robert, the son so recently given to the navy, was not married, but the other two each had a wife and children back in Michigan. It was difficult for the children. They hardly knew their fathers. Was Aunt Betty's husband in the service?

My aunt looked at Mama, then at the woman from Michigan. "My sister and I are both widows."

Mama's hand fluttered upward from her lap, like a bird startled in the night, then settled down again on her black purse.

Walking the aisles of the train, lurching away from our seats, away from Mama, I stood in the cold, cacophonous space between the cars, clutching the rail and trying to empty my mind.

By the second day of the trip, I was detraining at every stop where the train waited five or more minutes. Passing through the car, the conductor shouted information about these stops, warning passengers to return in time lest they be left behind.

Up and down platforms, brick or cobbled, in and out of depots modest or cavernous, I wandered, noting at one anonymous stop a fur-coated woman weeping, then a woman selling souvenirs dabbing at her eyes, and then a railroad porter and a Marine private, each crying. What was it? What had happened?

By the station clock, it was a quarter to three. But what had that to do with anything? Finally, I approached a man in a topcoat and fedora who seemed unmoved and asked, "Do you know why people are crying?"

Without apparent grief, he said, "Roosevelt's dead."

"Then *you* ought to be crying," I told him.

67

THE NIGHT WAS COLD as I stepped down from the train into Grandpa Browning's arms. I gulped astringent spring air and my lungs knew this air from all others. Home.

I helped Grandpa stow our grips in the back of the car. In the morning, we were coming back for the boxes.

At the house, Grandma had the radio tuned to Cedric Adams' ten o'clock news on WCCO. Although she was certain that FDR's Democratic Party was a tool of the Pope and Josef Stalin, Grandma's large nose was red and her eyelids puffy.

"He worked himself to death," she said, meeting us at the kitchen door, grabbing me and clasping me to her.

To smell Grandma's Lady Esther powder and her Noxzema, in concert with a lingering household bouquet of boiled ham and cabbage, was to step back across a threshold into another childhood.

Entering this familiar world, I was reunited with myself, and I was stabbed by a thousand knives of happiness. Everything leapt out to pierce me—the electric clock humming above the stove; the thick, coarse linen towel hanging on the back of the cellar door; Grandpa's after-dinner cigar still perfuming the dining room; and Grandma's electric percolator snorting and burping on the dining room sideboard.

A plate piled with sandwiches—ham stuffed into thick homemade dinner rolls—waited on the table, along with sliced dills heaped into a pickle dish, angel food cake squatting on a tall stand, and Malomars tumbling from a little opalescent bowl.

Before tucking in, I wandered through the living room, pulling off my coat and cap as I went, making sure that things were as I had left them.

"Come and eat now," Grandma called. "You must be starved."

Later, I climbed the stairs, carrying a warm brick wrapped in an old towel and sliding it between the bed sheets. Teeth chattering, I fetched my nightie and slippers from the grip and hurried along to the bathroom, the only heated room on the second floor. Back in the bedroom, I dug down into layers of quilts and stretched to find the brick.

Despite all this comfort, in the cold darkness above me Shirley's face floated, pale as snow.

Mama soon crept to bed, and Grandpa climbed the stairs a little later. Aunt Betty remained in the dining room with Grandma.

On the table between the two double beds, the luminous dial of the Big Ben alarm clock said twelve twenty-seven when Aunt Betty opened the door at the bottom of the stairs. The next time I looked, it was one forty-five. Shirley's face was still there on the ceiling.

Falling into a short night of restless sleep, I rode a train endlessly, glimpsing the faces of Shirley, Uncle Stanley, Alicia Armand, and President Roosevelt staring at me from backyards, fire escapes, station platforms, and trains headed in the opposite direction.

Waking the next morning before Mama and my aunt, I slid from bed, pulled on my slippers, and padded across the painted floor, which was cold and hard as ice.

Grandma sat at the dining room table, dressed and poring over the Minneapolis *Tribune* through the bottom of her bifocals. "You're up early," she said, glancing across the room at the desk clock. "Seven o'clock?" Through the upper half of her lenses she studied me. "Are you hungry?"

"I don't think so." I crossed to the bay window and sat on the low radiator.

"Cocoa and toast?" She rose.

In the kitchen, I stood with my back against the radiator, watching her at the stove, measuring cocoa, sugar, and finally milk into a beat-up pot. "What can you tell me about your mother?" she asked.

"What do you mean?"

"What happened to her?"

"Why don't you ask Aunt Betty?"

"Because I want to hear what *you* have to say. Get out the bread and make us toast."

"I don't know what's wrong with her. She's sick."

"How long has she been like this?"

"Not long."

"You don't sound very concerned." She glanced at me.

I could only look at her.

"She's your mother."

I said nothing.

"What's she done to *you?*"

She went on stirring the cocoa while I toasted and buttered bread. I wasn't hungry but I wanted to please Grandma. I must make small concessions, lay small offerings, because I couldn't tell her the truth about Mama.

"It's the war," Grandma said. "Nothing's ever going to be the same. Your Uncle Stanley dead thousands of miles away. Your mother and Betty off in California. I haven't seen you for three years. You've become somebody else, grown up, and I wasn't there.

"This family is flying apart, and when I'm gone it won't be a family at all. It's a terrible thing that's happening. To everyone—drifting around the country like cottonwood fluff." She groped for a handkerchief in her apron pocket.

She was frightened and distraught. I put my arms around her, but I couldn't think of anything hopeful to say. "I love you," I told her.

"It's not enough. It's not enough!" she cried, wrenching away, grabbing the pot of cocoa and carrying it to the dining room. "The world is flying apart, and nothing is glue enough."

I fetched the toast, cups, saucers, and plates, and we sat at the table. With the bread knife, I sliced the stack of toast diagonally, laying several triangles on Grandma's plate and sliding them toward her. She poured cocoa into our two cups.

The heavy oak table was round. As we ate, we bent slightly forward, tending toward the center. If a terrible gale swept through the house, carrying off curtains and beds, and if we clung to the curving rim of the table, the table holding our food, we would steer it through the sky like a ship and land it right again. That was the thing about a round dining room table.

68

THE NEXT DAY WAS SATURDAY and we rose at five and set out in Grandpa's Nash for Red Wing, Uncle Stanley's home and the place where a memorial Mass was being said for him at ten A.M.

Grandpa drove and Grandma sat beside him, while Aunt Betty, Mama, and I squeezed into the back seat. The day was chilly, thirty degrees by the thermometer outside the kitchen window, and the heater in the old car did not send much warmth into the back. Because Red Wing was a hundred and fifty miles distant, Grandma had brought a wool blanket to spread across our legs.

Aunt Betty, grown meticulous about her attire, complained about the pale green fuzz on her dark coat.

Grandma took umbrage. "When did you get so fussy?"

"It's just that . . . never mind."

"Mrs. Astor's horse," Grandma mumbled, frightened that Aunt Betty, like me, was becoming someone she didn't know. She was anxious in my aunt's company. She had come to me that morning asking which of two dresses she should wear, then which of two brooches, and were her shoes too run down at the heel?

The countryside looked unclothed and vulnerable beneath thin, grudging sunlight. Behind us, in the west, the sky was uncertain. By midday, clouds or even snow might overtake us.

Conversation was desultory. Grandpa noted the many potholes in the highway, which were especially annoying since new tires were impossible to get. Grandma wondered how Alf and Delia Weller were bearing up. A year or so ago, Alf had taken a bad fall, and bad falls at his age had a way of. . . . Well, a person didn't want to think.

Delia had been working at the Northern States Power Company but she would have to relinquish her job when the man she'd replaced came back from the war. "One whole letter was 'the office this' and 'the office that,'" Grandma said. "Job proud." Was that a note of jealousy? Or was it only that Delia had always been a pain in the neck?

I dozed. There was a strange kind of comfort in misunderstandings and differences that were old enough to have lost their teeth.

But there was little comfort in the memorial Mass at Holy Family Catholic Church. The building was freezing, due to conservation of precious heating oil, vital to the war effort. And since he was new to the parish, the priest had not known Uncle Stanley. Still, he did his best, telling us that my uncle was engaged in works brave and righteous and had likely been carried directly to heaven at the moment of his death. To think that Uncle Stanley had ascended directly to heaven was indeed comforting, if you believed in heaven.

After the service, we paraded down to the church basement, where a light lunch had been prepared by Delia's sodality. About fifty people gathered at long, cold tables.

Uncle Stanley's parents, standing at the foot of the basement stairs, "receiving," were a shocking sight. Five years ago, Alf had been a nondescript but healthy sixty. Now he hobbled on a cane, his suit hanging on him like a dust cover.

Delia, still a strapping woman, looked beaten and robbed. Belief in this world had escaped from them, as life itself sighs its way out of bodies.

We said our goodbyes in the church basement, Aunt Betty last, speaking low and with her back to us, but I heard enough to know that she was giving Alf and Delia Uncle Stanley's ten thousand dollar army life insurance. "It's what he wanted," she insisted.

The reassurance in her voice and the soft curve of her arms as they encircled the old people were maternal, and the Wellers nodded like children: Yes, yes, well, that's what we'll do then.

Mama, who had wept intermittently through the day, fell asleep before we were out of Red Wing. A few miles from Blue Lake she woke abruptly.

"Stanley played baseball when he was in school," she said, amazed that she hadn't known this until the morning's homily. "You remember, Betty, we were remarking what a beautiful body he had, and you—or maybe it was me—said he had the body of a baseball player."

"Yes."

In the front seat Grandma stirred, uneasy.

Back in Blue Lake, I hurried upstairs to change into my pajamas and visit the oil painting, unpacked yesterday from the boxes we'd brought from California. I had Shirley's picture as well, and they both stood on the bureau.

Shirley.

Downstairs, I spread the morning paper on the living room floor, but I found no news of Alicia Armand. I did find pictures of the train that had yesterday carried President Roosevelt's body from Warm Springs, Georgia, to Washington to lie in state. People along the route wept openly, saluted, and sang hymns. I wept, reading.

The stories included pictures of the new president, Truman. He looked very small compared with my memories of Roosevelt. But he also looked like your great-uncle Harry who taught you to ride a bicycle and bought you a ball and jacks without a special occasion, who sang silly songs from World War I and let you steer the car sometimes when he drove.

Before bed, I wrote short notes to Sally, Beverly, and Mrs. Stillman letting them know I was only an hour away. I was fluttery with happiness at the thought, and had to lay the pen down for a moment.

69

"Have you seen this movie star?" read the caption under a picture of Alicia Armand in the Sunday *Tribune*.

The article revealed a thickening plot. Several French citizens who had escaped from the Nazis and were living in Los Angeles had come forward to vouch for Alicia Armand. Her French was flawless. A perfect Parisian accent. That could not be learned, not by a girl from Queens, New York. One of the group had seen her perform, he was certain, with a provincial ballet company. "*Les Sylphides,* it was. Excellent." But Herman and Clarice Ayles were sticking to their story.

Near the end of the article, I read, "Los Angeles police are not ruling out foul play in Armand's disappearance. Following up on anonymous phone calls as well as other leads, 'We may find,' Lt. Greeve stated, 'that this is a murder investigation.'"

Sunday night, after the Jack Benny show, I found a pad of paper in Grandma's desk. At the dining room table, Grandma, Grandpa, and Aunt Betty were playing three-handed bridge while Mama sat nearby in a rocker, dematerializing.

In the living room, I wrote, "In the spring, as soon as the snow melted, Hilly began to build an addition to the cabin . . ."

. . . .

Monday morning, after breakfast, I bundled into warm clothes.

"Where are you going?" Grandma wanted to know.

"For a walk."

She looked displeased. "You ought to be in school, child."

"Aunt Betty said I didn't have to start till next Monday."

She huffed, returning to the letter she was writing.

I set out without a destination, only wanting to escape my silent mother and the mailman. If I'd been watching and waiting for the mail, finding no letter forwarded from Shirley was that much worse.

The skating pond beside the school had turned to ice puree, and the swings and slides stood in water. I waded through the soup in my galoshes and sat on one of the swings, letting the intense morning sun warm my face.

A girl about my age, looking for her lunch pail, called, "Who are you?"

"Lark Erhardt."

"Why aren't you in school?"

"We had a death in the family."

She nodded. "You're lucky."

Spying the lunch pail by the hand-over-hand, she grabbed it up and hurried back into the building.

The hand-over-hand made me think of the monkey bars, the boys, and Shirley. I ached to tell someone that she was missing, but the moment for confession had come and gone weeks ago. I sprang up from the swing and sloshed through the former skating pond, spraying frigid water.

I tramped along a sidewalk until it ran out, then followed a gravel road past the raggedy fringe of town, the tarpaper shacks and decaying cars, and finally the Good Night Dance Hall, drooping and peeling in the sunlight.

Half a mile ahead, on the crest of a hill, sprawled the Balm of Gilead Cemetery. Entering the gates, I bore to the right, discovering a family of Olsons. Picking my way among their headstones, I found no stone incised "Shirley." A good omen.

At the farthest end of the cemetery, the land dipped down to a little stream and away to farmlands that stretched to the horizon. In summer, meadow larks, mourning doves, blue birds, finches, and pheasants exuberated in the lushness.

The ice on the stream had broken up, and the sunlit water flashed optimistically. With cupped hands, I cried to the earth-circling clouds, "Shirley Olson, I love you!"

70

FROM TOWN CAME THE SOUND of the noon whistle.

I spun, pelting back the way I'd come, arriving home panting and pressing a fist into my side. At the curb on Cottonwood Street, a strange car was parked, an old Mercury, looking like a big black beetle.

I leapt the steps to the side door. The electric clock above the stove said twelve-thirty. Dinner was at noon.

"I'm sorry, Grandma. . . ." At the dining room door, I stopped. "Papa."

He rose and, circling the dining room table, lifted me in a bear hug. "Let me see you," he said, putting me down and standing back. "How come you're hunched over like that?"

"I have a stitch in my side from running."

"Well, sit down and have some food."

"Didn't you hear the noon whistle, child?" Grandma asked.

"I was way on the other side of town."

"How come you were 'way on the other side of town'?" Papa asked. "Shouldn't you be in school?"

"I told her she didn't have to go until next Monday," Aunt Betty said.

Pushing away a plate on which a few pie crumbs remained, Grandpa rose from the table. He had to get back to the tin shop. Extending a hand to Papa, he grunted, "Willie," then turned and snatched up the old beaked cap that looked like a railroad engineer's, slapping it onto his head.

"Pass me Lark's plate," Grandma told Aunt Betty, and she began filling it with pork sausages, mashed potatoes, and sausage gravy. "The green beans are there beside you," she said. "Willie, more pie?"

Papa passed his plate and Grandma slid a slice of cherry pie onto it. Aunt Betty poured more coffee and Mama played with her knife. Papa eyed her sideways.

"Your papa heard about Stanley's memorial service from—who was it, a trainman from Red Wing?" Aunt Betty said. "So he drove up here to see us. But he has to get back before the evening freight. Isn't that what you said, Willie?"

"That's right." Papa nodded, and again his glance slewed in Mama's direction. "I'd heard about Stanley being killed," he said, "from this same fellow who mentioned the memorial Mass. I sent a card to Stan's folks." He looked at each of us as if we were to note this in our account books.

"Even if I'd known about the Mass, I couldn't of made it. Art was out with bronchitis and I had to hold down the fort."

Art Bigelow was the depot agent and Papa's boss. "But I'd of appreciated knowing you were coming back here," he said, accusation in his voice. He would not put it more strongly for fear of irritating Aunt Betty, who clearly was in charge.

"Lark is my kid, and I like knowing where she is." His smile all around said, *You can understand that.*

"I had a lot on my mind, Willie," Aunt Betty told him.

"Yes, you did, I realize, with Stan and all. I didn't mean any criticism. Lark could of let me know you were coming."

"Lark's had plenty on her plate, too" my aunt noted, pausing to let that sink in. No direct reference to Mama, but the implication was there to be grasped.

Papa gave Mama a long look, then cast an inquiring glance at Aunt Betty, which she ignored.

"Arlene will rest for a couple of months before she comes back to California," she said. "I've been after her to change jobs for a long time. She's too capable for that kind of dead-end situation.

"I'm thinking of starting my own business when the war ends. I'm guessing it'll be over by the end of the year. Dress manufacturing—a small line for the carriage trade. I'm getting the background, I have the contacts, and I can get the financing."

Papa's mouth did not exactly hang open, but he was struck dumb.

"Los Angeles is the logical place to set up shop. The country's moving west. There's a labor pool and plenty of money. But I need Arlene's office skills. I can't be worrying about that end of things. I need someone I can trust to organize and run the office."

Like many people, Papa respected money and power. Although the business Aunt Betty had described might be small potatoes in some circles, in Papa's it was daunting. Aunt Betty had connections, and she knew where she was going.

"Now, Willie, I have to say something. All these threats have had a sad effect on Arlene. And they haven't brought you much satisfaction, either."

Papa looked askance at Mama. Was *he* responsible for the state she was in? Aunt Betty hadn't said that, but wasn't there an intimation? Something both reprehensible and flattering lay in such a possibility.

"I can't tell you what to do, Willie. But I think a legal separation is not too much for Arlene to ask. It would give both of you breathing space."

"And what about Lark?"

"A lawyer could work out an arrangement. You can each hire a lawyer and let them thrash it out. But it would be cheaper if you agreed to share one." She paused.

Tears sprang to Papa's eyes. "It's all gotten away from me, hasn't it?"

Aunt Betty said nothing. Surprisingly, neither did Grandma. Maybe *legal separation* was easier to swallow than *divorce*. And what was the alternative? Mama needed to be protected now.

Again, Papa's eyes darted toward Mama. "All right," he said, and a sigh shook him. "Shane. He's a Harvester lawyer, but Arlene always liked him. I'll talk to him."

"Have him call us this week," Aunt Betty said. "I'm leaving next Saturday. If I don't hear by Wednesday, I'll call him."

Papa nodded, frowning to hold back the tears.

"This way you'll salvage something, Willie. The other way you'd end up losing everything."

When it was time for Papa to leave, we all knotted around the door to say goodbye, even Mama. Grandma gathered him into her arms. "You're welcome here," she told him.

Aunt Betty kissed his cheek and promised, "We'll play fair, Willie."

And Mama admonished him not to drive fast.

I hugged him, wishing that I could pour forth vows and assurances it would please him to hear, but although I pitied him my heart was empty of tender words.

He dashed away, down the steps and out to the car. When he reached the corner, he tooted the horn and waved. We waved back.

71

ON FRIDAY MORNING, a letter from Jack arrived for Aunt Betty.

"And here's one for you, child," Grandma called.

Shirley? Holding my breath, I took the little envelope from Grandma. The return address was B.E., 138 Piñon: Miss Eldridge.

Dear Lark,

I miss your comings and goings, your visits to my house, and your inclusion of me in your family's affairs. Until the Project, Beau and I had lost all our family.

In addition to the substitute teaching, which fills many days, I have assumed your former duties with Cecil and Percy, taking them for a stroll when I return from school. They are funnier than Fred Allen, and quite as dour looking. The first three days after your departure, they sat on your stoop and whined when I took them for exercise. I had to be firm to get them to trot up the hill.

Would you believe that they have wrought a miracle?

The first time they saw darling Billy, they pranced around at the foot of his cage and barked until I thought Billy would die of fright. I put the cover over the cage until they were gone. The second time they came home with me, they headed immediately for the kitchen and set up the same racket. This time, Billy began to sing! I know it sounds unlikely, and his singing may only be a complaint, but I was deeply affected, and I take it as a sign.

Regarding Billy's namesake, I have a clue I'm following, which was among the many papers you and I sorted so assiduously. Not for naught, our labors. And Jack has given me some ideas about finding Mr. Bates should the current trail peter out.

Jack tells me he is planning to move to Los Angeles when the war ends. I believe he has a business venture in mind, though he wasn't prepared to go into detail yet.

When the war ends, I suppose everyone in the Project will scatter, although doubtless many will move no further than across town. The Project will be dismantled, don't you think, and real homes built in its place? When that happens, I will look for something close by. The school system has offered me a full-time contract in September, despite my age. They are desperate for teachers still, and expecting an even greater need when the war is over.

A letter from Beau arrived yesterday. He is someplace in the Pacific. While he is sickened by the killing, he does not regret the decision to enlist. Perhaps for the first time, he is looking forward to the future. None of this would have happened if we hadn't moved here.

Jack and I are taking turns caring for the gardenia bush. When you planted it, I said to myself, "It will never survive." Well, it's putting out all sorts of buds, more this spring than last, and earlier. Why am I surprised? You told me the bush had made up its mind to hang on!

What a shame that President Roosevelt has left us. He saw us through so much. It's a pity he didn't live to see the end of the war, which is coming soon.

I look forward to hearing about your trip and your new life. Greet your mother and aunt for me. I send my affection to you all.

Love,
Belle Eldridge

That afternoon, Apollo Shane, the Harvester lawyer, talked long-distance with Aunt Betty for a considerable time, hashing out terms of a legal separation between Mama and Papa. Aunt Betty had already taken me aside on Monday, after Papa left, to discuss how much time I wanted to spend with him.

The next morning, we all drove down to the depot to see Aunt Betty off on the train to Chicago, the first leg of her New York trip. She was dressed in a pair of tan trousers, an apricot shirt with a mannish cut, and a brown Eton jacket of her own design, which a San Diego tailor had executed. She wore a scarf of browns and golds tied loosely at her throat and looked like a fashion model.

Grandma was both proud and peeved. She bragged to her chums about her daughter's clothes and sophistication, but she could not bear the distance between them that the glamour represented. She feared being on the margins of my aunt's life.

On the platform, when her bags had been handed up into the car, Aunt Betty grasped Mama's shoulders. "You have to get your strength back."

Mama looked at her with bewilderment, but asked, "Did you mean it, about the new business?"

"I won't do it without you, Arlene."

Mama's face clouded, as if she were putting this through refractory mental machinery.

The conductor was urging Aunt Betty to board, and she gave us each a quick clasp, a wave, and was gone, up the steps and into the coach. We stood huddled and waving until the caboose disappeared around the bend.

As we climbed back into the Nash, Grandma asked, "The financing she was talking about with Willie? Where's it coming from?"

"I think maybe Jack," I said.

"Who's Jack?"

"He was our neighbor in the Project. He had a wife named Fanny, but she died."

"What do you think of him?"

"I like him. He reminds me of Alan Ladd, and he can fix *anything*."

Grandma turned toward me. "Do you think your aunt is interested in him?"

72

WHEN SATURDAY MAIL DELIVERY brought no word from Shirley, my stomach got queasy and heavy. At lunch Grandma said, "I went to a lot of trouble making that soup."

"It's fine, Grandma. I'm just not hungry."

"How can you not be hungry? You don't eat enough to keep a bird alive. What's gotten into you? You mope around, and you treat your mother like a stranger." Her hand clenched and unclenched on the dining room table.

Behind her bifocals, her eyes were moist. "Just because you're in junior high school doesn't mean you can turn your back on your mother."

I couldn't tell Grandma about Mama loving Uncle Stanley. In a family, you did not defend yourself at another's expense. The most you could hope was that history would vindicate you. It sometimes did, although not always in your lifetime.

Grandma heaved herself up, carrying an empty plate and soup bowl with her. In the kitchen, she slammed cupboard doors and clattered the drawers. When I found a towel to dry dishes, she snatched it away. "Go feel sorry for yourself someplace else."

"Go to hell!" I screamed. "You think you know so much, and you don't know anything!" Grabbing my coat, I ran out of the house.

. . . .

NOW I STOOD HANGING on the cyclone fence around the swimming pool in Chapman Park. Except for a mat of dead leaves, the swimming pool lay gray and empty. In less than two months, it would be cleaned, filled, and shuddering with noise—shrieks and laughter and the shrill of lifeguards' whistles.

It was almost impossible to believe that such a transformation could occur in six weeks: that the air would be cordial, the trees fat and green, and the grass shaggy and warm and stretching past the wading pool, the play equipment, the tennis court, and the softball field.

Southern California had no quarterly miracles, no opportunities for starting over. Not everybody cares to pay the cold, silver coinage of winter for a seasonal renascence, but for me it was a small price.

. . . .

AFTER A WEEKEND of frostbitten silence from Grandma, I was relieved to be enrolled in Blue Lake Public School, to be issued a pus-green gym suit that looked like a baby's romper, as well as textbooks and a locker on the third floor in which to keep them. In addition to my class schedule, I was going to tape a picture of Alicia Armand inside the locker door.

My first day in the new school was filled with curious, sidelong glances and scant conversation. The lockers on either side of mine belonged to boys who pretended not to see me. A pimply faced boy across the hall asked me in a carrying voice, "Where'd you get those clothes, a rummage sale?" My clothes were fine. He was just establishing my low place in the seventh-grade pecking order.

"Don't they make masks for people with your skin problem?" I called back.

On the way home from school, I stopped at the Ben Franklin five and dime to buy lined paper and a loose-leaf notebook. When I had found these, I wandered up and down the aisles, examining brassieres I didn't need and the latest popular phonograph records, which I surely didn't need since I had no phonograph.

Maybe I needed face cream. I fingered jars of Jergens and Ponds, then noticed the rack of magazines. The April *Stars of the Silver Screen,* written before Alicia Armand's disappearance, featured her on the cover. The photo was of her face only, the sort of picture photographers loved taking of Garbo. Alicia Armand's face conveyed that same purity, mystery, and inviolability.

I carried the magazine, along with the lined paper and three-ring notebook, to the front of the store. A group of girls from my new homeroom hung around the lipstick and cologne counter, but they didn't say hello.

I paid for the purchases out of my remaining dog-walking money and left the store, hugging the magazine to me. I had seen Alicia Armand in person, had been as close to her as I'd been to those girls with their muddy galoshes and Evening in Paris dreams.

The next morning I found a note on my locker door and knew it was from the pimply-faced boy. "My ma says you got nothing to be stuck-up about. Your ant almost had a baby with a guy named Miller who used to run the Ben Franclin."

Glancing down the hallway, I saw the boy and a couple of his pals standing by the stairwell watching me. I hung my coat and scarf on the peg in the locker and folded the note, shoving it into the pocket of my skirt. Grabbing up my math text and notebook, I slammed the locker, twirling the combination.

I headed directly toward the boys, my heart banging so hard I thought I might be having a mild heart attack.

Drawing abreast, I told the pimply faced boy, "I'll give your note to Grandma Browning, who may want to talk to your mother. Or maybe she'll just send the note along to my aunt to see whether she wants to have your mother arrested for slander."

The brass was pure Shirley. I hadn't any intention of adding to Grandma's worries, but I counted on the boy being gullible.

In homeroom after lunch, a note was passed to me. "I'll tell evryone I made it up about your ant. Dont tell your grandma about it. Please."

"I'll think about it," I wrote back. "Learn to spell."

Galloping out the main doors at three-fifteen amidst a roiling sea of students, I saw Mama standing at the end of the wide sidewalk. Her headscarf was untied, dangling, and ready to slip to the ground. Her hair was a rat's nest. Oh, God, I thought, what now?

She waited patiently by the street, smiling uncertainly.

"How come you're here?" I asked.

"The actress, the one we saw on the train?" She paused, near tears. "They think she's dead."

"What?"

"It was on Cedric Adams' noontime news," she said, groping for the name of the program. "I didn't want you to hear it from someone else."

We started across the street.

"It's a mistake," I told her.

"Maybe," she said, trying to sound hopeful.

I kept her moving, up onto the courthouse lawn, across the dry, winter-beaten grass.

She halted among the gaunt trees, recalling, "They found a body below the cliffs, up by . . . Mendocino. But they didn't find a head."

73

THE EVENING PAPER, which Grandpa drove me downtown to buy, carried the barest facts. I stayed up for the ten o'clock news on WCCO, although it added little, except that the body had been spotted by fishermen.

"Why do they think it's her?" I kept asking.

"They said she was wearing a jade bracelet like one Alicia Armand owned," Grandma said. "The housekeeper said it was hers, or like it." Grandma, who usually had no interest in the lives of movie stars, had been drawn to this story because Mama, Aunt Betty, and I had seen Alicia Armand in person, making the actress part of Grandma's world.

"I don't believe it's her," I told them.

"It's someone of her height and build," Grandma pointed out.

"Why would they . . . why would they cut off her head?" I asked. "It doesn't make any sense."

"So she couldn't be identified?" Mama ventured quietly. She was extending herself for my sake, reaching further than at any time since Uncle Stanley's death.

"Then why didn't they remove the jade bracelet?"

She shook her head, baffled.

"The news said these Ayles people were being flown to California to identify the body," Grandma noted.

"But nobody knows if they were Alicia Armand's parents," I told her. "They had a daughter named Alice Ayles. That's all anybody knows for sure." A new thought struck me. "What if this is the body of Alice Ayles, not Alicia Armand?"

We were sitting at the dining table. Grandpa was eating a bowl of bread and milk, his nightly bedtime snack.

"Life is like fiction," Mama said with wonder.

"Well," said Grandpa, who found a good deal of moonshine in this movie star talk, "I'm going to climb that big wooden hill." And he rose, carrying his empty bowl to the kitchen sink.

"Morning comes early," Grandma said, and followed.

While Grandma and Grandpa used the bathroom, Mama and I sat waiting our turn. "Most of the time, death is undeniable," she said. "But sometimes, we can make up our own ending." She smiled, radiant that she'd been able to share a great possibility with me.

Did she believe that Uncle Stanley's death was deniable?

I went to her and put my arms around her.

. . . .

AT SCHOOL THE NEXT MORNING, I overheard two girls in the biffy discussing the bizarre case, one telling the other, "I saw *Love Affair in London*. I can't believe she's dead."

"I saw her in person," I said.

"No kidding!" one of the girls said. "Where?"

I explained. Now I was the Girl Who Had Seen Alicia Armand.

During my last class of the afternoon, a student aide from the principal's office delivered a green slip of paper to Miss Hargrave and she delivered it to me. According to the slip, my mother had called at 2:34 p.m. Her message: "Meet me after school at the Koffee Kup Kafe. Important."

Oh, God. I couldn't endure another piece of important news. Was the body definitely Alicia Armand?

Suddenly I was exhausted, so tired I nodded off during the final five minutes of class. When the bell rang, I thought the building was on fire.

Mama was sitting in the last booth, watching for me. She half rose when she saw me, as though I might miss her among the other customers—three old geezers: retired farmers, or railroaders.

I pulled off my coat and hung it on a rack by the restroom. A bottle of Coca-Cola and a glass sat waiting when I slid into the booth. Oh God, what shock were they meant to allay?

"Close your eyes," Mama told me.

What was this?

"Surprise!"

On the table lay a manila envelope, the kind with a little string on the back that winds around a tiny cardboard button.

"Turn it over and look at the return address."

Shirley Olson c/o Mrs. John Ferguson, Riverton, Wyoming. I laid my head down on my arms.

"Would you like me to open it?" Mama asked.

"Yes," I whispered.

"There are two envelopes in here. The first one appears to be a letter from this Mrs. Ferguson. Should I read it?"

I nodded.

"Oh my God, honey, here's a check for two hundred dollars made out to you. Let's see, now, the letter says, 'Dear Lark, I am writing for Shirley because she insists that she is no good at letters. Well, I told her I would write this one and after that she was on her own.

"'We are all sorry that you have not heard from Shirley since she left San Diego. You must have been worried half to death. No one is sorrier than Shirley herself. But, these were the circumstances—

"'Shirley arrived in Riverton around Christmas to find that my husband and I were in Arizona where John's brother was taken ill. We have good help here at the ranch, hands who've been with us for years, so we stayed with my brother-in-law who was a bachelor, until his death on the twelfth of March. A good deal of paperwork followed and with one thing and another, we only got back here recently.

"'Meanwhile, Shirley had hitched a ride out to the ranch when she got to town. We never lock the place and when she saw that we weren't here, she let herself in. Shirley hid upstairs for fear she'd be sent back to San Diego if someone discovered her.

"'She is a very resourceful girl. She knew that we kept a lot of home preserves and other canned goods in the cellar. Once a day she scratched together food for herself, careful not to leave evidence, though she did hear Mrs. Higgins tell the hands that the bread and jam seemed to disappear by magic!

"'All this is to let you know that Shirley is well and doing fine. She's enrolled in town school and a bus picks her up in the morning and brings her back in the afternoon.

"'We had a storm last week that dumped a ton of snow on us. We got out the sledge and hitched up the horses and carried Shirley and several other children up to the main road. She did enjoy that.

"'Shirley has told us some of what happened to her in San Diego. It made us cry to hear it, and I know there's more she can't bring herself to talk about.

"'But whatever good happened to her there came from knowing you folks. She says you saved her life and I am sure that is true. Giving her the money you had saved—well, what can I say—I think you deserve a medal. I am enclosing a check to repay you but there just isn't enough money in the world to really do that.

"'We have a lawyer who is handling the legalities to make Shirley our ward and eventually our daughter, we hope. We never felt right about it when her folks left here, taking her with them, and now we find it hard to forgive ourselves, but we didn't know at the time what the right thing was.

"'It broke my heart when Shirley showed me the program from the concert in La Jolla where she played. The playing meant so much to her.

"'We have a piano here. My husband used to play when he was younger. Now he plays the radio, he says. At any rate, Shirley still has a musical ear and loves the piano. She's been composing little tunes, and we hope to encourage that.

"'I have one last thing to say and then I must close as it's nearly time to carry this to the box for pickup. Shirley and Mr. Ferguson and I would be tickled if you could visit us. Maybe next summer. I don't know what your family's plans are, but maybe they would not mind parting with you for a little while. Let us know if this is a possibility.

"'Yours truly, Helen Ferguson.'

"Shirley told us she'd gone to Texas," Mama said.

I nodded without raising my head.

"But she ran away to Wyoming instead."

Nod.

"And you gave her the money."

Nod.

Mama reached across the table, brushing a hand over my hair. "My, oh my," she said, but she wasn't angry. After a long moment, she said, "Here's Shirley's letter. Would you like to read it?"

She passed me a white envelope and I sat up. I slit the seal with my fingernail and extracted a folded sheet of lined paper.

Dear Lark,
How are you? I am fine. Come visit me in the summer.
I love you,
Shirley
P.S. Thank you.

FOR DAYS AFTER HEARING from Shirley, I was so happy I'd burst out laughing any old time—in the middle of algebra class or helping Grandma with supper.

Immediately, I wrote to let Aunt Betty know that Shirley was alive and well and living on a ranch in Wyoming. She, of all the grown-ups, was most concerned, and she would let the others know.

And I wrote a note to Mr. Trustworthy telling him the good news and sending along a couple of stories I'd been saving for him. But I never heard back. "I am away," the notice on the window had said.

I continue to write stories for him, but until I hear I will hold them.

Epilogue

LESS THAN THREE WEEKS after I heard from Shirley, the war ended in Europe. The two events are forever linked in my mind, as if Shirley's change of luck had been the feather required to tip the scales of world fortune.

In August, I stayed with Shirley in Wyoming, learning to ride a horse and milk a cow, asking a thousand questions, and sucking up every skill that might later prove useful.

On September 2, aboard the battleship *Missouri,* an agreement ending the war with Japan was signed. Days later, I turned thirteen, and the following week Mama left for California to help Aunt Betty and Jack set up My Lady's Fashions, "The acme of design and quality in women's fashions."

Since the new business would require round-the-clock work the first year, I was to remain at Grandma and Grandpa Browning's in Blue Lake, which was right and inevitable. My magnetic compass has always pointed toward Minnesota.

Papa and I got together once in a while, usually in Blue Lake. We were a strange, embarrassed pairing, a kind of accident of nature, but we tried to make the best of it.

And what of Alicia Armand? I went on scanning the papers for word, and even though a thin trickle of stories continued through May and June ("Mendocino body not that of missing actress, police confirm"), by midsummer the trickle dried up and the actress became part of Hollywood history, the latest of its unsolved mysteries.

But the truth is that she plodded through drifts of snow, pressing toward the door of a golden-warm cabin where Hilly, Baby Marjorie, Uncle Stanley, and a girl with big teeth waited.

FAITH SULLIVAN was born and raised in southern Minnesota. Married to the drama critic Dan Sullivan, she lived for twenty-some years in New York and Los Angeles, returning frequently to Minnesota to keep her roots firmly planted in the prairie. Since 1989, she has lived in Minneapolis.

Sullivan describes herself as a "demon gardener, flea marketer, and feeder of birds." Born into a family of women storytellers, she grew up in Lakefield, Minnesota, a town that she says is "a vague model" for the fictional Harvester. Sullivan began writing novels after her youngest child started school. Her first book, *Repent, Lanny Merkel*—a humorous novel about a high school reunion—was published in 1981 and was followed by *Watchdog* (1982), a psychological mystery, and a novel, *Mrs. Demming and the Mythical Beast* (1985). *The Cape Ann* (1988) introduced readers to Harvester, the setting of her two subsequent novels, *The Empress of One* and *What a Woman Must Do.* Sullivan also has taught high school history and written and acted for the stage.

More Fiction from Milkweed Editions

To order books or for more information, contact Milkweed at (800) 520-6455 or visit our Web site (www.milkweed.org).

Katya
Sandra Birdsell

My Lord Bag of Rice:
New and Selected Stories
Carol Bly

The Tree of Red Stars
Tessa Bridal

The Clay That Breathes
Catherine Browder

A Keeper of Sheep
William Carpenter

Seasons of Sun and Rain
Marjorie Dorner

Winter Roads, Summer Fields
Marjorie Dorner

Blue Taxis
Eileen Drew

Crossing Bully Creek
Margaret Erhart

Trip Sheets
Ellen Hawley

All American Dream Dolls
David Haynes

Live at Five
David Haynes

Somebody Else's Mama
David Haynes

The Children Bob Moses Led
William Heath

Pu-239 and Other
Russian Fantasies
Ken Kalfus

Thirst
Ken Kalfus

Ordinary Wolves
Seth Kantner

Distant Music
Lee Langley

Persistent Rumours
Lee Langley

Hunting Down Home
Jean McNeil

Swimming in the Congo
Margaret Meyers

Tokens of Grace
Sheila O'Connor

Roofwalker
Susan Power

Hell's Bottom, Colorado
Laura Pritchett

Sky Bridge
Laura Pritchett

Tivolem
Victor Rangel-Ribeiro

The Boy Without a Flag
Abraham Rodriguez Jr.

Confidence of the Heart
David Schweidel

An American Brat
Bapsi Sidhwa

Cracking India
Bapsi Sidhwa

The Crow Eaters
Bapsi Sidhwa

The Country I Come From
Maura Stanton

Traveling Light
Jim Stowell

Aquaboogie
Susan Straight

The Empress of One
Faith Sullivan

What a Woman Must Do
Faith Sullivan

Falling Dark
Tim Tharp

The Promised Land
Ruhama Veltfort

Justice
Larry Watson

Montana 1948
Larry Watson

Milkweed Editions

FOUNDED IN 1979, Milkweed Editions is the largest independent, nonprofit literary publisher in the United States. Milkweed publishes with the intention of making a humane impact on society, in the belief that good writing can transform the human heart and spirit. Within this mission, Milkweed publishes in five areas: fiction, nonfiction, poetry, children's literature for middle-grade readers, and the World As Home—books about our relationship with the natural world.

JOIN US

Milkweed depends on the generosity of foundations and individuals like you, in addition to the sales of its books. In an increasingly consolidated and bottom-line-driven publishing world, your support allows us to select and publish books on the basis of their literary quality and the depth of their message. Please visit our Web site (www.milkweed. org) or contact us at (800) 520-6455 to learn more about our donor program.

Interior design and composition by Barbara Jellow
Text set in Sabon, display in ITC Mona Lisa and Centaur Italic
Printed on acid-free 50 lb. HiBulk Cream paper
by Friesens Corporation.